KT-169-286

GHOST VIRUS

GRAHAM MASTERTON trained as a
newspaper reporter before beginning his
career as an author. Graham's credits as
a writer include the bestselling horror
novel *The Manitou* and the Katie
Maguire crime series, which became a
top-ten bestseller in 2012.

3011780347512 4

ALSO BY GRAHAM MASTERTON

The Katie Maguire Series

White Bones

Broken Angels

Red Light

Taken For Dead

Blood Sisters

Buried

Living Death

Dead Girls Dancing

Dead Men Whistling

Begging to Die

The Beatrice Scarlet Series

Scarlet Widow

The Coven

GRAHAM
MASTERTON

GHOST VIRUS

HEAD
of ZEUS

First published in the UK in 2018 by Head of Zeus Ltd
This paperback edition first published in the UK in 2019 by Head of Zeus Ltd

9 7 5 3 1 2 4 6 8

A catalogue record for this book is available from
the British Library.

ISBN (PB): 9781788545044
ISBN (E): 9781788545013

Typeset by Divaddict Publishing Solutions Ltd

Printed and bound in Great Britain by
CPI Group (UK) Ltd, Croydon CR0 4YY

Head of Zeus Ltd
First Floor East
5–8 Hardwick Street
London EC1R 4RG

WWW.HEADOFZEUS.COM

Tooting is a district of south-west London.
It has been settled since the 6th century.
Today its population includes
5 per cent Pakistani and 3 per cent Polish.
Its name is derived from the old verb 'to tout'
which means to 'watch out' or 'beware'

I

Samira had been staring into her dressing-table mirror all morning before she summoned up the courage to burn off her face.

You are not me, she whispered to herself. *Whoever you are, you are not me.*

She heard the clock in the living-room downstairs chime twelve, and that was when she stood up and walked over to the door. She turned the key and jiggled the handle to make sure that it was securely locked. Then she returned to her dressing-table and picked up the clear glass bottle of concentrated sulphuric acid that was standing next to her Rasasi Blue Lady perfume and Masarrat Misbah foundation and all her lipsticks and blushers and eye-liners.

Behind the cosmetics stood an oval framed photograph of Samira with her husband-to-be Faraz. They were standing outside the Mahabat Khan Mosque in Peshawar, in Pakistan, both smiling, Samira with her hand held up to shield her eyes from the sun. That photograph had been taken only three hours after she had first met Faraz, but she had been happy that they were going to be married. Although he had a large mole on his upper lip he was reasonably good-looking and soft-spoken and only four years older than she was.

When her father and mother had driven her to his family's house in Hayalabad, she had thought for one terrible heart-sinking moment that she was going to be given to Wasim, his fat sweaty forty-four-year-old cousin. Wasim had been sitting in the corner smoking and cramming saffron burfi into his mouth in between puffs.

But however suitable Faraz was, there would be no wedding now. Her parents could keep their dowry. They would have only her brother Jamal to worry about, as if Jamal wasn't enough trouble on his own.

She didn't look at herself in the mirror again. Instead she took the bottle of sulphuric acid in her hand and went to the window to stare down at their back yard. It was only about four metres wide, with a narrow flower-bed and a concrete path which led up to her father's toolshed. It was here, though, she had spent most of her childhood, ever since her family had arrived in England.

It was here that she had played with her dolls and dressed herself up in fancy costumes and pretended to serve tea in plastic teacups to her friends from Iqra Primary School.

She raised her eyes. It was a clear November day, with a washed-out blue sky and sunshine. An airliner sparked like a silver needle as it flew high across south London towards Heathrow Airport. Samira had wanted so much to go back to Peshawar and see more of the country where she was born. That would be impossible now. They wouldn't know who she was.

She sat down on the maroon satin bedspread that covered her single bed. The grubby stuffed lamb that she had been sent from Pakistan on her fourth birthday was lying on the pillow, with its pink ribbon and its Ziqi label, so she had always thought that its name was Ziqi. She reached out to pick it up but then she changed her mind. Even Ziqi wouldn't recognise her.

She lay back on the bed. In anticipation of her wedding next month she was wearing an orange shalwar kameez with an embroidered collar, with a long orange dupatta scarf hung over her shoulders. It was warm in her bedroom, almost stiflingly warm, but she was also wearing a thick grey peacoat, with wide triangular lapels.

It was already past time for the dhuhr, the midday prayer, but she knew that what she was about to do was in direct contravention of Allah's will. Whoever she was, she knew that Allah would forgive her, but she simply didn't have the courage or the strength to face herself any longer. All the same, she whispered '*Subhana rabbiyal adheem*' three times as she lay there. Then, '*Please Lord... please... don't let me suffer too much and too long.*'

She held up the bottle and unscrewed its yellow metal cap. She felt quite calm now, and her hand was steady. The acid had no smell, although she could remember being warned when she was at school not to sniff it, because its vapours could burn her nasal cavities.

She bunched up her dupatta and gripped it between her teeth, in case she screamed. Then, keeping her eyes wide open, she poured the acid slowly over her forehead. Instantly, she saw scarlet, and then jagged flashes of lightning, like demons dancing, and then total blackness. The burning sensation was so excruciating that she dropped the bottle and splashed even more acid down the side of her neck.

Her skin crackled and bubbled and melted, dripping down her cheekbones and onto her pillow. Although she was biting deep into her dupatta, she let out a hideous half-choked screech, arching her back and bouncing up and down on the bed in agony.

The pain grew even more intolerable, and she clawed at her face with both hands in a futile attempt to try to relieve it, but she succeeded only in pulling slithery lumps of flesh from her chin, and ripping off her lips like two fat glutinous slugs. She could feel her teeth being bared, and then the acid eating hungrily into her gums.

She shrieked, and dragged at her long black hair, wrenching it out in clumps.

All the same, her prayer was answered. The acid ate so rapidly through the nerve-endings under her skin that her face and her neck soon began to feel numb, and then her heart stopped. The half-empty acid bottle rolled off the edge of the bed onto the floor and Samira shuddered as if she were cold and then she lay still. Her flesh continued to crackle softly and dissolve, exposing her windpipe and her larynx, all the way down to the vertebrae in her neck, but Samira was in the hereafter, and felt nothing.

Nearly three hours went by. The pale daylight outside her bedroom window was beginning to fade before the front door downstairs was noisily opened, and her mother called out, 'Samira! We're home! Samira! Where are you, Samira?'

2

'You know what you are?' said Jerry. 'You're a pillock. That's what you are.'

'I was cold, that's all,' retorted the booming voice from inside the large green charity box. 'What do you expect me to do? Sleep in a fucking doorway?'

'Oh, shut it,' Jerry retorted. 'You was in there trying to nick stuff. You're about the fifth twat who's got himself stuck since they put it there.'

He gave the charity box a thump with his fist just to annoy the young man trapped inside and also to vent his own frustration about being called out on such a petty, pointless job. Ever since he had been sent down here to Tooting three months previously he had been handling nothing but anti-social behaviour and petty drug-dealing and racist stabbings by gangs of rival schoolboys.

Detective Superintendent Perry at New Scotland Yard had told him that he was being posted to the suburbs because he had a 'keen sense of smell for the streets'. What Jerry had actually smelled were the bribes that his fellow detectives had been pocketing for quietly dropping prosecutions against the Harris crime family in Hoxton, and they hadn't trusted him not to blow the whistle on them.

One of his fellow officers had pushed him up against the wall in the corridor and said, 'You know what your trouble is, Jerry? You're too fucking ethical. There's only two places for ethics, chum – the pulpit and the cemetery. Not here. Not in the Yard.'

Jerry paced up and down Fishponds Road with the collar of his brown leather jacket turned up and his hands thrust deep into his pockets. Two uniformed constables were standing on the corner by the Selkirk pub, stamping their feet to keep warm, but he knew that it wasn't worth him trying to go and have a matey chat with them. Like all the other officers at Tooting police station, they knew why he had been transferred here, and they wouldn't speak to him – not socially, anyway.

They were all waiting for the area representative from the charity collectors to arrive and unlock the box. These days, the quality of the clothes and the shoes being dropped into charity boxes was so good that it was worthwhile for hard-up druggies to wriggle their way inside them to steal whatever they could. The only problem was that the boxes were now designed so that once they had wriggled their way inside it was impossible for them to wriggle their way back out again.

Jerry checked his watch and said, 'Shit,' under his breath. He would be going off duty in less than an hour, and he didn't even know what he was doing here anyway. Detective Inspector French had told him to question the lad trapped in the box because stealing clothes from charity boxes was now developing into a major racket, and they needed to find out who was behind it.

In Jerry's opinion, though, this lad had only been stealing clothes to feed his own habit, and he wouldn't know a major racket from a minor ping-pong bat. Jerry reckoned the large-scale theft was being done by Lithuanians, and one Lithuanian in particular.

'How much longer?' the lad shouted out. 'I'm bursting for a piss in here.'

'Don't have a clue, mate!' Jerry shouted back. 'You'll just have to tie a knot in it!'

'You gotta get me out of here, I'm telling you! I'm getting claustrophobia!'

'That's a clever word for a thick dick like you!'

It was gradually beginning to grow dark, and one by one the streetlights flickered on.

'You gotta get me out! I'm going mental!'

'You were mental to climb in there in the first place! Pillock!'

'I'll make a complaint about you! What's your name?'

'Detective Constable Jeremy Thomas Pardoe. Make sure you write that down. Oh, sorry – I forgot you haven't got a pencil and paper and it's pitch dark in there!'

'I'll have you!'

'I should wait until I've got you out of there first, mate. You wouldn't want me to change my mind, would you? Bloody hell – you could be in there for *days* before anybody finds you! Or *weeks* even!'

'You bastard!'

Jerry walked away again and left the lad ranting. He had almost reached the Selkirk pub when a silver Volvo V40 came around the corner. It stopped next to the two uniformed officers and Jerry could see the driver leaning across to talk to them. They turned around and both of them pointed in his direction. The driver parked on the opposite side of the road and climbed out.

He had been expecting the usual bad-tempered prickly-headed bloke from the charity collectors, but this was a very petite young Asian woman in a dark grey trouser-suit and a black headscarf. She came across to him with a smile and said, 'DC Pardoe?'

She made him feel very tall and scruffy. 'That's me. What can I do you for?'

'They told me at the station at Mitcham Road that I would find you here.'

'Oh, yeah? You're not from the charity, are you?'

The lad inside the box banged loudly on the metal sides and shouted out, 'Get me out of here! Get me out of here! For fuck's sake get me out of here!'

The Asian woman glanced over at the charity box and said, 'No need for us to lock him up, is there? He appears to have done that quite successfully for himself.'

Jerry decided he liked this woman. Not only was she exceptionally pretty, with dark brown eyes that were almost cartoonishly large and full bow-shaped lips, but it seemed as if she shared his sense of humour.

'And you are...?' he asked her.

'Detective Sergeant Jamila Patel.'

'From—?'

'The Met, same as you. I've been working at the Yard for the past fourteen months.'

'Really? Surprised I never clocked you.'

'Is that meant to be a compliment?'

'No – just surprised I never clocked you, that's all.'

'You wouldn't have done. I was working with a specialist team on honour crimes.'

'Oh, you mean like women being stoned for adultery?'

'That's right. And, yes, it happens even here in England, more often than you'd think. I had a woman in Edmonton last week who had a twenty-four-kilo concrete block dropped on her head because she'd had an affair with her English tutor.'

'Bloody hell.'

DS Patel shrugged, as if she had to deal with cases as horrific as that every day of the week.

'Then of course we've had any number of young women being strangled because they refused to marry the man their parents wanted them to – or because they'd run off with a boy from a lower caste and brought shame on the family. And most of the cases are so hard to solve. Nobody saw anything. Nobody heard anything.'

'OK...' said Jerry, looking around. The lad inside the charity box had started kicking it now. 'So what are you doing here in beautiful downtown Tooting?'

'Well, first of all, DC Pardoe, I've come to collect *you*.'

'I'm on a shout. I'm supposed to be questioning this pill— I'm supposed to be questioning this suspect as soon as we can get him out of there.'

'You're excused.'

'What?'

'DI French told me to tell you that you're excused. He only sent you out here to give you something to do. But *I* want you because I've been sent down here to investigate what appears to be an honour killing, and before my team was set up, you successfully investigated three honour killings – two in Redbridge and one in Waltham Forest.'

'Yes, I did. But if you've got a team, why do you need me?'

'I *did* have a team,' said DS Patel. 'Unfortunately we were the victim of last month's budget cuts. That was the official explanation anyway. The truth was that it wasn't very popular with the Asian community leaders and they put pressure on the commissioner to disband it.'

'So now it's just you and me?'

'*Get me out of here! Get me out of here!*' screamed the lad in the charity box. '*I can't hold it any longer!*'

'Don't worry about him,' said DS Patel. 'Those two uniforms will take him into the nick for questioning, once he's out.'

Jerry went over and gave the charity box another thump with his fist.

'Sorry about this, mate! I'm going to have to leave you! I'll send somebody round in the morning to let you out!'

'No! *Noooo!* You can't do this! I'll suffocate! I'll die of cold! Please – I'm begging you!'

At that moment, a green Fiesta with only one headlight came up Fishponds Road. Jerry recognised it as the car belonging to the area representative of the charity collectors. It stopped right next to them, and the grumpy grey-haired driver climbed out. Underneath a beige windcheater he was wearing a brown Fair Isle sweater which he had put on backwards, so that the label was right under his unshaven chin.

'Evening, Ron,' said Jerry.

'Huh,' Ron retorted, dragging a huge bunch of keys from out of his windcheater pocket, and sniffing monotonously as he sorted through them.

The lad inside the charity box obviously hadn't heard him arrive, or the jingling of his keys, because he was weeping now, like a young woman in distress.

3

Sophie had just turned off the lights at the back of the shop and switched on the alarm when there was a frantic knocking at the front door.

She could see a white-haired woman in a long tweed coat standing outside, with two large black bin bags. She went up to the door and said, 'We're closed! Sorry!'

'What shall I do with these bags, then?' the woman asked her, exaggerating her lip movements so that Sophie could understand her through the glass. 'I can't take them back.'

'Just leave them there in the doorway,' Sophie told her.

'There's some very good-quality clothes in here, and some other bric-à-brac, too! It would be a shame to have them stolen!'

Sophie hesitated for a moment, and then sighed and said, 'All right... just hold on a moment!'

She went back to switch off the alarm, and then she returned to unlock the front door. The woman immediately bundled the two bags inside and dropped them onto the floor by the counter.

'That's got rid of that lot, thank God!' she said. Now that she was inside the shop, Sophie could see that she wasn't as old as she had appeared when she was looking in through the window. Her hair was white, but only because it was blonde and she had bleached it. Her ankle-length coat made her look older, too. She couldn't have been more than thirty-eight or thirty-nine, and very thin, with pale blue eyes and sharp angular cheekbones.

'My uncle's clothes,' she explained. 'He died three weeks ago and we've been clearing out his house. You can't imagine how much stuff he had! All of my aunt's clothes, too, and *she* passed away nine years ago. He hadn't thrown away anything. Not even her tights!'

'Well, if you have any more—' said Sophie. 'Especially sweaters and jackets, at this time of the year.'

'No, this is the last of it,' the woman told her. 'There's a lot of books but they're mostly in Russian and Polish and they're mostly medical. He was a doctor of something-or-other.'

'All right, well, thank you anyway,' said Sophie. 'I have to lock up now. My boyfriend will be wondering what's happened to me.'

The woman looked around the shop. 'You have it very *organised* in here, don't you? It doesn't even smell like a charity shop, if you don't mind my saying so. Do you get very busy?'

Sophie smiled. 'You'd be amazed. We're packed out sometimes, especially on Saturdays. But thanks, yes. I do try to keep it neat and tidy. Before I came here to Little Helpers I used to work in Selfridges, in the fashion department.'

She could tell that the woman was dying to ask her – *Selfridges? So how did you end up managing a charity shop, and in Tooting Broadway of all places?* Instead, she said, 'Well – thank you so much for taking those bags in. I never want to go back to that house again – like *never* in my whole life.'

She left, and when she went to lock the front door after her, Sophie saw her climbing into a black Mercedes saloon which had pulled up on the opposite side of the street. Although she had said that her boyfriend would be wondering where she was, there was no sign of Mike yet. He was almost always late picking her up these days, and three or four times lately she had been forced to take the 77 bus home.

She had been feeling for months now that she needed to change her life completely, but she had become so dependent on Mike, especially for money, that she couldn't see what she could do to break free. She was beginning to wish that she had never met him. Everything that she used to find attractive about him now irritated her, especially his habit of never answering when she asked him a question. She used to think his silence was masculine and moody. Now it made her wonder if he was simply thick.

As she went to switch on the alarm, she heard a scuffling sound. She stopped and listened. In the early summer, the back of the shop had been infested with rats. They had tunnelled in through the drains from the Turkish restaurant next door, and had been trying to make nests among the unsaleable clothes which were piled up waiting for the rag man. She had called in the council to exterminate them, and soon after that the Turkish restaurant had closed down. But perhaps they had found their way back in again.

There it was again: a sharp, distinct scuffling. It didn't seem to be coming from the back room, though. It seemed to be coming from one of the two black bin bags that the white-haired woman had just brought in.

Sophie went up to them and prodded each of them with her Ugg boot. She had once found a dead tortoiseshell cat in a bag of clothes that an elderly man had brought in, but never anything living. She was beginning to think that she had imagined the scuffling when she heard it again, and this time she was sure that she saw one of the bags moving.

Oh God, what if it is a rat? I mean, it must *be a rat – what else could it be?*

She didn't want to open the bag in case the rat jumped out at her. Perhaps she should carry the bag outside the shop and leave it by the dustbins until tomorrow morning. If the rat hadn't managed to escape by then, she could ask her volunteer Raymond to open it for her. Raymond had worked in an abattoir and wasn't squeamish about killing anything. He would squash wasps with his thumb.

She picked up the bag by its twist-tied top. It was quite heavy, but then the woman had told her that she was donating bric-à-brac as well as clothes. She carried it as quickly as she could to the doorway at the back of the shop which led through to her small office and the toilet and the storeroom where they steam-cleaned the clothes before they hung them on display. She prayed that she wouldn't hear that scuffling sound again or feel any movement inside the bag before she had managed to drop it by the dustbins.

As she made her way past the heap of clothes that were waiting for the rag man, her feet became tangled in an old velveteen curtain that had slid down onto the floor. She stumbled into the bag that she was carrying and it split wide open, so that jackets and dresses and shoes and corduroy trousers tumbled out onto the floor, as well as a cuckoo clock and a box of silver-plated teaspoons.

Sophie took a quick step back, fearful of a rat or some other creature running out, but after she had waited for almost half a minute, nothing appeared. She prodded a grey tweed coat with her foot, but there was still no movement, and no more scuffling sounds.

I know I didn't imagine that noise, but perhaps it was the cuckoo clock whirring, or simply the clothes settling down inside the bag.

Cautiously, she dragged the tweed coat out from the rest of the clothes, shook it, and laid it out on the table they used for ironing clothes that were badly crumpled. There was still no more scuffling, so she pulled out the corduroy trousers, and then two striped shirts and a dark green sweater with frayed holes in the elbows. She picked up the cuckoo clock, too. Its pendulum chains were twisted and its doors were jammed open. The cuckoo was trapped inside, with one wing broken.

Just the way I feel... like I'm stuck inside a stopped clock, unable to fly.

The bag also contained a knitted blanket which smelled strongly of Voltarol liniment, a pair of worn-out gardening gloves and at least a dozen odd socks, but Sophie also found two women's turtle-neck sweaters, one grey and one cream, both of which looked as if they had hardly ever been worn, and a woman's velvet jacket, midnight blue, with military-style braiding around the buttons.

She knew that she could get a good price for the sweaters, and she really fancied keeping the jacket for herself. She thought that it would look great with her skinny Mantaray jeans and her Red Herring ankle boots, and she would make a donation of £10 to the shop to cover the cost.

She finished emptying the bag. There was nothing else of any value in it, only a few old Penguin paperbacks with yellowing pages and a badly stained pair of oven gloves. No rats, no mice. Nothing that would account for that scuffling sound.

She took the velvet jacket into the curtained-off changing-room and tried it on in front of the mirror. It was slightly tight across the chest, because whoever had owned it had obviously been slightly less bosomy than Sophie, but she wouldn't have to button it up, and otherwise it fitted her perfectly. She thought that its military style suited her looks, too, because her mother was half-Polish and she was slightly Slavic-looking, with a round face and small feline eyes, and although her dark brown hair needed washing after a day in the shop, it was cut in a sharp geometric bob.

As she stood staring at herself in the mirror for some unaccountable reason she began to feel wistful, as if she had fallen out with a very close friend, or someone close to her had moved away, or died.

You need a break, she told herself. *Even if you can't change your life, you could at least take a few days off. You could go down to Sidmouth and see Mum and Dad. You know you always feel better when you can take some long walks by the sea.*

She peered at her reflection even more closely and she was alarmed to see that she had tears glistening in her eyelashes. Why did she suddenly feel so sad? But at the same time, she began to feel resentful, too.

Why did you do this to me? What did I do? You think I can't hurt you any more? You don't know the half of it!

To her astonishment, she gave a deep, suppressed sob, and the tears started to roll down her cheeks and drip off her chin.

Why am I crying? Why am I so upset and angry? Stop it!

She stepped out of the changing-room and started to take off the jacket, although she had only just taken her right arm out of the sleeve before she thought that perhaps she should keep it on, and wear it home. But without having it dry-cleaned? Whenever she bought clothes that had been donated to the shop, she always had them cleaned before she wore them. A whole legion of virulent bacteria were capable of surviving in second-hand clothes, as well as lice and scabies. Some infections like hepatitis and syphilis could even withstand repeated washing, and that was the reason that charity shops never sold second-hand underwear.

For some reason, though, Sophie felt reluctant to be parted from this jacket. It almost seemed to be pulling at her left arm to stay inside its sleeve, like an unhappy friend tugging at her and begging her not to leave her alone. She sniffed and wiped the tears from her face with the back of her hand and she was about to put her right arm back into its sleeve when she was filled with anger again.

You're such a coward! Only a coward would have treated me like this! But don't think you're going to get away with it! Oh, no!

She pulled the jacket off so quickly that its left sleeve was turned inside-out. She dropped it on the counter next to the cash register and stared at it, half-expecting it to jump back up at her.

She couldn't understand it. How had trying on a jacket disturbed her so much? It had given her a sense of terrible loss, but at the same time it had made her furious.

She lifted up the jacket and straightened out the sleeve. Surely it couldn't have been the jacket itself. Perhaps it was the way that she had looked when she had tried it on. Perhaps it had reminded her of some person that she had long forgotten. After all, she had imagined that she was shouting at somebody – somebody who had let her down somehow, somebody who had made her feel grief-stricken.

Don't think you're going to get away with it! she had told them, in her mind. But who were they? And what had they done to her?

She heard the sharp tapping of car keys at the shop's front window. She turned around and saw Mike, and for the first time in a long time she was actually pleased and relieved to see him. She went over and unlocked the door.

'Hi,' he said. As usual, he never explained why he was late, or apologised for it, but this evening she didn't mind so much. He was broad-shouldered and bulky, because he worked out almost every day and went to kick-boxing sessions every weekend, and after what she had felt in the changing-room, it was reassuring to have somebody around who could protect her. She still wished he didn't have his hair shaved so short up the sides. His face was broad, with a deeply cleft chin and a puggish nose, and she thought that his hairstyle made him look like a convict.

She could smell alcohol on his breath. That was why he was late. He had been drinking in the Gorringe Park with his friends from the estate agents where he worked.

'Aren't you ready?' he asked her, seeing that the back door was open and that the contents of the burst-open bag were still strewn across the floor.

'I won't be a moment,' she told him. She switched on the alarm and closed the door, leaving the sweaters and trousers and cuckoo clock where they were. As she passed the counter, though, she hesitated, and looked at the jacket.

'What?' said Mike. 'Come on, Soph, buck up – I'm parked on a double red line out there. That's a hundred and thirty quid fine!'

Sophie hesitated for a second longer, but then she picked up the jacket and folded it over her arm.

'You're not pinching that, are you?' Mike asked her. 'Just because I wouldn't buy you that coat from Next. It was too bloody expensive, that coat, and anyway it didn't suit you.'

'I'm going to pay for it. I've tried it on and I want it.'

'All right. Up to you. If you want to walk around dressed in second-hand clothes like some old bag-lady, go ahead.'

Sophie locked the front door of Little Helpers and then followed Mike to his red Subaru. She sat in the passenger seat with the jacket folded in her lap, and as they pulled away from the kerb, she felt almost as if it were snuggling up to her, like a pet cat, and she patted it.

It needs me, she thought. *I don't know why I feel like that, but it needs me, and it doesn't want to let me go.*

4

'I hope you've got a strong stomach,' said Jamila, as they turned into Rectory Lane.

'Don't worry,' Jerry told her. 'I only had an egg sandwich for lunch. I think that will probably stay down.'

They reached number 35. Four response cars and two police vans were lined up outside, and an ambulance was waiting around the corner in Southview Close. The pavement in front of the house had been cordoned off, and arc lights had been set up on tripods in the brick-paved front garden.

Jamila found a space to park further up the road, and then they walked back. They ducked under the blue-and-white crime scene tape and entered the house. Three uniformed constables in bulky stab-proof jackets were crowded into the narrow hallway, along with a coat-stand heaped with overcoats, so they had to breathe in and squeeze their way past. Off to the left, in the living-room, a female officer was talking to a plump Pakistani woman in a maroon headscarf and a skinny Pakistani boy of about seventeen or eighteen, with bulbous eyes and a straggly black moustache.

The house stank of fenugreek, and the walls in the hallway were clustered with pictures: traditional illustrations from Pakistani folk stories, family photographs, and landscapes of Peshawar and the Khyber Pass. Jamila peered at one of them and said, *'The Tale of the Cunning Siddhikari.'*

'Oh, yeah,' said Jerry. 'And what's a cunning Siddhikari when it's at home?'

'The cunning Siddhikari stole a merchant's treasure, persuaded a thief to hang himself from a tree, and bit the tongue off one of the merchant's servants.'

'I see. Just your average day in Pakistan, then.'

'DI Saunders is up in the bedroom,' said one of the constables, jerking his thumb towards the staircase.

'Don't tell me. Not Smiley.'

The constable said nothing but gave him a wry, sympathetic nod. Jerry had worked with DI 'Smiley' Saunders on only one case, a Somalian girl in Tower Hamlets whose boyfriend had stove in her skull with a steam iron. He had never met anyone so consistently miserable as DI Saunders in his life. If he won the jackpot in the lottery, he'd only grumble that he should have won it twenty years earlier, so that he wouldn't have needed to join the police force at all.

Jamila climbed up the steep hessian-carpeted stairs to the landing and Jerry followed her. In the back bedroom, one forensic officer was standing in the corner taking flash photographs while the other two were crawling around on their hands and knees, shining black light torches on every inch of the carpet. The room was filled with the crispy rustling of their white Tyvek suits.

DI Saunders from the Homicide and Major Crime Command was standing by the window in a putty-coloured windcheater, with his arms folded. He was tall, with slicked-back grey hair, near-together eyes and a sharply hooked nose. His mouth was permanently turned down, so that he looked like a disapproving bird of prey.

'Oh, you found him, then?' he said to Jamila. 'Hallo, Jerry. Long time no see.'

But Jerry didn't answer – didn't even hear him. All his attention was fixed on the body of the girl lying on the bed. She was wearing an orange shalwar kameez with a dupatta twisted around her shoulders, and both of her fists were clenched as if she were ready for a fight. She had copious waves of tangled black hair, but almost all the skin had been burned off her face so that it had become a scarlet mask. Her eyes had shrivelled into blind white mothballs inside their sockets and she no longer had a nose, only a triangular hole, so that every time the camera flashed Jerry could see inside the glistening red cavities of her sinuses. Her jaw had dropped open and her tongue was sticking out, a cluster of transparent blisters like bubble-wrap.

'Gordon Bennett,' said Jerry, shaking his head. 'She looks like something out of a bleeding horror film.'

'I did warn you,' said Jamila. Then she turned to DI Saunders. 'Have you talked any more to her mother and her brother?'

'Not yet,' admitted DI Saunders. 'To be honest with you, Jamila, I was waiting for you to come back before I did that. I don't know any Paki-speak and even when they're supposed to be talking English I have a job understanding what the eff they're on about. I don't know too much about their rituals, either, except that they won't eat with their left hand because they wipe their arse with it and they treat their women like shit.'

'Besides,' he added, 'I think we need to have a much clearer idea of exactly how she died before I started asking questions. Clive – tell DS Patel what you think happened.'

The forensic officer who was kneeling on the opposite side of the bed tugged down his face-mask, revealing a gingery Prince Harry beard. 'It was concentrated sulphuric acid. The bottle's still lying on the floor down there and that's what it says on the label. We're not taking that for granted, of course, and we'll be testing what's left of it, but the trauma to her face and the damage to the bedding – they're definitely consistent with H_2SO_4.'

'Tell DS Patel how it was done, though. It wasn't thrown at her, was it?'

'No, not thrown,' said the forensic officer. 'I mean, that's the way they usually do it, isn't it? – walk right up to them when they're standing or sitting and splosh it straight into their face. But this young lady, she was lying on her back right here on the bed. You can tell by the pattern of acid discoloration on her hair and the bedspread underneath her that it was poured over her while she was prone.'

Jerry leaned over the bed so that he could examine the young woman's glistening red face more closely. The flesh on her cheeks was all twisted and knotted, and in places the bones were exposed.

'If you're conscious, you're not just going to lie there and let somebody pour concentrated sulphuric acid all over your mush, are you?' he said. 'Maybe she was drugged with Rohypnol, or something like that. Either that, or there was more than one assailant. If she wasn't drugged, somebody would have had to pin her down.'

'There's no apparent bruising on her wrists,' said the

forensic officer. 'We'll know more, of course, once she's been taken to St George's for a full post-mortem.'

'All we know about her so far is that her name is Samira Wazir,' said Jamila. 'She's seventeen-and-a-half years old and a former pupil at Al-Risalah Secondary School. Her parents recently took her to Pakistan and judging by her orange shalwar kameez I'd say that they may have taken her there to meet her husband-to-be.'

'You mean an arranged marriage?' asked DI Saunders.

'That's the usual custom, yes.'

'So maybe she didn't like the look of this husband-to-be and said she didn't want to marry him.'

'That can be the motive for an honour punishment, yes,' said Jamila. 'But it's far too early to say in this case. We need to find out from her mother and her brother who she was supposed to be marrying, and whether she had any boyfriends here in the UK that her family didn't approve of. Or maybe she had a Pakistani boyfriend here who was angry that she was going to marry another man, and wanted to ruin her looks.

'It's even possible that she was being punished for something that her brother has done. That has happened many times in Pakistan. A man might commit adultery but it will be one of his sisters who gets punished for it. Sometimes she might be forced to marry the cuckolded husband, and often she'll be gang-raped, too, by all of the male members of his family.'

'Charming,' said the ginger forensic officer. 'I'm bloody glad I don't have to gang-rape the wife's sister. I wouldn't climb on her to hang wallpaper. Mind you, she'd probably enjoy it.'

'I'll go down and have a word with this poor girl's mother and brother. Jerry – come with me. It's important that I have a man with me, especially when I question her brother.'

'Where's her father?' asked DI Saunders.

'Still in Peshawar, doing business, so she said. He might have stayed there to arrange the wedding with her prospective husband's family – sorting out the dowry, maybe. We'll find out, anyway.'

Jerry and Jamila left the bedroom, but before he went out of the door Jerry took one last look at the girl lying on the bed. He was shocked but also fascinated by that gruesome face, with its wild mane of black hair spread out all around it, and by that blistered tongue poking out as if she were challenging anybody who dared to suggest that she didn't look beautiful. He had seen plenty of dead bodies during his nine-year career – some crushed, some charred, some bloated from the river – but none as horrifying as this. He would probably have nightmares about her, but he was trying to imagine what kind of sadist could have deliberately mutilated her like that, and wanted her to suffer so much agony. In the name of what? Religion? Or jealousy? Or family honour? How could it be honourable to kill a young woman by melting her face off?

Mrs Wazir was twisting her green dupatta nervously as Jerry and Jamila entered the living-room. Her eyes were bloodshot and swollen from crying. Jamal was standing by the window looking at the police cars out in the street and he didn't turn around when they came in. The young woman constable who had been sitting with them stood up and said, 'Do you want me to wait outside, ma'am?'

'No, stay,' said Jamila. 'It'll be good experience for you. Mrs Wazir – this is Detective Pardoe. He's been seconded from Scotland Yard. He's very experienced in dealing with domestic incidents so you can be quite open with him.'

'What do you mean, "domestic incidents"?' demanded Mrs Wazir, using her dupatta to wipe her eyes. 'This had nothing at all to do with my family. Like I told you before, my son Jamal and me, we had both been away for two days when this happened, visiting my cousins in Redbridge.'

'Mrs Wazir, our forensic team have now examined all of the doors and windows in this house, and there is no sign of forced entry. This means one of four things. Either Samira's assailants possessed a key, or had borrowed one; or Samira knew them and invited them into the house; or they forced their way in once she had opened the door, whether she knew them or not.'

'That is only *three* things,' said Mrs Wazir.

'Well, I think the fourth is obvious. She was assaulted by a member or members of her family.'

'That is an outrageous suggestion,' said Mrs Wazir. 'If you repeat such a thing I will be forced to call our solicitors.'

'Please,' Jamila told her, 'I'm not trying to be offensive, or make false accusations, but I have to consider every possibility, or else I wouldn't be doing my job. I'm sure you can understand that.'

'I can only understand that you are trying to accuse me of burning my own beloved daughter's face with acid. Can you imagine what it was like for me, to find her like that? I shall never sleep again as long as I live.'

'She was wearing an orange shalwar kameez, which suggests to me that she was soon to be married,' said Jamila.

'Yes. This is true. The reason we took her to Peshawar in September was to meet her husband-to-be. He is a very fine upstanding young man from a good family, and Samira liked him and was very happy that she was going to be his bride.'

'Does she have any boyfriends here in Tooting?' asked Jerry.

'She has friends who are boys but not what you would call a boyfriend. She was a virgin.'

'You're sure about that?'

'Quite sure.'

'How about her brother here – Jamal, is it? Do you know if your sister had any boyfriends?'

'My sister did what she was told,' said Jamal, without turning around.

'That's not what I asked you.'

'I don't know. I don't know any of her friends.'

'Can you think of anybody who might have wanted to harm Samira for any reason at all? Had she upset one of her girlfriends, maybe?'

'You will have to ask them,' said Mrs Wazir. 'Her best friend is Aqeelah Abdali. She lives in Streatham somewhere. I expect you will be able to find her address from Samira's telephone book.'

'Was Samira planning on further education?' asked Jamila. 'Going on to college maybe, or university?'

'What do you mean?' said Mrs Wazir. 'She was going to be married.'

Jerry was tempted to ask Mrs Wazir why being a wife meant that she couldn't continue her studies, but he decided to keep his mouth shut.

'What has she been doing since she left school?' he asked her.

'Helping me in the house mostly. Sometimes to make herself a little money she worked in the evenings at Saravanna Bhavan restaurant in the High Street.'

Jamila noted that down, and then she said, 'How about Samira's health? Had she said anything to you about being worried or depressed or not feeling well?'

Mrs Wazir thought about that, and then shrugged. 'I will say that for the past week she was very quiet, and I didn't see much of her. In fact she went out almost every day and she would come back late and go straight up to her room.'

'Did you ask her if there was anything wrong?'

'I knocked at her door, yes, and asked her if she was all right, but she said everything was fine.'

'She didn't join you for meals, or come downstairs and watch television with you?'

'No. When I told her that supper was on the table she said that she had already eaten at the restaurant.'

Jamal came away from the window. His black hair was brushed up into a point and his moustache looked false, although he had the beginnings of a curly beard, too. He was wearing a dark green zip-up fleece with the nickname *Pak Shaheens* on it for the Pakistani national football team, and skinny black jeggings.

'Come on, Mum,' he said, in a strong South London accent, 'why don't you tell them that you and Sam was always shouting at each other anyway? You was always arguing and slamming doors.'

'Is that true, Mrs Wazir?' said Jamila. 'You and Samira weren't getting on?'

Mrs Wazir threw up her hands and said, 'Pfff! What do you expect? Mothers and daughters always argue. And Samira could be very stubborn. That was why we thought it was time that she was married. To be married would teach her to be obedient, like a woman should be. But my heart still bleeds for her, I can tell you. I cannot believe that I will never see her again. I cannot believe it!'

She pressed her dupatta to her eyes, and shook her head in disbelief and grief.

At that moment DI Saunders appeared in the doorway and looked around the living-room in his bird-of-prey way, left and right, as if he expected to see mice scurrying along the skirting-boards that he could pounce on.

'How's it going, sergeant?'

'I think we're done for tonight, sir,' said Jamila. 'We'll come around again in a day or two, Mrs Wazir, when you've had more time to get over the shock, and we've had time to talk to Samira's friends and assess exactly what happened to her. If you like, I can arrange for a volunteer from Victim Support to come and visit you.'

Mrs Wazir raised one hand to acknowledge that she had heard her. Jamal just stood there with his hands in the pockets of his fleece and a bored expression on his face, as if he couldn't wait for Jerry and Jamila and the young woman police officer to leave.

They had to wait for a moment while two paramedics carried a stretcher past the living-room and up the stairs. As they stood in the doorway, Jerry said, 'Where's that coat gone?'

'What coat?' asked Jamila.

'There was a grey coat on that coat-stand, on top of all of those other coats. It's not there any more. There's a red coat on top now.'

'I can't say that I noticed it.'

'No, there was definitely a grey coat on top. I remember it because it was just like a coat I used to have when I got my first motorbike.'

'I can't seriously see anybody half-inching it,' said DI Saunders. 'It probably dropped off and they've hung it up somewhere else.'

The police officers who had been standing in the hallway had stepped out into the front garden so that the paramedics could get past, and were chatting and stamping their feet to keep warm.

'Did any of you see what happened to that grey coat?' Jerry asked them, as he and Jamila came outside.

They all shook their heads. 'What grey coat?'

'There was a grey—' Jerry began, but then he said, 'Never mind.'

'Not suffering from optical illusions, are we, Jerry?' asked DI Saunders, as they walked back up the road to their cars.

Jerry was strongly tempted to say, '*You actually smiled when you said that, "Smiley"*,' but he decided against it. He was becoming quite proud of his self-restraint these days. But he was still convinced that he had seen a grey coat on top of that coat-stand, and if nobody had taken it, where had it gone?

5

Sophie was woken up by Mike's snoring. He always snored, but he snored even louder and more elaborately when he had been drinking. Each exhalation started softly, like a motorboat puttering across a lake, but it would gradually grow into a harsh, rabid growl, and finish up with an off-key squeal.

She turned her head to look at the digital clock beside the bed. It was 3:41. Because of Mike's snoring she never slept well, and she wondered if that was one of the reasons why she had been feeling so depressed lately.

She lay there for a while, while Mike snored on and on, with an occasional snuffle. The streetlights were shining through the gap in the curtains, so that a shadowy pattern of leaves was dancing on the ceiling. She couldn't stop thinking about the blue velvet jacket, and the way that she had felt when she had tried it on. *Bereaved*, strangely, but furious, too.

She had left the jacket on the sofa in the living-room downstairs. Maybe if she went down and tried it on again, she would understand why it had made her feel so sad and so angry. The more she thought about it, the more she knew that she needed to do it. Anyway, she wouldn't be able to go back to sleep, not with Mike snoring so loudly. She could try on the jacket and make herself a mug of warm chocolate Ovaltine and listen to Adele on her headphones.

She folded back the duvet and climbed out of bed. She was naked, but their maisonette was always warm, and neither she nor Mike ever wore anything at night. He was always so hot and sweaty, in any case, and she had to change the sheets at least twice a week because they smelled so sour, especially if they had been having sex. Not that they had been having sex very often – not for the past three or four months, anyway.

She felt her way across the darkened landing and down the stairs, and once she was in the living-room she closed the door behind her and switched on the table-lamp. There was just enough space in the living-room for a tan vinyl two-seater sofa, one armchair and a glass-topped coffee-table. A 55-inch television was mounted on the wall, and Sophie could see herself reflected in its black shiny screen as she crossed the room to pick up the jacket. She thought she looked like a ghost of herself, pale and out of focus.

Perhaps that's what I've become, staying with Mike. Nothing more than a ghost.

She tried on the jacket, and this time, because she was naked, she could feel its wrinkled silk lining across her back, cool and slippery, but slightly clinging, too. She had to admit that it was still too tight for her across the bust, although she managed to fasten the middle button out of three. There was something about it that she hadn't noticed when she had first tried it on – probably because there was lily-of the-valley air freshener in the Little Helpers shop to mask the smell of second-hand clothes and yellowing paperbacks. The velvet had a faintly bitter aroma to it, as if its last wearer had been standing close to a bonfire. She sniffed one sleeve and there was no doubt about it. It had absorbed the pungency of charred wood.

She closed her eyes. She could picture the smoke billowing across the owner's garden, and hear the crackling of burning timber. Although she had no idea why, it made her feel both angry and pleased with herself.

There – you've got what you deserved. Did you really think that I was so weak that I wasn't going to punish you?

She opened the living-room door and stepped out into the hallway. She didn't care now if the light from the living-room shone upstairs and woke Mike up. It might make him annoyed, but even if he started shouting at her, so what? She preferred his shouting to his snoring – at least when he was shouting he was recognising that she existed.

She stood in front of the long wall mirror at the bottom of the stairs and admired herself. She thought the jacket gave her style, and sophistication, and a certain authority, too – the look of a woman who commanded attention whenever she walked into a room. Somehow it made her prettier, too. Mike had once called her 'suet-pudding-face' when they had been having one of their rows, but now her cheekbones seemed more angular. Perhaps it was only the subdued lighting in the hallway that lent her that look, but her jawline seemed stronger, too, and more clear-cut.

She held her breath and listened. She heard Mike snuffling again, and it sounded as if he had said something, but after a few seconds he continued snoring, although his snores no longer ended in that oboe-like squeal.

What makes you think you can treat me with such contempt, as if I'm nothing? Just because you've been paying the rent and you've lent me money, what makes you think that I don't deserve to be loved, and respected, and given my freedom?

She stared at herself in the mirror for almost half a minute, only blinking twice. Her eyes still had that feline slant to them, but she thought they looked wider, and a much darker brown, as dark as polished mahogany; and there was an intensity in them which she had never seen before. Not just pride, although she could see pride as well – pride in her personality and pride in her appearance. Most of all she saw cold determination.

Nobody is ever going to trap me again. Nobody is ever going to grind me down, so that I have to live the same tedious life, day after day, afraid to express myself, afraid to disagree. This is where it ends.

Sophie went back through the living-room to the small kitchenette, switching on the fluorescent lights. The dishes from last night's Indian takeaway were still soaking in the sink, with a greasy orange film on the surface of the water. She had intended to wash them up before she went to work in the morning. Mike wouldn't do them, even though he didn't have to leave for the office until 9:15.

She opened the second drawer down in the kitchen cabinet. This is where they kept the tongs and the slotted spoons and the potato-peeler, as well as the cooking knives. She took out a wooden-handled carving knife, as well as two smaller knives.

Her heart was beating hard, but she felt mentally calm and completely focused, unlike the white-skinned ghost of herself that she had seen in the television screen. She knew exactly what she was going to do and how she was going to do it, and she also knew that nothing in the world was going to change her mind.

She left the lights on and quietly climbed the stairs. On the landing, she paused to make sure that Mike was still snoring. He had drunk three cans of Peroni before they had gone to bed, and who knows how much he had drunk in the pub with his friends after work.

She eased open the bedroom door and crept inside. As quietly as she could, she laid the three knives down on the bedside table, next to the digital clock, and then she went across to the fitted wardrobe. Mike's ties were hanging on the back of the door, and she picked out two of them. One was his favourite: the Tooting & Mitcham Darts Club tie. The other was the flowery tie she had bought him for his birthday, which he had never worn. He had said that he didn't want to look like a screaming gay.

She sat down on the bed next to him, so close that she could smell the stale alcohol on his breath. He stirred, and snorted, but still he didn't open his eyes. She eased up his right arm until his hairy wrist was resting against one of the rails of the brass headboard. Then, quickly and deftly, she looped the darts club tie around it and fastened it in a constrictor knot. His armpit smelled so foetid that she had to hold her breath while she tightened it.

After she had secured his right wrist, she went around the bed and tied up his left wrist. Then she folded down the pale green polycotton bedspread as far as his knees and wedged it deep underneath the mattress on both sides of the bed, so that he wouldn't be able to kick.

When she was ready, she stood looking down at him. He was still snoring, but somewhere in his subconscious he must have been aware that his movement had become restricted, because his breathing became shallower and quicker, and he started to twist his body from side to side. Sophie guessed that, as drunk as he was, it wouldn't be long before he woke up.

She picked up one of the two smaller knives from the bedside table. It was a paring knife, with a blade only about three inches long, but very sharp. She sat down close to him and positioned the point above his right eyelid, until it was almost touching it.

Look at you, helpless now. Why did I ever think that I loved you, you selfish uncaring pig? I gave you everything – my devotion, my body, my money – and how did you treat me in return? Like some kind of slave. I don't think you even recognised that I was a real person, with my own feelings and my own ambitions. God, you're ugly. Ugly in spirit, ugly in appearance. Just ugly.

She gripped the handle of the paring knife as tightly as she could and stabbed him through his eyelid. Blood and optic fluid burst out onto his cheek, and he opened his other eye in shock.

'*Aaah!*' he screamed out. He tried to reach down to pull the knife out, but all he succeeded in doing was tugging the constrictor knot even tighter. '*Aaaah!* My eye! My fucking eye! What's happening? Sophie, my eye! Something's stuck in my eye! Jesus Christ, Sophie! Sophie, what's happening? I can't move my arms! Sophie, help me! What's going on? Sophie, there's something stuck in my eye and I can't fucking open it! It hurts, Sophie! *Jesus!*'

Sophie said nothing but sat beside him watching him struggle. She left the knife-blade sticking in his eyelid, so that he couldn't open it, and even if he had been able to, she had pushed the point right into the optic nerve at the back of his eye, and blinded him.

Although he was pinned by the tightly tucked-in bedspread, he tried to hump himself up and down and wrench his arms free, staring at Sophie with his bulging left eye, but all she did was stare back at him calmly as if she were thinking about something else altogether, like what she was going to wear to the shop today.

'Sophie!' he screamed. 'Sophie, what have you done to me? Get this thing out of my eye! Please, Sophie! Get this fucking thing out of my eye! Sophie!'

Eventually Sophie stood up and walked around to the other side of the bed. She sat down again, and picked up the second small knife. She reached across and gripped Mike's right ear, digging her sharply pointed thumbnail into the lobe, so that he couldn't move his head. Then she held the knife over his left eye, as close as she had held the first one. Mike roared and struggled, but she gripped his ear even tighter.

'Don't do it, Soph! Please, I'm begging you! Don't do it!'

He screwed his eyelid shut, but not because he wanted to. It was an involuntary response, to protect his eye. Sophie took a deep breath and stabbed him so hard that she felt the point of the knife jar against the bone of his eye-socket. Again, optic fluid bulged out from under his lashes and dribbled in glutinous blood-streaked teardrops down his cheek.

Mike screamed again, although it was more of a howl of utter despair. Sophie said nothing, but let go of his ear and sat watching him as he shook his head from side to side, with knife-handles sticking out of each eye.

'Soph, for the love of God! Call an ambulance! Call an ambulance!'

Sophie didn't answer him, but picked up the carving knife and stood up. She didn't really feel like Sophie at all. She knew that she *was* Sophie, but would Sophie have done anything like this – and would Sophie have enjoyed it so much? Because stabbing Mike in the eyes had made her feel excited, and strong, and *triumphant*. At last she was getting her own back for every time that he had insulted her, or slapped her, or simply ignored her when she had asked him a question. And blinding him – this was more than winning an argument. Now he would never be able to treat her with such contempt, ever again.

He stopped begging her to call for an ambulance, because he had obviously realised that she wasn't going to do it. Instead, he started to cry, and his crying was high-pitched and pathetic.

'Oh, shut up!' Sophie snapped at him. 'You're not a child!'

That was exactly what he had said to her, the last time he had slapped her.

She leaned over and laid her hand flat on his stomach. He jerked, as if her hand were red-hot.

'What are you doing? What are you doing to me, Soph? For Christ's sake, what are you doing?'

He wasn't fat, but his stomach bulged slightly because he drank so much. It was covered with a fan of black hair which she had once thought was sexy, but which she now found vaguely repulsive. She bent her wrist downwards so that the carving knife was pointing two inches below his breast-bone. She wondered how deeply she would need to cut, but then she thought: *You know how deeply. You've done this before. An inch is enough.*

He started crying again, but then she pierced his skin with a soft popping sound and started to cut into the fatty tissue and the muscle underneath. As she slowly sliced downwards, his crying rose into a hideous warbling shriek, like a parody of some tragic Wagnerian opera.

'No! Soph! No, Sophie! Aaaahhh! Stop! No!'

But Sophie carried on cutting through the layers of his abdominal wall until his small intestines came swelling out, and then his large intestines. She cut as far down as his pubic hair, and then stopped, and laid the knife back on the bedside table. She was aware that Mike was still pleading with her, but she closed her ears to it. She didn't care if he was in pain. However much he pleaded, what she was doing to him was irrevocable.

She plunged both of her hands into the warm slippery coils of his small intestines. It was difficult to hold onto them, because they were as soft and flaccid as freshly boiled cannelloni, and her carving knife had nicked them in places, so the sour stench that rose out of them made her retch. But she dragged them out, pulling them across the side of the bed until they were hanging down onto the carpet.

She stood up. She remained calm, but her stomach kept clenching and unclenching with nausea. She went across the landing to the bathroom, tugged on the light, and turned on the taps in the basin to wash the blood off her hands. As she did so, she stared at her reflection in the mirror and thought: *You look extraordinary. You're almost beautiful. But you don't look like me. Who are you?*

She was still staring at herself when she became aware that Mike was still whimpering and pleading for her to save him. She could hardly believe it. She had blinded him and disembowelled him – shouldn't he be dead by now?

She dried her hands and went back into the bedroom.

'Soph,' Mike croaked at her, and she could actually see his lungs inflating and deflating like two pink balloons. 'I love you, Soph. Help me.'

'Help you?' said Sophie, in disbelief. 'Help you?'

She picked up the sticky-handled carving knife again and went around to the opposite side of the bed. She knelt on the mattress and screamed into his face, '*Help* you! After the way you've treated me? *Help* you?'

She stabbed him in his open mouth. The carving knife split his tongue in half and the blade became jammed in between his lower front teeth, so that she was unable to pull it out.

She climbed off the bed and stood back, panting.

If all the arrogant uncaring men in the world knew that this would be their punishment for mistreating the women in their lives, wouldn't life be different?

She went to the window and drew the curtains. It was still dark outside, and it had started to rain.

On the bed, Mike gave one last cackle as his lungs collapsed.

6

Jerry was eating a chicken-and-mushroom slice at his desk in the corner of the CID room when Jamila came in. Today she was wearing a black trouser-suit and a purple silk headscarf.

'Ah, there you are,' she said. 'Is there something wrong with your phone?'

'Yes, it's called "switching it off for five minutes so I don't have to answer it with my mouth full".'

'You should eat a proper breakfast before you come to work.'

'I would, if I had somebody to cook it for me.'

'You're wearing a wedding ring. I thought you were married.'

'I was. It was something to do with the hours I had to work, and the fact that she took a fancy to the manager of our local Waitrose. With him, she could have regular sex *and* a ten per cent discount on her weekly shop. How could I compete with that?'

'Do you have children?'

41

'One. A little girl. Alice. She's two-and-a-half. I'm allowed to see her once a fortnight.'

'Life can be very hard to bear sometimes.'

'Are you speaking from experience?'

Jamila didn't answer that, but said, 'The pathologist just called me, from St George's. He says he has something unusual to show me.'

'Oh, yes? Like what?'

'He said we should go the hospital and see for ourselves. He couldn't describe it over the phone.'

'What about Saunders?'

'He's stuck up at the Yard this morning. Some kind of policy meeting. But he'll be down here later.'

Jerry looked at his half-eaten pastry.

'Take it with you,' said Jamila. 'I'll drive. I wouldn't want you to go hungry.'

'No, you're all right,' Jerry told her. He opened his desk drawer and dropped the chicken-and-mushroom slice on top of a report on local vandalism.

*

Dr Fuller impatiently checked his wristwatch when they arrived, although he said nothing.

'Traffic,' Jerry explained. 'Burst water-main on Longley Road.'

'I have three dead drug-addicts waiting for me,' said Dr Fuller. 'It would be nice to get them all wrapped up before lunch.'

He was a big, untidy man, Dr Fuller, with a wild comb-over covering a scalp that was freckled from thrice-yearly Mediterranean cruises and half-glasses that looked as they were going to drop off the end of his snubby nose at any

42

second. His lab coat was done up with all the wrong buttons and his trousers were an inch too short, so that Jerry could see that he wasn't wearing any socks.

He had a slight cast in his pale blue eyes so that Jerry couldn't be sure if he was looking at him or Jamila.

'DS Patel said you had something strange to show us.'

'Well, it's something I've never come across before, let me put it that way, and I've been carrying out post-mortems for thirty-three years.'

Dr Fuller led them along the corridor with his shoes squeaking. The mortuary was as chilly as a church, with high clerestory windows. A young lab assistant was washing a metal dish in the sink, making a loud clattering noise and singing to herself. Three autopsy tables were lined up along one side of the room, and a fourth was standing in the centre. Its stainless steel covers were folded down on either side and its downdraught ventilation system switched on, so that anybody who leaned over it wouldn't be breathing in formalin.

Samira was flat on her stomach with her arms by her sides. Both her head and her buttocks were covered with neatly folded green cloths. Jerry and Jamila approached the autopsy table and stood looking down at her, although neither of them could see anything unusual. It was a plump young Pakistani woman's bare back, with a sprinkling of moles and some bruising around her shoulders where blood had pooled after her death, but that seemed to be all.

'So... what's so strange?' asked Jerry.

'You're not looking closely enough,' said Dr Fuller. 'Here... use this. This might help.'

He handed Jerry a large white magnifying glass with an LED light. Jerry switched it on and examined Samira's back through the lens. The light illuminated a forest of fibres, so fine that they were almost invisible. Each was less than a centimetre long, but they were protruding from almost every pore.

Jerry passed the magnifying glass to Jamila.

'What the hell are all those hairs?' he asked Dr Fuller. 'Was she growing herself a winter coat or what?'

'They don't... they don't look like hairs to me,' said Jamila. 'At least not the natural hairs that this poor girl would have grown. Look at the hair on her head, it's jet black.'

'It's not her natural hair,' said Dr Fuller. 'And she's not growing it. It has no roots.'

Peering through the magnifying glass, Jamila carefully pinched one of the fibres between finger and thumb and pulled it out. 'It comes out quite easily,' she said. 'Not much resistance at all.'

'So what is it?' asked Jerry. 'If she's not growing it, how did it get into her pores? Even pushing one hair into one pore would be hard enough, and there are hundreds of them – *thousands*, even. Gordon Bennett – it takes me about half an hour to thread a needle.'

'I've carried out a preliminary analysis,' said Dr Fuller. 'Of course the forensic unit will be able to do a much more comprehensive check. But it's not hair at all. Not human hair. It's a mixture of wool and polyester.'

'*What?*'

Dr Fuller poked his half-glasses more firmly onto the bridge of his nose. 'No doubt about it. It's the sort of fibre that clothes are made out of. Somehow it seems to have penetrated her skin. Her back, mainly, but her arms, too, and her sides, and her breasts and her stomach.'

'Do you have any idea how that might have happened?' asked Jamila.

'Absolutely none, I'm afraid,' said Dr Fuller. 'I've come across quite a few cases in which people have exhibited allergies to certain fabrics, such as nylon or pure wool. They've had rashes and spots and sometimes they've become very ill. But I've never seen anybody who appears to have been *invaded* by a fabric before, not like this unfortunate girl.'

'What's your next step?' asked Jamila.

'I'll take further samples including a section of skin with the fibres embedded and send them up to Lambeth Road to see what they make of it. The cause of death was almost certainly cardiac arrest brought on by shock, but that's hardly surprising when you consider what was done to her face. I'll be setting up some further tests, though, to see if these fibres didn't contribute in some way to her demise. Perhaps they caused some chemical reaction that dramatically lowered her blood pressure.'

'They're just wool and polyester; how could they do that?'

'They contain elements of a synthetic disperse dye, too. That's a man-made dye frequently used to colour clothing, especially clothing with a polyester content.'

'The fibres are *dyed*? What colour?'

'Some variety of grey, as far as I can make out. Pigeon grey, dove grey. Something like that.'

*

Jerry and Jamila left St George's and drove back to the station. They were both silent for most of the way, but as they turned into Mitcham Road, both of them spoke at once.

'I hate bloody inexplicable mysteries,' said Jerry.

'How can a *fabric* attack a woman?' said Jamila. 'It makes no sense at all.'

As they went up in the lift to the CID room, Jerry said, 'It was grey. And that coat was grey, the one that went missing.'

'The one that you *thought* went missing.'

'I know it went missing. I distinctly saw it when we first entered the house, and by the time we left it had gone. And it was grey.'

'That's not even a coincidence.'

'Well, perhaps it isn't. But I'd still like to know where that coat went.'

'In that case, why don't you go around to the Wazirs and ask them if they know where it is. Then maybe you'll stop nagging me about it.'

'I just have a feeling about it. I don't know why. It could be that her mother or her brother got rid of it because it was evidence that it was one of them who poured acid in her face. Maybe one of them was wearing it when they attacked her, and some of the acid splashed onto it.'

'You really are clutching at straws, Jerry.'

'I know. But I have OCD when it comes to circumstantial evidence. We had a case in Tower Hamlets last summer and there was only one shoe in this missing woman's bedroom and we couldn't find the other shoe anywhere. I looked everywhere for that bloody shoe, and in the end I found it. It was jammed underneath the passenger seat of her husband's car. He'd knocked her out, dragged her out of the house, and driven all the way down to Leigh-on-Sea so that he could hire a boat and chuck her into the estuary.'

'Go on, then, if it's bothering you that much. But DI Saunders has arranged a media conference for twelve noon and you need to be back in time for that.'

'What are we going to tell them? It wasn't an honour killing, after all. They were trying to turn her into a magic carpet and something went wrong?'

'Jerry—'

'Sorry. It's just that it gets my goat sometimes, all this pussyfooting round the Muslim community.'

'Jerry – we respect your religion. We ask only that you respect ours, in return.'

'I don't have a religion. I gave it up about the same time that I gave up smoking.'

'We don't smoke, either.'

'Oh, don't you? I thought you were still burning embassies. Sorry – sorry! Bad joke!'

'It's probably just as well for you that I don't get it.'

'Embassy cigarettes? Never heard of them? Never mind.'

'I'll see you at twelve.'

7

David unlocked the front door of the bungalow and stepped inside. The hallway smelled airless and damp. He was about to call out, as he always used to, 'Hallo! It's all right! It's only me!' but of course he didn't need to – not now, nor ever again.

All the same, under his breath, he whispered, '*Hallo! It's all right! It's only me!*'

He went into the living-room. The curtains were half-drawn, so that it was gloomy in there. His mother's knitting was still lying on the seat of her armchair, a half-finished sleeve in pond-green wool. She had promised him a new sweater for his birthday, as she always did every year, but this year, thank God, he wouldn't have to pretend he liked it.

This was the first time he had visited the bungalow since the funeral last week. He had been making excuses to himself why he couldn't have come earlier, but the reality was that he had been dreading it. The smell of urine-soaked seat cushions. The chipped china ornaments and the murky reproduction landscape paintings. The kitchen with its blocked sink and its tannin-stained teacups and its dinner-plates that hadn't been washed properly, so that they still carried a crust of month-old gravy round the rim.

Worst of all were his memories of growing up here. David was an only child, and his father had died of a stroke when he was eight, so he had spent all his adolescent years here alone with his mother. Netty, her name was – a selfish, bitter, domineering woman who never had a good word for anybody.

Strangely, she had been almost beautiful when she was young, in a sharp-jawed way, and she had kept her looks into her old age. But dementia had taken hold. Up until her late sixties she used to pin up her hair into an immaculate French pleat, but gradually she had allowed it to grow tangled and filthy. Her clothes became spattered with the food that she had dropped, and by the age of seventy-eight she was incontinent.

A carer from social services had visited her every day, but she had spent only about twenty minutes tidying up and changing the bed and microwaving her lunch for her. It wasn't surprising that she hadn't stayed longer. Netty had done nothing but insult her and complain that she was ugly and useless and a fat black cow.

David had been appalled by her racism. When he was seventeen he had a black girlfriend, Millie, from Streatham, but he hadn't dared to bring her home.

He went through to his mother's bedroom. In here, too, the curtains were half-drawn, so he pulled them open. The small garden outside was overgrown with weeds and heaped with sodden leaves. A concrete gnome was surrounded by dead bracken, so that only his faded blue hat was visible.

David looked over at the bed with its thick brown- and mustard-coloured cover. The pillow was still indented from his mother's head, and the sheets were still stained and wrinkled, untouched since her body had been lifted out of it. In the corner, her dressing-table was crowded with jars of foundation and crumpled tubes of anti-wrinkle cream. The mirror was so dusty that the bedroom appeared as if it were filled with fog.

He had come to the bungalow with the intention of clearing up everything in it – emptying drawers and taking down curtains – so that it was ready to be put on the market. But now that he was actually standing here, all of that brisk efficiency had drained out of him. He felt as helpless as he had when he was a boy, overpowered by his mother's relentless malevolence.

Don't you dare touch anything – this is my *house, not yours!*

He went across to the fitted wardrobes and opened one of the sliding doors. All of his mother's dresses and skirts were hanging in there, some of them filthy. Her lilac tweed suit he remembered from when he was a teenager, as well as the long green dress with the cowl-neck collar which she had always worn to what she considered were 'special occasions', like his school concerts and midnight Mass on Christmas Eve.

On the right-hand side, every shelf was untidily stuffed with her sweaters and cardigans, which she had once folded with almost obsessive neatness, and with her underwear, her withered roll-ons and her laddered tights. He was about to slide the wardrobe door shut when he noticed the black fisherman's sweater which his mother had knitted for his father, for his birthday, the year before he had died.

David had always thought it was the best sweater that she had ever made – mainly because his father had insisted on it being black, and not custard yellow or pond green or salmon pink like most of her knitwear. All the same, his father and mother had argued ferociously about something on his birthday – David couldn't remember what it was – but after that argument his father had refused to wear the sweater.

His mother had kept it, though, and on wintry days she had worn it herself, even though it was much too big for her.

David tugged it out from under the other sweaters. It was untouched by clothes moths, and it was clean, so his mother probably hadn't worn it for years. He had been thinking of buying himself two or three new sweaters for the winter, and if he kept this one, it would save him a bit of money. His solicitors' partnership hadn't been doing too well lately, and he was in arrears with his mortgage, although he hadn't told his wife Evie that he was almost broke.

His mother's death had actually come as a relief, not just because he would no longer have to visit her two or three times a month and listen to her demented insults, but because she had left him nearly £17,000 in savings and shares and the bungalow would fetch at least £475,000, if not more. Her jewellery would be worth a couple of thousand, too.

He took off his brown corduroy jacket and tugged the sweater over his head. It smelled faintly of the perfume his mother used to wear, but he found that nostalgic rather than off-putting. Perhaps she hadn't been as hard on him as he remembered. She had been left to fend for herself with an eight-year-old boy to take care of, after all, and with only her child support to feed and clothe him.

He looked at himself in the foggy dressing-table mirror. The sweater fitted him so well it could have been made for him. It was warm, and it relaxed him, so that he no longer felt so hostile towards his mother, and the bungalow seemed less depressing, and more homely.

Now you understand what I went through, putting up with that ungrateful father of yours, and bringing you up, you obnoxious boy. I never even wanted you in the first place. You were an accident, and a tragic accident, as far as I was concerned.

'I was an accident?' said David, out loud. 'You didn't want me?'

What am I doing, he thought, *talking to myself?* But perhaps he *had* been selfish, when he was a boy. Because the two of them had always argued so much, he had blamed his mother for his father's death, without once thinking what pain and loneliness she must have suffered. No wonder her tongue had seemed so sharp at times.

He shrugged on his jacket again, but he kept the black sweater underneath. He didn't know why, but it gave him confidence, and certainty, and a feeling that he was in charge of his life again – and that was a feeling that he had been losing lately, with his partnership doing so badly. Nelson & White had lost several crucial actions in court, and because of that their reputation had suffered and business had dried up.

He left his mother's bedroom and went into the bedroom that had once been his. His mother had been using it to store suitcases and deckchairs, as well as her ironing board and vacuum cleaner and cardboard boxes filled with all kinds of junk, from burned-out lightbulbs to ten-year-old women's magazines. His single bed was still there, with its shiny blue quilt, and his poster of David Bowie was still stuck on the wall beside it, although the bottom half of it had been ripped off.

This was where you hid yourself and never thought about how lonely I was. This is where you listened to your cacophonous music and masturbated every night. Oh, don't think I didn't know! I found all your Mayfair *magazines! And you thought that I was being hard on you?*

David stood in the doorway with his mind in a turmoil. He felt as if he was seeing this room through his mother's eyes now, and remembering what it was like when he came home from school and closed the door and stayed there all evening, only emerging to eat his supper in the kitchen and never say a word to her, except to grunt.

You know what I should have done? I should have come into your room one night when you were sleeping, and suffocated you. Why didn't I?

David found that his eyes were filling with tears. He blinked, and they blurred his vision, so that all the junk in the bedroom seemed to dance.

'I'm sorry,' he said. 'I didn't realise. I really didn't know.'

He was still standing there wiping his eyes when his iPhone warbled. He sniffed and took it out of his pocket. It was Evie calling him. There was a picture of her on his screen – dark-haired and petite and smiling, with red and yellow balloons in the background.

'How's it going?' she asked him.

'Why?'

'What do you mean, "why"? I just want to know how it's going, that's all. Do you want me to come around and help you? I've finished all my shopping now.'

'Why should I need any help?'

'Well – there's an awful lot of rubbish in that house to clear out, isn't there?'

'What do you mean, "rubbish"?'

'All that old furniture, of course, and bedding, and curtains, and your mother's clothes.'

'They're not rubbish! How dare you call them rubbish?'

'David – what's the matter with you?'

'Nothing's the matter with me. Why?'

'You don't sound like yourself at all. And why are you being so aggressive?'

'You'd be aggressive if you'd had to put up with all the bad feeling that I've had to put up with.'

'Honestly, David, I don't have a clue what you're talking about. Has it upset you, clearing out your mother's stuff? I know she was a horrible old bag but you shouldn't let her get to you. Not now – now that she's dead. Why don't you call it a day and come home? We can both of us go back there on Saturday and clear it out together. Or I'll do it by myself, if it throws you off so much.'

'Oh, you think I'd let you do that?'

'David – please, come home. You're sounding so weird.'

David stood silent for a few moments.

'David?' said Evie, but then he ended the call without answering her.

Yes, I'll come and see you, Evie. And I'll show you what I do to anybody who insults me. I've done it before and by God I'll do it again.

8

When Jerry arrived at the Wazir house on Rectory Lane, he found three uniformed constables taking down the police line tapes and the last two members of the forensic team packing up their van ready to leave.

'How's it going?' he asked the PCs.

'Pretty much sorted,' said one of them. 'Not sure I need to go for a curry anytime soon, though. I feel like I've been breathing in balti for the past two days.'

Mrs Wazir was sitting in the living-room with a short bald Pakistani man in a shiny black suit.

'This is my husband's brother Nadeem,' said Mrs Wazir. 'Samira's uncle.'

Nadeem put down his teacup and stood up, holding out a podgy hand with three gold rings on his fingers.

'How is your investigation progressing?' he asked.

'Well, it's early days yet,' said Jerry. 'I've just come around to see if I can tie up one or two loose ends.'

'Samira and my family were very close,' said Nadeem. 'My brother has to be away on business in Pakistan sometimes for weeks at a time, so Samira often used to come round to spend the evening with us, and weekends too. I am mortified that she is gone. Truly mortified.'

'When was the last time you saw her?'

'Late on Saturday afternoon. She had been working at the restaurant and she called in to give us some kebabs. She said she was tired so she didn't stay long.'

'How was she, apart from tired? Did she seem upset about anything?'

'I have to say that she didn't seem like her normal self. I don't exactly know how to describe it, but she was very distant. It was like her mind was somewhere else. But maybe that was just because she had been working hard all day. That restaurant can get very busy at weekends.'

'So... what were the loose ends that you wanted to tie up?' asked Mrs Wazir. It was obvious that she was keen to get rid of him.

'Had Samira complained to you at all about skin irritation?'

'I don't understand the question.'

'Did she tell you that she'd been feeling itchy at all, or sore?'

Mrs Wazir shook her head. 'Nothing like that. She had beautiful skin, like silk.'

'OK. Another thing was – I saw a coat on top of the coat-stand when I came here yesterday. A short grey overcoat.'

'Yes, that was Samira's.'

'She was wearing it the last time I saw her,' put in Nadeem.

'It was hanging on top of the coat-stand when I arrived here, but by the time I left after talking to you and your son, it had disappeared.'

Mrs Wazir frowned. 'What do you mean? It should still be there. Nobody would have taken it.'

'I'm sorry, Mrs W, but it had gone, and it's not there now.'

Mrs Wazir stood up, gathering up the folds of her abundant black dress. She went out into the hallway and started to lift the coats off the coat-stand, hanging them one by one over the banisters. After a few moments she came back, frowning.

'You are right. It isn't there. I can't think where it could be. I can't imagine that anybody would have stolen it. It was only second-hand. She bought it from one of those charity shops.'

'You're absolutely sure you didn't remove it yourself, for any reason?' Jerry asked her.

'Why should I? And how could I? All the time that you were here yesterday, I was sitting in this room, with that policewoman, too. And so was Jamal.'

'Do you know which charity shop she bought it from?'

Mrs Wazir sat down again. 'I don't know the name of it, but Samira used to buy several things there, because she said it was always clean, and didn't smell like some charity shops. And of course everything was very cheap. She bought gloves there, and scarves, and I think once she even bought some boots.'

'Would you know where it is?'

'Yes... on the Mitcham Road, in between Kentucky Fried Chicken and Sabina's, where she used to buy her make-up. But I don't see how this will help you to find out who killed her.'

'It's just routine procedure, Mrs W. We have to follow up every possibility, no matter how remote it might seem. Maybe her assailant saw her wearing that coat and mistook her for somebody else. It does happen.'

Nadeem said, 'Do you know when her remains will be released for her funeral? We like to bury our dead as soon as possible after death.'

'I'll talk to the pathologist and let you know. I believe he's nearly completed his post-mortem so it'll probably be Monday at the latest. Meanwhile – that's about all for now. I may have to get back to you once we have some more information, but now I can leave you in peace.'

'I will never know peace again,' said Mrs Wazir. 'Every time I close my eyes I will see my beloved Samira with her face in ruins.'

*

It started to drizzle as Jerry drove down to the Mitcham Road, so that the pavements were wet and shiny. It was a long straight high street with shops and restaurants on either side, as well as the Tooting Granada cinema, a massive white art deco building which was now a bingo hall. In between KFC and Sabina's cosmetics he found Little Helpers Charity Shop, and he parked on the red line outside. He could see a traffic warden eyeing him from a distance, but he couldn't be bothered to walk up and tell him that he was a police detective on duty.

In the front windows of Little Helpers stood three dummies dressed in coats and Puffa jackets, as well as an assortment of dolls and toys and second-hand books. Jerry walked in and realised at once why Samira had said that it didn't smell like an ordinary charity shop. There were Yankee Candle reed diffusers on the shelves, and through the open back door he could see an elderly volunteer steam-cleaning a pair of corduroy trousers that were hanging up on a rail.

A young woman was standing behind the counter, counting the money in the cash register. She had a short brunette bob and she was wearing a tight blue velvet jacket. She had plum-coloured circles under her eyes but Jerry couldn't decide if she was tired, or if the circles were make-up.

'I'm looking for the manager,' he said. He glanced outside and saw that the traffic warden had already pounced on his car and was taking a photograph of it.

'That's me,' the young woman replied, looking up at him quickly but then going back to counting her handful of £5 notes.

Jerry took out his ID card and held it up in front of her. 'Detective Pardoe, Tooting CID.'

She looked up again, and it was plain that she was irritated because he had made her lose count. She didn't say anything but started counting again from the beginning.

'I'm wondering if you recall a Pakistani girl buying a short grey winter coat from you, not so long ago.'

'Why? Has something happened to her?'

'I'm just making some general inquiries, that's all.'

'Well, if it's who I think you're talking about, then yes. I don't know what her name is but she comes in here quite often. She's not missing, is she?'

'She's deceased, as a matter of fact.'

The young woman nodded, almost as if that was what she had been expecting to hear. Jerry was surprised that she didn't ask when Samira had died, or how.

'It's her coat I'm interested in,' he told her.

'Her coat?'

'Do you have any record of where it came from? Who brought it in?'

'Why?'

'Because it would help us with our inquiries, Miss, that's all.'

'I don't usually ask for names and addresses when people bring in donations. I happen to know who brought that particular coat in, though, because he makes cash donations, too, and I have to keep a record of those for tax. It was Mr Stebbings. His wife died about two months ago and he donated a whole heap of her clothes.'

'Do you have his address?'

The young woman put down the banknotes that she was holding and took out a black accounts ledger from a shelf underneath the counter, every page stuffed with receipts. Her tightly pursed lips gave Jerry the impression that she felt she was doing him an enormous favour.

'Here,' she said. 'He last made a cash donation on August the twenty-fifth. He makes regular donations because his son had cerebral palsy. That's why this shop's called Little Helpers.'

'Because it helps kids, you mean?'

'No. It's because cerebral palsy used to be called "Little's Disease" after the man who first studied it, William Little.'

'Well, well. You learn something every day. Are you going to give me Mr Stebbings' address?'

'Here. Number fifteen, Furzehill Drive.'

'Thanks. And can I have *your* name, please?'

'Why do you need my name?'

'In case I have to explain to Mr Stebbings who gave me his address, and for my report.'

'Sophie – Sophie Marshall. Is that your car outside? You've just got a ticket.'

9

Evie was in the kitchen chopping up onions when David came home.

'Oh, you're back,' she said.

David came into the kitchen and stared at her. 'Yes,' he said. 'What does it look like?'

Evie put down her knife. 'David, what's wrong? You sounded so strange on the phone. Has something upset you? Tell me.'

'Nothing is wrong, Evie. Nothing at all, except you.'

Without saying anything else, David walked out of the kitchen and into the living-room. He picked up the remote control and switched on the television, but almost immediately he switched it off again and threw the remote control across the room, so that it clattered into the beige tiled fireplace.

Evie came into the room, wiping her hands on her apron. 'David, what on earth's the matter with you?'

'You're always bloody nagging, that's what's the matter with him. You think you've got him under your thumb, but that's where you're mistaken, my girl. That's where you're very much mistaken.'

'"*Him*"?' said Evie. 'Who's "*him*"? I'm talking about *you*.'

'There you are!' David retorted. '*That's* how much you don't care about him! Pretending you don't even know who he is! Well, I think it's time to put an end to your little game, don't you? You should never have married him in the first place! I *told* him! Didn't I tell him? But oh no, you played your tricks and he believed you! But now we can put an end to all that!'

David stalked across to Evie and loomed over her. At first she stood her ground, but his eyes were so glassy and his grin was so deranged that she took a step back, and then another.

'David, have you been smoking something? I don't know what's wrong with you but I'm calling the doctor.'

'Oh, there's nothing wrong with him, Evie. Not now, anyway. All that was ever wrong with him was *you*. But now that's all going to change! Oh, yes!'

David seized both of her arms and shoved her back against the door-frame, so that she banged her head hard.

'*David!*' she screamed at him, but he shoved her again, and then again, until she managed to twist herself around and wrench her arms free. 'What are you doing? Have you gone mad?'

David didn't answer but tried to grab her again, ripping the sleeve of her blouse. She smacked his face, hard, and then turned around and tried to escape into the kitchen. Before she could slam the kitchen door shut, though, David collided with it and flung it wide open.

'*You trapped him, didn't you?*' he screeched at her, as she dodged around the kitchen table. His voice was unnervingly high, like a furious woman. '*You trapped him and then you kept him under your thumb, you selfish little bitch!*'

Evie feinted to her right, but when David came around the table towards her, she ducked to her left. She had almost made it to the door when she caught her foot against the leg of one of the kitchen chairs, and stumbled. David caught up with her and gripped both of her shoulders before wrapping his left arm around her neck, almost choking her.

'*David!*' she gasped, trying to pull his arm away. 'David, for God's sake!'

But David pulled her even closer, until she was squeaking for breath. Then he reached across to the wooden board where she had been chopping onions and picked up the five-inch knife that she had been using. He twisted her around and then he stabbed her in the lower back, as hard as he could. The point of the knife crunched into the disc between two of her lumbar vertebrae and severed her spinal cord. She let out a muffled whinny and her knees gave way, although David kept his arm around her neck so tightly that she didn't collapse.

'You thought he was spineless, did you?' David hissed in her ear, and he sounded even more like a woman than he had before. 'You thought you were the only one with a backbone, did you? We can see about that, can't we? We can certainly see about that!'

With that, he started to tug out the knife, although it was lodged so tightly in her spine that he had to wrestle it from side to side before it came free. Evie said nothing. She couldn't breathe and she couldn't feel her legs at all. She could only think that she was dreaming this, and it wasn't happening. Any second now she would be back chopping onions for the beef casserole that she had been making for their supper. Any second now she would hear David's key in the door and it would be David as he always was, cheerful and resilient, in spite of their money worries.

But David kept his choke-hold on her, and now she could feel him breathing harshly into her hair. He tensed, and then he stabbed her again, just as hard as he had the first time, but in the middle of her back this time. She flinched, and murmured, but she was in shock now, and close to blacking out.

'Girls like you, they think they can get away with anything,' said David. 'They think that they can treat their husbands any way they like – as if they're something unpleasant that they've trodden in. It's time girls like you were taught a lesson, that's all I can say.'

He pulled out the knife and then he stabbed her yet again, between the shoulder-blades. By now the back of her pale pink gingham dress was soaked in blood, and she was sagging so much that David was finding it hard to keep her upright. He stabbed her one last time in the back of the neck, and then he lowered her lifeless body onto the kitchen floor. Their tortoiseshell cat Maggie approached her and stared at her in bewilderment, and then looked up at David as if she were saying, *What have you done?*

David laid the bloody knife back on the chopping-board. His heart was beating hard but he felt truly vindicated now, as if a long-standing score had been settled. He left Evie lying where she was and went to the sink to wash his hands. Then, shaking the drops off them, he went through to the bedroom and sat down on the end of the bed, staring at himself in the wardrobe mirror.

You've wanted to punish Evie for so long, and now you've managed it. Justice has been done! She took him away from

you even though you had nobody else to take care of you.
When did she ever once think about you, and how your heart
would be broken?

He stood up and went so close to the mirror that the tip of
his nose was almost touching it. He couldn't believe how much
he looked like his mother. Even his mouth was turned down,
in the way that her mouth always was, as if she disapproved
of everything. And he had that impenetrable look in her eyes,
just like the look she had, as if she were hiding how much she
hated the world and everybody in it.

He would have to work out how he was going to get rid
of Evie's body, but he didn't want to think about it now.
After that surge of triumph, he was beginning to feel deeply
tired, both physically and emotionally. It had been a long and
difficult day, and Evie had struggled hard. Stabbing her in the
spine hadn't been easy, either: he had sprained his wrist.

He shrugged off his corduroy jacket. There was blood on
the sleeves, which he would have to wash off himself, because
he couldn't take it to a dry-cleaners. How could he possibly
explain it? *Oh, I was butchering a pig, as you do when you're*
wearing your best corduroy jacket.

Next, he reached behind him to pull the black sweater
over his head, but as soon as he had grasped the back of the
collar, he stopped, and let it go again. *I don't want to take*
this off yet. This makes me feel more secure. It reminds me so
much of my mother. She used to wear it, and it helps me to
understand her. It's almost as if she's here, with me, still alive,
and with Evie gone, who else have I got?

David sat down on the bed again and took off his shoes and
socks, followed by his trousers and his boxer shorts. Then he
carefully lay down on the white candlewick bedspread, his
knees drawn up in a foetal position, and closed his eyes.

He didn't fall asleep, but he continued to lie there, for hour after hour, with his eyes still closed. He was pretending to be dead. Being dead meant that he was no longer responsible for anything.

Maggie came to the bedroom door and mewed because she was hungry, but all he could think was: *Go away. I can't hear you. I'm deaf to the world. I'm dead.*

10

Before the media conference at noon, Jerry and Jamila briefed DI Saunders on what little progress they had made so far.

DI Saunders stood staring out of the window at the station car park two floors below and Jerry wasn't even sure that he was listening to them.

After a while, though, he turned around and said, 'It could have been some kind of an allergy.'

'You mean the fibres in her skin?' Jerry asked him.

'Well, I don't know, do I? But I can't see what those fibres have got to do with her having concentrated sulphuric acid poured over her face.'

'The only prints on the acid bottle were hers, guv,' said Jerry. 'It could have been that the fibres were hurting her more than she could bear, and she wanted to end it all.'

'Jerry – just because the only prints on the acid bottle were hers, that doesn't mean that nobody else handled it. And if she couldn't stand pain, why would she choose the most painful possible way of killing herself? She'd take an overdose, wouldn't she, or jump in front of a train? It's only a five-minute walk to Streatham Common station.'

'I seriously don't think it was an honour killing, sir,' said Jamila.

'You don't? Why?'

'Because it seems that she was happy to be marrying the man that her parents had chosen for her, and because her mother is so deeply distressed about her dying. The father, of course, is still in Peshawar, but apparently he will be back before the weekend, and we can interview him then.'

'I've found out where her coat came from,' said Jerry. 'It was donated to a charity shop opposite the Granada and Samira bought it from there. I'll be going round this afternoon to talk to the fellow who donated it.'

'Quite honestly, I don't know what the point of that is,' said DI Saunders.

'The fibres embedded in her skin were grey, and her coat was grey. I'm just checking to see if there's any connection.'

'Jerry – she died because acid was poured over her face. Perhaps it was self-inflicted but as I say, there doesn't seem to be any logical motive for her killing herself. There was no suicide note, and no indication that she was depressed. Everything points to an honour killing.'

'We know that less than sixty per cent of suicides leave any kind of note, guv,' said Jerry. 'And her uncle said that the last time he saw her, after she had finished at the restaurant, she was very tired and seemed to be distant. That was the word he used – "*distant*".'

'Perhaps she'd knocked back a few sneaky drinks while she was working,' said DI Saunders.

'She was a Muslim, sir,' put in Jamila. 'Muslims don't drink alcohol.'

'Oh, they *say* they don't,' said DI Saunders. 'I went to a police conference in Dubai last year and if some of those Arab officers weren't drinking whisky then there must be some special soft drink there with the same label as Johnnie Walker.'

'Well, whatever; Dr Fuller has sent a skin sample to Lambeth Road for forensic tests,' Jerry told him.

'All right,' said DI Saunders. 'But don't spend too long chasing this coat. I never heard of anybody being driven to kill themselves by a coat before. And where is it, anyway, this coat? Didn't you say it went missing?'

'That's right, sir. At the moment I'm working on the possibility that one of Samira's friends or relatives came around while we were there and took it.'

DI Saunders raised one sceptical black eyebrow and it looked like a crow suddenly taking off from a telegraph wire.

'Well, I don't know *why* they took it, do I?' said Jerry. 'Maybe they wanted it for sentimental reasons, like a souvenir. Or maybe Samira had promised to give it to them.'

'I think you're wasting your time, Jerry,' said DI Saunders. 'You'd be far better employed trying to find out which of the victim's relatives did it, or who they paid to do it.'

'Is that what you're going to suggest at this media conference?' asked Jamila. 'If so, I think that you'll be treading on very thin ice, racially speaking.'

'I'm simply going to say that one of our lines of inquiry is the possibility that it was an honour killing. There's no point in pretending that it couldn't have been, and if there's any witnesses out there who can tip us off about who might have done it, they need to know what we're looking for. We'll be offering the usual reward for any information leading to a conviction.'

'The Pakistani community here in Tooting is very proud and very tight-knit,' said Jamila. 'At the moment we have excellent relations with them. I don't want us to put their backs up, that's all. There's a word in Punjabi which roughly translates as *omertà*, or keeping schtum. We don't want that.'

At that moment there was a knock at the office door. It was Sergeant Bristow from the desk downstairs, a thin, morose man with large ears and a comb-over. He was always helpful but he had no sense of humour at all. Jerry always thought he looked as if he ought to be the manager of a shoe-shop.

'DC Pardoe? Ah – there you are. You asked me to tell you when that lad who got himself stuck in that charity clothes box was going to be questioned. It'll be about one-thirty, in interview room two. DC Willis will be doing the honours.'

'Great, sarge, thanks,' said Jerry.

'What's all that about?' asked DI Saunders. 'It sounds like you've got some bee in your bonnet about second-hand clothes.'

'No, sir – it's not connected with the coat. It's a long-running case I've been working on with DI French, on and off. This Lithuanian geezer, Jokubas Liepa, he's been operating a racket in stolen charity donations for over a year now, but he's a bugger to nail down. People leave bags of clothes and shoes and toys and stuff outside their front doors for the charities to come around and collect, but Liepa sends a couple of vans round at the crack of dawn and picks them all up before the charities can get there.'

'You wouldn't think it was worth the effort, would you?' said DI Saunders.

'What? No, you've got to be joking! It's more than worth the effort. It's worth *thousands* – tens of thousands! Liepa sends most of the clothes off to Lithuania, where they either get cleaned and restructured and modernised, or else they get ripped apart and re-spun into new fabric. Shoddy, they call that.'

'Oh well, good luck with that,' said DI Saunders. He checked his Rolex and then said, 'Time for our media briefing. Let's make it a *brief* briefing, shall we? And I don't think we'll mention the fibres in the victim's skin, not until we get a full report from forensics. And I don't think we'll mention the coat, either.'

'If it appears on the media that we're looking for it, guv, there's every chance that someone might come forward and let us know what's happened to it.'

'Yes, and there's every chance that some reporter will ask us *why* we're looking for it, and we won't be able to give them a coherent answer. Jerry – I want *focus* on this case, and the focus as far as I see it is on an honour killing. Why do you think we sent DS Patel down here? I know we have to be thorough, but everything else is just a diversion.'

'Sir – I wasn't necessarily sent down here to prove that this *was* an honour killing,' said Jamila. 'I was sent down here because I have the experience and the ethnic background to recognise if it really was an honour killing or not. At this stage of our investigation, like I said, I have considerable doubts that it was. If she was happy about her arranged marriage, what was the motive?'

'We don't know that yet,' said DI Saunders. 'Maybe it wasn't her own family that killed her – maybe it was somebody acting on behalf of her intended husband's family. Maybe they weren't happy about *him* marrying *her*. Or maybe it was somebody acting on behalf of another family who wanted *their* daughter to marry him. His family are pretty wealthy, aren't they? That would have made him quite a catch for a girl who lives in a terraced house in Tooting.'

He paused, and shrugged, and then he said, 'There's endless possible motives for an honour killing, DS Patel. Maybe she had a boyfriend here in Tooting who was jealous about her getting hitched to some fellow in Pakistan and decided to mess up her looks. Maybe that was all he intended to do, but it all went too far, and she died.'

'You have a very vivid imagination, sir,' said Jamila.

'Oh no, I don't. The things that people do to each other, DS Patel, and the reasons why they do them, they're beyond *anybody's* imagination, mine included. Why do you think I have a reputation for being such a miserable git?'

Jerry thought, *Blimey, he actually knows that he's a miserable git, and accepts it. There's no answer to that.*

*

As DI Saunders had demanded, the media briefing was very brief indeed. Only five journalists had turned up: a middle-aged reporter from the *Wandsworth Guardian* with a blocked-up nose and a hacking cough and two stringers from the *Daily Mail* and the *Sun*, as well as a young woman from *Nawa i Jang*, the Pakistani weekly, and a bored-looking man in an anorak from BBC-TV London News.

'Are you looking for anybody in connection with Samira Wazir's death?' asked the stringer from the *Mail*. 'Like, was it an honour killing?'

'We're exploring every avenue,' said DI Saunders. 'That includes the possibility that it was an honour killing, or a deliberate assault that may have had more serious consequences than the perpetrator intended.'

'Is it conceivable that it was suicide?' asked the young woman from *Nawa i Jang*.

'As I say, we're keeping an open mind,' DI Saunders told her. 'We're still waiting for the results of some further forensic tests, and these may take several weeks.'

'Were there any signs of a sexual assault?' asked the stringer from the *Sun*.

'Not so far,' said DI Saunders. 'Her mother claimed that she was a virgin, but then it's highly unlikely that she would have confided in her mother about losing her virginity, isn't it?'

The young woman from *Nawa i Jang* put up her hand. 'Is it possible that it was a racially motivated attack? There has been some tension in Tooting lately between different ethnic groups. That black boy who was stabbed last week at Tooting Broadway station, and that fire at the Svaadisht Khaana restaurant?'

'I really can't say,' said DI Saunders. 'All I know is that the Wazir family seem to be well integrated into the local community and they've received no threats that I'm aware of.'

He paused and looked around. 'Is that all? This is an ongoing investigation and we're appealing for anybody who has any information to get in touch with us, no matter how inconsequential that information might seem to be. Thank you, and good afternoon.'

'Did Ms Wazir have any history of mental illness?' asked the reporter from the *Wandsworth Guardian*.

'Mental illness? Not that we're aware of.'

'It's just that I found details on Google about a similar case in 2010. A nineteen-year-old Pakistani girl in Balham poured petrol over her head and set fire to herself. She survived, even though she was severely disfigured, but she told her doctors that she had wanted to destroy her face. She said that she had been possessed by an evil female spirit called Pichal Peri, and that her face was changing so that she was beginning to *look* like this Pichal Peri, with staring eyes and sharp teeth. Apparently this belief in possession is quite common in Pakistan. Even quite educated people in the cities will blame mental instability on demonic possession.'

'Well, thank you for that,' said DI Saunders, without making any attempt to mask his impatience. 'That gives us one more avenue to explore. Demonic possession. Terrific. I'll see if I can get in touch with Father Karras.'

11

Jerry bought himself a cup of black coffee from the coffee machine before he went down to the interview room. The young man who had been trapped in the charity box was bent over the table with his forehead resting on his hands. DC Derek Willis was sitting opposite him, reading through the incident report, and moving his lips while he did so. A uniformed constable sat in the far corner with his arms folded, yawning from time to time.

Derek Willis was a large overweight man in his early forties, with a short grey buzzcut and a roughly hewn head that resembled a half-finished granite sculpture. He was wearing a grey suit as tight as a sausage-skin and his neck bulged over his shirt collar. Jerry had worked with Derek on three or four cases, and while he wasn't at all imaginative, he was thorough to the point of being obsessive. In fact his fellow officers called him 'OCD Willis'.

When Jerry drew out a chair, Derek dropped the incident report onto the table and said, 'Ah, Pardoe. You know this young chap already, I gather.'

'We've talked,' said Jerry. 'This is the first time I've met him face-to-face.'

The young man looked up, too. His face was dead white and foxy-looking, and his hair stuck up. He wore a silver stud earring and he was covered in tattoos, all the way up to his neck. In appearance, he reminded Jerry of Sid Vicious, and he gave off the same air of rebellious vulnerability.

'They got you out of there, then?' said Jerry. 'I would have let you stay there for a week or two, and just fed you on salt-and-vinegar crisps and corned-beef sandwiches.'

'That ain't funny,' the young man retorted.

'It wasn't meant to be. The only funny thing about it was you getting yourself stuck. I mean, that was hilarious.'

'For the record, son, can you confirm your name?' said Derek, although he had all of the young man's personal details on the incident report right in front of him.

'Billy. Billy Jenkins.'

'Address?'

'Number eight, Dewar House, Tooting Grove.'

'How old are you, Billy?'

'I was seventeen in June.'

Jerry sipped his coffee, staring intently at Billy all the time. Then he said, 'Didn't you realise you were going to get stuck in that charity box? There's even a warning notice on the outside, saying don't attempt to climb inside.'

Billy shrugged. He started scratching the back of his left hand, and then his skinny bare arm.

'What's the matter, Billy?' asked Derek. 'Got the itch, have you?'

'I could do with some stuff, man. I'm feeling really pukish.'

'What kind of stuff?'

'Anything.'

'What are you on? Crystal meth? Coke? Or just good old common-or-garden smack?'

Billy looked at Jerry appealingly, and said, 'Cheese, mostly. But anything. Otherwise I'm going to throw up, man, honest.'

Cheese was a mixture of heroin and Benylin cough mixture. Jerry had seen a lot of it around lately, especially in schools. It was highly addictive, but it did tend to make its users vomit.

'That's all right,' said Derek. 'I can call for a bucket if you really need it.'

'Please,' said Billy. 'Just one hit to stop me from itching.'

'Well, answer me some questions first, and then we'll see what we can do. To begin with, were you trying to rob that charity box off your own bat, or did somebody tell you to do it?'

Billy shook his head. His nose was running and some clear snot was flung across his cheek. Derek reached across for the box of tissues which they always kept in the interview room.

'Here, blow your nose. And answer my question. Somebody told you to do it, didn't they?'

'No, but I needed the money.'

'What for?'

'To pay off my debt, man. I'm so deep in the shit it's untrue.'

'How much?'

'Three hundred quid.'

'For cheese? Is that it?'

'Most of it, yeah. Some of it just for food and bus fare and stuff.'

'Who do you owe it to? All the same person or more than one?'

'About fifty quid to my girlfriend. The rest to somebody else.'

'Somebody else?' asked Jerry. 'Somebody else like who?'

Again, Billy shook his head, and kept on shaking it. 'I can't tell you, man – I can't! If I tell you, he'll fucking kill me for being a snitch. Either that or cut my fucking tongue out. He's done it before, I know he has.'

'Never mind,' said Jerry. 'I believe I know who you're talking about. It's Jokubas Liepa, isn't it? Liepa the Weeper, they call him, don't they, because he always pretends to cry when he's doing something really nasty to someone, like nailing their balls to the kitchen chair they're sitting in.'

'I'm not saying nothing.'

'It *was* him, though, wasn't it? Who else would accept second-hand clothes in payment for a drug debt? The Weeper's the only man who's got the organisation to turn second-hand clothes into cash.'

'I need some stuff, man. I mean it. I'm dying here.'

'I'll see what I can do. But it *was* Liepa, wasn't it, who sent you after those clothes?'

'He didn't tell me to do it. I was just walking past and I saw this woman shoving shoes and sweaters and all kinds of good stuff into that box, and I decided to give it a go. I've done it loads of times before and I've never had no trouble – never.'

'You must be aware, though, that they've adapted almost all of the charity boxes lately,' said Derek. 'Once you're inside, son, there's no way that you can get yourself out. Not without a key, anyway.'

'Didn't you read the warning notice on the side?' put in Jerry. 'You *can* read, can't you?'

'Course I can fucking read. I come second in English, at school. Mind you, the rest of the class was all Pakis.'

'Let's try to be ethnically inclusive, shall we?' said Derek.

Billy hesitated for a moment, biting at his thumbnail. Jerry had the feeling that he was going to come out with more, so he said nothing and waited.

Eventually, Billy said, 'This is going to sound like I'm off my nut or something.'

'Go on,' said Derek. 'I'll be the judge of that.'

'It sounds cracked but I swear it's true, and it weren't the cheese or nothing.'

'I'm listening.'

'The reason I thought it was going to be OK to climb in there, right – the reason was, I heard somebody else inside it.'

'You heard somebody else inside it?'

Billy nodded. 'I don't know what they was saying. It was more like singing than talking. Like a woman singing.'

'So you thought – if there's somebody else in there, it's got to be OK to get out?'

Billy nodded again.

'And you don't think it was the cheese singing to you, or whatever other shit you'd been taking?'

'I heard them, honest. I heard them as clear as I can hear you now. But it wasn't even like proper singing. It was just "*ooh-wooh-ooh*".'

'But once you'd managed to climb inside, there was nobody there?'

'No. I was the only one in there.'

'So how do you account for hearing that voice?' asked Jerry.

'I can't. But I swear on the Bible I heard it, and it wasn't inside my head or nothing. It was inside the box.'

'All right,' said Jerry. 'You thought you heard a voice singing or "*ooh-wooh-oohing*" or whatever inside the charity box. But even before you heard it, it was your specific intention to steal clothing and shoes so that you could take them to Jokubas Liepa as part-payment for the money you owed him for drugs?'

'You won't say nothing to Jokubas, will you? He'll fucking kill me. Even if I'm in prison he'll pay somebody to kill me.'

'I'll have to have a word with Inspector Callow,' said Derek. 'He may decide to let you off with a caution.'

'If we do that, though, we might have to make some conditions,' added Jerry. 'We could well expect you to give us more information on the Weeper and how he's running his business these days.'

'I seriously need some stuff, man,' said Billy. His white face was glossy with sweat now, as shiny as if it had been coated in clear varnish, and he was trembling and scratching and shuffling his feet and his nose was running again.

'I'm afraid I'll have to talk to Inspector Callow about that, too,' Derek told him. Then he turned to the uniformed constable and said, 'That's it for now, thanks. Can you take him back to his cell? And give him a blanket. I think he could do with a little security, right now.'

12

Jerry was buttoning up his coat when Jamila came into the CID room.

'Going out?' she asked him.

Jerry was about to say, *You'd make a good detective, you would*, but then he remembered that Jamila outranked him and he didn't know if she could handle sarcasm.

'I'm going to have a word with the bloke who donated Samira's coat to the charity shop. I just want to know if his late wife noticed anything funny about it.'

'I'll come with you. I've got nothing better to do.'

'OK. You haven't heard anything from Lambeth Road yet?'

Jamila shook her head. 'You know how long they usually take. I doubt if we'll get any results from them for weeks.'

They drove up to Furzehill Drive. Number fifteen was a corner house, overlooking Furzedown Recreation Ground, a rhomboid of wet green grass with swings and a roundabout. The sky was overcast and it was still drizzling, and so the only person on the recreation ground was an elderly man in an anorak, walking his Labrador.

Jerry rang the doorbell. They waited almost half a minute but nobody answered, so he rang it again. This time the front-room curtain was drawn aside, and a grey-haired man in a mustard-coloured cardigan appeared, frowning at them. Jerry took out his ID and held it up, and mouthed the word '*Police*'.

The man opened the door. He was sixtyish, with brambly grey eyebrows and a downturned mouth. He was wearing baggy grey trousers, and Jerry noticed that his slippers didn't match. One was brown corduroy and the other was black leather.

'Yes?' he said, holding onto the edge of the door as if he didn't want to open it any wider and let them in.

'Mr Stebbings? I'm Detective Jerry Pardoe and this is Detective Sergeant Jamila Patel. Can you spare a few minutes?'

'What's this about?'

'It's about your wife, Mr Stebbings.'

'What about my wife? She's gone now. You're not accusing her of anything, are you? She was always breaking plates but I don't think she ever broke the law.'

Jerry couldn't work out if this was meant as a joke, but Mr Stebbings didn't appear to be smiling so he ignored it.

'Actually it's about her coat. That short grey coat you donated to Little Helpers.'

'What about it?'

Jerry looked up at the sky and held out his hand. 'Do you mind if we come inside and talk about it? We're getting a bit wet standing here.'

Mr Stebbings opened the door and stepped back to let them in. Inside, the house was chilly and dark and smelled of cigarette smoke and stale cat food. There was a framed engraving hanging in the hallway of the death of Nelson.

'Come through,' said Mr Stebbings, and led them into the living-room. An obese brindled cat was sleeping on one of the armchairs so he pushed it off, and it sulked away under the glass-topped coffee-table. On top of the table there was a plate with the remains of Mr Stebbings' lunch on it, which looked as if it had been sausages and baked beans, judging by the orange sauce and the lump of spat-out gristle on the side of it.

Jerry reluctantly sat on the armchair where the cat had been sleeping, while Jamila sat on the end of the sofa. Mr Stebbings sat on the opposite end, with his knees so close to Jerry's that they were almost touching.

'So what about her coat?' asked Mr Stebbings. Jerry could see that his fingers were stained amber with nicotine.

'Do you know where she bought it?'

'No idea. It wasn't new, though. She liked to scour the charity shops. You know, Oxfam and Cancer Research, shops like that. She never liked spending money, that was her problem. Well, one of her problems.'

'What were her other problems?' asked Jamila.

'Oh, you know, women's problems. One minute she'd be sobbing her heart out and the next she wouldn't even talk to me.'

'After she bought the coat, did you notice any change in her behaviour?'

Mr Stebbings stared at Jerry as if he had insulted him. 'No!' he snapped. 'What do you mean?'

'I'm interested to know if the coat appeared to have any effect on her, that's all.'

'It was a bloody coat. Apart from the fact that she hardly ever took the bloody thing off, no, it didn't have any *effect* on her. Why would it?'

'When you say she hardly ever took it off, did she wear it in the house?'

'Yes – well, the cost of heating these days. Our last gas bill was more than four hundred quid.'

'I'm sorry to bring this up, Mr Stebbings,' said Jerry. 'But can you tell us the cause of your late wife's death?'

'She drowned. Drowned in the bath. I was out that evening, playing darts. I always told her not to have a bath on her own, when I wasn't there, because she was prone to fainting fits. I came home about half past ten, and there she was, lying under the water. I fished her out, and tried to give her the kiss of life, but the bathwater was freezing cold so she must have been there for hours.'

'I'm sorry,' Jerry told him. 'That must have been a terrible shock for you.'

'Well, thirty-four years we'd been married. The last couple of years were a little difficult. I won't pretend that they weren't. But – yes, it was a shock.'

'When you found her, did you notice anything unusual about her skin?'

Mr Stebbings gave Jerry another hostile stare.

'What do you mean, "unusual"?'

'Did you notice any fibres, for example?'

'Fibres? I don't know what you're talking about.'

'Fibres – you know, like fine hairs growing on her skin.'

Mr Stebbings shook his head. 'Still don't know what you're talking about.'

'All right, then. That's all we wanted to ask you. We'll leave you in peace.'

Jerry and Jamila stood up. Mr Stebbings looked up at Jerry and said, 'I don't understand what you come here for, to be honest with you.'

'We needed to check out one particular line of inquiry, that's all.'

'Inquiry into what? I mean, what does my late wife's coat have to do with anything? It was a bloody coat. She wore it so often I was sick of the sight of the bloody thing, but that's all.'

'I'm not at liberty to tell you why we're interested in your late wife's coat, Mr Stebbings,' Jerry told him. 'But thank you anyway for your time, and for being so cooperative.'

Mr Stebbings stood up, too. Close up, his breath smelled strongly of tobacco. 'Well, if you won't tell me, you won't. But I won't pretend I'm not bloody baffled, because I am.'

When they left Mr Stebbings' house, it was raining much harder, and they ran to get into their car. After they had climbed in, and Jerry had started the engine, Jamila said, quietly but firmly, 'He was lying.'

'What?'

Jamila turned to him. Jerry surprised himself by thinking how pretty she was, with those large brown eyes and those full, pouting lips.

'He was lying about finding her in the bath like that. He was telling the truth about going out to play darts, but that was only to give himself an alibi. It wouldn't surprise me if he drowned her himself – either before he went out, or after he came back. Before, most likely.'

'So how do you know that?'

'Let's just say I have a talent.'

'I'm sorry? A talent?'

'It's one of the reasons I decided to become a police officer. I can always tell when somebody isn't telling the truth.'

'How? Do you see their nose growing longer?'

'It's not a joke, Jerry. I shouldn't really have told you, but if you're right to have suspicions about this coat, then you need to know that our Mr Stebbings is a liar. The coat made him very angry for some reason, and he knew exactly what you meant when you asked him about the fibres.'

'So how can you be so sure?'

'If I tell you, you won't believe me. I know that Mr Stebbings lied to us, but let's just leave it at that. I agree with you now that we need to find out what happened to that coat, and if possible find the coat itself so that we can examine it.'

'Why don't you try me?'

'What do you mean?'

'Why don't you try telling me how you know that he was lying. Maybe I *will* believe you.'

'You won't.'

'How do you know? I'm extremely gullible. I believe they've found a statue of Elvis on the Moon.'

'You won't believe me because you're not superstitious like we are. In Pakistan we believe in supernatural causality. Many of us believe in witches and jinns and evil spirits called *bhoot*. Even our former president Zardari used to have a black goat sacrificed every single day to protect him from demons.'

Jamila pulled down the neck of her light grey sweater and lifted out a small black pouch on a string. 'I have worn this all my life. It's called a ta'wiz and it contains words from the Qur'an. It keeps me safe from evil.'

'That still doesn't tell me how you're so sure that Mr Stebbings was coming out with a load of porkies.'

'Before I was born, my father helped to save the life of a woman who was accused of being a witch. Some local men believed that she had caused a fire which had destroyed several of their houses, and so they were going to cut off her fingers and put out her eyes with a pointed stick and then pour petrol all over her and set her alight. But my father who was the district policeman got to hear of this, and he rescued her before the men could hurt her.

'She came to visit us soon after I was born, so my father told me, and she admitted that she really was a churail, or a witch, but that she cast only good spells. She cast a spell over me, when I was in my crib. She said that it would give me the power of knowing when people were trying to deceive me, and that would help to keep me safe. It was her way of thanking my father for saving her life.'

'Well, it's a good story,' said Jerry. 'But you still haven't told me *how* you know they're trying to deceive you.'

'For as long as they're lying, their eyes go totally black. Black and shiny, like black onyx. I suppose it means that their words are empty. Sometimes their lips turn black, too, and when I see that I know that what they're telling me is not only meaningless, but poisonous.'

'And did Mr Stebbings' eyes go black?'

Jamila said, 'Yes. As soon as he said that his wife had drowned in the bath, they went totally black, shiny black, and they stayed black until he had finished answering your questions about the fibres.'

'How about his lips? Did they go black?'

'No. I think that he was only trying to deceive us, not to harm us.'

Jerry sat and watched the rain dribbling down the windscreen. 'I don't know what to say, DS Patel. I believe you, but then again how *can* I believe you? His eyes turned black? I mean, *really*?'

'It was the power that the churail gave me. A sixth sense, just like seeing and hearing and tasting and smelling and touch.'

'So you're telling me that he was lying when he was talking about the fibres, too?'

'Definitely. And that's what makes me feel that we have to locate that coat, if only to rule out the possibility that it had anything to do with Samira Wazir or Mrs Stebbings both being murdered – that's if they *were* murdered.'

Jerry sat and thought for a moment longer. Then he said, 'Do you know something? I need a drink.'

13

Sophie could smell Mike as soon as she opened the front door.

She knew that people's bodies started to decompose from the very moment they died, but she had never realised that they could smell as strong as this. It was like a gas escape mixed with the stench of rotten chicken, and it filled the whole house. Her mouth filled with bile, and she gagged, and gagged again, and then she hurried through to the kitchenette and brought up a mouthful of half-digested cheese roll into the sink.

Almost immediately, though, she went back and closed the front door. She couldn't have the neighbours complaining about the smell. They were always moaning that she was playing her music too loud, or that she hadn't sorted her rubbish and put it in the right recycling bin. Before she knew it, they would have some council official knocking at her door.

She dropped her bag on the couch in the sitting-room, and then she went into the small downstairs toilet, took out her handkerchief and sprayed blossom-scented air freshener into it. Holding it up to her face, she climbed the stairs to the bedroom.

Mike looked worse than she could have imagined. His face was glistening grey, with the two knives sticking out of his eyes. His intestines were already bloated, and they had turned the colour of pale greenish pasta. The sheet underneath him was soaked in yellow fluid.

Sophie went over to the window and opened it to let in some fresh air. It was still raining, and she could hear the water splattering from the broken gutter right above her. After a while she turned around and looked at Mike. Even though the sight of his disembowelled body revolted her, she still felt that she had given him what he deserved: an agonising and undignified death, almost sacrificial. But now she would have to find some way to dispose of him and clean up the bed.

She went downstairs to the kitchenette and took her yellow latex gloves out of the drawer. Back upstairs, she opened the airing cupboard and tugged out her oldest duvet cover, which was purple, with even darker purple flowers on it.

Unfolding the duvet cover, she laid it out on the bedroom floor. She gagged again as she turned Mike over, and she had to grip her stomach for a moment and take two or three deep breaths. When she had recovered, she rolled him off the bed and onto the carpet. He landed on his side with a heavy thump, and all his intestines slithered around her feet like escaping snakes, with liquid squelching and balloon-like exhalations of gas.

It took her nearly twenty minutes to insert Mike's stiff, chilly feet into the duvet cover and then heave and tug and wrestle the rest of his body into it. She managed to pull the knife out of his left eye, but the knife in his right eye was lodged so tightly that she had to leave it where it was. Finally she bent his head forward, with a loud cracking sound from his neck, so that she could fasten all the buttons along the opening of the duvet cover.

'There, Mike,' she said, triumphantly. 'No undertaker would have given you a shroud as pretty as this.'

Little Helpers owned their own van, which they used to collect furniture and other large donations. It was mainly used by one of Sophie's volunteers, Jeff, but she had driven it herself several times when Jeff had been off sick. She could borrow it this weekend and take Mike's body down to Ashdown Forest, in Sussex. She knew a small country road there called Kidd's Hill where she could drag him into the undergrowth, and with luck nobody would ever find him.

She stripped the sheets and the mattress cover off the bed, and dropped Mike's bloodstained pillow next to his body. She was relieved to see that the mattress had only been slightly stained, so that she would only have to scrub it with bleach and turn it over.

There was nothing more she could do tonight. She left the bedroom window open and closed the door. She would have to sleep downstairs on the couch, but that would be a small price to pay for having rid herself of Mike.

Down in the kitchenette she washed her latex gloves and pulled them off, and then she washed her bare hands. She didn't feel like eating anything, especially since the house still smelled of Mike's insides, a pungency that she could actually taste in her mouth. However she had half a bottle of pinot grigio in the fridge. She poured herself a large glass and went through to the living-room.

I've won, she thought. *I've won, and I am never ever going to allow another man to treat me the way that Mike treated me. Just who did he think he was dealing with? Didn't he*

realise that one day I would have had enough of his arrogance,
enough of his contempt, and enough of his snoring?

She switched on the television. She had a choice between a
celebrity quiz show and a nature programme about baboons
and the local London news, and so she left it on the nature
programme and muted the sound. She took a sip of her wine
and then she tried to shrug off her blue velvet jacket.

It was then that she found that the jacket seemed to be
stuck to her.

She tugged at the lapels, and tried to pull it off her shoulders,
but somehow it felt as if it was clinging to her. She pulled at
it harder, and this time it actually *hurt*, the same kind of skin-
tearing pain that she felt when she had her legs waxed. She
pulled harder still, and this time the pain was too much to
bear. It brought tears to her eyes and she said, *Oww-ahh!*
out loud.

*How can it be stuck to me like this? It feels like I have
hairs on my back but of course I don't have hairs on my
back. Maybe there was some sort of glue in the lining, and it's
melted, because it was so hot in the shop today.*

She gripped the collar with her left hand and tried with
all her strength to wrench the jacket off her right shoulder.
With a soft crackling sound, it came away, but she felt as if
her shoulder had been scraped with glasspaper. She yelped,
and panted for breath, but then she took hold of the collar
with her right hand, and prepared herself to rip that side
off, too.

*Why are you doing this, Sophie? Why not leave the jacket
on? It fits you so well. It's like your second skin. Do you
really think you could have taken your revenge on Mike if
you hadn't been wearing it? The jacket is me, Sophie, not
you. How do you think you found all that strength? Do you*

really believe you could have blinded him and gutted him all by yourself?

Sophie turned and stared at herself in the mirror over the fireplace. *What am I thinking? Whose voice is that, in my head? I feel like I'm talking to myself, but I'm not, am I? There's somebody else inside me. Oh my God! There's somebody else inside me!*

She slowly approached the mirror and stared at herself even more intently, still keeping her grip on the collar of her jacket. The face in the mirror bore some resemblance to Sophie, like two sisters might resemble each other, but it wasn't her. This face had sharper-cut cheekbones and a squarer jaw, and a much higher forehead.

You see? This is who you really are now. That's why you must leave the jacket on, at least for now.

Sophie stepped back from the mirror, almost tripping over the edge of the hearth-rug. She was hyperventilating now. She had never felt so frightened in her life. She had been threatened once by a madwoman on the Tube, a stinking woman with jagged teeth who had sworn at her and said that she would rip her face with her fingernails. But she had never been threatened like this – not by *herself* – or somebody who looked like her, but wasn't.

She let out a hoarse, high-pitched scream, although she was panicking so much that she couldn't hear it. At the same time she tore the jacket off her back and then dragged the sleeves off, and threw it across the room. She felt a ripping pain across her shoulders, and her hands and her forearms were smothered in blood. Her back felt wet, and when she twisted around to look at herself in the mirror again, she saw that her short-sleeved cotton blouse was soaked in blood, too.

She staggered across to the couch and picked up her bag, fumbling inside it for her iPhone, so that she could call for help. Before she could find it, though, she saw that the jacket seemed to be moving. It was hunched up, and it was crawling slowly towards her, its empty sleeves dragging it across the floor.

When she saw it inching its way towards her, she dropped her iPhone and stumbled out of the living-room. She saw herself reflected in the mirror in the hallway, her face white and her blouse drenched in blood, and she could do nothing but whimper at her reflection in pain and terror. She looked back and the jacket had reached the living-room door, pulling itself along as if there were somebody invisible inside it, creeping along on their hands and knees.

She opened the front door and tottered outside, almost losing her balance on the concrete steps. As weak and frightened and disorientated as she was, she managed to turn around and slam the front door shut behind her, just as the jacket reached one of its sleeves out towards the doormat.

She took three unsteady steps past the dustbins, so that she managed to reach the front gate, but then stars prickled in front of her eyes and the street went black and she fell forward onto the wet pavement outside her house, and lay there on her side, in the rain.

She was lying there for more than five minutes before a passing taxi stopped, and the driver climbed out and bent over her. She could hear the knocking sound of its diesel engine.

'What's happened, love? Has somebody stabbed you?'

She opened her eyes. All she could see was the pavement and the taxi-driver's shoes. It was still raining, and she felt chilled to the bone.

'*Save me,*' she said.

She heard the taxi-driver talking on his mobile phone. Then she felt him cover her up with his anorak.

'Who did this to you, love? Is this where you live? Is he still inside?'

'Don't go in there,' she whispered.

'What? I didn't get that.'

'Don't go in there. Whatever you do, don't go in there.'

*

Jerry was almost back at his rented flat, turning the corner from Tooting Bec Common into Prentis Road, when his iPhone pinged. He pulled into the side of the road and took it out.

'Jerry? DI Saunders.'

'Don't tell me. Somebody's handed the coat in.'

'No, nothing like that. Well, I don't know – maybe something like that. We've had a call from St George's. A young woman's been brought into A&E with severe skin abrasions and apparently she's raving about her injuries having been caused by her jacket.'

'What?'

'Sergeant Bristow sent a couple of PCs over to talk to her, but they called in to say that they couldn't make head nor tail of what she was on about. She's quite badly injured, though, and the doctor who examined her said she had fibres adhering to her skin. As far as he could make out, it was the tearing away of the fibres that caused her abrasions. That's the reason I'm calling you.'

Jerry inhaled deeply. He was exhausted after a long day, and apart from his half-finished chicken-and-mushroom slice, he hadn't had anything to eat. After he and Jamila had visited Mr Stebbings he had felt like going to the pub for a pint and a packet of porky scratchings but of course Jamila didn't drink alcohol – nor eat pork, either.

'So – where are you now?' asked DI Saunders. 'Do you want to get yourself over to St George's and find out what this young woman is ranting on about?'

'Yes, sir. OK, sir. I'll get back to you as soon as I can.'

14

Jerry had to sit in the hospital waiting-room for nearly an hour while the young woman was having her injuries sterilised and dressed. He read a day-old copy of the *Daily Express* and a year-old copy of *Country Life* and then he texted Jamila to tell her where he was and what he was doing. She didn't answer, so he assumed that she was out having a meal somewhere. He felt jealous. He could fancy an Indian curry, especially a chicken tikka masala.

He was still thinking about ordering a takeaway when a young neatly bearded Indian doctor came into the waiting-room.

'Detective Pardoe?'

When he heard the word 'detective', a middle-aged man on the other side of the waiting-room looked across at him with hostility. The man's face was bruised and unshaven and he smelled strongly of drink.

Jerry said, 'That's me. How is she?'

'Come and see for yourself. I have to say that her injuries are most unusual.'

Jerry followed the doctor along the corridor to A&E. Behind the curtains that lined one side of the room, a woman was sobbing and a child was grizzling, both in miserable harmony. The doctor took Jerry to the very end of the room and drew back the curtains that surrounded the young woman who claimed that she had been hurt by her jacket.

Jerry recognised her immediately. 'Bloody hell,' he said. 'It's you.'

Sophie was lying back on her pillows, her eyelids flickering as if she were nearly falling asleep. Her face was waxy and pale, and she seemed to be having trouble in breathing.

'Hallo, Sophie,' said Jerry. 'It's me again – Detective Jerry Pardoe from Tooting police station. You remember me, don't you?'

Sophie nodded, still taking little sips of breath as if she were trying to stop herself from crying.

There was a plastic chair next to the young woman's bed and Jerry pulled it over and sat down. 'What happened to you, Sophie? The doctor told me that you've got some really bad scrapes on your back.'

Sophie nodded again, and her eyes filled with tears.

Jerry waited for a moment, and then he said, 'You told the nurses your jacket did it. What did you mean by that?'

'I couldn't take it off,' Sophie whispered.

'You couldn't take it off?'

'It was like it was stuck onto my skin. I pulled it and pulled it and in the end I got it off, but it hurt so much.'

'When you say it was stuck to your skin—?'

Sophie pulled up her bedsheet to wipe her eyes. 'I was so scared. It was like I was me but I wasn't me. It was like the jacket was telling me what to do.'

'Sorry, love. I'm not too sure I understand you.'

Sophie closed her eyes for a moment, trying to summon up the strength to tell Jerry what she had done. When she opened them again, and saw him sitting beside the bed looking at her sympathetically, she let out a bleat of sheer anguish.

'He upset me, but I didn't mean to hurt him! Not like that! I swear I didn't mean it! It wasn't me!'

'Who are you talking about, Sophie?'

'Mike, my boyfriend,' she wept. 'We weren't getting along very well, but I didn't mean to hurt him as much as that! I never would have done that to anyone, no matter how they treated me!'

'You hurt your boyfriend?'

'Yes. But it wasn't me.'

'All right, it wasn't you,' said Jerry, taking hold of her hand. 'But what exactly did you do to him?'

Another long pause, and then Sophie whispered, 'I killed him.'

'He's *dead*?'

'Yes.'

'You're sure he's dead?'

'Yes.'

'How did you kill him?'

'I stabbed him in the eyes and then I cut him open.'

Jerry took out his iPhone and his notebook. 'Sophie... I'm going to write down what you tell me, and also record it. I have to caution you too, love. You do not have to say anything. But it may harm your defence if you do not mention when questioned something which you later rely on in court. Anything you do say may be given in evidence. Do you understand that?'

'Yes. But it wasn't me. I did it. I killed him. But the jacket made me do it.'

'When did this happen?'

'Yesterday night. He was asleep and he was snoring and I stabbed him in the eyes and cut him open.'

'Where is he now?'

'He's still at our house, ninety-six Lavender Avenue. He's in the bedroom. I was going to get rid of his body but then I took off the jacket and I hurt myself so much and the jacket came after me.'

'Excuse me? The jacket came after you? I don't follow what you're saying.'

Sophie clutched Jerry's hand so tightly that her fingernails dug into him. She sat bolt upright in bed even though it must have hurt her back, and her face was distorted with anger and fear.

'*It wasn't me!*' she screamed. '*It was the jacket that made me do it! And when I took it off—!*' Her screaming subsided, and she dropped back onto her pillows. 'When I took it off, and I was bleeding so much, it came after me. It was crawling after me, like it didn't want me to go.'

The doctor and two nurses appeared, drawing back the curtain.

'Is everything all right here, detective?' asked the doctor.

Jerry stood up. 'I think Sophie here is still suffering from shock, doctor. I think she needs a good night's sleep and some time for her injuries to start healing.'

'She has already been given a sedative,' said the doctor. 'Don't worry, she will be very well looked after.'

Sophie looked up at him and said, 'You do believe me, don't you?'

'Yes, Sophie. I believe you. I'll go round to your house when I leave here and make sure that everything's OK. You don't happen to have a key, do you?'

'No. I left it inside. But watch out for that jacket. It could still be right behind the front door.'

'I'll take care, I promise you.'

'Don't try to put it on, whatever you do. It's the same jacket I was wearing in the shop.'

'In that case, no chance. Far too small for me.'

'I killed Mike,' said Sophie. 'I killed him, but it wasn't me. You have to believe me.'

'All right, love. Don't get yourself all worked up. I'll come back later.'

Jerry left the A&E department and walked back to the hospital's main entrance. The doctor came with him.

'She is claiming that she *killed* somebody?' the doctor asked him.

'Her boyfriend. She says she stabbed him.'

'She is in a state of hysteria. We can't really work out yet how she sustained her abrasions, but there were fibres implanted in her skin, and it would appear that her injuries were caused when these were forcibly pulled out. There are still quite a few remaining. Whatever happened, she has been left extremely traumatised.'

'What kind of fibres are they?'

'They appeared at first to be very fine hairs, but of course it would be extremely unusual for a female to have hairs all across her back and her shoulders and her arms. Even when a woman is suffering from hirsutism the hairs are usually thicker and darker. I thought at first she might have polycystic ovary syndrome, but when we examined the hairs more closely we could see that they were not hairs at all. We haven't had the time yet to carry out a conclusive analysis, but as strange as it may seem, my opinion is that they are some kind of thread, like silk.'

'Silk? OK. If you can let us have a sample, doctor, I'll send it to our forensics experts.'

'Of course,' said the doctor.

They had reached the main door now. As Jerry was about to leave, the doctor said, 'She was really telling you that she had killed somebody? Do you believe that this is true?'

'I have no idea. Like you say, she's in a state of hysteria. But there are two officers posted outside and I'll ask them to liaise with your security people in case she gives you any trouble or tries to leave before we've fully investigated. In any case, I'll be back here myself to talk to her again – tomorrow morning at the latest.'

The doctor looked dubious, but then he shrugged. 'I have dealt with some very strange cases,' he said. 'But this is the strangest case I have come across so far. Who can weave silk into a woman's skin?'

*

He was driving back to the station when Jamila texted him. *Did u want me?*

He called her back on his hands-free phone and told her about Sophie and her confession that she had murdered Mike.

'I'm going to go around to her house with a couple of uniforms and a bosher. It's possible that she's simply gaga and making the whole thing up. It could be that she's been smoking or snorting something or popping Molly. We won't know until we take a butcher's.'

'I'll meet you at the station. I've just come back from a meeting with the Asian Women's Resource Centre.'

'Oh. I thought you were out having a curry. I was jealous.'

'Really? One day I will cook you one of my curries. I make a wonderful keema.'

'If I knew what a keema was, I'd probably be drooling.'

Jamila was waiting for him in the CID room when he got back. She looked as tired as he felt, but they went immediately down to see Sergeant Bristow to arrange for uniformed back-up.

'What's the SP?' asked Sergeant Bristow.

'Suspected stiff,' Jerry told him.

'Don't forget your Vick's, then,' said Sergeant Bristow. He was referring to the strong mentholated vapour rub which was often dabbed by undertakers and pathologists on their upper lip to mask the smell of corpses.

Two PCs were out on patrol close to Lavender Avenue where Sophie lived, and they arranged to meet up outside her house in fifteen minutes. They had a battering ram on board their patrol car – what Jerry called a 'bosher' – so they would be able to open Sophie's door without any trouble.

'So what's this Asian women's thing all about?' Jerry asked Jamila, as he drove them to Lavender Avenue.

'I've been involved with it for over a year now,' said Jamila. 'It's partly a social group, partly an information centre, and partly a refuge where Asian women can go if they are being abused or battered by their husbands.'

'Sounds very worthy.'

'Oh, it is more than worthy, Jerry. It saves some women's lives.'

When they reached Lavender Avenue, they found that the patrol car was already parked outside Sophie's house. It was a small terraced property with a pebble-dashed frontage, typical of thousands of suburban houses built around South London in the 1930s. An elderly man and a woman were standing in front of the house next door to watch what was going on. The man was even holding a cup of tea and smoking a cigarette.

'Nothing to see here, chum,' said Jerry, as he passed them by.

'Always screaming and shouting, those two,' the woman retorted, as if that justified them standing outside and rubbernecking.

'Yeah, nothing but a bloody nuisance,' her husband put in. 'The times we've called the council.'

'Well, we might want to talk to you later,' said Jamila. 'Meanwhile, my colleague is quite correct. There is nothing for you to see.'

The two constables were a burly black officer and a small red-haired WPC. The black officer was cradling the red Enforcer battering ram like a babe-in-arms and waiting patiently by the yellow-painted front door.

Jerry rang the doorbell and knocked, just in case Sophie had been hallucinating and her boyfriend was still alive and unharmed, or somebody else had come round to the house.

'What – there's supposed to be a body inside?' asked the WPC.

'A young woman was brought into St George's with serious contusions,' Jerry told her. 'She said that she'd murdered her boyfriend. Stabbed him in the eyes, that's what she said, then sliced him open.'

'Oh, I'm looking forward to this,' said the black officer.

Jerry rang the doorbell again. They all waited another fifteen seconds, and then he said, 'OK. Bosh away.'

The black officer swung the battering ram and knocked the door open with one hard blow, cracking the cheap Yale lock away from the frame. He gave it a kick to open it wider, and immediately they smelled the ripe gassy smell of death.

'*Urghh*,' said Jamila. 'I believe your young woman was telling you the truth.'

The woman constable waved her hand in front of her face and said, 'God. I hope I'm not going to throw up. I just had a Big Mac.'

Jerry switched on his flashlight and pointed it inside the darkened hallway. As Sophie had told him, the blue velvet jacket was lying crumpled on the floor.

'That jacket,' he told Jamila, shining his flashlight on it. 'Take a picture, could you, skip?'

'What for?' asked Jamila, although she took out her iPhone and photographed it, as he had asked her.

'I'll tell you later. But it's one of the reasons why Smiley wanted *us* to follow this up. I mean, DI Saunders,' he added, turning to the two constables with a stern expression, in case he had given them the impression that they too could refer to him as 'Smiley'.

Jerry looked into the living-room, and then the kitchenette. The smell of decomposition was so strong that it was difficult to tell where it was coming from. He opened the small downstairs toilet but there was no dead body in there.

'Upstairs, I reckon,' said the black officer.

Jerry climbed the steep, narrow stairs. He checked the bathroom, and then he opened the bedroom door. It was chilly in there, because the window was open, but the stench was overwhelming. He shone his flashlight onto the floor, and there was the purple duvet cover with the dark purple flowers on it, and from the way it was bulked up, it was obvious what was inside it. The lower folds of it were shining wet, and the beige carpet next to it was stained dark yellow.

Jerry cupped his left hand over his nose and mouth and wished that he had taken Sergeant Bristow's advice to bring some Vick's vapour rub. He pulled his black forensic gloves out of his coat pocket and snapped them on, finger by finger. Then he stepped carefully into the bedroom and crouched down beside the duvet cover. Jamila watched him from the doorway.

Laying his flashlight down on the carpet, Jerry unbuttoned the duvet cover, lifted it up and peered inside. He could see the back of Mike's neck, and his shoulders, and when he lifted it higher he could just make out some of his greeny-yellow intestines, all piled up in his lap. He couldn't see Mike's face, because his head was bent so far forward, and he didn't want to touch him until the forensic experts had taken photographs of him *in situ*, so he was unable to determine if Sophie had been telling the truth about stabbing him in the eyes. He dropped the duvet cover and stood up.

'She wasn't lying about one thing,' he said, peeling off his gloves. 'She's cut him open.'

Jamila shuddered, and said, '*Yuck.*' Then she said, 'I'll contact forensics. There's nothing else we can do here, not at the moment.'

'I'll call Sergeant Bristow for some more back-up,' said Jerry. 'And I also need to make sure that we're keeping an eye on that Sophie. We don't want her doing a disappearing act before we arrest her.'

The two constables were waiting downstairs in the living-room. They didn't need to ask if Jerry and Jamila had found the victim's body.

'She wouldn't have had far to go to get rid of him, would she?' said the black officer. 'London Road Cemetery's just round the corner, and there's a wheelbarrow in that garden over the road there.'

Jerry tried not to give him a smile. 'Let's get the front of the house taped off, shall we?' he said. 'We don't want any nosey neighbours wandering in.'

He took another look around the kitchenette and the living-room, but there was nothing in either room to indicate that Sophie and her boyfriend might have been fighting before they went upstairs – no broken plates, no cushions thrown around. As he came back out of the living-room, though, he saw that the blue velvet jacket was no longer lying in the hallway.

'Hey!' he called to the black officer, who was outside the front of the house now, unwinding a roll of blue-and-white police tape. 'Did you move that jacket?'

The black officer shook his head. 'I saw it was gone but I thought you'd taken it.'

Jamila was outside, too, by their car, calling the forensic service. Jerry went out and said, 'You didn't pick up that jacket, did you?'

Jamila finished her call and frowned at him. 'Of course not. I haven't touched anything.'

'It's gone. It's not there any more.'

'This is ridiculous,' said Jamila. 'This is exactly like what happened at the Wazir house. It can't have disappeared on its own. Maybe one of those neighbours took it when we were upstairs.'

'Well, I'll ask them. But why would they?'

Jerry went next door. The neighbours were still standing in their front yard, smoking and chatting to another neighbour who had just joined them.

'Haven't seen a blue velvet jacket, have you?' Jerry asked them.

All three of them stared at him in bewilderment.

'I was wondering if you happened to see a blue velvet jacket lying in the hallway next door – and, ah—'

'And *what*, mate?' asked the husband, blowing out smoke.

'No, never mind,' Jerry told him.

'Blue velvet jacket, mate?' said the husband. 'Nah.'

15

Jamie couldn't believe his luck. He had limped into the alley between Tooting Public Library and the Subway sandwich shop so that he could relieve his bursting bladder when he saw the grey coat lying crumpled in the library's side doorway.

Although it had been raining for most of the afternoon, the coat had been sheltered by the doorway and when he picked it up, Jamie found that it was only slightly damp. He could see that it was a woman's coat, from the way it buttoned up, but he was narrow-shouldered and skeletally thin, apart from his swollen belly, and he could tell that it would easily fit him.

The temperature had dropped below 5 degrees now, and Jamie was wearing only a thin green cotton sweater and a faded denim jacket and jeans with holes in the knees. He had tried to go into the Long Room pub to warm himself up, but the barman had refused to serve him and told him to sling his hook. It had been a long time now since Jamie had been aware of how badly he smelled, and he hardly recognised himself when he saw himself reflected in shop windows, because he had never grown a full ginger beard when he was younger.

There had been a time when he had been a barman himself, at the Castle. But then Damon had moved into the flat that he had been sharing, and Damon had been a smack addict. Within only a few weeks, he had tempted Jamie into trying smack, too, and after that Jamie's life had swiftly and progressively fallen apart. Now he could barely remember the days when he used to have a job, and money, and a car, and a pretty blonde fiancée called Carole.

He had managed to find a room for three months at the Thames Reach homeless centre but then he had scrapped with another addict over drugs and he had been forced to leave. Since then he had been sleeping in shop doorways and begging and shoplifting in branches of Maplin's to raise the £100 he needed every day for smack. Most days he wasn't able to raise enough, and he would spend hours sitting in the library quaking with cold and hunger and withdrawal symptoms.

But now – God must have looked down from Heaven and seen how cold he was, and sent him this thick grey coat.

He shrugged it on, and after he taken a long piss against one of the library's dustbins, he buttoned it up, and raised the collar, too. He looked up at the narrow strip of grey sky in between the buildings and said, 'Thank you, Lord. I always knew that You hadn't forgotten me.'

He walked back out onto Mitcham Road. His coat would not only keep him warm, it would enable him to go into the Carphone Warehouse shop on the corner of Tooting Broadway and slip three or four new mobile phones in its pockets. God was not only protecting him from the cold, He was helping him to feed his habit.

He had only been shuffling along the pavement for two or three minutes, though, when he began to feel as if this new coat was prickling his back. It wasn't a pleasant prickling, either – it felt as if lice were crawling all over his skin, and he had experienced that often enough since he had been sleeping in hostels and homeless shelters and out on the streets.

He was passing the Primark store so he went into the doorway and unbuttoned the coat, with the intention of taking it off and giving it a shake. Maybe the coat had been left in the alley because it was infested. If it was, he could take it into the launderette and put it in a tumble dryer for fifteen minutes or so. That would be enough to kill the lice. He had done it before after he had shared a bed with a girl he had picked up on Oxford Street. His friend Marcus had warned him that she was 'a lousy lay' and he hadn't realised that he meant it literally.

As hard as he tried, though, he found that he couldn't pull the coat off. It wasn't too tight, but it felt as if it were stuck to his skin, and his sweater was stuck to his skin, too. He pulled at each of the cuffs to see if he could drag the sleeves off, but the coat was firmly stuck to his arms. Two women paused before they entered the store to watch him in amusement as he twisted and turned and tried to reach over his shoulders to pull the coat off his back.

'Having trouble, love?' one of them asked him. 'Not practising for *Strictly Come Dancing*, are you?'

He gritted his teeth and shook his head. He tugged at the coat even harder, but when he did that, he felt as if he were going to rip off a whole layer of skin, and it hurt so much that he had to stop. He stood in the shop doorway panting with pain and frustration, and with every second that passed, the prickling sensation across his back and his shoulders grew worse.

A few more passers-by stared at him, but he looked so dirty and scruffy that none of them stopped to ask him what was wrong.

Jesus, this wasn't lice. Lice were bad enough, but this was worse. Maybe the coat was infected with scabies, or infused with some kind of corrosive chemical. It was only about ten minutes' walk to St George's Hospital. Maybe he should go to A&E and ask for a doctor to help him to peel it off.

He sat down for a while with his back against the shop window, hoping that if he relaxed and calmed down the prickling sensation would fade. Very gradually, it did. At the same time, though, he began to feel light-headed, as if he might faint. He looked around at the street – at the shoppers walking past, and the cars, and the buses – and for a few seconds they all looked like a photographic negative. The clouds in the sky and people's faces all appeared to be black, while the road and the pavement and all the shop windows had turned a foggy white.

He felt different inside himself, too, as if his whole body had been emptied out through his feet, and he had been filled up with somebody else altogether.

Why are you so surprised? You're not Jamie. Why did you always believe that you were? You kept on thinking that you were Jamie and look what happened to you. Now you're back to being yourself and everything's going to be better. Not only better, but wonderful.

He managed to lever himself onto his feet. Leaning against Primark's window he stared at his reflection and he was baffled but also fascinated by what he saw. He thought he looked more like a woman than a man, even though he still had his ginger beard. In fact, somehow, he *knew* that he was a woman. His irises were normally pale green, but now they were dark and glittering, and his eyes were much wider. His eyebrows were finely plucked and uptilted. His sweater felt tighter, and when he lifted up both hands and felt his chest, he discovered that he had breasts. He squeezed them, again and again. *I have breasts. I have* breasts? *What am I? Who am I?*

He still felt swimmy and off-balance. In spite of that, he didn't feel frightened. It seemed as if this metamorphosis had been a long time coming, and it was only confusing him because it had happened so unexpectedly, right in the middle of Tooting on a busy Thursday evening, with so much traffic going past and so many people staring at him.

He started to walk slowly towards the junction with Tooting Broadway, limping slightly with one foot and dragging the other. Across the road he could see the Carphone Warehouse on the corner.

I need to go in there and half-inch some phones.

Ah – that's what Jamie would have done. But you don't need to do that. You're a woman. You don't need to steal any more. You have other ways of making money.

What other ways? How can I be a woman? I'm Jamie. I'm a man.

You were a man, Jamie. But not now.

I don't care what I am. If you say I'm a woman, I'm a woman. All I need now is a fix. I have to get myself a fix or else I'm going to have a fucking heart attack and die right here in the street.

I told you. You have other ways of making money. Look around you.

Where? What?

Jamie turned around, tilting so much that he nearly lost his balance and fell over. About a hundred metres along the

Mitcham Road he saw a bespectacled black-bearded Sikh man in a blue turban standing by the bus stop. The man was wearing a short beige raincoat and carrying a briefcase.

There you are. A prospective client. I'll bet he doesn't get enough of it at home.

What do I say to him? I can't take him anywhere because I don't have anywhere to take him.

Just ask him if he'd like to come round the back of Primark with you and you'll make him happy.

I don't know. I'm scared. What if he just tells me to get knotted?

He won't. But if he does, all you have to say to him is OK, it's your loss. You'll regret it when you get home and see your big fat ugly wife all wrapped up in her sari.

Jamie's brain was in a turmoil. He couldn't believe that he was arguing with himself, and yet the woman inside him was so strong and demanding and his own physical need had reached screaming pitch. He saw dazzling flashes of white light in front of his eyes, and the pavement felt as if it were heaving beneath his feet like the deck of an ocean liner.

He walked up to the Sikh and stood in front of him, swaying. At first the Sikh tried to ignore him, but Jamie was standing so close to him, and grinning at him with such a lewd expression on his face, that at last he said, 'Go away.'

'Don't you fancy some fun?' Jamie asked him.

'What are you talking about, fun? Go away.'

'I thought you might like a quickie.'

'*What?* Go away, please.'

'We could go round the back of the shops. Only a tenner.'

'Please go and leave me alone. I don't give money to beggars in the street.'

'I'm not begging. I'm offering you a service. Only a tenner for the best BJ you've ever had. And quick, too. I'll make sure you don't miss your bus.'

'For the last time, please go away,' the Sikh told him. 'If this is supposed to be some kind of a joke, it is not at all funny. You smell very bad and I am not interested in anything you have to offer.'

Jamie leaned closer to him, and took hold of the lapels of his raincoat. 'Don't you think I'm beautiful? You ought to see me naked. If you saw me naked, you'd be interested.'

The Sikh put down his briefcase and twisted Jamie's wrists. 'Get your dirty hands off me and leave me alone!' he shouted at him.

Jamie let go of his lapels but slapped him hard on the shoulder. 'You ungrateful bastard!' he screamed, and his voice was as high as a woman's. 'You wait till you get home and see your big fat hideous wife! Then you'll wish you'd come behind the shops!'

By now, a small crowd had gathered around them, although nobody stepped forward to intervene. The traffic next to the bus stop had been at a standstill, but suddenly it started to move, and a police car came past them. The Sikh stepped off the pavement and rapped on its window.

'Please – I need some assistance here,' he said. 'This fellow is bothering me and making indecent propositions.'

The woman PC in the passenger seat peered across at Jamie, who was swaying and leering and clutching the front of his coat with both hands, as if he had breasts.

'All right, sir,' said the WPC. The police car drew in to the side of the road and she climbed out, followed by a burly male officer.

The woman PC went up to Jamie and said, 'This gentleman says that you're being a nuisance.'

Jamie pouted at her coquettishly. Her head seemed to grow enormous and then shrink to the size of a tennis-ball. 'A nuisance? I was offering him a service, that's all!'

'What kind of a service?'

Jamie pointed over his shoulder to the shops behind him. 'A quick BJ, behind Primark. Only a tenner. He didn't have to get so angry about it. The thing is, the thing is – oh Christ, I need a fix. I really need a fix.'

The male officer looked down at Jamie. He seemed to tower over him, blotting out the sky, and when he spoke his voice boomed and echoed, as if Jamie were down at the bottom of a well.

Maybe that's where I am – down the bottom of a well, like that girl in The Ring.

'You offered him a blowjob?' said the male officer.

'What's so funny?' Jamie challenged him, but then he staggered sideways and it was only because the male officer caught his elbow and held him up straight that he didn't fall onto the pavement and hit his head.

'I think you'd best be coming along with us,' said the WPC. 'Can you tell me what your name is?'

Jamie frowned at her. 'My name?'

He thought long and hard but the inside of his head was churning over like wet concrete in a concrete-mixer and the strobe lights kept shimmering in front of his eyes and the WPC kept growing larger and smaller. He began to think that she was repeatedly running away from him and then running back again.

'No,' he mumbled. 'I can't remember my name. I'm not even sure who I am. It's the coat.'

The WPC said, 'I'm arresting you on a charge of importuning for an act of gross indecency in a public place.' She cautioned him; and then between them, she and the male officer opened up the door of the police car and heaved Jamie onto the back seat.

'Blimey,' said the male officer, waving his hand in front of his face. 'He don't half pen-and-ink.'

16

David was woken by the doorbell chiming. He opened his eyes and stared at the bedroom wallpaper with its florid red roses. At first he couldn't think where he was.

Where am I? Whose bedroom is this? How did I get here?

He sat up. The doorbell chimed again, and then a woman's voice called out, 'Evie? Evie, are you there?'

Somebody wants to see Evie, but you know what you've done to her. Punished her – taken your revenge, and about time too.

He climbed off the bed, crossed the landing and went downstairs, although he lost his footing near the bottom. He banged loudly down the last three or four stairs and had to grab at the newel post to stop himself from falling over.

The doorbell chimed yet again, and the woman knocked and called out, 'Evie? It's Bella! You're not still in bed, are you?'

He opened the front door. A freckle-faced woman in a white raincoat and a headscarf was standing in the porch, holding a large tapestry bag.

She took one look at David and said, 'Oh! David! Sorry!'

It was then that he realised that he was wearing only the black sweater that he had found at his mother's house. He pulled it down at the front to cover himself.

'Is Evie there?' asked Bella, keeping her head turned away so that she wouldn't have to look at him.

'Evie? No. Evie's, er… Evie's gone to see her sister.'

'Gone to see her sister? She didn't say anything to me. We were supposed to go out shopping early today. They've got a sale on at Morley's.'

'Her sister's not too well. I don't know what's wrong with her. But she asked Evie to go up to Watford and take care of the kids.'

'Why didn't she ring and tell me?'

'I have no idea. I don't know when she'll be back, either.'

Bella reached into her raincoat pocket and took out her mobile phone. 'I'll give her a call. I can't believe that she didn't tell me that she couldn't come shopping this morning.'

She prodded at her phone but David said, 'It's no good ringing her. She left her phone behind.'

Bella turned her head now and stared at him. 'She left her phone behind? *Evie?* I don't believe it!'

'She was in a hurry, and she was very upset about her sister.'

'Well, have you got her sister's number? You must have her sister's number.'

'Sorry, I don't. Evie keeps all her numbers on her phone and I don't know her password.'

'What's her sister's surname? You must have her address. I could find her number from directory enquiry.'

'Atkins, I think. Or maybe it's Watkins. I'm not entirely sure. And I don't know her address. She only moved to Watford in March and I've never been there.'

Bella stayed in the porch for a few moments, looking exasperated. Then she said, 'What about her sister's husband? Do you know where he works?'

'I haven't a clue. I think he's a solicitor, something like that. Listen – why don't you wait until Evie rings you? She's bound to, sooner or later.'

'I'll have to, won't I? I don't see that I've any alternative.'

With that, Bella walked away. She clanged the wrought-iron gate behind her to show her disapproval and crossed over to her bright yellow Fiat 500. There was another woman sitting in the back seat and David vaguely recognised her as one of Evie's friends. He couldn't remember her name but he remembered that she never stopped talking.

He closed the front door and went through to the kitchen. Evie was lying on her side staring at the grey-tiled floor, the back of her dress looking like a map of North and South America in dried brown blood. Her eyes were open but they had turned milky. Maggie the tortoiseshell cat was prowling around, clearly unable to understand why Evie didn't stand up and feed her, as she usually did. She looked up at David and mewled.

You can starve for all I care, you perishing nuisance. Evie knew that you were allergic to cats, didn't she? but she insisted on having one. 'Who will I have for company when you're at work?' And that had been a double-edged question, hadn't it, because you hadn't been able to have children. And whose fault had that been? His – because of having such a low sperm count.

David felt a tinge of sadness that Evie was dead. After all, they had enjoyed nearly seven years together, and for most of the time they had been happy, although she had always desperately wanted children. That had caused endless low-level friction between them, because she had often had dreams that she was pregnant, or that she had actually given birth. She had once claimed that she had heard their child laughing in another room – the child they would never be able to have. But David had been dead set against a sperm donor. That would have been like allowing his wife to have sex with another man, and the child would never have been his.

He looked at the slices of onion on the chopping-board. They had all dried up now, but there were plenty more onions in the vegetable rack. Carrots, too, and half a swede, and he knew that there were beans in the fridge. He could carry on where Evie had left off, and make a stew himself.

He crouched down beside her, and gently laid his hand on her shoulder. If he cooked a stew, that could not only provide him with three or four decent meals, it could solve the problem of what to do with her body. He could cut her up neatly, and package her, and freeze her remains, and over the coming months he could keep the promise that he had made to her on the day that he had proposed to her. 'You and me, the two of us, let's become one.'

Her bones? Well, he could smash up her bones with a hammer and then flush them a little at a time down the toilet.

He stood up. He felt pleased with that plan, especially since it would have secretly delighted his mother so much.

Evie was never right for him. Never had his class. Now she's going to end up what she was always destined to be. Human waste.

He opened the cutlery drawer and took out a sharp thin-bladed boning knife. While Maggie watched him, he knelt down on the floor and lifted Evie's dress up over her right hip. He cut the elasticated waistband of her tights and pulled them down as far as her knees. When he gripped her thigh between finger and thumb her flesh felt soft and yielding. With the point of his knife he marked a rectangle into her skin, about fifteen centimetres by eight, and he used this as guidelines to slice deep into her flesh, until the tip of the blade jarred against her femur.

Carefully, he cut out a large lump of flesh. It was paler and fattier than he thought it was going to be, and there was very little blood, but of course her heart had stopped beating and she had no circulation. Once he had worried the lump away from her thighbone he lifted it up in the palm of his hand and smelled it, and when Maggie saw him doing that she licked her lips. He had read that cannibals claimed that human flesh tasted like pork – that's why they called it 'long pig' – but this didn't smell like pork at all, or any other meat that he had ever eaten. The closest he could think of was veal.

He scraped the dried-up onion slices off the chopping-board and laid the lump of flesh onto it. Before he started preparing his stew, though, he knelt down beside Evie's body and finished undressing her. He grunted with effort taking off her dress because she was so floppy, and she seemed to be so much heavier than when she was alive. At last, though, he managed to bundle up her dress and her tights and her apron and toss them over to the far corner of the kitchen. When he rolled her over onto her stomach to unfasten her bra, he saw the tiny angel's wings that had been tattooed between her shoulder-blades the day after he had proposed to her.

'I've done that because I feel I'm in Heaven,' she had told him. If only she had realised how soon she really would be.

He opened the door to the utility room and dragged Evie's body inside. Next to the washing-machine stood a large chest freezer, and he unlocked it and opened up the lid. He had to take out at least a dozen bags of frozen roast potatoes and broad beans and chicken drumsticks before there was enough room for Evie. He dropped them all on the floor. He could either throw them in the dustbin or scatter them over the lawn at the back of the house. The pigeons and the squirrels would soon eat them.

Grunting again with effort, he lifted up Evie's body and lowered her into the freezer. He tried to do it with some reverence, as if he were setting her down to rest in a coffin. She lay there naked, her skin dead white, her lips slightly parted, staring up at him with those milky unfocused eyes. He was reminded of that pre-Raphaelite painting of Ophelia, drowning in the river, except that Ophelia was surrounded by flowers and weeds, and Evie was lying amongst packets of frozen prawns and Bird's Eye peas.

He closed the lid of the freezer, locked it, and went back into the kitchen. He took out the largest of their frying-pans, put it on the hob, and poured a tablespoonful of olive oil into it. While the oil was heating up, he sliced the lump of Evie's flesh into cubes. It was quite stringy, and made a crunching sound when he cut it.

As soon as the oil was smoking, he dropped the cubes of flesh into it, and stirred them around. They were quickly sizzled to a golden-brown, and when they had all been seared, he tipped them out onto a piece of kitchen towel. The smell was meaty but light, and again he was reminded of veal. It made him feel seriously hungry, and of course he hadn't eaten since lunchtime yesterday, and that was only a pig cheek sandwich in the Trafalgar Arms.

Why bother making a stew? You could try this right now.

He picked up a cube of flesh. It was crisp on the outside and it did smell good. He hesitated for a moment, and then he bit into it, and chewed it. It was still a little tough, and it squeaked at first between his teeth, but the flavour was savoury and delicious.

I'm eating my wife. I'm eating Evie. She was a human being and I loved her and now I'm eating her. I'm actually eating her.

Aren't you proud of yourself? There's not many husbands who would have the nerve to do what you did, no matter how often they may have felt like it.

And I'll bet there's hardly any husbands who would deny their wives a Christian burial by passing them through their digestive tract instead.

Still chewing, David walked out of the kitchen, with Maggie following him and tangling herself between his ankles, mewling for something to eat. He stared at himself in the mirror by the front door. He had dark circles under his eyes and he was still wearing nothing but the black sweater that his mother had knitted. The sweater felt itchy across his back and around his elbows, but he had no inclination to take it off.

He watched himself chewing, moving the piece of flesh from one side of his mouth to the other. *I'm eating my wife. This lump of meat that I have in my mouth, this is Evie.*

He chewed more slowly. He closed his eyes and wondered if he ought to spit the meat out. But then, after a long pause, he swallowed it.

17

When Jerry arrived at the station that morning, he was surprised to find that DI Saunders was already sitting at his desk. He was tapping at his laptop with a cup of macchiato from Mud's growing cold beside him.

'I wanted to make an early start,' DI Saunders told him. 'I've got an important lunch later, up in the City.'

Jerry didn't ask him what kind of a lunch he was going to, but he could guess. DI Saunders was a Freemason, and he had heard that the masons were holding a series of fundraising events to buy a new air ambulance. All the same, he looked even more miserable than usual.

'Dr Fuller's just sent the preliminary report from forensics,' he said. 'Both on Samira Wazir's skin sample and the fibres that were taken from Sophie Marshall. Here I've printed a copy out for you.'

He picked up a sheet of paper and handed it over.

'I hate to admit it, Jerry, but it seems like you may have been right to be suspicious about Ms Wazir's missing coat... and Ms Marshall's jacket, too. The fibres in Samira Wazir's skin sample were definitely a mixture of wool and polyester, and the samples from Ms Marshall turned out to be silk. But both samples also contained traces of human DNA – and not the same DNA as Ms Wazir and Ms Marshall, and not the same as each other.'

Jerry quickly scanned the report from the forensics service.

'But how did the fibres get into their pores?' he asked. 'They don't say anything about that here.'

'They're still running tests. In other words, they haven't got the faintest. I spoke to Dr Fuller on the phone and he said that the only way they could have penetrated her pores was if they had been alive, like worms, or some other kind of parasite that gets under your skin. I asked him if he'd been watching too much *Doctor Who* lately.'

Jerry didn't answer. The expression on DI Saunders' face was so bereft of any trace of humour that he couldn't think what to say.

'On the other hand, it may not be so much of a science fiction story as it sounds,' DI Saunders went on.

'Really?' said Jerry.

DI Saunders stood up. 'A druggie was brought in late yesterday afternoon for importuning and threatening behaviour in the Mitcham Road. He's wearing a short grey coat that matches the description of Ms Wazir's coat. He's down in the cells right now. Apparently he was suffering so badly from withdrawal symptoms last night that they had to call in a doctor to give him a shot of methadone. He's sleeping it off right now.'

'But he was wearing Samira Wazir's coat? Or one that looks like it?'

'He still is. And that's the whole point. We can't get it off him. It's like it's stuck to him with superglue. Except that it's not superglue. It's the fibres of the coat. They've penetrated right through his sweater and into his skin. The doctor said that if we tried to pull it off him, half of his skin would probably come away with it, and he could die of shock.'

'So the odds are, it's the same coat?'

'It seems like it. Once we've removed it, we'll run Ms Wazir's mother down here to identify it. I'm just waiting to hear that he's conscious, and then we can interview him and send him over to St George's and see what they can do surgically to get it off him.'

'Sophie Marshall sold that coat to Samira Wazir at her charity shop. She should be able to identify it, too.'

'Well, yes. Not that she's going to count as a reliable witness. DS Patel's going to be interviewing her again this morning. She's still insisting that it was her jacket that encouraged her to murder her boyfriend.' He circled his finger around his head to indicate that he thought she was loopy.

Jerry said, 'How about that appeal about the jacket that the press office put out? It was on *London Tonight* yesterday, wasn't it? Have we had any response to that yet?'

DI Saunders shook his head. 'I have to tell you, Jerry, I'm not at all sure how to handle this. Ms Wazir's coat – all right, what happened to her was bizarre, but maybe there was some kind of infestation in the fabric, like Dr Fuller suggested. We could have put that down to an isolated incident. But then we get Ms Marshall's jacket, and it's almost the same story over again. On top of that, both garments immediately went missing from the crime scene, almost as if—'

He paused, and Jerry finished what he was obviously going to say. 'I know. Almost as if they ran off by themselves. That's what Sophie Marshall told me… She said her jacket came after her.'

'It's bonkers, isn't it?' said DI Saunders. 'It's totally bloody bonkers. It *seems* to be bonkers, anyway, but the trouble is, there's going to be a perfectly simple and reasonable explanation, and when we find out what it is, we're going to look like complete cretins for suggesting that a coat and a jacket could run around all by themselves. It's like what happened to DCI Charlie Meredith, do you remember? He was totally convinced that a baby girl had been abducted by foxes, and all the time it turned out that her mother had suffocated her and buried her in the back garden. Ruined his career, that did, and he ended up dying of a heart attack in Woolworth's. I don't want the same to happen to me.'

Jamila came in, wearing a smart navy-blue trouser-suit and a blue Hermès headscarf. She smelled of patchouli perfume.

'Good morning, gentlemen,' she smiled. 'I dropped in to see Mrs Wazir on my way here this morning, just to see how she is coping. She is still deeply upset by the death of her daughter, of course. Her husband will be coming home this afternoon so I'll go back there later and see what he has to add, if anything. But Mrs Wazir told me that she now remembers something strange that happened on the day before she and her son went off to see her cousin. That was also the same day that Samira came home with the coat.'

'Strange?' asked DI Saunders. 'Strange like what?'

'Strange like she went upstairs to tell Samira to come down for her supper, because that was one day when she hadn't eaten at the restaurant. She was just about to open her bedroom door when she heard what sounded like Samira talking to another woman.'

'OK. So who was she, this other woman?'

'That was what was strange. She listened for a while, and then she knocked and went in, but only Samira was there, nobody else. She told Samira that she thought she had heard her talking to somebody, but Samira didn't say anything. She didn't confirm it and she didn't deny it.'

'Did she hear anything of what Samira and this imaginary woman were talking about?' asked Jerry. 'I used to have an imaginary friend called Bill, and we used to jabber all the time, him and me. Bill used to speak very *gruff*.'

'She couldn't hear exactly what they were saying,' said Jamila, 'but according to Mrs Wazir, Samira sounded as if she was really upset about something, and this other woman sounded very cross and demanding. She was *nagging*, that was how Mrs Wazir put it.'

'Well, that's something to note in your report,' said DI Saunders. 'I don't know if it throws any more light on who poured acid over our victim, or if it was self-inflicted. I'm still leaning towards an honour killing, but perhaps it's an indication that the balance of her mind was disturbed.'

'There's one more thing,' said Jamila. 'Samira was wearing her new coat at the time.'

'In her bedroom?'

Jamila nodded. 'It seems unusual, doesn't it, to say the least? That's a very warm house. *Too* warm, for my liking. So why would she be wearing an overcoat?'

'Funny, that,' said Jerry. 'That kid who got himself stuck in the charity box, Billy Jenkins, he said he heard a voice inside the box, but when he climbed inside there was nobody there.'

'Well, maybe he did,' said DI Saunders. 'But he was out of his brain on smack, wasn't he?'

'Was Samira still wearing the coat when she came down for her supper?' asked Jerry.

'No, but Mrs Wazir says that she ate her supper very quickly, and hardly spoke, and couldn't wait to leave the table and get back up to her bedroom again.'

DI Saunders sat down again with his hand over his mouth, thinking. Then he pushed a copy of the report from the forensic service across his desk and said, 'You'd best read this.'

While she scanned it, he told her about the addict who had been arrested in Mitcham Road, and how he appeared to be wearing Samira Wazir's coat, or at least a coat that looked very much like it.

'Jerry and I were discussing this when you came in. How bloody mystifying it all is. And what Mrs Wazir told you hasn't helped. If anything, it's made it even *more* bloody mystifying.'

'There's still no sign of Sophie Marshall's jacket?'

'No,' said Jerry. 'I only hope that if anybody finds it, they don't try it on. I don't fancy finding any more bodies with their guts hanging out.'

'Well, Sophie's had her breakfast, so I'm going down to interview her now,' said Jamila. 'Are you coming, Jerry?'

DI Saunders said, 'Text me when you've finished. Especially if she admits to it. I should be back here about four o'clock in any case. And perhaps you can have some thoughts about how we're going to present this to the press.'

'I think I'm going to agree with what you said yesterday, sir,' said Jerry, although he could hardly believe that he was saying it. 'Don't let's say anything about the coat or the jacket until we're sure we know exactly what we're talking about.'

★

Sophie was looking dazed when a young woman officer brought her into the interview room. Her hair was tousled and she had a blue blanket draped over her shoulders.

She was seated at the table opposite Jerry and Jamila, while the woman officer went over and sat in the opposite corner.

'Hallo, Sophie,' said Jamila. 'How are you feeling this morning? Did you sleep?'

Sophie blinked at her, and frowned, as if she were speaking in a foreign language.

'We're going to ask you some questions, Sophie, and we're going to record your answers. Do you understand that? You've already been cautioned, but I want you to be clear that you understand your rights. You know that you don't have to say anything, but anything you do say can be used as evidence in a court of law, and if you rely for your defence on something that you don't tell us now, it could count against you.'

Sophie continued to frown at her as if she couldn't understand a word.

'Can you confirm your full name, please?' asked Jamila.

'What difference will it make, who I am?' Sophie retorted.

'I just need you to confirm your full name, for the record.'

'I'm not telling you.'

'Are you Sophie Jean Marshall, of Lavender Avenue, Tooting?'

'What difference will it make, if I am?'

'Until yesterday, were you co-habiting at Lavender Avenue with Michael Lewis Brent?'

'She was, yes.'

'When you say "she", do you mean you?'

'I mean her.'

'Who's she?'

'She's the one who killed him. But after the way he treated her, I don't blame her.'

'Do you admit that you murdered Michael Lewis Brent?'

'She did. It was her. You can blame me for it if you like, but you don't have any proof, do you?'

'Sophie, your fingerprints are on the handle of the knife that was stuck in Michael's left eye, as well as a knife that was stuck into his right eye and then removed, and also on a knife that was used to cut open his stomach.'

'Yes, but they're *her* fingerprints. Not mine.'

'Sophie, you *are* her. You're one and the same person. Those fingerprints match yours.'

'I don't know how that can be. You're lying. You're making it up. You're trying to trick me into saying it was me who murdered him, aren't you?'

'I don't have to trick you, Sophie. All the evidence points to the fact that it was you. Apart from your fingerprints on the murder weapons, there was nobody else in the house except for you, and we have witnesses who can testify that they saw nobody else enter or leave the property during the time-frame when Michael was killed.'

'They're mistaken, because *I* was there. Either that, or they're lying. They never liked her. They were always complaining because of all the shouting. But it wasn't her fault, it was Mike's. You can't blame her for killing him. I don't know how she put up with him for so long. He was a pig.'

'All right, *you* were there, as well as Sophie,' said Jamila. 'Can you please tell me who you are?'

'No,' said Sophie. 'You said I didn't have to say anything if I didn't want to.'

'I warned you that it would harm your defence if you relied on something in court which you refused to tell us now.'

'I won't need to, because I didn't do it, and you can't prove that I did.'

Jamila reached across the table and switched off the recorder. 'That's it,' she said. 'It's clear that we're not getting anywhere. I'm going to send you for a psychiatric assessment to determine if you're capable of understanding the charges against you.'

Sophie stared at her wide-eyed. '*What?*' she screeched. '*Are you saying that I'm mad? Is that what you're saying? I'll show you who's mad!*'

She stood up, so that her chair fell backwards onto the floor with a loud clatter. Then she climbed up over the table and seized Jamila's right arm. Jamila smacked at her with her left hand and tried to push her away, but Sophie lifted up Jamila's right hand and bit into it, just below her thumb, so hard that blood spurted out. Jamila let out a yelp of pain, and shook her hand away, and as she did so Jerry reached out and dragged Sophie off the table and onto the floor.

The woman officer pushed Sophie face down onto the carpet and forced her knee into her back. Then she twisted Sophie's arms behind her, unclipped the handcuffs from her belt and snapped them around Sophie's wrists.

'Don't you worry! Don't you worry!' Sophie shouted. 'That was only the first bite! I'll eat the rest of you yet, you cow! I'll eat every last scrap of you and pick my teeth with your bones!'

Between them, Jerry and the woman officer pulled Sophie up onto her feet. Jamila had pressed the panic button and two more uniformed officers burst their way into the interview room.

Sophie threw her head violently from side to side and spit flew out of her mouth. 'I'll eat the rest of you yet, you miserable bitch! I'll chew you and swallow you and digest you and you'll become me! Then you'll know who murdered Mike! *Then* you'll know! But it'll be too late for you then, won't it? Far too late! Just let me get my teeth into you, you bitch! You won't stand a hope in hell!'

The three officers dragged Sophie, still screaming and kicking, back to her cell. Jerry looked at Jamila's bleeding hand and saw that Sophie had bitten her right through to the bone. He pulled three tissues out of the box on the table, folded them up into a pad, and pressed them against the teeth-marks.

'You're going to need stitches, or butterfly bandages at least, and sterilising, too,' he told her. 'God knows what's wrong with that girl, but you don't want to catch it.'

Jamila's lips were pursed and she was wincing with pain. She nodded, and Jerry could see that she was trying hard not to cry. If she hadn't been his superior officer, he would have hugged her and kissed her and told her that she was going to be fine.

18

Laura rinsed her muesli bowl and left it in the sink. Then she went through to the bathroom to brush her teeth. It was a dull grey morning and when she saw herself in the mirror over the washbasin she thought that she was looking tired and old.

She had been head teacher at St Blandina's primary school for four years now and this term had been her hardest. Three of her best teachers had left to get married and the Ofsted government inspector had given her school an 'inadequate' rating. Her dyed-brown hair was dry and wiry and she had pouches under her eyes and deep lines on the sides of her mouth. And to think she had once been the prettiest girl at her teacher training college.

She was just about to start brushing her teeth when she heard a rattling, scuffling sound from out in the hallway. She listened, still looking at herself in the mirror. The rattling continued, and it seemed to be coming from the cupboard where she hung up her coats and kept her outdoor shoes.

At first she thought it might be an airlock in the central heating pipe – but that always made a knocking noise. This was softer and quicker, almost *furtive*, as if there were somebody trying to hide themselves behind the coats.

She put down her toothbrush, went across to the cupboard and opened the door. Three coats and two jackets were hanging on a rail, and her shoes and boots were neatly arranged in wooden compartments. The rattling and scuffling had abruptly stopped, although she was sure that the coats were swaying slightly on their hangers.

She left the cupboard door open while she went back into the bathroom to brush her teeth. Although she couldn't understand why, she couldn't help feeling that she was no longer alone in her flat. She was on the point of calling out, 'Who's there?' until she thought to herself: *Don't be ridiculous. Both the front and the back doors are locked and all the windows are shut. Nobody could have got inside without my knowing.*

She gave her hair a quick primp, and then she went back to the cupboard and lifted out her thick brown tweed coat. As soon as she had put her arms into the sleeves, and before she had even started to button it up, she felt a hard jolt, as if somebody had come up behind her and grabbed her by the shoulders. She gasped, and stumbled forward, so that she collided with the frame of the bathroom door on the opposite side of the hallway, hitting the right side of her forehead.

Half-stunned, she tried to turn around to wrest herself free from her attacker, but she was dragged bodily back into the cupboard. She fell among the other coats and jackets, and the impact of her falling made their sleeves flap up and almost smother her. She struggled to free herself, but they kept flapping up as if they were alive, and they were trying to wrap their arms around her.

She reached over her shoulder with her left hand to push off whoever it was who had seized her, but it was then that she realised that there was nobody there. It was her *coat* that was gripping her. It had fastened itself onto her shoulders and her back and it was clinging to her as if it were three sizes too small.

She took hold of her right cuff and tugged it, but she simply didn't have the strength to pull it off. She jerked it again and again, harder and harder, but she still couldn't budge it.

She stood still, and took several deep breaths. The coat was so tight that it was making her feel panicky. *I can't think why it's suddenly got so tight, but if I can't take it off normally, I'm going to go to the kitchen and get my scissors and* cut *it off.*

The other coats and jackets were still swaying, even though she was standing still, and the sleeve of her khaki raincoat suddenly flipped up over her shoulder and brushed itself against her cheek. She took two or three unsteady steps forward to get out of the cupboard, and staggered towards the kitchen as if she were drunk. The coat was even tighter now, and she felt that it was going to break her collarbone and force her shoulder-blades together, and she was finding it hard to breathe.

She opened the drawer in the kitchen and took out the scissors she usually used for cutting chickens, and string. As she was about to cut into the left-hand cuff, though, she hesitated.

Why does she want to take it off?

It's hurting. It's far too tight. It's making me feel panicky.

Tell her to relax. Tell her that she doesn't need to worry. The coat is her and she is the coat. It won't hurt her so long as she understands that.

How can I be a coat? I don't understand.

We're like conjoined twins now, she and me. I can enter into her, and then we'll be together, the two of us – inseparable. I know she's not happy at the moment. I can feel it. I know that she's tired and disappointed. But I can give her the life that I once had. I can come back, through her.

Laura slowly lowered the scissors and then she laid them back in the drawer. She was right. The coat didn't feel as if it were crushing her any more. In fact it seemed to fit her perfectly. All she could feel was a prickling sensation across her shoulders and down her back, but that wasn't altogether unpleasant. In a strange way, it was slightly erotic.

She left the kitchen and went back to the cupboard in the hallway. She looked at the coats and the jackets hanging there, and she thought: *You're alive. You're my brothers and sisters. Don't worry – we'll find people like Laura for you, too. People you can embrace. People who will give you back the lives you've lost. You've suffered enough. Now it's your time.*

The coats and the jackets swung on their hangers as if they were silently showing their approval.

*

She parked her Mini Clubman at the back of the school and went inside.

St Blandina's was a large red-brick Edwardian building on the corner of Hillbury Road overlooking Tooting Bec Common. It had been named for the Christian martyr who was the patron saint of young school-children. St Blandina had been half-roasted on a red-hot grille and then wrapped in a net and thrown into an arena to be tossed by wild bulls. Lately Laura had been feeling that she had been suffering almost as much. Not only did she have to deal with Ofsted inspectors telling her how much her school needed improvement, but she had to cope with carping parents and dim supply teachers and spoilt, arrogant, misbehaving children.

From today, everything's going to be different. From today, she's not going to take any more nonsense from anybody. She wasn't born in this world to suffer, not like I did.

She walked along the parquet-floored corridor to her office. She could hear children chattering and laughing in the classrooms, and some of them slamming the lids of their desks.

Why does every school smell the same? she thought. *Of paints and paper and children's wee and whatever's being cooked in the kitchen for lunch? I hate the smell. It makes me feel nauseous. It makes me feel trapped.*

There were seventy-seven children in the school at the moment, between the ages of four and seven. Before the Ofsted report there had been over a hundred, but now it was difficult to make ends meet, financially, and she had been forced to cut down on educational trips and on school dinners, too. Some of the parents had complained that the meals were smaller than they used to be, but most of the children left half of their food anyway, with one or two obese exceptions.

As she reached her office, Leta Clover came out of her classroom, making a point of looking at her watch. Leta was a young supply teacher, originally from Jamaica, with a cornrow hairstyle and huge gold earrings.

'What time are we going to start lessons, Miss Miller? My class is getting very restive.'

'Oh, excuse me,' Laura retorted. 'Are you pointing out that I'm ten minutes late? I *am* sorry to have kept you waiting so long! I'm only the head teacher and your employer. How silly of me to assume that I could come and go whenever I pleased.'

Leta's mouth dropped open. Laura had never spoken to her so sarcastically before – not to her, nor to any of her supply teachers. Usually she made a special effort to keep them happy, and to make them feel appreciated, mainly because really good supply teachers were so scarce.

'Prayers in five minutes,' said Laura. 'And can I hear some girls in your classroom screaming? I won't have screaming. Go back in there and sort them out.'

'They're only playing,' said Leta.

'They don't come here to play, they come here to learn. They can play when they get home. Now go and tell those girls to keep the noise down.'

'Well, yes. If that's what you want.'

'It's a school rule. No screaming. And no running, either. I don't want running.'

'Anything else?' Leta challenged her.

'Yes. No impertinence. I won't have impertinence. Either from the children, or from you.'

Leta was obviously ready to answer her back, but she managed to restrain herself. Without another word she turned around and went back to her classroom, slamming the door behind her.

Right, thought Laura. *That's the end of your career at St Blandina's, young madam!*

She went into her office. There were seven or eight letters waiting on her desk. She quickly sorted through them. Bills, most of them, although there was also a letter from Ofsted about her NTI – notice to improve. She tore it in half, and then tore it in half again, and dropped it into her wastepaper basket. Then she stared at the other letters for a moment before picking them up and tearing all of them in half, too.

She's in charge now. Properly in charge. She's not going to allow anybody to make demands on her or tell her what to do.

She sat down at her desk, opened her laptop, and began to write out a letter to parents informing them of her new school rules. If a child was defiant, the parent would be expected to come immediately to the school and remove him or her for the rest of the day. Children who refused to eat their lunch would have to sit at the table until it was finished, even if it meant sitting there until home time.

She could hear the children chattering and laughing as they were ushered into the large hall at the front of the school which was used for assemblies and for meals. Once they had all passed her door, she stood up and went after them, still wearing her coat. The school was well heated, but she didn't want to take it off, and guessed that she probably couldn't, although she had no inclination now to try. She felt that the coat was part of her. The coat *was* her.

19

When she entered the hall, the children were all sitting cross-legged on the floor, with their four teachers sitting on chairs, two on either side. They were all talking and giggling and nudging each other, and one boy was throwing rolled-up paper pellets. None of them stopped when Laura came into the room.

'Simon,' she said, coldly.

The boy who was throwing paper pellets took no notice.

'*Simon!*' she snapped.

He stopped, and grinned at her. 'Yes, miss?'

'Go to the toilet,' she told him.

'I don't need to go, miss.'

'I don't care. Go to the toilet, close the door, and stay there until I say that you can come out.'

All the children burst out laughing, including Simon, although his laughter was more uncertain.

'What makes you think that I'm joking?' said Laura. 'Go to the toilet now and stay there, otherwise I will phone your mother and tell her that you've been misbehaving and she has to take you home.'

The laughter died away. The children could see by the expression on Laura's face that she was serious. Simon stood up and stepped over the other children on his way to the door. His eyes were filled with tears and his mouth was turned down in misery.

Once he had gone, Laura said, 'Listen to me, all of you! There will be no more talking during prayers. Not today, not tomorrow, not ever. There will be no more talking in the corridors. There will be no more running. When you go outside to play, there will be no more shouting and screaming. You have come here to school to learn, and two of the most important things that you are going to learn are good behaviour and respect for your elders. I don't care what your parents allow you to do at home. That's none of my business. But here, at St Blandina's, you will do what you are told. Do you understand that?'

There was silence from the children. Laura could see the teachers giving each other quizzical looks, and Leta shrugging and pulling a face as if to say, 'Don't ask me!'

'*Do you understand that?*' Laura repeated.

'Yes, Miss Miller,' the children chorused. Some of the younger ones sitting in the front looked completely bewildered, while others looked frightened, and two or three of them gave a little shiver.

'Right, you can go back to your classrooms now,' said Laura.

Susan Lawrence put up her hand. She was in charge of the six-year-olds, and had been teaching at St Blandina's since it first opened.

'No hymns today, Miss Miller? No prayers?'

'We're not singing or showing our devotion to some imaginary deity, thank you,' said Laura.

'But – this is a Christian school, isn't it?'

'Do you believe in ghosts, Susan?' asked Laura.

'Well of course not, but—'

'Ghosts are imaginary. God is imaginary. We don't have conversations with ghosts because that would be absurd, and we don't sing ridiculous songs to God, because that would be equally absurd. These children are here to be educated, not deluded. Now, everybody back to your classrooms!'

She clapped her hands and all the children stood up and filed in silence out of the room, some of them glancing at her worriedly. What had happened to the warm and smiling head teacher who had led them yesterday in singing 'Jesus Wants Me for a Sunbeam' and 'Arky Arky'? Most of the children had never been spoken to so harshly in their lives and Laura could tell by the way that some of the older ones were smirking that they thought she had been play-acting. *Well, they would soon find out.*

★

At 10:30, Natasha Bell knocked at Laura's office door. Natasha was a small, shy young woman who looked after the nursery class. She was pale and plump but quite pretty, with her hair always twisted up in a bun. The four-year-olds all loved her.

'I'm just going for my doctor's appointment now,' she said, cautiously.

Laura carried on typing for a few moments, but then she looked up and said, 'What doctor's appointment?'

'The one I told you about yesterday, Miss Miller. For my IVF treatment.'

'Did you? How long are you going to be?'

'The rest of the day, as I told you.'

'So who's going to be taking care of your class?'

Natasha gave her an awkward smile. 'Well, *you* are. You said you would. You said it wouldn't be a problem.'

'Are you *sure* I said that?' Laura's fingers were still poised over her keyboard, as if she were determined to continue writing her letter.

'I've had to wait three months for this appointment,' Natasha told her. She was beginning to sound desperate. 'If I miss this one, I don't know when I'll be able to get another.'

'So you want a baby?' said Laura. 'I would have thought you were heartily sick of small children by now. Sick to the back teeth.'

'Please, Miss Miller. My husband's come to collect me and he's waiting outside.'

Laura looked at the screen of her laptop for a moment, and then she switched it off and closed it. 'Very well. I can't have you thinking that I'm an ogress, can I? Who's looking after the little darlings at the moment?'

'Gemma's keeping an eye on them for me. She's given her own class some colouring to keep them out of mischief.'

Laura stood up. Natasha was disturbed to see that she looked much taller than usual, and even though she had her back to the window, and the light was behind her, her face seemed different, with a chin that was broader and squarer, and with much smaller eyes. She was still wearing her brown tweed coat, and Natasha felt like asking her if she was feeling the cold, but she was in such a strange and prickly mood that she decided not to.

Natasha left; and Laura trudged upstairs. There were two classrooms on the first-floor landing – the nursery class and the seven-year-olds. Laura had arranged it like that so that the older children could be asked to help with the infants whenever it was necessary – like taking them to the toilet, which they needed with irritating frequency.

Gemma Watts was standing in front of the children when Laura came in, singing 'The Wheels on the Bus Go Round and Round'. Most of the children were joining in, although two or three of them were staring blankly at nothing at all and picking their noses, and a ginger-haired boy was standing on his chair and waving his arms from side to side as if he were conducting the singing.

'Thank you, Gemma,' said Laura. 'I think we've had enough of this cats' chorus. You can go back to the Sevens now.'

Gemma's cheeks flushed. She was a big young woman, wearing a long dark brown cardigan and an oatmeal tartan skirt. Usually, she was very outspoken, and had her own strong ideas about educating small children, and she was never afraid to tell Laura what they were. Now, though, she didn't answer back. She was still unsettled by the way that Laura had spoken to the school at prayers this morning, and there was something else that she found even more disturbing. Laura seemed to have grown until she was nearly as tall as she was, even though she wasn't wearing high heels, and her face was oddly mask-like and expressionless. Laura actually frightened her.

She left the classroom and Laura closed the door behind her. It was obvious that she had made an impression on the children this morning, too, because they were fidgeting and whispering and staring at her apprehensively, when normally they would have been laughing and larking about. The ginger-haired boy, though, was still standing on his chair waving his arms and singing.

'Luke,' said Laura, quite quietly. 'Get your feet off your chair and sit down properly.'

Luke took no notice and started to sing 'Old King Cole', clapping his hands.

'*Luke!*' snapped Laura. 'I won't tell you again! Stop that horrible howling and get your feet off your chair and sit down properly!'

Luke continued to ignore her, so she marched up to him, picked him up and carried him over her shoulder to the front of the classroom. He screamed and kicked in anger and embarrassment, but she was far too strong for him. Some of the children laughed but others were clearly terrified, especially the very little ones, and they sat round-eyed and silent.

Luke carried on struggling and screaming '*No! No! No! Let me go! Let me go! You're horrible! Let me go!*'

Laura said, 'Shut up, you little runt! You asked for this!'

She let him down onto his feet, but she kept a tight hold on his collar while she unlocked one of the windows. Once she had swung it wide open, she lifted Luke up again and forced him over the windowsill. Then, without any hesitation, she pushed him out. He let out an extraordinary noise that sounded more like a gargle than a scream and then he was gone.

It was over twenty-five feet down to the narrow concrete pathway at the side of the school, and it was fenced off from Hillbury Road with spiked iron railings. Luke dropped onto the railings with a thud and a crunch, because the spikes penetrated his ribcage. After that he hung there, with his arms and his legs outstretched, looking more like a ginger-haired doll than a real boy.

Six or seven of the children got up from their tables and rushed to the window. The windowsill was too high for them to see out, but a little Somalian girl with her hair tied up in four bouncy plaits dragged a chair over and climbed up onto it. The rest of the children stayed where they were, too shocked to understand that Laura had actually thrown Luke out. One of them started to cry, and then another, and another, until almost all of them were wailing.

'Luke must be hurt, miss!' said the little Somalian girl. 'He's stuck on the fence! We have to go down and save him!'

'Luke got what he deserved for being disobedient!' Laura retorted. 'Now get down from that chair and go and sit down, Bishaaro, and the rest of you – *the rest of you* – stop that crying! I said, *stop it at once*!'

'But Luke is *stuck*!' Bishaaro protested. 'We have to save him!'

'You want to go down and save him?' said Laura. 'All right – you go down and save him!'

With that, she picked up Bishaaro and even though she struggled and kicked, she pushed her out of the window, too. Bishaaro let out a shrill scream and tried to snatch the handle to save herself, but then she dropped straight down, bouncing off Luke's body and rolling to one side, so that the railing spikes pierced the back of her neck and she hung there, still alive, unable to utter a sound, but thrashing her arms and her legs as if she were swimming the backstroke.

Now the whole class was moaning and crying. Laura stood in front of them and shouted, 'Shut up! Do you hear me? Stop that appalling racket! If you don't stop bleating, you'll *all* go out of the window!'

The classroom door was thrown open and Gemma Watts came bursting in.

'What on earth is going on, Miss Miller? Why are all the kids crying?'

'Mind your own business and get back to your class!' Laura told her.

But one of the little girls pointed to the open window. 'Luke and Bishaaro!' she sobbed. 'Miss Miller threw them out!'

'Gemma – I told you to go back to your class!' Laura repeated, but Gemma went over to the window and looked out.

'Oh my God,' she said. 'Oh my *God*, Miss Miller, what have you done?'

'They were misbehaving! They got what they deserved!'

'Henry!' said Gemma, turning to the children. 'You're the class monitor! I want you to take everybody downstairs to the dining hall and I want you to tell Miss Lawrence and Miss Clover what's happened! Go on, everybody, off you go, quick as you can!'

'You can't do this,' said Laura. 'This is my school and my children. Everybody stay where you are!'

But the children were already hurrying out of the classroom, whimpering in panic, almost tripping over each other to get away. When Laura tried to go towards the door to stop them, Gemma stood in her way. She took her mobile phone out of her cardigan pocket and prodded out 999.

Laura tried to get past her, but Gemma sidestepped and blocked her again.

'Ambulance,' she said, into her phone. 'Ambulance and very quickly, please. St Blandina's School next to Tooting Bec Common. And police, too, please. Two children have been thrown out of a window and impaled on railings. Yes. I'm going to look at them now but I think they both may be dead. Yes, I'll stay on the phone.'

Laura stood and watched her without saying a word.

They have no idea, do they, that children need discipline? No wonder the world is in such a mess, with so much violence and so much civil disobedience. People need to be taught right from the beginning to do what they're told, or suffer the consequences.

Laura sat down at her desk. Behind her on the chalkboard there were pictures that the children had drawn of the animals going two by two into Noah's ark.

Gemma went to the window. She could see that Susan Lawrence was already outside, along with two passers-by, trying to lift Luke and Bishaaro off the railings. She closed the window and locked it and dropped the key in her pocket.

'I want you to stay here until the police arrive,' she told Laura.

Laura smiled and shrugged and said, 'The police won't blame her. The police will understand. Children can't be allowed to run riot. You know that as well as she does.'

20

Jerry was eating sausages and baked beans in the station canteen and reading the sports pages of *The Sun* when Jamila came in. Her right hand was bound up in a thick white bandage, like an enormous mitten.

'How's the mauler?' he asked her, as she sat down beside him.

'Oh, fine. No serious damage, but they've given me a tetanus shot and they gave Sophie a point-of-care test to make sure that she didn't have HIV. We'll be sending her to Springfield later today.'

Jerry said, 'I'll tell you, sarge, these cases are making me feel like admitting myself to Springfield.' Springfield University Hospital was the main psychiatric centre in Wandsworth, and a maximum security facility for dangerous mental patients. When it was first opened in 1840, it had been called the Surrey County Pauper Lunatic Asylum.

'Well, perhaps we'll get some sense out of our druggie,' said Jamila. 'I've just had a call from St George's and they've managed to separate him from his coat. He's still anaesthetised but they reckon he should be *compos mentis* in two or three hours.'

'What about the coat? I mean, I've been thinking about it, and it's more like it's *alive*, isn't it, rather than infested? And the same with Sophie's jacket.'

'The coat's gone off to forensics. We should know within a day or two how it managed to stick itself to his skin.'

'Do we know who he is yet?'

'Not yet, but we've circulated his picture around all of the local homeless shelters and charity soup kitchens and drug dependency clinics. The *Evening Standard*, too.'

'This is all going way beyond your specialised field, isn't it?' said Jerry. 'I mean, it's looking less and less likely that Samira was the victim of an honour killing, isn't it?'

'What are you suggesting? That I should quit? I think I'm already too deeply involved. Besides, even though I don't personally believe that it was an honour killing, there is still a remote possibility that Samira was murdered by a member of her family. Until we understand what effect her coat might have had on her, I think it would be premature for me to consider withdrawing from this investigation – or from the Sophie Marshall case for that matter. Supposing the coat somehow changed her feelings about marrying the man that her parents had chosen for her, and they resented it?'

Jerry prodded his last remaining sausage. 'I think Smiley's right about this. It's one hundred per cent bonkers.'

They were still talking when Sergeant Bristow came into the canteen. 'Ah, Jerry! I don't mean to interrupt your lunch, but DS Morgan thought you ought to know about this female suspect we've just brought in. He said something about her case having similarities to the cases that you've been working on.'

'"Similarities"?' asked Jamila. 'What kind of "similarities"?'

Sergeant Bristow checked the note he had scribbled down. 'She's the head teacher at St Blandina's private primary school – Laura Jean Miller, aged forty-five. About an hour ago she threw two children out of the window of an upstairs classroom, a boy of four years old and a girl of just five. Both of them were impaled on railings outside the school and were fatally injured.'

'Bloody hell,' said Jerry, and put down his fork. 'Did she say why?'

'They were misbehaving and they had to be punished, that was what she said. But she also said that it wasn't her who did it – even though there were no other adults in the classroom at the time. And that's one of your similarities. She said it was her coat that threw them out of the window, not her.'

Jerry looked at Jamila. Jamila said, 'Her *coat*? What kind of a coat is it?'

'Fairly ordinary brown woman's overcoat, that's all. About knee length. She's still wearing it.'

'Can't we take it off her?'

'She refuses, absolutely refuses, and when a WPC tried to remove it, she found that she couldn't. It's like it's stuck to her. Same as that homeless bloke who was brought in this morning.'

'We need to have a word with this woman,' said Jamila. 'Has she been cautioned?'

Sergeant Bristow nodded. 'We've taken down all of her personal details but DS Morgan isn't going to proceed with a formal interview until she's been assessed by a doctor.'

Jamila stood up. 'Of course,' she said. 'But I would like to see her at least. Are you coming, Jerry?'

Jerry put his knife and fork together and folded his newspaper. 'Lost my appetite, anyway.'

*

Laura was lying on her side in her cell when Jerry and Jamila came in. Her eyes were open but she showed no sign that she had seen them.

'Laura Miller?' said Jamila.

Laura still didn't respond, so Jamila sat down on the blue vinyl mattress next to her and laid her hand on her shoulder.

'Laura Miller?' she repeated, very gently.

Laura looked at her for a few seconds, and then said, 'Who are you? What do you want?'

'I'm Detective Sergeant Jamila Patel. Is it all right if I have a word with you?'

'If it's about those children I have nothing to say.'

'No, Laura. It's not about the children. It's about you.'

'What about me?'

Laura lifted up her head and Jamila stood up, so that Laura could swing her legs around and sit up straight. She squeezed her eyes shut a few times, as if she were in pain, and then opened them again, although she kept them fixed on the cell door opposite, hardly blinking at all, and didn't look either at Jerry or Jamila.

'We haven't been able to take off your coat,' said Jamila.

'It's *her*, that's why.'

'What do you mean by that? Who's "her"?'

'*Me*, of course,' said Laura, as if Jamila were unbelievably stupid. 'She's me and I'm her and the coat is both of us. That's why you can't take it off.'

'The officer who arrested you... you told her that the children were misbehaving and that they needed to be punished.'

'I told you. I'm not going to talk about the children.'

'I understand that, Laura, but I just need to know who punished them – you or her?'

'It wasn't me.'

'So *she* punished them, not you? Even though she's you and you're her?'

'It was the coat.'

'All right, it was the coat. We won't trouble you any more, Laura. Get some rest. The doctor's coming in a while to see if we can get it off you.'

'You can't get it off me. It's me.'

'Well, we'll just have to see. I'll come back and talk to you later.'

'Listen! They think they can do and say whatever they like, those children. It's the parents. I blame the parents. But you can't let them get away with it. Otherwise they'll grow up to be hooligans.'

'But those two little children are dead now, Laura. They're not going to be able to grow up at all.'

'It's no good blaming me. At least I didn't try to eat them. She would have eaten them, given the chance.'

'She would have *eaten* them? What do you mean by that?'

'Nothing. I'm not answering any more questions. My head's too noisy.'

'Laura—'

'No. I'm not saying any more. And neither is she.'

Jerry and Jamila left the cell and the duty officer locked the door. Jerry turned to Jamila, spinning his index finger around his head and letting out a whistle.

'Nutty as a fruitcake, just like the others. But that's three of them now, all blaming their coats for what they've done, and all of them with fibres from their coats stuck into their skin. Four, if you count Samira Wazir. There's no way that's a coincidence.'

'Once we manage to take off Laura Miller's coat and send it to forensics, I think we need to have a meeting with Dr Fuller,' said Jamila. 'Like DI Saunders said, there has to be some logical explanation for this. My grandmother in Peshawar used to warn me about jinns, and she terrified me. She said that if I wore perfume at night, a jinn would be lured by the smell into my bedroom and stick to me while I was asleep, and I would never be able to get free of him. But that was only a story. This is something quite different – if only we could understand what.'

'Some granny you had, scaring the crap out of you like that,' said Jerry. 'My granny used to tell me the story of Goldilocks and the Three Bears, and that was frightening enough. Whenever she tried to say "who'sh been shleeping in my bed?" her false teeth fell out.'

As they were walking along the corridor, DC Willis came plodding towards them.

'Jerry... just the man! Young Billy Jenkins says he's got something you might like to hear. I get the impression he wants to do a deal.'

'Couldn't he tell you?'

'No... he reckons he can only trust you. He reckons if he told me, I'd only use it as evidence against him – and yes, well, he's probably right. I would, the little sniveller.'

'OK,' said Jerry, and then he turned to Jamila and said, 'I won't be long, sarge. I'll catch up with you in a bit.'

He found the duty officer, who was just about to sneak out

of the back door of the station for a quick cigarette in the car park, and asked him to open up Billy's cell for him. Billy was sitting hunched on his bunk, shivering and twitching and looking even more like the last days of Sid Vicious than he had before. His cell smelled as if he had been sweating and breaking wind all night.

'Wotcher, Billy!' said Jerry, trying to sound cheerful. 'How's it going? Are we treating you all right? Had your lunch, have you?'

'I need to get out of here, Mr Pardoe. I really do. I'm going barmy.'

'DC Willis said that you had something you wanted to tell me.'

'Yes, but only if you promise to let me out.'

'I can't promise until I've heard what it is, Billy. It could be something I already know, like the price of Marmite after Brexit.'

'It's about Liepa. But you must never let him know that I told you. I mean like, not *ever*.'

Jerry sat down on the bunk next to him. 'OK, I'm listening. But don't take too long, it smells of farts in here. What have we been feeding you on? Cauliflower curry?'

'Tomorrow's Thursday, isn't it?'

'That's right, because today's Wednesday. Bloody hell – and to think I called you thick!'

'Yes, but this Thursday is collection day for Cancer Research. You know, for people to put out bags of old clothes and shoes and stuff and the Cancer Research van goes around in the morning and picks them up.'

'I know. Go on. What about it?'

'The thing is, Cancer Research always get the best-quality stuff, and much more of it than anybody else, even the NSPCC, I suppose because everybody knows somebody who's had cancer. But Liepa's been missing their collection days for a while, on purpose, because he knows you've been watching him.'

'I'm not saying we have and I'm not saying we haven't.'

'Well, *he* reckons you have, which is why he's been leaving out the Cancer Research collection days, in case you catch him in the act.'

'I get it. *In flagrante delicto.*'

Billy had no idea what Jerry meant, but all the same he said, 'Tomorrow Liepa's going to go for it, though. I was supposed to be going with him, to help him out. He's got four vans, plus himself in his estate car, and they're going around Streatham and Mitcham and most of Tooting, all before it gets light.'

'What time are they setting out?'

'Half past three, from his house.'

Jerry thought for a while, and then he said, 'OK... if I let you out, you'll be able to go with him, won't you? And you'll be able to text me as soon as he's picked up some bags. In fact, just one bag will do. That's all I'm going to need to nick him.'

'You won't say that I grassed on him, will you? He'll nail me to the fucking wall and set fire to me.'

'No, Billy. I promise you that, on whatever's left of my honour. I'll go to see Inspector Callow now and see what I can do to get you bailed.'

Billy shivered, as if a goose had walked over his grave. 'You won't be too long, will you? I have to get out of here, Mr Pardoe, or else I'm going to have a fucking heart attack. I mean it.'

Jerry clapped him on his bony shoulder. 'Don't you fret, Billy boy. I'll run all the way.'

*

Jerry hurried towards the lift to take him up to Inspector Callow's office just as the doors were closing. Sergeant Bristow was already inside the lift and held the doors open for him.

'Thanks,' said Jerry. 'Going up to see Callow?'

Sergeant Bristow held up a sheet of notepaper. 'We're looking to make a forced entry, that's all. Some woman reported that she was supposed to be going shopping with her friend this morning, but her husband said that she wasn't at home because she was visiting her sister, who was supposed to be sick.'

'I see. So what's the problem?'

'The woman said the husband was acting peculiar and wearing nothing but a sweater and exposing himself.'

'Oh, well. There's nothing like a tasty sausage first thing in the morning. What's she complaining about?'

'The husband said his wife had left her mobile at home, but this woman thought this was suspicious, and so she looked up her friend's sister's number and phoned her. Her sister said she wasn't sick at all and that she hadn't seen her friend in weeks.'

The lift arrived at the second floor and Jerry and Sergeant Bristow started walking along the corridor towards Inspector Callow's office.

'She called the husband's work to talk to him again, but apparently he hadn't shown up,' said Sergeant Bristow. 'We had a car just around the corner from where the husband lives so I got them to knock at the door and have a quick word with him – only to check that there hadn't been some kind of domestic.'

'And, what? Nobody at home?'

'Oh, there was somebody at home all right. There was no answer when the uniforms knocked but they could see a man watching them from behind the bedroom curtains.'

'Weird. But then some people have a phobia about the police knocking at their door, don't they? I can't for the life of me think why. Listen – do you mind if I go in first? I only want the OK to let that bin boy out on bail.'

They had reached Inspector Callow's office. The door was open and they could hear the inspector barking loudly at somebody on the phone.

'No problem at all, Jerry,' said Sergeant Bristow. 'Be my guest.'

21

At 6:15 that evening, when it was beginning to grow dark, two police cars arrived outside the Nelsons' semi-detached Edwardian house on Franciscan Road. Four uniformed officers climbed out and went to the front door, three male PCs and one female, and loudly knocked.

'Mr Nelson! Mr David Nelson! Police! Can we have a word, please?'

There was no answer, so they knocked again.

'Mr Nelson! If you fail to let us in, we have a warrant to enter the premises by force!'

This time, nobody looked out of the upstairs window, but one of the officers checked his iPhone and said, 'That's his car parked outside, that silver Audi. Even if he's out, he hasn't driven anywhere.'

'Well, let's give him one more chance,' said one of his fellow PCs, and knocked seven or eight times, so loudly that a dog-walker across the road stopped to see what all the noise was about, and a woman in an apron came out of the next-door house and said, 'What's going on?'

'Do you happen to know if Mr Nelson is in?' the officer asked her.

'I haven't seen him go out, if that's what you mean.'

'What about Mrs Nelson?'

'I haven't seen her all day either, although I usually do.'

'Haven't heard any arguing between them, by any chance?'

The woman shook her head. 'No, but you don't hear anything in these old houses. The walls are too thick. You could scream blue murder and nobody would hear you.'

'All right, ma'am, thank you,' said the officer. 'If you don't mind going back inside now.'

The woman reluctantly went back into her house, but almost immediately she drew back the net curtains in her living-room window so that she could watch what was going on.

One of the officers went back to his car and came back swinging a bright red battering ram, but he had only just stepped into the porch, when the front door suddenly opened. David appeared, whey-faced, unshaven, his hair tousled, and still wearing the black sweater that he had taken from his mother's house, although he was also wearing a pair of droopy grey boxer shorts.

'Mr David Nelson?' asked the officer.

'Why? What do you want him for?'

'Took you long enough to answer us knocking, didn't it, sir?'

'So? I was busy. What do you want?'

'We've had a report that your wife may be missing, sir.'

'Missing? Who told you that?'

'I can't tell you at the moment, sir, but would you mind telling us Mrs Nelson's whereabouts?'

'What do you mean, "whereabouts"? She's here at home.'

Maggie the cat came padding to the front door. She looked up at the police officers and mewed, as if she were trying to tell them something.

'All right if we have a quick word with Mrs Nelson, sir?' asked the officer.

'With his wife? No. She's indisposed.'

'We do need to see for ourselves that she's here, sir. If she's indisposed, WPC Bennett here can go and check on her.'

'No. He can't have her disturbed.'

'Sorry, sir. Who's "he"?'

'David. He can't let you see her and that's all there is to it. Goodbye.'

David started to close the front door but the officer jammed his boot into it.

'Sorry, sir, but you'll have to let us see your wife. We have a warrant.'

David tried to close the door again but this time the officer leaned his shoulder against it and pushed it wide open. David raised both hands in surrender and took three or four steps back into the hallway. 'All right. You win. Police brutality. I'll have to see what the local paper has to say about this.'

WPC Bennett came up to him. She was blonde and square-jawed with her hair fastened in a French pleat and almost as tall as he was, with broader shoulders. 'Is Mrs Nelson upstairs in bed, sir?'

'No. No, she's not.'

'You said that she was indisposed.'

'Yes. But she's in the kitchen.'

WPC Bennett squeezed her way past him, and two of the other officers followed her, although the fourth officer stayed where he was and blocked the front door. It seemed unlikely that David might try to run away. He was prickly but he was outwardly calm, and he was wearing only his black sweater and his shorts, and his feet were bare. In spite of that, the officers had known suspects to sprint off down the street stark naked, rather than face arrest.

The officers went into the kitchen. An unwashed dinner-plate and two saucepans were stacked in the sink, and the table was cluttered with a crumpled-up copy of the *Daily Express* and empty yogurt pots, as well as an assortment of dirty cutlery and a hacksaw. Two twisted brown-stained tea-towels were lying on the floor. What struck the officers most, though, was a strong smell of singed hair. That, and the fact that there was nobody there.

'So – where is she?' demanded WPC Bennett.

David came into the kitchen, smiling at her. 'He told you, didn't he? She's indisposed. But she's looking at you. Even if you can't see her, *she* can see you!'

'I'm sorry, sir. I don't understand you.'

David pointed to the microwave oven underneath the kitchen cabinets. WPC Bennett frowned at it. It wasn't switched on, so there was no light inside, but she could make out a pale shape behind the laminated glass door. She turned to her fellow officers, who shrugged, and so she went over and opened it.

Inside, on a plate, was Evie's head. Her cheeks were bloated and her lips were blood-red and her hair had been frizzed up by the heat of the microwave. She looked like some terrifying Gorgon.

WPC Bennett couldn't believe at first that she was looking at a real head but then she saw that the skin around Evie's neck had been jaggedly cut, and that congealed orange fluid was pooled on the plate around it.

'There she is,' David said, in a harsh voice that sounded thick with catarrh. 'Fully defrosted and ready for cooking! You know what they say, don't you? If you eat somebody's brains, you inherit all of their memories... everything they've ever experienced, everything they've ever learned! Mind you, I don't know what he'll get from eating Evie's brains... She wasn't the sharpest tool in the box! But then neither was his hacksaw, as you can see! He wasn't much of a solicitor, and I don't think he'd make much of a butcher, either!'

Without a word, one of the officers came around the kitchen table, twisted David's arms behind his back and handcuffed him. David offered no resistance at all, and kept on smiling.

His fellow officer went out into the hallway and called in to the station for immediate back-up, as well as a forensic team and an ambulance. WPC Bennett pulled on a pair of latex gloves and closed the oven door. Evie's eyes had been poached until they were totally white like quail's eggs, but they still had tiny pinpricks for pupils, and she found her stare too unnerving.

'Where's the rest of her, Mr Nelson?' she demanded, trying to keep her voice steady.

David jerked his head towards the utility-room door. 'He put her in the freezer. She's all there, I promise you, apart from a bit of leg. The key's right there, on the table. Go and look for yourself.'

'Did you kill her?'

'Evie deserved it! She'd been asking for it, for months.'

'Why?'

'Because of her endless complaining, and I mean *endless*! He'd had enough of it, as simple as that, and who can blame him? All right, yes, granted – his practice was going through a difficult patch, and he wasn't bringing home much money, if any at all. But a husband needs support when times get hard, doesn't he, not nagging. *Sympathy* – not slagging off! So – yes, David taught her a much-needed lesson.'

'Mr Nelson, you *are* David.'

David stared at WPC Bennett in complete incomprehension. When he didn't answer, she started to caution him.

'David Nelson, I am arresting you on suspicion of murdering your wife, Mrs Evie Nelson. You do not have to say anything, but it may harm your defence—'

'For God's sake, how many times do I have to tell you that I'm *not* David!' David shrilled at her. 'Take these handcuffs off me and go away, all of you! I need to eat! I'm ravenous! Why do you think I was defrosting Evie's head?'

'Sir – if you're not David Nelson, then who are you?'

'His mother, Jeanette Nelson. Well, Netty they usually call me. Do I even *look* like a man?'

'To be perfectly frank with you, sir – yes, you do. And whatever you're calling yourself, you're still under arrest for murder.'

One of the officers had gone into the utility-room with the key to the freezer. He came out again now, swallowing hard and pressing his hand against his stomach to suppress his nausea.

'She's in there all right, Sal. What's left of her, anyway.'

David looked as if he were about to say something, but then he changed his mind and gave a petulant shake of his head, as if he couldn't be bothered to explain himself to any of these fools.

They won't be able to prove it was me, so I don't know why they're even bothering. Let them take me to court. They'll only be wasting their time. But I wish they'd get the hint and go. I need to eat, badly.

David glanced towards the microwave. His insides were beginning to feel chilled and watery, as if his intestines were melting away, and he was losing his grip on reality.

I'm going to faint if I don't eat soon. I'm going to disappear.

He didn't pay any attention to what WPC Bennett was saying to him. All he could think of was taking Evie's head out of the microwave and splitting her skull in half so that he could spoon out her brain and slice it up and melt some butter in the pan and fry it. Dear God, he could almost *taste* it.

'Mr Nelson – do you have anything to *say?*' WPC Bennett asked him, sharply, as if she were repeating herself.

David stared at her. 'Please,' he said. 'If you don't let me eat, I'm going to die again.'

'They'll give you something to eat at the station, once you've been formally charged.'

Despite the officer's attempts to keep him upright, David sank to his knees, sobbing.

'I don't want to die again. Please. Not again. You don't know what it's like.'

The officer who had been blocking the front door came into the kitchen and said, 'Back-up's arrived.'

'*You don't know what it's like!*' David screamed, and his eyes were bulging with terror. '*You've never died, so you don't know what it's like!*'

22

Mindy was walking her Yorkshire terrier Sprout across Furzedown recreation ground when she saw the blue velvet jacket hanging on the railings. Although it was a grey, still day, one of the jacket's sleeves was flapping, almost as if it were waving to her.

She stopped and watched it for a few moments. Sprout tugged at his thin red leather lead and then looked up at her impatiently. He had seen a black Labrador by the entrance to the recreation ground and he was eager to go and have a sniff.

'Wait, Sprout,' said Mindy. 'I want to have a look at that jacket. See its arm waving? Maybe there's a squirrel stuck inside it!'

Mindy was nine – a thin, pretty girl with a brunette bob and a turned-up nose. In her red and yellow zig-zag sweater with its floppy hood and her ankle boots she looked like a character from a 1920s children's storybook. Today was a school day but she was recovering from a cold and so her mother had let her have one more day off.

She walked over the grass to the railings and peered at the jacket closely. She had to tug Sprout to come with her, because he kept his fluffy little head turned towards the Labrador.

Now the sleeve had stopped waving, and it hung limply. The jacket was so expensive-looking that Mindy couldn't think why its owner had left it in the recreation ground. Perhaps she had hung it up on the railings while she watched her children play on the swings, but it was a chilly morning, so why would she have done that? And how could she have walked off without realising that she had left it behind?

Perhaps one of her children had fallen off the roundabout and hurt himself, and she had rushed him to hospital. Perhaps she had suffered a fainting fit and some kind stranger had offered to drive her home. Mindy was always making up stories to explain the world around her, although she sometimes found out that the reality was even stranger. Once she had seen two men walking along Tooting Broadway carrying a stuffed brown bear between them, a real one, and she had invented so many different explanations for that, although she had never found out where they were taking it, or why.

The Labrador had disappeared now, and Sprout turned his attention back to Mindy. When he looked up at the jacket he made a thin falsetto whining noise in his throat, like he always did when he was frightened, and tried to back away. But as soon as he saw that she was about to lift the jacket off the railings, he started to bark, and he kept on barking, high and sharp and almost hysterical. He circled around and around, trying to pull her away, and became hopelessly tangled up in his lead.

'Sprout! Stop it, will you! Don't be so stupid! It's only a jacket!'

She smacked at him with the end of the lead but he still wouldn't stop barking and turning around in circles.

'Sprout! Stop it! If you don't stop it I won't give you any rabbit sticks when we get home!'

Sprout kept on barking so Mindy tied his lead to the railings. He jumped up into the air again and again and he almost throttled himself with his collar.

Mindy lifted up the jacket. The lining was snagged on one of the spikes on top of the railings, but she managed to twist it free without tearing it too much. As she did so, she felt a strange but exhilarating sensation of being set free, like finishing school on the last day of term, or arriving at the beach on her holidays and running across the sand towards the sea.

She ran her fingertips over the velvet and the nap was so soft and luxurious that she had to try the jacket to see it fitted her. Although she was skinny, she was tall for a nine-year-old, and while the jacket had quite broad shoulders, it had a cinched-in waist and she was sure that she could get away with wearing it. It would look fantastic with the Hollister high-rise super-skinny jeans which she had been given for her last birthday, the ones with the shredded knees.

She took off her zig-zag sweater and hung it on the railings before she tried on the jacket and buttoned it up. It was two sizes too big for her, and the sleeves were too long, but it gave her a tingle of pleasure across her back and down her arms, and she felt that it belonged to her – as if it had been hanging on the railings waiting especially for her to come walking past – her and nobody else.

She reached into the pocket of her sweater to take out her mobile phone and admire herself. Then she took a series of selfies, posing and pouting like Kim Kardashian. A middle-aged man wheeling his bicycle along the path called out, 'Lovely, love! You ought to be a model!'

Mindy turned round to him and shouted back, 'Piss off, you pervert!'

The man stopped, obviously trying to make up his mind if he ought to answer back, but then he saw that two young mothers with pushchairs were approaching him, and he wheeled his bicycle away without saying anything.

You see? She's always been sweet and polite and done whatever she's told, but now she can be strong, too, and stick up for herself.

But 'piss off' – that's rude!

He asked for it. She's only nine and out on her own. Who knows what he might have done to her next, the lecher?

Mindy felt that the jacket was becoming tighter and tighter, and actually clinging to her skin through her long-sleeved T-shirt. It was so tight that she was finding it difficult to breathe, but the sensation was pleasurable, too, in a way that she had never experienced before, and it made her feel grown-up and excited.

So what is she going to do now? Go home and see her mother? It's about time she told her mother what she really thinks of her.

Why? What's Mummy done wrong?

Oh, come on! Think about it! She may be her mother but that doesn't give her the right to tell her how to behave every minute of the day, and to make her bed and tidy her room, and help with the laundry. Why should she? She's nine now, and an independent person. She can stop her mother taking her to St Nicholas' every Sunday, for a start. God doesn't exist, so why waste an hour in a chilly church singing stupid songs about fighting the good fight and listening to some boring vicar talking about forgiveness? If anybody needs to ask for her forgiveness, it's her mother.

Mindy untied Sprout from the railings and tugged him away, even though he was still barking and furiously trying to shake himself free from his collar. She left her zig-zag sweater behind on the railings, and one of the young mothers called out, 'Hey! Sweetheart! Is that jumper yours?'

Mindy waved her arm at her dismissively and called back, 'Get stuffed and mind your own business!'

'Oh – charming!' said the young mother. 'Why don't you go home and wash your mouth out with soap and water!'

'Didn't you hear me?' Mindy retorted. 'I said get stuffed and I meant it!'

The two young mothers shrugged and pulled faces at each other and carried on walking. For a few moments Mindy stood watching them go, and then she made her way to the entrance, almost bursting with self-satisfaction.

See! That was telling them, wasn't it? She's found her true voice at last!

*

It was beginning to grow dark by the time Mindy came down the alley beside her house in Nimrod Road and into the kitchen through the back door. Her mother was ironing sheets and pillowcases and her father's shirts for the office.

'Mindy!' said her mother. 'Where on earth have you been? I've been ringing you and ringing you! Isn't your phone working? I was going to call the police if you didn't come home soon!'

'Oh, yes, why?' said Mindy, dropping Sprout's lead on the kitchen table. 'Don't you think she's quite capable of looking after herself?'

'*What* did you say? And where did you get that jacket you're wearing? And where's Sprout?'

'What do you care?' Mindy replied, walking towards the door that led to the hallway.

Her mother put down her iron and caught hold of Mindy's arm. She looked so much like Mindy that they could have been sisters, if there weren't twenty-four years between them.

'Where have you been, Mindy? Where's Sprout? What's happened? And why are you wearing that awful jacket? Where's your sweater?'

Mindy stayed perfectly still, but stared straight ahead of her, as if she intended to keep on walking out of the kitchen as soon as her mother let go of her.

'So what is it now?' she asked. 'Insult the way she dresses, as well as everything else she does, like her homework, and her piano playing, and her dancing?'

'Mindy – where's Sprout? What have you done with him? Have you lost him? What's going on, darling? Please – tell me!'

Mindy looked up at her at last. 'Just like she said to those busybodies in the park – get stuffed and mind your own business!'

Mindy's mother slapped her across the face, and then immediately said, 'I'm sorry! I'm so sorry! I didn't mean to hurt you! But you have to tell me what's happened, Mindy! Why are you talking like this?'

Mindy's left cheek was flushed scarlet, but she gave her mother a dismissive smile, as if she had expected to be slapped, and couldn't care.

'Mindy, for the love of God, darling! I really didn't mean to hurt you! But you've come home hours and hours late, wearing some completely strange jacket, and there's no Sprout with you, and all you can do is answer me back as if I'm some kind of a stranger.'

'She's had enough, that's why,' said Mindy.

'Why do you keep calling yourself "she"? Have you had an accident or something? Has somebody attacked you?'

'If you had experienced even a tenth of my suffering, you would feel the same way as I do,' said Mindy. Her voice sounded different now, low and measured, and her mother thought her eyes looked different, too – not wide and round and innocent, but curiously feline, and filled with a kind of weary malevolence. They were the eyes of somebody who had been punished by life, and was not going to forgive those who had hurt her, or anybody.

'Mindy, let's go through to the sitting-room. I'm going to call Daddy.'

'Oh, yes? And what do you think the great and wonderful Daddy is going to do? He's as hopeless as you are, you stupid bitch.'

Mindy's mother wasn't tempted to slap her face again. She was seriously worried now. She held onto her arm and guided her into the living-room and switched on the light. Over the beige-tiled fireplace there was a row of framed photographs, most of them of Mindy from when she was a baby, and always smiling her coy, shy smile, as if she couldn't believe that she was pretty enough for anybody to want to take a picture of her.

'There, sit down,' said Mindy's mother, leading her over to the sofa. 'I think you've had a shock and we need to find out what it was. Why don't you take off that horrible jacket? I mean, where did it come from? It doesn't look very clean.'

'No,' said Mindy, staring around the room. 'I hate this wallpaper. Green! Why did you choose *green*, of all the disgusting colours?'

'Well, sit down at least.'

'No.'

You see? She doesn't have to be obedient. She can defy her mother and there's nothing that her mother can do about it. Her mother won't slap her again. Slapping her like that made her feel worse than Mindy.

Mindy's mother sat in the armchair next to the fireplace and took her mobile phone out of her apron pocket. She rang her father's number and he answered almost immediately.

'Hi there, love! What's up? I'm right in the middle of a meeting, I'm afraid.'

'Peter, it's Mindy. Something awful's happened to her but I don't know what it is and she won't tell me.'

'What do you mean, "something awful"? Has she been hurt?'

'I don't think so, not physically. But she took Sprout out for a walk at three o'clock and she's only just come back. There's no sign of Sprout and she's wearing some peculiar second hand jacket instead of her sweater. And she's saying such meaningless things. She keeps talking about herself in the third person, as if she's somebody else.'

'And she won't say what's happened to her?'

'No... she told me it was none of my business. In fact she was ruder than that.'

There was a long pause, and then Mindy's father said, 'She hasn't been raped, has she?'

'I don't think so, no. But then she won't tell me anything.'

Mindy had been standing with her back to her mother, but now she turned around and said, 'I know what he's thinking. Typical father. He thinks she was raped, doesn't he? Just because he'd secretly like to have sex with her himself. All fathers do. They look at their little daughters naked in the bath and if their wives weren't around they'd love to touch them.'

'Peter,' said Mindy's mother. 'I think you'd better come home now. And I think we might have to call the police.'

'Oh, you want to call the police?' Mindy challenged her. 'And what good will that do? You think the police are going to go looking for a Yorkshire terrier and a sweater? You don't think they've got one or two things more urgent to attend to?'

'Mindy—' her mother began.

'No, Janet! You can't go on interfering in her life any more! She's found her strength now! She has me and I have her! We're one and the same! Nothing you do or say is ever going to be able to change that!'

Mindy's voice rose to a scream. She bent forward so that her face was only two or three inches away from her mother's and her mother could feel her spit on her cheeks.

'It's all going to be different from now on! You're never going to give her orders again and you're never going to treat her like a child! She's a woman because I'm a woman and we're one and the same! She's going to come and go as she pleases! Not only that, she—'

Mindy hesitated, and held her left hand to her stomach. She retched, and a long string of saliva dripped from her lips.

'Not only that—' she repeated, but then she stopped again, and retched even louder, with a sickening noise.

For three or four seconds she stood leaning over her mother with her eyes closed and her cheeks bulging, as if her mouth were filling up with bile. Then she shuddered and vomited directly into her mother's lap, a stringy torrent of red, half-chewed meat and tangles of wet tan and black fur.

She heaved again and again and all her mother could do was hold onto her shoulders with both hands and try to suppress her convulsions.

At last she sank to her knees onto the carpet and stayed there with her head bowed, sobbing. Her mother looked down at the grisly mess in her apron and she could tell by the fur and the liquorice-black fragment of snout what it was.

'Dear God in Heaven,' she whispered. 'Oh, Mindy. What's got into you, my darling? *Who's* got into you?'

23

'So what's the plan with this what's-his-name, this Lithuanian bloke?' asked DI Saunders.

Jerry said, 'It's simple enough. We stake out his gaff early in the morning and when he sets off on his rounds picking up charity bags we nab him.'

DI Saunders came away from the window. It was dark outside now and he must have been admiring his own reflection.

'I'm just wondering if it's worth it,' he said. 'I know you said he makes a fair bit of money out of it, but if the clothes are being given away for free anyway, it's not exactly the crime of the century, is it? It's no worse than scavenging through a council rubbish tip and making off with a second-hand toilet.'

'It's depriving Cancer Research of valuable funds,' said Jerry. 'If your mum was diagnosed of cancer, how would you feel about some Eastern European tosser making off with the money that could have been used to save her?'

'My mum *was* diagnosed with cancer,' said DI Saunders. 'She passed away last Christmas.'

'Oh. Sorry. Wouldn't have said that if I'd known. But you get what I'm getting at.'

'Well, all right. But it seems like a slightly dubious use of our resources when we have more important cases to cope with. Like for instance Samira Wazir and Michael Brent and those two poor kids who got chucked out of their classroom window.'

'We're right on top of all of those investigations, sir,' put in Jamila. 'Samira Wazir's father is back from Pakistan now and we've arranged to interview him at his house at six o'clock. We'll be meeting Dr Fuller as soon as he's completed his latest tests on the fibres from the coats and the skin samples from the victims.'

'And when will that be?'

'We don't know for sure, sir. He's waiting to get some more results from Lambeth Road, so it could be tomorrow or the day after. It depends. It could take weeks. But there's not much more we can do until we understand how the clothing affected the suspects' state of mind – if indeed that is what motivated them. Dr Fuller is also running new toxicology tests to see if there are traces of any mind-altering drug in the suspects' bloodstreams.'

'Well, keep on breathing down his neck, won't you?' said DI Saunders. 'I've got the bloody media chasing me every five minutes and they're getting on my nerves. We're having to be so cagey about these cases they can smell that there's something fishy about them.'

He stood looking at Jerry and Jamila with one hand lifted as if he were about to say something else. Eventually, though, he shrugged, and went back to his desk, and started prodding at his keyboard.

'We'll be sure to let you know as soon as we have anything conclusive, sir,' said Jamila.

'Yes, OK,' said DI Saunders. His tone of voice was such that it was difficult to tell if 'yes, OK' was simply an acknowledgement, or a statement of fact, or an order – as in, *yes, OK, you will, because you'll bloody well regret it if you don't.*

*

As soon as the lift doors opened on the ground floor, Jerry and Jamila heard a woman screaming. Two officers hurried past them in the direction of the cells, and almost immediately Sergeant Bristow appeared, bustling back towards his reception desk.

'What's up?' asked Jerry. 'It's not that schoolmistress, is it? I thought she'd gone off to St George's to have her coat cut off her.'

'You'd think it was, wouldn't you?' said Sergeant Bristow. 'But it's a bloke.'

'What? A *bloke*? He sounds just like my Auntie Doris!'

Sergeant Bristow stopped and came back. 'You remember that call I was telling you about this morning?'

'Of course, yes. The woman who rang in and said that her friend was missing?'

'That's the one. We got the go-ahead from Callow to force an entry, but as it turned out we didn't have to, because her husband was at home. And – so was she, because her husband had stabbed her to death and hidden her body in the freezer.'

'*Jō ki hairāna hai!*' said Jamila, shaking her head. 'That's just incredible!'

'Oh, it gets worse,' Sergeant Bristow told them. 'After he'd killed her he cut a lump off her thigh and cooked it and ate

180

it, and when we got there, he'd cut her head off and was defrosting it in the microwave. He said he wanted to cook and eat her brain, and he got all narky when we wouldn't let him.'

'I feel sick,' said Jamila.

'And that's him screaming?' asked Jerry.

'That's him, believe it or not,' said Sergeant Bristow. 'DC Willis and DC Baker are with him now. They've been trying to get him to strip but he's not having it – says he can't take his sweater off because it hurts.'

'It *hurts*?' said Jamila. 'Why?'

'I haven't a clue, but DC Baker's asked me to call for a doctor. First of all we get that ice-cream stuck to his coat, and then that teacher, now we've got him, screaming about taking off his sweater.'

'Let's go and take a butcher's,' said Jerry.

While Sergeant Bristow went off to reception, Jerry and Jamila walked quickly along the corridor to the cells. David had stopped screaming now but he was sobbing bitterly and he still sounded like a woman.

The duty officer was standing outside the cell with his arms folded looking bored.

'Come to see Madame Butterfly, have you?' he asked.

'If you've no objection,' said Jamila, coldly, and the duty officer fumbled with his keys and opened the door for them.

David was sitting on his bed, his hands covering his face, his shoulders shaking. He was still wearing his black sweater and his grey boxer shorts and one bare foot was crossed over the other, more like a miserable woman than a man.

DC Willis was standing with his hands in his pockets and a look of total frustration on his face, like a parent whose three-year-old child is standing at the top of a playground slide, refusing either to slide down it or climb back down the steps.

DC Jean Baker was a young, chunky woman with short red hair, a face the colour of a pink party balloon and a tight bottle-green suit. Jerry always thought she could have been Ed Sheeran's baby sister.

The two uniformed officers were there, too – PC Ted Jonas, in his shirt-sleeves, as broad-shouldered as a rugby full-back, and PC Wilkinson, older and greyer, with a paunch.

'Ah, Jerry,' DC Willis greeted him. 'And DS Patel. I think we might have another case of Stuck Clothes Syndrome. He won't take his sweater off himself and he screams like an effing soprano every time we try to do it for him.'

'What's his name again?' asked Jerry.

'David Nelson. He's been formally charged with doing his wife in, and cautioned. He hasn't asked for a brief, although I reckon he needs a nut doctor more than a lawyer. The trouble is, he keeps talking about himself in the third person.'

'The third person?' asked Jamila. 'What do you mean by that exactly?'

'He's admitted that David Nelson killed his wife and ate part of her leg, and he's admitted that he decapitated her with the intention of eating her brain. But he keeps insisting that he's not David Nelson.'

Jamila turned to Jerry and said, 'Just like Sophie Marshall. Just like Laura Miller, that teacher. Both of them quite freely confessed to the murders that they had committed, didn't they, but both of them claimed that it wasn't actually them. Oh, and that addict, too, the one who was brought in for importuning. It's like they're all suffering from schizophrenia.'

'I think we need to leave this bloke alone until he's been seen by a doctor and we've had a full report from forensics,' said Jerry. 'It's obvious he's in some kind of a freaky mental state, unless he's putting it on, and somehow I don't think he is.'

He sat down beside David and laid a hand on his quaking shoulder.

'David? Can you hear me, David? Do you want to tell me how you're feeling?'

David didn't answer at first, but gradually his sobbing subsided and he gave a deep bubbling sniff. He lowered his hands and stared at Jerry with puffy, reddened eyes.

'I can't take it off,' he whispered, as if he didn't want anybody else to hear. 'She won't let me.'

'Who won't let you, David?'

'My mother. She won't let me.'

'Your *mother*? Why won't she let you? Where is she?'

David closed his eyes for a moment, and then shuddered. When he opened his eyes again, his expression had changed from miserable pathos to naked hostility.

'What's it to you?' he demanded, and his voice was shrill again, almost a scream. 'Why don't you go away and mind your own business, whoever you are?'

'Detective Constable Jerry Pardoe, if you must know, and you're under arrest for murder. You're not doing yourself any good by squawking at me.'

'It wasn't me. It was David. How many times do I have to tell you?'

'You *are* David. You killed your wife and you started to eat her.'

'There's no law against eating human flesh.'

'I know that. But there's a law against killing people so that you can do it.'

'But it wasn't me, and you can't prove that it *was* me.'

Jerry took his hand away from David's shoulder and stood up.

'There's no point in carrying on with this,' he said. 'Let's wait until a doctor's seen him. If you ask me, he needs to go off to Springfield, too.'

'Given up, have you?' David challenged him.

'For now,' Jerry told him.

'You need to feed me. I'm starving. If I don't get something to eat soon, I'm going to be very sick, and then you'll regret it. You're supposed to take care of people in custody.'

'We can bring you some sarnies later, OK? I assume you don't have any food allergies, do you? And you're obviously not a vegetarian.'

'Don't you mock me, young man,' said David. 'I'll dig your eyes out and fry them unless you're careful.'

Jerry ushered Jamila out of the cell and the others followed them. DC Willis said, 'I'll keep you up to date, Jerry, once the doctor's taken a shufti at him. I mean, don't ask me what the bloody hell's wrong with all of these nutters. I've never come across anything like it.'

They were all walking back to the reception area when they heard a hideous screech from David's cell. It was more than a cry of protest – it sounded like somebody being tortured. They all looked at each other, wondering if they ought to go back and see what was wrong, but then David screeched again, and shouted out, '*No! No! You can't do that! You can't do that! Stop! Stop, you can't do that! No!*'

They all hurried back to David's cell. The duty officer had already lifted up his huge bunch of keys and was trying to unlock the door. Meanwhile David kept on shouting and whooping in agony. The last time Jerry had heard anything like it was when he had visited an abattoir in East London and heard pigs being killed.

'What's the hold-up?' he snapped. 'Just get the fucking door open!'

'The key won't turn!' said the duty officer.

'What do you mean, the key won't turn? Here!'

Jerry pushed him aside and tried to turn the key himself, but it wouldn't budge.

'You're sure this is the right key?'

'Of course I'm sure. It's just bloody jammed.'

Jerry lifted the viewing flap and inside the cell he saw that David was standing up with his back towards the door, and that he was trying to wrench his black sweater over his head. He had managed to lift it as far as his shoulders, and he was desperately trying to claw it up further, but in doing so he had ripped off all of his skin. His entire back was raw and glistening red, and he was throwing himself from side to side and twisting himself around in what must have been unbearable pain. Drops of blood were flying all around the cell like a swarm of scarlet flies.

'*Stop!*' he screamed. '*You can't do that! You know what will happen if you do that! You'll kill me! I can't die again! You'll kill me!*'

In spite of his obvious suffering, he gave the sweater one last heave. He managed to pull it right off, but at the same time he tore all the skin from his upper body and his arms, and it dangled from the inside of the sweater in long bloody shreds.

'*You bastard!*' he screamed. '*You little bastard!*'

With that, he pitched over sideways and disappeared from sight.

'Call for a bus!' said Jerry. 'And go and fetch a bloody crowbar!'

He tried turning the key again. At first it remained stubbornly stuck, but when he jiggled it once more, the lock smoothly clicked and the door swung open, almost as if somebody invisible had pushed it.

Jerry stepped into the cell, followed closely by Jamila and DC Willis. David was twitching and shaking and mumbling. Jerry crouched down beside him, although he couldn't touch him. He had ripped away more than just the top layer of skin. At least five or six out of the seven layers had been torn off, right down to the dermis and even the hypodermis in places, so that his body fat and muscles were exposed, and were glistening with interstitial fluid.

'David,' said Jerry. 'David, there's help on the way.'

David's eyes opened, but then they rolled back into their sockets so that only the whites were showing. He was in deep shock, and Jerry knew that it would be more than a miracle if he survived until the paramedics arrived.

Jamila said, 'Maybe his sweater did the same thing as those two coats. How else did he manage to pull off so much skin? Maybe its fibres had stuck themselves into his pores.'

'Well, maybe,' said Jerry. 'Where is that bloody sweater, anyway? I thought he dropped it straight down on the floor.'

Jamila looked around. Then she said, 'There – right under the bed.'

The black sweater was bunched up in the darkness underneath the bed, so close to the wall that they wouldn't have seen it if they hadn't been looking for it. Jamila bent down and reached out for it, but immediately she jumped back and yelped out, 'Ō naraka! It moved!'

'You're kidding me,' said Jerry.

'I swear to you, it moved!'

Jerry leaned over and looked under the bed. At first the black sweater lay there perfectly still, but then after a few moments he thought that he saw its shoulders hump up, and one of the sleeves slide forward as if it still had an arm inside it.

'It's a rat,' he said. 'I'll bet you anything that's what it is. A rat's got inside it.' He stood up and called out to the duty officer, 'Malcolm – had any rats in here lately?'

'Rats?' said the duty officer. 'No, Jerry, never had no rats. Had some pigeons up in the roof-space last month, but that's all.'

DC Willis was outside the door, talking to forensic services on his mobile. DC Baker had disappeared off to reception. She had said that she was going to meet the paramedics when they arrived, but Jerry guessed that she hadn't wanted to stand around here looking at David's grisly torso any longer. He had always prided himself on his cast-iron stomach, but the sight of a man whose entire upper body was nothing but scarlet muscle and exposed tendons and yellowish fat was beginning to make him feel queasy, too.

He bent down and looked under the bed again. The black sweater appeared to have crept forward a few inches. It was inside-out, glistening wet with blood and festooned with parchment-like ribbons of David's skin. But it was only a sweater. It couldn't be moving on its own.

He reached out for it, but as soon as he touched it, it recoiled, and then it came scuttling out from underneath the bed like a huge crippled spider.

'Jesus Christ!' Jerry shouted. 'Derek – watch out!'

DC Willis turned around and saw the black sweater running jerkily across the floor towards him, and he took two stumbling steps backwards in disbelief. The duty officer saw it, too, and stood with his mouth open as it carried on running jerkily up the corridor, leaving behind it a patchy trail of blood and fragments of David's skin.

Jamila was almost screaming. 'It's alive, Jerry! *Iha asabhava hai!* How can it be *alive?*'

Jerry didn't answer, but stepped over David and pushed his way past DC Willis. He caught up with the sweater before it could reach the reception area, and stamped on it. In immediate response, its sleeves flung themselves up and clutched at his ankle. They twisted themselves around his lower leg, around and around, and clung onto him tighter than a tourniquet. He kicked the sweater twice more, as hard as he could, and shook his leg again and again – so violently that he lost his balance and fell back against the wall, jarring his shoulder.

The duty officer came running up and stamped on the sweater, too. After he had trodden on it six or seven times, its sleeves went limp and unfurled themselves from Jerry's shin. It lay flattened and sodden and totally still.

Jerry rubbed his shoulder and said, 'Thanks, Malcolm. Jesus.'

They both looked down at the black sweater and then at each other. Neither of them could believe what had just happened. Jerry said nothing more – even swear words wouldn't have expressed how he felt.

DC Willis came up to join them, although Jamila had stayed to watch over David. DC Willis crossed himself.

'I didn't know you were a left-footer, Derek,' said Jerry.

'I'm not,' said DC Willis. 'But if that wasn't the bloody Devil at work, then I don't know what the hell it was.'

The duty officer prodded the sweater with his foot. 'I don't get it. There's fuck-all inside it. But it was beetling along, wasn't it? Like – I don't know – like a beetle.'

Jerry said, 'Go and find somebody to keep an eye on it for us, will you, Malcolm? I don't want it running off again before forensics have had a chance to take pictures.'

Just then, DC Baker came back, followed by two paramedics in bright yellow high-viz jackets.

'Mind where you're walking,' Jerry cautioned them, and pointed to the sweater on the floor. The paramedics looked back at him blankly, but all the same they skirted around it.

Jerry and DC Willis waited by the sweater until the duty officer came back with another PC, a young officer with a fuzzy blond moustache and a protuberant Adam's apple.

'We've called forensics,' said DC Willis. 'But we just want you to watch this sweater until they get here.'

'You want me to *watch* it?' the young PC asked him. 'In case what?'

'In case it tries to run away,' said Jerry. 'If it does, step on it. Hard.'

The young PC started to laugh, but when he saw that Jerry was serious, he stopped abruptly, and said, 'All right. Got you. If it tries to run away, step on it.'

'*Hard,*' said Jerry.

Jamila came out of David's cell and walked up to him. Her expression was serious and she shook her head. 'He's gone, Jerry. There was nothing they could do for him.'

'Oh, well. After what he did, he was probably going to be banged up for the next forty years, anyway.'

Jamila looked down at the sweater. 'This is just like Sophie Marshall's jacket. What did she say? It came crawling after her. And where did her jacket go, after we found it in the hallway?'

'I know,' said Jerry. 'And it wasn't Sophie who killed her boyfriend. The jacket did it. I can't get my head round this.'

'This is worse than my grandmother's stories about the jinns,' said Jamila. '*Much* worse, because this is real. This sweater – it ran away like a giant tarantula, yet it's made of nothing but wool. How could that be?'

'Don't know, skip. I can't imagine what Dr Fuller's going to tell us, but personally I can't think of any logical explanation for it at all. Well – except that it's witchcraft.'

24

Jerry and Jamila waited until four technicians from the forensic service had arrived, all of them waddling around in their white Tyvek suits, taking photographs of David's cell and the corridor outside, and samples of the blood and fluids from the walls and the floor.

Eventually David's body was wheeled away on a trolley, covered by a blue plastic sheet, and the black sweater was picked up with tongs and sealed in a corrugated cardboard evidence box. The sweater had shown no more signs of life – no more twitching – and although Jerry felt that he should have told the forensic team that it had tried to run away from them, he couldn't find the words. Neither could Jamila or DC Willis or the duty officer. They looked at each other as one of the forensic experts stuck tape around the evidence box, in tacit agreement that they would wait until Dr Fuller had examined the sweater and compared it with his findings from the overcoats.

It was nearly nine o'clock now. Jamila had phoned Mr Wazir and asked if he preferred to postpone his interview with them until tomorrow, but Mr Wazir told them that he would rather get it over with this evening.

'Are you up for it, Jerry?' she asked him. 'You're not too shaken up?'

'Stirred, but not shaken,' said Jerry. 'Come on, let's do it. There's no way I'm going straight home now for a beer and a box set and a cosy night's kip.'

*

Mr Wazir was a neat, bald man, with a small black moustache and several gold teeth. He was wearing an immaculate white shirt and a Peshawar Green Cricket Club tie. He led Jerry and Jamila into the living-room while Mrs Wazir retreated into the kitchen. There was a strong aroma of cardamom in the house, and before Mr Wazir closed the door, they could hear the sound of frying.

They sat down. Mr Wazir had very small feet in maroon corduroy slippers. Jerry felt that they should have taken off their shoes, but Mr Wazir didn't ask them to. He seemed calm and detached and more business-like than emotional.

Jamila cleared her throat. 'First of all, Mr Wazir, we have to offer you our condolences on the tragic loss of Samira.'

Mr Wazir nodded, but said nothing.

'We know that you want to hold a funeral as soon as possible,' Jamila went on. 'The pathologist has advised me that her remains can be released tomorrow. If you can just let us know which funeral directors you've chosen.'

'She was a most happy young woman,' said Mr Wazir. 'Always laughing, always singing. I have never known anybody so happy.'

'She was happy to be getting married?' asked Jamila.

'Oh, yes. We were careful to choose a husband who was both handsome and reliable, and would treat her well. After all, she was brought up here in UK, and we knew that she would not tolerate a man who did not respect her. She told me that she was so delighted to be marrying Faraz.'

'We understand that Samira and her mother used to argue a lot,' said Jerry.

'My wife is very traditional in her beliefs. She believes in obedience to your elders. In UK, girls do not think that way so much, so there was bound to be friction. But my wife would never have lifted a finger to harm her.'

'So who do you think might have killed her?'

'I have no idea at all. Like I told you, she was happy to be marrying Faraz, and she had no jealous boyfriends. She had friends who were boys, naturally, but as her mother probably told you, she was *ika anavi'āhī*.'

'Pure,' said Jamila, for Jerry's benefit.

'Do you think she committed suicide?' asked Jerry.

'Why would she?' Mr Wazir retorted. 'She was happy and she was beautiful and everything in her life was perfect. Somebody killed her but I cannot think who it might have been. To be frank with you, isn't that *your* job, to discover who did it?'

*

'These cases are beginning to get me down,' said Jamila, as they climbed into their car and buckled up their seatbelts. 'All the forensic evidence so far suggests that there was nobody else in the house when Samira had acid poured over face, and like her father said, everything in her life appeared to be perfect. Except, of course, the fibres in her skin.'

'Well, you know what old Sherlock Holmes's motto was, don't you?' said Jerry, as he started the engine and pulled away from the kerb.

'Yes, but Sherlock Holmes didn't find himself dealing with coat fibres that grew into people's skin and sweaters that ran along the floor like spiders.'

'Do you fancy a nightcap?' Jerry asked her. 'I only live down the road here. I know you don't touch booze, but I could make you a cup of tea. My daughter Alice comes to stay over sometimes, so I could even stretch to a mug of cocoa.'

'You have coffee? I would really love a strong cup of coffee. I want something to keep me awake tonight, or else I know what will happen. I will have terrible nightmares about giant spiders.'

'I'll make you a triple espresso. That should stop you from sleeping for about a week.'

*

Jerry's flat was on the first floor of a grey concrete block of flats on the corner of Prentis Road. Before he opened his door he said, 'You'll have to excuse the catastrophic mess. I have a really nice Polish girl who comes around once a week and tidies up for me, but she's been away this week. Her sister's getting married or her grandpa's died, something like that.'

He switched on the lamps in the living-room. It was furnished with a cream vinyl couch cluttered with newspapers, two mismatched armchairs, one green and one orange, a huge flat-screen television and an oak coffee-table that was crowded with empty Stella Artois cans and scribbled-in notebooks and a half-empty packet of paprika crisps.

Jamila took off her coat and Jerry hung it over the back of one of the chairs.

'Don't worry,' she said. 'Myself, I'm obsessive but I've seen much worse. My brother's house looks like World War Three. Mind you, he has three small boys.'

'You're not married?' Jerry asked her. 'I mean, I noticed you're not wearing a ring, but not everybody does.' He held up his hand and said, 'I still wear mine. It keeps away the women who have a kinky thing for detectives.'

'No. My parents wanted me to marry a cousin of mine, Zartash, who is a businessman in Islamabad and quite wealthy. But he is much older than me and anyway I simply didn't like him, so I flatly refused. My father was upset at first but when I told him that I admired him so much that I wanted to join the police force myself he gave in.'

'And now?'

'I had a long relationship with a social worker when I first started at the Met but in the end we grew apart. Now I have friends who are men but nothing serious.'

'You're a very attractive woman. I'm surprised.'

Jamila blushed and looked away. 'What about that treble espresso?' she said.

Jerry hesitated for a moment and Jamila looked back at him in a way that told him she wasn't at all upset by the compliment that he had paid her, in spite of being his superior officer. They were off duty now, after all, and she gave him the feeling that she liked him, too. Maybe she had a weakness for tall scruffy Englishmen with dirty blond brushed-up hair and blue eyes.

He went into the kitchen and switched on his De Longhi coffee machine. Then he took a can of Stella Artois out of the fridge and popped the top. Jamila followed him into the kitchen and looked around.

'Well, at least your kitchen is tidy,' she smiled. 'Not just tidy, in fact – absolutely spotless!'

'That's because I hardly ever cook. My toad-in-the-hole was legendary but it's not something you cook for one.'

'Well, I did promise to cook you my keema. Minced mutton curry with peas and potatoes.'

'Believe me, skip, I'll take you up on that. I'll even bring my own spoon.'

Once Jamila's espresso had been poured out, they went back into the living-room and Jerry cleared away some of the old copies of *The Sun* so that they could sit together on the couch. Jamila tucked her legs under her and held her cup in both hands as she sipped it and Jerry couldn't help thinking how defenceless and pretty and endearing she looked.

But they both knew that this wasn't a time for flirting, or even for seeking consolation in each other's company. Both of them could see nothing in their mind's eye but David's flayed and bloody body, and the black sweater trying to escape along the station corridor.

'I believe in the supernatural,' said Jamila. 'You know – poltergeists that throw pots and pans across the room, and tip over chairs. But you never think you are actually going to witness it.'

'Come on – there has to be a scientific explanation for what happened,' Jerry told her. 'Maybe it's some kind of chemical reaction. I don't know.'

'But it's the way it seems to be *spreading*, like an epidemic. First Samira, and then Sophie, and then our down-and-out, and then Laura Miller, and David. I know all of these cases have different characteristics. It looks very much as if Samira killed herself, instead of attacking other people, and our junkie didn't actually try to hurt anybody – although maybe he didn't get the chance before he was caught. Every one of them, though, had fibres from their clothing piercing their skin. So what can we conclude from that? That their clothing was contaminated? With what? What on earth makes the fibres of your coat or your sweater stick into your pores and turn you into a schizophrenic?'

'I've been thinking that too, skip. But it could be that we're looking at this the wrong way round. Maybe they'd all been taking some kind of drug that sucked the fibres into their skin – like osmosis or something. There are so many weird new party drugs around these days – Pink, for instance. They're strong enough to knock out an elephant. I mean, some of them like Carfentanil were actually formulated to knock out elephants, so maybe they're strong enough to pull your coat fibres into your skin. Who knows? Let's just hope that Dr Fuller can give us a clue.'

'If not – perhaps DI Saunders was right, and we need to call for an exorcist,' said Jamila. 'And—'

'And what?'

'And when we're together like this, away from the station, don't call me "skip". My name is Jamila. In Africa the name means "chaste", and in Arab countries it means "beautiful in appearance and behaviour".'

'It suits you. "Jerry" is either a German, or a petrol can, or a crap bit of building.'

Neither of them laughed, but they looked at each other for several seconds without saying anything, and a silent message passed between them, although both of them understood that it was a message that they might never have the chance to tear open and act on.

Jamila finished her coffee and stood up. 'I should go, Jerry, and you have a very early start tomorrow morning, don't forget. Good luck with Liepa the Weeper.'

'I'll drive you home. Where are you staying?'

'In Merton, with a friend from the Asian Women's Association. But I'll call for an Uber. You've been drinking and you've been through enough stress for one day.'

It took only ten minutes for the taxi to arrive. Jerry took Jamila outside and opened the car door for her. The night was growing chilly now and they could hear a train rattling in the distance.

Jamila paused and lifted her face to him and Jerry kissed her on the cheek.

'We have a saying in Pakistan,' said Jamila. 'It is better to risk humiliation than to stay silent about your feelings. One day there may be nobody there to listen to you.'

25

Mindy's father came downstairs and into the living-room, where her mother was standing with her arms tightly crossed over her breasts as if she were feeling cold.

'She's fast asleep,' he said. 'She doesn't seem to be running a temperature but she still won't take off that jacket, and I couldn't force her to.'

'What are we going to do?' asked her mother. 'Perhaps we should have taken her to A&E.'

'What – and sit in the waiting-room for six hours, only to have some junior doctor tell us that she's just had some surge in her hormones?'

'She's *nine*, Peter. She's nowhere near puberty yet.'

'You don't know these days, do you? There was a bit in the paper yesterday about some twelve-year-old girl having a baby.'

'Peter, she *ate* Sprout. She ate him raw! I don't know if she killed him or not before she ate him, but that's not a symptom of precocious sexual development. That's insanity.'

Mindy's father sat down, and her mother sat next to him, taking hold of his hands.

'Maybe we should take her to a psychiatrist,' he said. 'You said that she was talking like it was somebody else who ate Sprout, and not her. Maybe it's genetic. My grandmother went doolally when she was in her eighties, and started having these long conversations with people who weren't there.'

'Yes, but that was probably senile dementia. Girls of Mindy's age don't get senile dementia.'

They didn't speak for almost three minutes. Eventually, though, Mindy's father said, 'Look – let's go to bed and get some sleep. We can work out what to do tomorrow morning. Right now I'm absolutely knackered and I can't think straight.'

'How am I going to sleep?' asked her mother, desperately. 'And even if I can, what if she tries to get out of the house? She said that she was going to come and go as she pleases, and nothing I could do would stop her.'

'I'll take the key out of the kitchen door and double-lock the front door so that she can't get out. And of course I'll set the alarm. Take a Nytol. You look absolutely shattered.'

'Mindy's my little girl, Peter,' her mother sobbed. 'I don't want to lose her.'

Her father held her close and kissed her forehead. 'You won't, darling. This is just some temporary aberration. Maybe she fell over when she was taking Sprout for a walk and knocked her head or something. And she's just getting over that really bad cold, remember. Maybe her temperature shot up and affected her brain, like heat stroke. That can make people confused, and make them vomit, too. I bet she'll wake up tomorrow morning and won't even remember what happened.'

'I just wish we could take that horrible jacket off her.'

'I know. But she'll probably want to take it off herself tomorrow. The best thing we can do now is let her sleep.'

Mindy's mother wiped her eyes with her fingers and then nodded. 'All right, then. Let's go to bed. I think I will take a Nytol, yes. But you *will* hear her, won't you, if she wakes up?'

'Wasn't I always the one who used to wake up and feed her in the middle of the night, when she was a baby?'

'And poor little Sprout. It's all so sad. Dear God – I hope she didn't hurt him too much.'

Mindy's father and mother went upstairs to bed, leaving a single lamp alight in the living-room, so that the upstairs landing was dimly illuminated. While her mother undressed and went to the bathroom to brush her teeth and take a sleeping pill from the medicine cabinet, her father stole into Mindy's bedroom and leaned over her bed to make sure that she was still breathing evenly.

She was lying with her back to him, with only her legs covered by her duvet. The blue velvet jacket had ridden up a little, but it was still clinging tightly across her shoulders. Mindy's father knew that he wouldn't be able to tug it off her without waking her up.

He was about to tiptoe out of the bedroom when Mindy spoke.

'Have to— have to *eat* soon,' she mumbled.

Her father stood utterly still, wondering if she had woken up or was talking in her sleep. Her breathing continued, steady and even, and she didn't move, so he assumed that he hadn't disturbed her. As he started to creep towards the door, though, she spoke again.

'Not having *them* telling me what to do. Who do they think they are?'

'Mindy?' her father whispered. But she didn't answer, and she didn't stir, and so he crept out of her bedroom, leaving the door two or three inches ajar.

*

She had taken two Nytol tablets but it still took Mindy's mother nearly an hour to fall asleep. Her father dropped off almost immediately, as he always did when he was upset or distressed. It was like a defence mechanism, and tonight her mother envied him more than she usually did. He kept twitching, though, and letting out little gasps, and so she guessed that he might be having a nightmare.

She could have woken him, but if she did he might find it hard to get back to sleep, and perhaps he needed this nightmare to work out his anxiety.

She kept picturing Mindy spewing Sprout's half-chewed remains all over the living-room carpet. *I'll never be able to forget that*, she thought. *I'll have that image playing over and over in my mind's eye for the rest of my life. And I can still hear her heaving, too.*

When Mindy had at last finished vomiting, coarse and curly dog-hairs were trapped between her teeth. For all her mother knew, they still were.

She dropped off at last, lying on her back in her long white nightdress with her hands clasped as if she were the effigy of a saint on top of a tomb. She didn't twitch and she didn't murmur and her breathing was almost silent.

After a little more than half an hour, the bedroom door swung open, in the same way that the door of David Nelson's cell had swung open, soundlessly. Mindy was standing outside on the landing, still wearing the blue velvet jacket. She taken off her tights when she went to bed, she had kept her knickers on. She was breathing deeply, as if she were walking in her sleep, but her eyes were wide open, even if she had a fixed and glassy stare.

She came into the bedroom and stood beside the bed on her mother's side. In her right hand she was holding a yellow plastic-handled craft knife with a snap-off blade. In her left she was holding a claw hammer.

I heard you two talking downstairs. You think I'm insane, do you? You think you're going to take me to a psychiatrist to find out if I have a split personality? Well, I have for now, but every hour that passes there's less and less of Mindy and more and more of me. As soon as I've eaten my fill, I'll be back to being myself – all of me, and Mindy will be gone. Vanished, like everybody has to vanish one day, except us – the lucky survivors. That's if you can call it lucky to die, and have to find yourself a host so that you can live again.

She felt completely calm, although she was a little sad, too. Not sad for Mindy, or Mindy's father and mother, but for herself, that her life had come to this.

I would say a prayer for you, if I believed that prayers ever do anybody any good.

You're not going to hurt them, are you? I love them.

Of course I'm not going to hurt them. They won't feel anything.

But what are you doing with that cutter thing, and that hammer?

I can't let them tell me what to do. And they don't have the right to tell you what to do, either.

But they're my mummy and daddy!

All the more reason. Mothers and fathers should respect their children. They should be endlessly grateful that their children have chosen them to be the ones to give birth to them. Think of all the men and women who can never have children.

Mindy came up close to her mother. She laid the hammer on the bed next to her, and then she carefully turned down the Peter Pan collar of her nightgown. Her mother still didn't stir.

Sliding out the blade of the snap-off knife, Mindy positioned the triangular point just over her mother's larynx. She took a steadying breath, and then she pushed the point as deep as she could into her mother's neck. It made a faint popping sound as it went in. Her mother jerked, and gasped, but then Mindy dragged the blade all the way down as far as the pillow, so that she sliced through her mother's platysma muscle and severed her carotid artery and her jugular veins. Her neck gaped open like some hideous second mouth, and blood flooded out in a crimson torrent, drenching her nightgown and soaking the sheet undcrneath her. As her heart pumped out more and more blood, Mindy was spattered, too, all over her face and her T-shirt and her jacket.

Mindy's mother let out a bubbling, whistling sound, and flapped her arms up, trying to reach the gaping wound in her neck. Her father sat up instantly and said, 'What? *Janet!* What's going on?'

He saw all the blood pouring out of Mindy's mother's neck, and stared at Mindy aghast. 'Jesus! What have you done? Janet! Janet, hold on!'

Mindy stood watching him impassively as he dragged up the duvet and pressed it against her mother's neck. The rose-patterned duvet cover was sodden with blood in an instant, and her father realised with a howl of grief that there was nothing that he could do to save her. He pulled back the duvet and tried to cover her neck with his hand, but it was hopeless. Blood gushed out between his fingers with every beat of her heart.

'Janet!' he begged her. 'For God's sake don't die! Janet!' Then he looked up at Mindy and screamed at her, 'Dial nine-nine-nine! Dial nine-nine-nine! It's the least you can do, you little monster!'

As he turned back to look down at Mindy's mother again, Mindy picked up the hammer that she had left on the bed beside her. She lifted it high above her head with both hands, paused, and then swung it down to hit her father as hard as she could on the back of his head. It made a loud *clock* sound, and he collapsed on top of her mother, stunned but not completely knocked out. When he tried to lift his head again, though, Mindy hit him again, and then again, and when he rolled over sideways, she quickly went around to the opposite side of the bed and beat his head until she heard his skull crack. Then she turned her attention to his face, knocking five or six circular dents into his forehead and breaking the bridge of his nose. Lastly, she smashed his mouth and his chin and his jaw, until his lips burst open and his bloody teeth were scattered across the sheet.

He grunted every time she hit him because he was concussed but not dead. As soon as she had finished with the hammer, though, she picked up the craft knife again and sliced the side of his neck. A fountain of blood sprayed up almost six inches into the air, soaking his pale green pyjamas.

Mindy stood back and watched with that fixed glassy look in her eyes as her mother and her father rapidly bled out. In the half-darkness, the whole bed glistened with blood. She wondered abstractedly if she should take a strip of flesh from each of them now, while they were still alive and warm, or if she should wait until they were dead.

You ate that dog raw, didn't you, and that made you sick.
It would be better to cut off some nice lean pieces and cook
them, like that casserole you made at school. Think how good
that would taste, and how much more you could eat.

I loved them, but now they're dying, both of them.

Yes – but they loved you more, and what they're giving you
now is a whole new life.

I feel sad for them.

No you don't. One generation always has to sacrifice their
lives for the next. That's the way of the world. That's what
they were born for. This is their destiny.

There was a long silence inside Mindy's mind. She felt as if
she were standing on the edge of an endless desert, at night,
with a thin cold wind blowing across it. A young girl in a blue
velvet jacket was walking away from her, into the darkness,
becoming smaller and smaller, and that young girl was her.

Who are you? she asked, but even though she waited and
waited, she was given no answer.

26

Three unmarked patrol cars and two vans were already lined up outside the station when Jerry arrived. Eighteen officers were shuffling their feet on the pavement, waiting to set off, all of them swaddled in stab-proof vests and high-viz jackets. It was 2:05 a.m., and so cold that it looked as if all of them were smoking.

DI French had called this Operation Weeper, and the cars and the vans were code-named Weepers One to Five.

Jerry parked behind one of the vans. DI French saw him arrive and came over to talk to him, and so he put down his window.

'Right, Jerry,' said DI French, with a sharp sniff. 'Operation Weeper is a go. We're going to catch the bastard in the act this time. We've got a reporter and a cameraman from BBC London News here too, so this is going to be something of a publicity coup.'

DI French was short and stocky, with grizzled grey hair and the look of a boxer who had retired after twenty unsuccessful years in the ring. He was wearing a tightly belted grey raincoat and his breath smelled of the cigarette that he had just thrown away.

He had been passed over time and time again for preferment, and these days he was only allocated cases which were more of a public nuisance than serious crimes. He was hoping that arresting and prosecuting Jokubas Liepa for stealing charity donations would win him media attention and public gratitude and a last chance of becoming a DCI. Jerry thought that no matter what he did he didn't have a hope in hell of being promoted, but he kept that to himself.

'OK, Jerry, you'll go to Du Cane Court and give us the heads up as soon as he sets off. It's him I want, Liepa. I don't care about any of his minions. Once you know where he's headed, Weepers One, Two and Three will box off the area and move in as soon as he's lifted his first bag. Before we give him a tug, though, he must have lifted at least one bag, and it must be an official Cancer Research bag, not just any old black dustbin bag. Wait until he slings it into the back of his van, closes the doors and starts to drive off. Before that, don't for God's sake give him any reason to think that you're tailing him.'

Jerry gave DI French the thumbs-up and said, 'Got you, sir,' as if they hadn't already discussed this operation yesterday afternoon, over and over again, in tedious detail. DI French never grew tired of the sound of his own voice, and if he ran out of things to say, he would simply repeat himself.

Starting up his engine and turning around, Jerry drove back through the centre of Tooting and then north-east towards Balham High Road. The streets were deserted apart from two drunks staggering along Tooting Broadway. Jokubas Liepa lived in a top-floor flat in Du Cane Court, an expensive art deco block built in 1936 which had been the home over the years to numerous famous actors and singers and comedians. Hitler was supposed to have had his eye on it for his living quarters after he had conquered England, and that was why the Luftwaffe's bombers had left it unscathed during World War Two.

When he arrived outside Du Cane Court, Jerry saw that three large Transit vans were parked nose-to-tail in the layby outside, two white and one pale blue. He drove past and parked a few yards further up the road, by the bus stop, so that he could see them in his rear-view mirror. He called DI French on his R/T and told him that he was in position.

'OK, Jerry, roger that,' said DI French. 'Just don't give him any reason to think that you're tailing him.'

'No, sir. I won't.'

Almost twenty minutes had passed before a gang of eight or nine men came out from the entrance to the flats, all of them shaven-headed, and all of them walking with that aggressive shoulder-swinging strut that characterised so many criminals. Jerry sometimes wondered why they didn't just wear a T-shirt saying *I Am A Thug*. Most of them were dressed in windcheaters or black leather jackets and jeans, although the tallest of them was wearing a long camel-hair overcoat with the collar turned up and a dark brown scarf wrapped around his neck.

This was Jokubas Liepa – Liepa the Weeper. He was handsome enough to be an actor, with sharply defined cheekbones and an angular jaw, although he was deathly pale and his deep-set eyes had a sinister glitter, so he probably would have been cast as a villain. His long dark hair was swept back into waves, which made him look even more like a thespian who had just stepped off the stage, instead of what he really was – a racketeer who had made a fortune by half-inching second-hand clothes.

'Liepa's on the move,' said Jerry, into his R/T. 'He's getting into the pale blue van, registration RB02 UOH. He's sitting in the front passenger seat.'

'OK, Jerry, roger that.'

'The vans are setting off now, all three of them. The first one's done a U-ey and he's heading back towards the Broadway. The second one's turning left into Balham Park Road. Liepa's turning immediately right into Elmfield Road. I'll give him a few seconds and then I'll be after him.'

Jerry waited until the pale blue van was out of sight, and then followed it into Elmfield Road. The bulb had gone in its nearside brake-light, so it was easy for him to identify it from a distance, although there was scarcely any other traffic around at this time of the morning. He switched off his own lights so that Liepa's driver would be less likely to notice him in his mirror.

'He's turning south now on Cloudesdale Road, even though it's a one-way street and he's heading in the wrong direction. He's only crawling along now, and that probably means that he's looking out for charity bags on people's doorsteps.'

'Right,' said DI French. 'We can start boxing him in now. I'm going to position Weeper Two and Weeper Three on the streets running parallel to Cloudesdale Road on either side – one on Childebert Road and another on Foxbourne Road. Weeper One will drive up ahead of him on Bushnell Road, but heading in the same direction as he is, and stay ahead of him until he picks up a bag. Then it can stop and reverse and block him.'

'Right, sir. Roger that.'

Jokubas Liepa's pale blue van continued to creep southwards on Cloudesdale Road at about five miles an hour, but so far none of the residents had left charity bags out for them to steal. Jerry was just about to tell DI Finch that it looked as if both they and Liepa and were wasting their time when he saw Liepa's single brake-light flare red, and his van came to a halt.

The back doors of the van were flung open and one of the leather-jacketed men jumped out. He jogged over to the second-to-last house on the left and picked up a bulging white plastic bag that had been left in the porch. Even from a distance Jerry could see that it carried the blue-and-pink 'C' symbol of Cancer Research.

'Weeper's a go,' he told DI Finch. 'They've picked up a bag – they've slung it in the back of the van – the doors are shut – they're starting off again.'

'That's it, then, Jerry! Wait till Weeper One has blocked him, then hit him where it hurts!'

Jerry stayed about fifty yards away from the back of the pale blue van. It continued to creep forward until the van code-named Weeper One came speeding in reverse out of Bushnell Road, straight across the junction with Ritherdon Road, and collided with it. Even at this distance, with his car windows closed, Jerry could hear the smash of metal and glass. The pale blue van jumped up like a startled animal and the impact jolted it backwards at least five feet.

Whoever was driving the pale blue van, though, had quick reactions. As soon as Weeper One had crashed into it, he shifted into reverse and started to steer it backwards, stamping his foot so hard on the accelerator that smoke poured out from its tyres.

What he didn't realise was that Jerry was right behind him. Jerry stamped on his accelerator, too, and sped forward, hitting the back of the pale blue van with a deafening bang. His air-bag blew up in his face, splitting his lip and almost knocking his front teeth out.

Half-stunned, he managed to force the door of his car open and climb out, although he fell onto his hands and knees on the pavement, and it was only by reaching out for the bars of a wrought-iron garden gate that he managed to heave himself up onto his feet. Three uniformed officers had left Weeper One and were approaching the pale blue van. One of them was armed with a Heckler & Koch semi-automatic carbine. The other two were carrying halogen flashlights and shining them into the van's shattered windscreen.

'Step out of the vehicle!' one of them shouted. 'Step out of the vehicle now and keep your hands where we can see them!'

The doors of the pale blue van remained shut, and there was no answer.

'I said, step out of the vehicle!' the officer repeated.

Two of the officers had now reached the sides of the van, while the officer with the carbine stood in front of it with his weapon raised. As one of the officers went to open the passenger door where Jokubas Liepa was sitting, the driver of the van revved the engine and the van surged forward with a scream that sounded almost human. The van hit the officer with the carbine with a thump, and carried him forward, half-stuck and half-clinging to its radiator grille.

It smashed into the back of the police van, Weeper One, and with a complicated crunch the officer was crushed almost completely flat below the chest. His carbine clattered to the ground and lay in the blood that gushed from his body like an ornamental fountain.

'*Back up! Back that van up!*' shouted one of the officers, hoarsely. '*Jesus Christ, you've fucking killed him!*'

But the leather-jacketed van driver opened his door and climbed out, holding up both hands in surrender. 'Sorry, boss. Engine's conked out.'

By now, though, the other officer had run back to Weeper One, jumped into the driving seat and started it up. He drove it slowly forward so that the crushed officer slid down from between the two vans, and his colleague could take hold of him and lower him onto the road.

Jerry picked up the carbine, sticky as it was, and approached the open driver's door. Jokubas Liepa was still sitting in the passenger seat, his arms folded, staring straight ahead of him at the milky, opaque windscreen. If anything, he looked bored.

'*Liepa!*' Jerry shouted at him. 'Get your arse out of there! Get your arse out of there *now!*'

Without turning to look at him, Jokubas Liepa opened his door and climbed out of the van, straightening his coat collar with an air of nonchalance. Jerry circled around the back of the van and confronted him.

'Down on the floor!' he ordered him. He was so shocked and angry that he was almost screaming.

Jokubas Liepa looked down at the pavement with distaste, and then back at Jerry.

'You heard me!' Jerry repeated. 'Down on the floor! Arms and legs spread!'

'I promise you that it was accident,' said Jokubas Liepa. 'My driver's foot must have slipped on the pedal. I didn't order him to do it, and that's for sure.'

'I said – get down on the fucking floor,' Jerry told him, much more calmly this time, but he cocked the carbine to show that he was serious.

Jokubas Liepa shrugged, hitched up the knees of his trousers, and carefully laid himself face down on the pavement. 'I promise you, it was total accident,' he said again, lifting his head up so that his cheek wouldn't be touching the concrete. 'I am as distressed as you are.'

'Shut it,' said Jerry.

Just then, Weeper Two and Weeper Three came roaring around the corner from opposite directions. They blocked off the road and their officers came scrambling out.

The officer who had moved the van came up to Jerry looking grim.

'I've called for a bus, Jerry. Not that there's much fucking point.' He covered his mouth with his hand for a moment, and then he said, 'Whitey. I can't believe it. It's his little lad's third birthday on Saturday and Maureen's expecting another one in April.'

Jokubas Liepa raised his head again.

'I'm sorry. It was accident.'

'I'll give you an accident where it hurts the most, mate,' the officer snapped at him. 'You'll be coughing your balls up by the time I've finished with you.'

27

Mindy was turning the corner into Moyser Road when she felt the first spots of rain. She brushed them off the shoulders of her jacket and looked up at the clouds, wishing that she had thought to bring her mother's umbrella with her.

She was on her way to Budgens store to buy some tinned tomatoes and mixed herbs, so that she could make her casserole. She had been taught how to prepare it in her cookery class at school, although at school they had used chicken breasts.

Mindy was feeling so hungry that she had retched over the toilet several times since waking up this morning, but after her experience with Sprout she couldn't face eating anything raw. That was why she had decided on the one recipe that she knew how to cook. When she had proudly brought her casserole home for her mother and father to taste, they had both told her how much they liked it, and that made her feel much more at ease about what she was going to do. At least they were going to be cooked in a dish that they enjoyed.

She went into the store and bought everything that she needed, as well as two Mars bars and a box of Bakewell tarts. She had seven pounds in coins which she had taken from the jar in which her mother kept her loose change.

As she came up to the counter to pay, the Pakistani shop assistant smiled and said, 'No school for you today, miss?'

'School?' she frowned. 'I haven't been to school for years.'

'Oh. They teach you at home then?'

'I have no idea what you're talking about. Why don't you just mind your own business?'

'Well, I'm sorry, miss. But there's no need for you to be so rude.'

Mindy counted out the money she owed him and placed it on the counter. 'There,' she said. 'Five pounds sixty-five. It's a pity it won't pay for you to go back to wherever you came from.'

The shop assistant opened his mouth as if he were about to say something, but then he thought better of it and simply shook his head. Mindy left the shop and started to walk home, although by now a fine soft rain was falling across the road like a funeral procession of nearly invisible ghosts, and she knew that she was going to get soaked through. She would have to use her mother's hair-dryer to dry her jacket, because she wouldn't be able to take it off. Not that she *wanted* to take it off – it felt as much a part of her now as her own skin.

She had almost reached the corner of Nimrod Road when a silver BMW drew up alongside her, and the passenger window was put down. A grey-haired man in thick-rimmed glasses leaned over from the driver's seat and called out, 'Hey there, darling! Need a lift, do you? It looks like you're going to get yourself drowned out there!'

The collar of her jacket was already sopping, and Mindy knew how stiff velvet went when it got wet. She said, 'Yes, thank you! I only live just around the corner!'

'Hop in, then,' the man told her, and she opened the door and climbed into the passenger seat.

'Halfway down Nimrod Road, just past Spalding Road,' she told him.

'Well, you're the pretty one, aren't you?' said the man, grinning at her. She reminded him of her Uncle Jim, with a bulbous nose and a prickly grey moustache. He was wearing a Tattersall shirt with a brown tie and a grubby khaki windcheater. Unlike her Uncle Jim, who had reeked of cigarette smoke and Voltarol liniment, this man had liberally sprayed himself with Lynx Dark Temptation, which smelled like chocolate, although Mindy could still detect a strong underlying odour of unwashed armpits.

'You won't mind, will you, if I nip home first?' the man asked her, as he pulled away from the kerb. 'I forgot my bloody phone, that's the trouble, excuse my French. It won't take a second for me to find it. You can come in and see my goldfish. I've got some really rare goldfish. One of them's worth more than a hundred pounds. Can you believe that? A hundred pounds! Just for a tiny little fish!'

He didn't wait for Mindy to answer, but drove straight past the intersection with Nimrod Road and carried on south-east along Moyser Road until he reached Pretoria Road, which was another long street with red-brick Victorian terraces on either side. He turned left, and drove another two hundred metres before he pulled in and parked outside a house with a luridly green front door.

'I'll wait for you,' said Mindy.

'Oh. I can't let you do that, darling. I'd get into all kinds of trouble for leaving a minor unattended in my car. Besides, don't you want to see my hundred-pound goldfish? It's a twisty-tailed tosaku.'

Mindy was about to say, *I'm not in the least bit interested in your twisty-tailed tosaku. And besides, I'm not a minor.* But then she thought: *He doesn't know that. And I'm hungry. And perhaps he needs to be taught a lesson for picking up a young girl off the street with who knows what in mind.*

'All right,' she said, and opened up the car door.

'Good girl,' said the man, and climbed out of the car himself.

It was still raining, and so the man put his arm around her shoulders and hustled her quickly up to the green front door. He took out his door key and inserted it into the lock, but before he turned it he looked around as if he were making sure that none of his neighbours had seen him. Then he opened the door and almost shoved Mindy inside.

The house was gloomy and smelled of damp and something else sweetish and unpleasant, like unwashed socks. It didn't look as if it had been redecorated since the 1960s, because the maroon and yellow wallpaper was faded and the paint on the interior doors was peeling.

'In here,' said the man, and ushered Mindy into the living-room, where there were two sagging Parker Knoll armchairs and a worn-out brown sofa. The man took off his windcheater and hung it over the back of one of the armchairs, and then he went over to the beige tiled fireplace and switched on a three-bar electric fire.

'Want to be nice and toasty, don't we?' he said, chafing his hands together. Then he said, 'Oh, yes! This way for the twisty-tailed tosaku!'

He led Mindy through to the open-plan dining-room, where the goldfish tank was standing on top of a cheap walnut sideboard. Outside, she could see a small back garden, densely overgrown with nettles and bindweed, with a broken deckchair lying on its side next to a weathered plastic gnome. The man stood behind Mindy and placed his hands on her shoulders, gently massaging her with his thumbs.

'My name's Barry, by the way,' he told her. He spoke in a soft, hoarse voice, so close to the top of Mindy's head that she could feel his breath in her hair. 'What's yours, darling? You're a very pretty girl, aren't you? Very, very pretty. You should be a model, do you know that?'

'Which one's the twisty-tailed tosaku?' asked Mindy. 'The water's all dirty and I can't see any fish at all.'

'What's your name, darling?' Barry asked her.

'Varvara. But I can't see any fish.'

'Varvara? That's an unusual name, but beautiful. I'll have to clean the tank out, won't I, Varvara? Then you'll be able to see all the fish. Would you like me to take some photos of you, Varvara?'

'What? Why?'

'Why? Because you're so pretty. And if I took some photos I could send them off to a magazine and you could be a famous model. How about that? Wouldn't your daddy and mummy be proud?'

'No, they wouldn't.'

'Oh, I'll bet they would be. Their pretty young daughter Varvara, in a magazine. Why don't I go and fetch my camera?'

Mindy thought for a moment, and then she said, 'All right, then.' There was no expression in her voice at all. She had already been working out what she was going to do from the moment that Barry had pushed her in through the front door.

'You'll be famous, I promise you!' said Barry. 'It's upstairs, my camera, so I won't be a moment. Why don't you take that jacket off, for a start?'

Mindy didn't answer. Barry turned her around and grinned at her again and gave her a wink. Then he left the room and ran upstairs. His footsteps quickly crossed the bedroom above the dining area, and she heard a wardrobe door bang.

You poor deluded fool. I've known so many men like you. And I know what they want from naïve young girls.

There was a door on the right-hand side of the dining area. She went over and opened it, and as she expected, she found herself in the kitchen. It was narrow and dirty, with a rust-stained sink and a draining-board heaped with crumpled shirts and underpants waiting to be washed. The enamel gas stove was at least forty years old, with three dented aluminium saucepans sitting on top of it.

Mindy opened one drawer after another, until she came across what she was looking for: a small wooden-handled paring-knife. She pressed the edge of the blade against the ball of her thumb, and even though she would have liked it to be sharper, it would have to do. She didn't care how much pain it caused Barry, being so blunt. He deserved it, and she was so hungry by now that she could have been sick, if her stomach hadn't been empty.

She dropped the knife into the pocket of her jacket and returned to the dining-room. A few moments later, Barry came back downstairs, whistling tunelessly and swinging a Leica camera with a flash attachment. By now Mindy was peering into the fish tank as if she really believed that there were any goldfish in it.

'You haven't taken off your jacket, darling,' said Barry, setting down the camera on the dining-room table. 'Do you want me to give you a hand with it?'

'No,' said Mindy, without looking away from the fish tank. She could see a phantom reflection of her own face in the dark green glass, but it didn't look like her at all. It looked older, and more secretive. It looked *sly*.

'You'll have to take the jacket off,' Barry told her. 'These photos, you know, they've got to be glamorous.'

Now Mindy turned around to face him. 'What do you mean?'

'Well, come on, you're a girl, you know what glamorous means. *Sexy*. I know you're only young but that's what makes you so attractive. You've seen those girls from *Love Island* and those reality shows like that. And some of those women on Facebook like your Kim Kardashian. They know they're pretty and they like to show themselves off. That's what the magazines are looking for. Glamour. Especially the online ones.'

Mindy came up very close to him. She was only four feet six inches tall, and he was five feet nine, so she had to tilt her head back to look up into his face. In turn, he had to look down at her so that his double chin bulged over his shirt collar.

'So what is it you want me to do?' she asked him, and again her voice was completely expressionless – so expressionless that even Barry was slightly thrown off, and hesitated before he answered her.

'Well, *you* know!' he blustered. 'You've seen these girls, haven't you? They pose in their bikinis, don't they, and their underwear? They take these selfies in their bathrooms, in their bras and their knickers. That's what the magazines are looking for.'

Mindy said nothing but kept on staring up at him.

'I mean, you're obviously too young to be wearing a bra,' he continued. 'You're wearing knickers, though, aren't you? Or perhaps you're not. I know some young girls don't. But the magazines like that, too. We could take a few pictures without your knickers. You wouldn't mind that, would you? All perfectly innocent. And you're very, very pretty.'

Mindy still said nothing, and still kept staring up at him.

'How about taking your jacket off, for a start?' said Barry. 'Let's start off with some fashion-type shots, and see how those go. Then we can think about a few glamour shots afterwards.'

Mindy beckoned to him with her left index finger.

'What?' he said, and leaned forward with his hand cupped to his ear, expecting her to say something. Instead, she took the paring-knife out of her pocket, swung her arm sideways and stabbed him in his bulging neck. Then she tugged the blunt blade down towards her so that it ripped a ragged two-inch hole in his grey-stubbled skin.

She missed his carotid artery, but blood still spurted out of his neck, soaking his collar and splattering his sleeve. He took three or four staggering steps backwards, pressing his right hand against his neck and waving with his left as if he were waving Mindy goodbye.

'You— *gah!*' he choked. 'What have you— *gah!*'

He took another two steps backwards, and fell onto the sofa, his eyes bulging and his whole right hand as red and shiny as a rubber glove.

'Ambulance,' he gargled, and a bubble of blood swelled out from between his lips and popped. 'Nine nine nine. *Please.*' He had been grey before but now he was ashen with shock.

Mindy came into the sitting-room and stood over him.

'No,' she said.

Barry shook his head. He tried to speak, but the knife had penetrated his trachea and he was choking on his own blood. He coughed, and a fine scarlet spray settled all over his face.

'*Am*—' he began, but then he coughed again, explosively, before wheezing his breath back into his lungs. Mindy could hear the blood crackling in his lungs.

She knelt down beside the sofa and laid her left hand on the fly of Barry's grey chinos. She gave him a squeeze and then she smiled at him.

'Well, well, Barry. How about that? You're still half hard. It got you all excited, did it, thinking about pretty little Varvara with no knickers on?'

Barry shook his head wildly from side to side. He was beyond denying it. He was desperate for some way to stop himself bleeding, and for air.

Mindy put down the knife and started to tug at Barry's zip with both hands. He gargled and tried to hump his hips sideways but she pushed him back against the seat-cushions and said, 'Keep still, Barry! You're not the twisty-tailed tosaku! Not that you really *have* one, do you, you fibber! I'll bet you don't even have a tin of sardines in that tank! Twisty-tailed tosaku – I ask you!'

Barry was panicking too much to notice how Mindy's voice had changed. She no longer sounded like a nine-year-old Tooting schoolgirl at all. Every word was harsh, and cutting, in what used to be called a BBC accent, although some of her flattened vowels gave her away, like 'twisty-telled.' She sounded more like a seventy-eight-year-old Eastern European immigrant who had learned to speak English from the radio, and imagined that she was upper-class.

Mindy puckered her mouth in disgust as she reached into Barry's open fly. She scooped out his penis, which was already beginning to shrivel, and stretched it upward as far as she could. Barry made no attempt to stop her. His eyelids were fluttering and blood was running from the side of his mouth.

Picking up the paring-knife, Mindy cut into the side of Barry's penis, slicing through the skin and then the spongy tissue inside. Because the knife was so blunt, she had to saw hard to separate the last stubborn web of skin, but then Barry was left with nothing but a ragged stump. For a few seconds it pumped out blood, but then his veins went into spasm and the bleeding was reduced to a steady leakage which gradually spread across the front of his chinos.

Mindy stood up, holding Barry's severed penis between finger and thumb. She dangled it in front of his face, and said, 'Look, Barry! Look! You won't have any more problems with young girls now! Don't fall asleep, Barry! Look!'

Barry opened his eyes and tried to focus, but Mindy could tell that he didn't understand what he was looking at. Because he had been keeping his hand pressed against his neck, she could see that the flow of blood had subsided, and it gave her a shiver of satisfaction to think that he could well survive this ordeal. Not only would he never be able to assault a young girl again, but he would have to explain to his doctor what had happened to him. What could he possibly say? That his hedge-trimmer had slipped while he was gardening in the nude? That he had decided to castrate himself?

She left the sitting-room and went through to the kitchen. She dropped the paring-knife in the sink and then she opened up the overhead cupboards one after the other until she found a willow-pattern plate on which she could place Barry's penis. She thought that it looked more like a purple-headed slug than a part of a human body, and she could almost imagine it crawling off the plate and painfully trying to hump its way across the draining-board.

She washed the blood off her hands in cold water, and then she opened the fridge to see if she could find some butter. The fridge contained nothing but five tomatoes, a litre of milk and some curled-up luncheon meat. In one of the cupboards, though, she found a half-empty bottle of sunflower oil. She took it out and poured a little into the bottom of one of the saucepans.

When the oil was hot, she tipped Barry's penis into it. It sizzled sharply and shrivelled up even more. She prodded it with the handle of a wooden spoon so that it would crisp evenly all round, and wouldn't burn. It smelled like the pork *katleti* her grandmother used to fry in Serpukhov when she was a girl, only a little younger than Mindy. It brought back so many memories of who she had been before she died, and she could feel her true personality flooding even faster into Mindy's mind. It was like a dam breaking apart, so that Mindy's nine years were swirled helplessly away as her seventy-eight years of pain and hate and suffering came pouring out.

Once Barry's penis was fried, she lifted it out of the saucepan and dropped it back onto the willow-pattern plate. She carried it into the sitting-room and she was pleased to see that Barry now had his eyes open, although he was still lying on his back on the sofa and his face was still so white that it looked as if it had been dusted with flour.

She knelt down beside him again, and held up the plate so that he could see it clearly.

'Please,' he croaked, and coughed up more blood. 'Ambulance. Please.'

'Do you know what this is?' she said.

Barry tried to focus on it, but then he shook his head.

'This is you. This is your *wacek*. And this is your punishment for thinking that you could have your way with me. Your punishment but my reward. You know what we say in Vilnius? *Głód nie jest ciotką. Nie przyniesie ci ciasta.* That means, hunger is not your aunt. It will not bring you a pie. If you want a pie, you have to cook it for yourself.'

'Who are you?' said Barry.

Mindy picked up his penis and smiled at him. 'You poor sad man! What a клоун you are! My name isn't really Varvara, I can assure you of that. And I am not what you think I am. Look into my eyes. Who do you see there, Barry? Who do you see?'

With that, she bit into his glans and started to chew it with her mouth open so that he could watch every bite. It was much more gristly than she had expected, and after she had chewed it for two or three minutes it had lost all of its pork-like flavour. She shifted it from one side of her mouth to the other, and eventually she had to swallow it, stringy and lumpy as it still was.

Barry's eyes closed again, and he started to shudder. Mindy sat beside him for a few minutes longer, but then she put down the plate and stood up. She didn't feel like eating what was left of his penis, even though she was still hungry, and what was the point if he wasn't conscious, and couldn't see her doing it? When her mother had beaten her, when she was a child, she had always made her stand in front of the long mirror in the hallway so that she could witness her own distress.

She reached into the inside pocket of Barry's windcheater and took out his brown plastic wallet. She found two £10 notes, a £5 note and an Aqua credit card, as well as his driving licence and a photograph of a woman with frizzy brown hair and a squint. She took the money and dropped the wallet onto the floor.

'*Do widzenia, głupcze!*' she said to Barry. 'Goodbye, you fool! Have a happy life!'

She went to the front door. She would have to retrieve her shopping from Barry's car, but then she could walk home and start to make her casserole. Her house was only about five minutes away, and from what she had seen from the sitting-room window, the rain seemed to have eased off now.

As she reached up to the handle the doorbell rang. She hesitated for a moment, but then she opened the door a few inches and looked around it to see who was out there. It was a black woman police officer, in uniform.

'Are you all right, young lady?' the WPC asked her.

'Sorry. What do you mean, "all right"?'

'Can I speak to the man who lives in this house?'

'Why?'

'Are you related to him?'

'No.'

'If you're not related to him, can you tell me what you're doing here?'

'I'm just leaving. I have to go home.'

'Where's home?'

'Just round the corner. Nimrod Road.'

'What's your name, love?'

'Mindy.'

'Can you tell me why you're here? One of the neighbours saw you entering the house with the man who lives here, and she was concerned. Is he still here? I'd like to speak to him, if I may.'

'Why?'

'Let me come in, please. I only want to have a few words with him, just to make sure that everything's OK.'

'There's nothing wrong. I have to go home now.'

'Yes, love. But why are you here?'

'He gave me a lift because it was raining.'

'All right. But I still need to talk to him. It won't take long.'

'You can't.'

'Why can't I? He is still here, isn't he?'

'Yes, but you can't speak to him.'

The WPC said, 'I'm sorry, Mindy, but I'm going to have to come inside and talk to him. He's known to us, that's why. I can't tell you what he's done but it gives me reasonable grounds to enter the property and ask him some questions.'

'Don't you need a warrant?'

The WPC frowned at Mindy and said, 'How old are you, love?'

'Nine.'

'Nine? Really? When I was nine I had no idea what a warrant was. But since you're asking, I can enter the property if I have a reasonable suspicion that a breach of the peace may have been committed or is about to be committed and that the offender is the owner or occupier and still on the premises.'

'He didn't touch me, and I have to go home now.'

The WPC said, 'Come on, Mindy, don't make this difficult.'

Mindy said nothing, but looked across at Barry's car, wondering if she could run across and grab her shopping before the WPC could stop her. After a few seconds' thought, though, she decided that she probably couldn't, and in any case the WPC would chase her up the street. She let go of the door and stood with her back against the wall, so that the WPC could step inside.

'Where is he, Mindy?' the WPC asked her.

Mindy nodded towards the sitting-room door.

'Mr Williams!' the WPC called out. 'This is the police! Can you hear me? I'm coming in to have a quick word with you!'

She entered the sitting-room while Mindy remained in the hallway, her back still pressed against the wall, her eyes closed. There was no point in trying to run away. The WPC would only follow her home, and then they would find her father and mother. At least she could say that she had stabbed Barry in self-defence, because he had threatened to strip off her clothes and take pornographic pictures of her. His camera was still there on the dining table, as proof, and she wouldn't be at all surprised if he had a computer with indecent images of young girls on it.

Almost at once, the WPC came back out of the sitting-room, her mouth wide open in shock.

'My God, Mindy, what happened to him? Who did that to him? Was there somebody else here? Or did he do it himself?'

Before Mindy could answer, though, she switched on her R/T and made an urgent call for paramedics and for back-up. Then she said, 'Stay there, love. Please don't move. There's help on the way.' She went back into the sitting-room and Mindy could only assume that she was trying to stem the bleeding from Barry's neck and his severed penis.

She was bored now, and she was still painfully hungry. It was more than a feeling that her stomach was empty. It was a gnawing sensation as if parasites were crawling inside every bone in her skeleton and devouring the marrow. Her pelvis, her thighbones, her ribcage. She felt as if they were inside her skull, too. If she didn't feed them, she didn't know how long she would be able to survive, and she didn't want to go back to being dead.

To distract herself from her hunger, she started singing a nursery rhyme that her mother used to sing.

'There was a gypsy who had a long nose
She was asking how to shorten her nose!
She was told to buy some butter
Put it on her nose, and then
Cut it with an axe!'

28

Jokubas Liepa was bored, too. When Jerry looked at him through the spyhole in his cell door he was elaborately picking his nose and frowning at what he had managed to excavate.

'Right,' Jerry said to the duty officer. 'Let's have him out of there before he starts digging his brains out.'

The duty officer opened the cell door and Jerry stepped inside. 'Mr Liepa?' he said, with exaggerated politeness. 'If you'd be so kind as to accompany me to the interview room, we're all set up to ask you a few pertinent questions.'

'I did not order Herkus to put down his foot,' said Liepa. 'I would not have been such reckless.'

'Well, you can explain that when we formally question you,' Jerry told him. 'Your brief's arrived, so we're all ready to go. Laurence Shipman from Shipman and Bridges. He's not exactly cheap, is he? I bet he charges you a ton just to say good morning.'

PC Jonas was waiting outside the cell, and between them he and Jerry escorted Liepa along to the interview room. DI French was waiting there, talking to an urbane-looking man in a dark blue three-piece suit. He had shiny dyed-black hair, this man, severely combed back, and a large bland face with piggy eyes.

'How are they treating you, Jokubas?' he asked, as soon as Liepa sat down.

'They should not have arrested me,' said Liepa, staring at Jerry. 'I have done nothing wrong whatsoever.'

'I'm afraid that's not the way we see it,' said DI French. 'You and your associates set out on an expedition with the deliberate intention of stealing clothes which had been donated to Cancer Research in their official bags and which therefore had already become the property of Cancer Research. This expedition was carried out under your direction and therefore you were ultimately responsible for the theft of every bag regardless of whether you physically picked it up yourself.'

'I'm sorry to interrupt you,' put in Laurence Shipman. 'My client Mr Liepa was simply being given a lift by one of his acquaintances, and he was not aware when the vehicle stopped momentarily that another of his acquaintances had removed a bag of clothing from the doorstep of a nearby house.'

DI French opened up a plastic folder on the table in front of him. He picked out three sheets of a witness statement that were stapled together and held them up.

'We've already interviewed Mr Herkus Adomaitis who was the driver of the vehicle in which your client was a front-seat passenger. We've also questioned Mr Ignas Gabrys who was in the rear of the vehicle and who took the bag of donated clothing from the said doorstep. Both men independently stated that your client was the instigator and organiser of this expedition to steal Cancer Research bags, and that the sample act of theft of one bag was carried out with his full knowledge and approval.'

Jokubas Liepa banged the table with his fist. 'And you took notice of what those bastards said to you?' he protested. 'They are just stupid people – thick as shit! They can't even read or write! They are not even in UK legally, so of course they will say anything so that you don't send them back to Lithuania! And so what if one bag of old clothes was taken? What was it worth? Hardly nothing at all! This is all ridiculous!'

'My client is absolutely right,' said Laurence Shipman. 'Neither of the two gentlemen you are talking about can be considered to be reliable witnesses. And the value of what Mr Gabrys took was minimal. Come on, detective inspector, let's be realistic. Offenders who steal far more than a bag of old clothing are usually let off with nothing more than a caution.'

'Excuse me, Mr Shipman,' said Jerry. 'This wasn't just a case of nicking some second-hand sweaters. In the process of arresting your client and his monkeys Police Constable Stephen White lost his life, and as you very well know your client has been charged with manslaughter.'

'Well of course I was coming to that,' Laurence Shipman replied. 'My client deeply regrets the death of the officer involved, I can assure you. He can't even begin to express how sorry he is. However the fact remains that he was only a passenger in the vehicle which struck and killed the unfortunate officer, and he is firmly of the belief that the driver's foot slipped on the accelerator pedal and that the officer's death was nothing more than an accident. A regrettable accident – but an accident nonetheless.'

'This is true,' put in Jokubas Liepa. 'How can you accuse me of killing this policeman when I am not even sitting in the driving seat? That is like accusing me of killing somebody who is knocked down by a bus, when I am doing nothing more than sitting up on the top deck reading the paper.'

DI French nodded, as if he agreed with what Jokubas Liepa was saying. But then he picked up the witness statement again, and waved it slowly from side to side.

'The problem is, Mr Liepa, that your driver Mr Adomaitis has said in his sworn statement that you ordered him to put his foot down and run the officer over. Your exact words were, *Eik, nugalėk bustardą!*'

Jokubas Liepa furiously shook his head. 'That is craziness! He's lying to you! He's lying through his dirty teeth! All he wants to do is save his own skin!'

'Well, that's as may be,' said DI French. 'But Mr Gabrys claims that from the back of the van he heard you give the very same order to Mr Adomaitis – *Eik, nugalėk bustardą* – word for word – and as I mentioned the two of them were interviewed independently.'

'My client has nothing further to say at this juncture,' put in Laurence Shipman, very smoothly. 'Obviously he will be challenging the veracity of these two statements. As he suggested, Mr Adomaitis and Mr Gabrys are clearly anxious to mitigate their own culpability for PC White's demise. The two of them may well have had the opportunity to concoct this story between them before they gave you their statements. It certainly sounds like it.'

'And your Lithuanian accent, it's rubbish!' said Jokubas Liepa.

'My apologies, Mr Liepa,' said DI French. 'But you'll have plenty of time to give me some Lithuanian elocution lessons, won't you, while you're waiting to go up in front of the court.'

'I'll be applying for bail, naturally,' said Laurence Shipman, tucking his papers into his £2,500 Berluti briefcase. Jerry noticed that his fingernails were manicured, and shiny.

'Good luck with that, Mr Shipman,' DI French told him, closing his plastic folder.

Jerry was beginning to realise how much DI French was relishing this prosecution. If he had been able to charge Jokubas Liepa with nothing more than stealing charity bags, there would have been only a slim chance of him winning his longed-for promotion. But if he succeeded in getting him sent down for the manslaughter of PC Stephen White, that would be a different matter altogether. He would be regarded as a minor hero – not only in Tooting but the whole of the Met.

*

After Jokubas Liepa had been returned to his cell, Jerry made his way upstairs to the canteen for a cup of tea and a bacon sandwich. He had only just sat down, though, when Jamila came into the canteen and crossed over to his table, looking intensely worried.

'What's up, skip?' he asked her.

'That blue velvet jacket's turned up again.'

'You're having a laugh, aren't you?'

'No. Some young girl's wearing it, or perhaps I should say that the jacket's wearing her. She's stabbed some fellow in the neck and cut his thing off.'

'His thing? You mean his— ?'

Jamila nodded. 'He was lucky not to bleed out. They've taken him to St George's for emergency surgery.'

'When was this?'

'Only about half an hour ago. Willis and Baker went up there, but as soon as Baker saw the jacket she gave me a call.'

235

'Is the girl still wearing it?'

'Yes. And I told Baker to make sure that she didn't take it off.'

The girl behind the canteen counter called out, 'Jerry! Your sarnie's ready!'

Jerry stood up and said, 'Shit. Sorry, love. Duty calls. Castration before bacon. Where are we going?'

'Pretoria Road, if you know where that is,' said Jamila. 'The girl's still there. She won't give her full name and she won't say where she lives.'

'Bloody hell. This day gets crapper by the minute.'

29

Mindy was sitting in the back of an unmarked police car with DC Baker sitting beside her. There were two other patrol cars parked on the opposite side of Pretoria Road, and five uniformed officers standing in Barry's front garden talking to DC Willis, including the black WPC who had first rung the doorbell.

Jerry parked awkwardly behind the unmarked car and he and Jamila climbed out. DC Willis came over and said, 'Hi, Jerry. Definitely looks like another case of your Stuck Clothes Syndrome. But you're not going to believe what she did.'

'Well, she cut off his dinkle, didn't she?'

'She didn't just cut it off, Jerry. The paramedics were looking around for it, in case there was a chance it could be sewn back on. But they could find only half of it, and that half of it was fried.'

'It was what?'

'That's right. Fried. And what's more, it had teeth-marks in it. So I think we have to assume that she was halfway through eating it.'

'Jesus. Thank God I didn't have time for that bacon sarnie.'

'You think it's another case of her clothes being stuck to her,' said Jamila.

'Definitely. We're not one hundred per cent sure she's wearing the same jacket as that Marshall girl, but it fits the description. It's dark blue and it's velvet and it's got braid around the buttons. And most of all she keeps insisting that it was the jacket that stabbed him and cut off his dinkle, and not her.'

'Do we know her name?' asked Jamila.

DC Willis shook his head. 'She won't tell us and she won't give us her home address, either. She's got a bag of shopping which she won't let go of, and that's come from Budgens which is only just up the road there, so I doubt if she lives very far. The neighbour who called us, Mrs Harris, she's the local curtain-twitcher. She knows that Mr Williams is on the sex offenders' register, and so she keeps a beady eye on him. He's twice been convicted of indecent assault of a girl under the age of twelve, and he still has a month left to run of a six months' suspended sentence.'

'What did the paramedics say about his injuries?'

'Life-changing but not life-threatening. Once he's out of surgery we should be able to talk to him. I've bagged up the knife that the girl must have used to stab him, and the CSEs should be here in a minute. They'll be able to take dabs off the saucepan in the kitchen and the plate that she used to serve up his willy.'

Jamila said, 'Let's go and talk to her. We need to find out where she found that jacket and we also need to know if it's really stuck to her, like it was with Sophie Marshall.'

She went over to the unmarked car and tapped on the window. DC Baker climbed out and said, 'I've been asking her all kinds of questions but she hasn't said a word.'

'OK. Let me try,' said Jamila. 'Jerry, do you want to come and sit in the front?'

She sat down in the back seat next to Mindy while Jerry opened the door and sat in the front passenger seat.

'You don't have to be frightened,' Jamila told Mindy. 'My name is Jamila and this is Jerry and both of us are here to help you. We just need to know why you had to stab that man. Did he try to hurt you?'

Mindy didn't answer for almost ten seconds. Then, lowering her eyelashes and with her fingers laced together as if she were praying, she said, in a whisper, 'It wasn't me who stabbed him.'

'If it wasn't you, then who was it? There was nobody else in the house, was there?'

'Yes.'

'There was somebody else there? Who was it? Do you know?'

'Varvara.'

'Varvara? What kind of a name is that?'

'I don't know.'

'But it was a woman?'

'Yes.'

'And what are you saying? That this Varvara did the stabbing?'

'Yes.'

'So where is she now? Did she run away?'

'No. She's still here. But she's asleep.'

'She's still here? Where? I'm not sure I understand what you mean.'

Mindy turned to Jamila and looked at her steadily.

'Can't you see her? She's inside me. She's asleep and she's all bunched up but she's inside me.'

Jamila glanced at Jerry, and Jerry said, 'Where did you get that jacket, darling?'

Mindy leaned forward and spoke so softly that Jerry and Jamila could hardly hear her. 'I found it in the park.'

'Why are you whispering?' asked Jamila.

'Because I don't want to wake up Varvara. She'll be angry if she hears me talking to you.'

'So why don't you tell us your name?' said Jerry.

Mindy hesitated, and then she spelled it out for them. 'M – I – N – D – Y.'

'All right,' said Jerry. 'And can you tell us where you live?'

Mindy closed her eyes, as if she were making sure that the presence that she could feel inside her was still unconscious. Then she spelled out her address in Nimrod Road.

'Nimrod Road, OK,' said Jerry. 'And that's where you live with your mum and dad?'

Mindy shook her head. 'No,' she whispered. 'Not any more.'

'What do you mean, "not any more"?'

Mindy's eyes filled with tears, and her mouth turned down with grief.

'They're dead!' she blurted out. 'She killed them! Varvara killed them! And I'm supposed to go home and cook them!'

As soon as she had said that, she jolted, and her head jerked back and hit the seat. She lifted both of her hands like claws and dragged the two sides of her jacket even more tightly together. Her eyes rolled back in her head so that only the whites showed, and she bared her teeth in a grimace that would have been laughable if she hadn't been convulsing so

240

violently and her feet hadn't started drumming on the floor like a child in a terrible tantrum.

'You're not listening to that stupid girl, are you?' she hissed at them. 'What can a girl like that know about death and pain and sickness? How can a young girl understand what it is to die? *Kormit – yedinstvennyy sposob vernut'sya k zhizni!*'

Once she had spat out those words, she stopped convulsing. Her head dropped forward and she tilted sideways against the car door.

Jamila shook her and said, 'Mindy? Mindy? Can you hear me, Mindy?'

Mindy didn't respond, but her chest was still rising and falling, and when Jamila touched her fingertips against her neck to check her pulse, she nodded to Jerry that it felt quite normal.

'Jean can take her straight to hospital,' she said. 'The sooner we get this jacket off her the better. I'll call Dr Fuller and make sure that he's available.'

Jerry climbed out of the car and beckoned to DC Baker and to one of the uniformed officers. When Jamila had finished speaking on her iPhone to Dr Fuller's secretary, she climbed out, too. Mindy remained slumped against the door, breathing harshly with her mouth open, and dribbling.

'Straight to A&E,' said Jamila. 'But make sure they know that Dr Fuller's coming in specially to take care of her. And tell them in no circumstances to try to take any of her clothes off until he gets there.'

DC Baker and the uniformed officer drove off with Mindy to St George's, leaving Jerry and Jamila standing on the pavement.

'Bloody hell,' said Jerry. 'What she was shouting, that sounded like Polish. Something like that, anyway. I'm not very hot on my Eastern European languages.'

'Yes, Polish,' Jamila told him. 'One of my uncles had a Polish business colleague. He kept trying to touch me up and I hated him. But – there's no prize for guessing where we're going now. If Mindy had been lying when she told us that her parents were dead, I would have seen it in her eyes.'

Jerry held out his hand and looked up at the clouds. It had started raining again. 'Do you know what, skip?' he told her. 'This has gone way beyond a joke now. How the hell can we arrest second-hand clothes?'

30

The front-door lock of the house on Nimrod Road was only a simple Yale, and Jerry was able to open it with his skeleton key. As soon as they had stepped into the hallway, they knew for certain that Mindy had been telling the truth about her parents. The house was thick with the smell of death – that sweet, ripe, faecal odour that filled their lungs every time they breathed in.

'Jesus. Forgot the Vick's again,' said Jerry, pressing the back of his hand against his nose and mouth.

They looked into the living-room. The curtains were drawn and it was dark and chilly in there. A copy of the *Daily Mail* was lying on the couch so Jerry went over and checked the date.

'Blimey, only yesterday's. If I was going by the Jimmy, I'd have guessed they'd been dead for at least three days.'

They went through to the kitchen. The pale green venetian blinds were closed and one of the taps was dripping. On the counter beside the hob there was a large orange casserole dish, with its lid off, and a sharp kitchen knife lying beside it.

Jamila said, 'Do you see those? Are you thinking what I'm thinking?'

'Don't,' said Jerry. 'I'm feeling pukish enough already.'

'Well, me too. But come on. The parents must be in one of the bedrooms.'

Jerry went back out into the hallway and started to mount the stairs. 'Do you know something? My old dad wanted me to join him in his plumbing business.'

'Really?' said Jamila. 'Why didn't you?'

'I told him, "I'm not spending my life unblocking other people's stinky toilets." Gordon Bennett, if only I'd known.'

The first bedroom at the top of the stairs was Mindy's. Her bed was unmade, with a crumpled *Frozen* duvet cover and large posters on the walls of Justin Bieber and Harry Styles, each with felt-tip kisses drawn around their heads, like a cloud of black moths. Mindy's laptop was sitting on her desk, still open, and above her desk there was a shelf crammed with books. Jamila quickly checked the titles, to see if any of them were subversive or inappropriate for a nine-year-old, but they were all Harry Potter and Jacqueline Wilson.

'Oh, well, here goes nothing,' said Jerry, and pushed open the door to the parents' bedroom.

The smell was so rank that Jamila retched. She shook her head and said 'Sorry.'

Mindy's mother and father were lying side by side on the bed. Their blood-soaked sheets and duvet had been dragged off them and lay in a heap at the foot of the bed. Her father's pyjama jacket had been unbuttoned to expose his chest, and his trousers had been pulled down to his knees. Her mother's nightgown was bunched up around her neck. Scores of transverse slices had been cut into their stomachs and their thighs, as if somebody had been playing mad games of noughts-and-crosses all over them with a sharp knife. They smelled so foul because in several places their abdomens had been pierced right through, which allowed the gases to escape from their putrefying intestines. Her mother's right breast had been partially severed, so that its spongy tissue hung to one side, exposing a white glint of ribs. Beneath her father's flaccid penis there was nothing but a soggy cavity.

Jerry and Jamila stood on opposite sides of the bed looking down at this carnage in silence. Eventually, with her hand covering her face, Jamila said, 'I have seen this kind of mutilation before, when a child has murdered its parents. They castrate the father, in denial of where they first came from, and they cut off the mother's breast, in denial of having been nurtured.'

'Yes, but this isn't just some kid taking it out on her parents, is it?' said Jerry. 'This is the same as all the others, isn't it, trying to make out they're possessed? "It wasn't me, it was my coat, or my jacket, or my sweater." And this Mindy girl, she was saying that there was someone else inside her.'

Jamila nodded. 'Varvara, whoever Varvara might be.'

'And all this cooking and eating – what's that all about? Zombies like a bit of human flesh for dinner, don't they, like in *Night of the Living Dead* or whatever. But zombies don't fry their victims before they eat them, do they? Apart from that zombies are not only dead, they're not real, either.'

'Well, there have been cases of cannibalism when victims have been cooked,' said Jamila. 'There was that German who advertised for a volunteer who actually wanted to be eaten, do you remember that? He ate about twenty kilos of some young man, sautéed in olive oil and garlic, and he even set the table with his best cutlery and candles and everything.

And my father told me about several isolated incidents in Pakistan, but it was mostly children who were eaten, because their parents were starving.'

'Isolated incidents, exactly,' said Jerry. 'But like we've agreed, this is a bleeding epidemic.'

He quickly took several photographs with his iPhone and then they left the bedroom and went back down to the living-room. Jerry called in to DI Saunders, and caught him just before he was going out to lunch.

'How's it all going?' asked DI Saunders. 'You can fill me in later – I'll be back for a media conference at four.'

'Sorry, guv. You're not going to like any of this,' said Jerry. He told him about Mindy and Barry, and how they had found Mindy's dead parents. When he had finished describing the condition of their bodies there was a long silence from DI Saunders – so long that Jerry thought that he might have been cut off.

'Bugger,' said DI Saunders, at last. Then, even more emphatically, 'Bugger.' Then, very testily, 'All right, Jerry. I'll get things organised at this end and then I'll come up to see for myself. But if any media come sniffing around, don't say a word to them, right? I still haven't worked out how we're going to present this publicly without causing widescale panic.'

'OK, guv. Got you.'

Jerry and Jamila went outside and stood by the front gate. It was raining, but at least the air smelled like wet privet and car exhaust, and not of decomposing bodies. Jerry wished that he hadn't given up smoking. A cigarette would have helped to calm him down, and it would have blotted out the smell and the taste of death. He could almost believe that he had been chewing human flesh himself.

Jamila said, 'Do you know something, I have no confidence at all now that Dr Fuller will be able to give us all the answers. Or even half the answers.'

'The trouble is, skip, who the hell can?' Jerry asked her. 'Who's an expert on clothes that have a life of their own?'

Jerry hadn't completely closed the front door behind them, but out of the corner of his eye he became aware that it was gradually shuddering open again. He turned around, thinking that the breeze must be blowing it, but with a bang it was suddenly flung wide. A black child-like figure came bursting out, its arms flapping, turning immediately to the left and running across the small York stone garden.

Jerry shouted out, 'Hoi! You! Stop!' and went after it.

The figure leapt over the low brick wall that separated Mindy's house from the house next door, and dodged around the silver estate car that was parked in their driveway. It started to run down the road, still flapping its arms, and the way it ran was extraordinary, as if it were being blown by a gale-force wind. Its coat-tails billowed, and its belt waved free, and as Jerry began to catch up with it, he realised that it had no legs. It was flying, not running, and when he was nearly close enough to reach out and seize it, he saw that it had no head, either.

It was nothing but a black raincoat, tumbling through the air by itself.

Jerry stumbled and tripped himself up and almost fell over, stupefied and shocked by the weirdness of chasing an empty raincoat down the street. But he felt angry, too. *It's a fucking raincoat, that's all, with nobody inside it, and I'm running after it like a total twat.*

After a hundred metres his heart was thumping and he was gasping for breath, but he began to gain on the raincoat, and at last he managed to reach out and snatch its collar. He thought that he would simply be able to shake it and fold it up, but it twisted violently around and flailed at him with both of its arms. He staggered back and fell off the kerb into the road, jarring his shoulder. The raincoat carried on attacking him as if it were hysterical with rage, lashing at his face with its buckled cuffs and beating at him with its coat-tails as if they were wings. He felt as if he were being attacked by a furious black swan.

'Skip!' he shouted out. 'For Christ's sake, skip! Jamila!'

But Jamila was already running towards him, and she was carrying a small black wrought-iron gate which she must have lifted off its hinges from one of the houses along the street. As soon as she reached him, she lifted the gate in both hands and beat it down on the raincoat's back, again and again. An elderly woman on the opposite side of the road stood watching her with her mouth wide open.

Jamila hit the raincoat eight or nine times, and once she hit Jerry's knuckles, too, and he shouted out, 'Ow! Shit!'

The raincoat must have been able to feel her beating it, because it jolted with every blow as if there were somebody inside it. Jamila swung the gate at an angle and hit it as hard as she could across the shoulders, first left and then right, and after the second blow it sagged. Its sleeves fell flat, and it collapsed.

Jerry threw the raincoat onto the ground and climbed back to his feet. He gave the raincoat a kick, and then another, but it lay limp and wet on the tarmac and showed no more signs of stirring into life. Jamila propped the gate against the nearest garden wall. She looked as shocked as Jerry felt, and she was breathing hard, too.

'This is insane,' Jerry panted. 'This is just fucking insane. But I owe you one, skip. I really owe you one. I mean, that was inspired. "Detective sergeant uses wrought-iron gate to kill raincoat." That's going to be front-page news.'

'No, it's not,' said Jamila. 'We're not going to tell anybody, Jerry, because it's madness. What do you think the media would say? They'd make out that we'd been smoking something.'

Jerry gave the raincoat another prod with his toecap, but it still didn't move.

'Yes, well, you're probably right. In any case Smiley would go apeshit. He's already tearing his hair out about how to present this to the press – and to the commissioner. He wouldn't want her to think that he was heading up an operation run by a bunch of loonies.'

'Let's get this coat back to the house,' said Jamila. 'I'd better put this gate back, too, before I arrest myself for vandalism.'

Jerry cautiously bent down and took hold of the raincoat's sleeve. He was sure that he felt it flinch, but he dragged it along the wet pavement behind him, and it didn't struggle or try to tug itself away from him.

When they got back to Mindy's parents' house, he pulled it in through the front door, intending to shut it in the cupboard under the stairs. He had only taken one step inside, though, when he looked up at the staircase and stopped dead.

'Skip,' he said, quietly.

Jamila came through the door behind him.

'*Bismillah*,' she whispered.

From top to bottom, the staircase was crowded with clothes – dresses, sweaters, jackets and trousers. But they hadn't just been strewn down the stairs, they were crawling down it, as if they were alive. A green turtle-neck sweater had already made its way down as far as the hallway, and it reached out with one of its sleeves for Jamila's ankle.

Without a word, Jerry and Jamila backed quickly out of the front door and into the porch. Jerry hesitated for two or three seconds, and then he tossed the black raincoat back inside, and slammed the door.

'It's not possible,' said Jerry, shaking his head. 'I'm asleep, and this is a dream. Well – no it's not, it's a nightmare.'

'It is possible,' Jamila told him. She was clenching her fists and her voice was very level, but Jerry could tell that she was shocked and upset. 'It is possible in the same way that all spirits are possible.'

'I don't get you.'

Jamila looked up at him. He had yet to see her expression so serious. 'Just because people in the West have lost their belief in their God, and everything that cannot be explained by science, that doesn't mean for a moment that they no longer exist. I believe that ghosts exist, Jerry, and I believe that evil spirits exist, and that they can possess anything and everything – not only human beings. They can hide themselves inside animals, as any dog or cat owner will tell you. And they can hide themselves inside inanimate objects, too. Where do you think the story of Aladdin and the magic lamp came from?'

'Skip, these are clothes. These are Levi jeans and Marks & Spencer jumpers.'

'It makes no difference, Jerry. I didn't want to believe this, either, but we have to face reality. There is an infection spreading around this area, like Asian flu, or Ebola. I don't know what Dr Fuller has found out, but I'm convinced now that this infection is spiritual, rather than viral.'

'So you reckon these clothes have got infected with spirits, and when people put them on, the spirits infect them, too.'

'Of course I have no way of telling for certain, but what other explanation can there be?'

'I don't know,' said Jerry. 'Maybe the Russians are putting something in our water and we're all hallucinating.'

He looked back at the front door, wondering what was going on behind it. What would happen to those clothes if they couldn't escape from the house? Would the spirits that possessed them eventually leave them, or fade away, or die? Or would they remain dormant, waiting for some unsuspecting victim to put them on, so that they could come to life again?

'It's urgent that we find somebody who has knowledge about this sort of thing,' said Jamila. 'DI Saunders thought he was joking when he talked about calling in Father Karras. But that's the kind of person we need.'

'An exorcist?'

'How do I know? These spirits may have nothing to do with Christianity or Islam or any other religion. Viruses can't be exorcised by priests, or shamans, or mullahs. Maybe this infection can't be cured by prayer or holy water, either.'

31

Eight uniformed officers arrived first, in three patrol cars, including Sergeant Bristow. They had just started to cordon off the front of the house when two white vans from the forensic unit turned up, and after ten minutes more, DI Saunders appeared, in an unmarked dark blue Vauxhall Insignia. He was wearing full dress uniform, and as he climbed out of the car he put on his cap. The lunch that he had been forced to cancel had clearly been with somebody important.

Jerry and Jamila were standing side by side in the porch and so far they hadn't let anybody into the house.

'What's the SP?' Sergeant Bristow asked them.

'The crime scene's a bit unusual, that's all, skip, that's all,' said Jerry. 'It could be hazardous and we want DI Saunders to give us the thumbs-up before we go in again.'

'What do you mean, "unusual"?'

'What went on at the nick with that Nelson bloke and his runaway sweater – it's similar to that. Only worse.'

'You're not pulling my leg, are you?'

'Yes, of course I am. That's why we're standing out here soaked to the skin and freezing our arses off waiting for Smiley to show up. Oh look – here he is now.'

DI Saunders manoeuvred his way through the small crowd of uniformed officers and forensic experts and came up to the front door.

Without any preamble, he said, 'What's the problem? What are you all doing out here?'

'There's been a development, sir, since DC Pardoe called you,' said Jamila.

'What kind of development?'

Jamila explained that Mindy's parents' clothes appeared to have made their way downstairs by themselves, in the same way that David Nelson's sweater had crawled along the corridor at the station. She didn't tell him about the raincoat, and how Jerry had run after it down the road. She had decided that she would leave that until later, when they had contained this situation, and he was calmer.

'So there's clothing inside, all over the floor?' asked DI Saunders.

'Yes, sir.'

'And it didn't occur to you that there might be somebody else in the house, apart from the deceased, who might have slung it all around while you were outside?'

'No, sir.'

'Did you search every room, apart from the parents' bedroom?'

'Only Mindy's, sir.'

'So there could have been somebody hiding in another room and you wouldn't have known?'

'That's possible, sir, except that I actually saw some of the clothing move by itself. A sweater tried to touch my foot.'

DI Saunders took off his cap and stared into it as if he expected it to be filled with raffle tickets. 'A sweater tried to touch your foot,' he repeated.

'Yes, sir.'

'Well, we have officers here now with batons and Tasers and at least two of them are armed. I think they'll be more than a match for a few rogue woollies.'

'Whatever you decide, sir.'

'Two people have been murdered on these premises, DS Patel, so I decide that we gain access as a matter of urgency and investigate the crime scene.'

Jerry took out his skeleton key again and unlocked the front door. He pushed it wide open and they all looked inside. The clothes were still there, piled up on the floor and halfway down the stairs. None of the coats or jackets or sweaters appeared to be moving, although Jerry noticed that the raincoat was lying by the kitchen door, much further away than he had thrown it.

DI Saunders stepped into the hallway and sniffed. 'How long deceased, did you say?'

'Not even twenty-four hours, guv,' said Jerry. 'But they've both suffered penetrative wounds to the abdomen, apart from all their other injuries. Hence the Dame Judy.'

DI Saunders bent down and picked up the green sweater that had reached out for Jamila's ankle. He turned it this way and that, and shook it, and then he dropped it again. Next, he picked up a brown herringbone jacket from the stairs, and held that up, too.

'Well, Jerry, however they got here, there's not much life in them now, is there?'

'No, guv. Not unless they're playing dead.'

DI Saunders didn't answer that. Instead, he said, 'All right, then, let's take a look at the victims. Sergeant Bristow! The CSEs can come in now. Tell them to start by taking pictures of all of these clothes.'

With that, he mounted the stairs, taking care not to step on too many of the trousers and shirts and sweaters that had tumbled down them. Jamila raised her hand and was about to remind him that he ought to be wearing Tyvek booties, but then she decided to leave it. Considering the mood he was in, there was no future in antagonising him even further.

Jerry looked at her and pulled a face. Up until today, DI Saunders seemed to have accepted that some kind of highly unusual virus had infected the clothes that had been clinging to their four murder suspects, as well as Samira Wazir and the drug-addict who had been arrested for importuning. But now Jerry had the distinct impression that he was trying to dismiss any suggestion that anything weird was going on. Perhaps he was under pressure from his senior investigating officer, his SIO. More likely he was afraid of ridicule in the media, and jeopardising his chances of being promoted to DCI. He didn't want to end up stagnating, like DI French, with nothing to look forward to except an early retirement.

Jamila shrugged and said, 'The evidence is all here, Jerry. He'll have to believe it.'

'Oh, I think he does,' said Jerry. 'He just doesn't want to face up to it, any more than we do. That raincoat didn't really run down the road on its own, did it? A gust of wind blew it, that's all.'

'Come on,' said Jamila, and started to climb up the stairs. Jerry followed her.

Jamila was only halfway up when they heard DI Saunders shout out, 'Holy Christ! Get off me!' He sounded hysterical.

They hurried up the rest of the stairs, along the corridor, and into the parents' bedroom.

Jerry said, 'Jesus.'

DI Saunders was sprawled on his back on the bloodstained bed. Mindy's father was kneeling on the bed next to him, gripping his wrists and holding him down, while her mother was leaning over him, wrenching at the front of his uniform jacket and trying to bite his face.

Jerry was so stunned that he simply stood in the doorway for a second, not knowing what he could do. These two people had been murdered, he had seen them both lying dead, and yet they were attacking DI Saunders with such ferocity that he couldn't fight himself free.

'For Christ's sake, Jerry, get them off me!' DI Saunders screamed at him.

Jamila turned around and shouted, 'Sergeant Bristow! Sergeant Bristow! We need back-up here, urgently!'

Jerry crossed the bedroom to the dressing-table and picked up the heavy padded stool that was tucked underneath it. He lifted it up and hit Mindy's mother on the back of the head with it, hard. She dropped sideways, and rolled off the bed onto the floor, but she was clenching DI Saunders' left earlobe between her teeth, and as she fell she tore part of it away. Blood squirted down the side of his neck and he screamed out, 'Fuck!'

Jerry lifted the stool again and hit Mindy's father on the shoulder. Mindy's father lurched to the left, but he kept his hold on DI Saunders' wrists. A thin yellow string of mucus was swinging from his lips.

Jerry hit him again, much harder, on the side of his head, which was already dented from the hammer-blows that Mindy had given him. This time he toppled onto the floor, his arms and his legs lifted like a dog that has fallen onto its back.

DI Saunders heaved himself up off the bed, one hand clamped against his ear. Three of the buttons had been torn from his uniform jacket and it was spattered with blood. Jerry gave him a hand to get up onto his feet, and he stood there dazed, clearly unable to grasp what had just happened to him.

Mindy's father was beginning to pick himself up from the floor, and Mindy's mother was already kneeling up on the opposite side of the bed, almost as if she were praying. Their faces were both bloated and bruised, and her father's forehead and nose were so badly smashed in that he looked as if he were wearing a Halloween mask. Their eyes were open, although they had turned that dark grey oxidised colour that pathologists call tache noire, so it was difficult to tell what they were looking at, or even if they could see at all.

Mindy's father was still wearing his pyjama jacket, although his trousers had now fallen down round his ankles, but Jerry could see that the sleeves of a dark brown sweater were now wrapped at least twice around his neck, with the rest of the sweater covering his shoulders.

He looked across at Mindy's mother, whose bloodstained nightgown had dropped down to cover her. Twisted around her neck were the sleeves of a long black evening-dress – knotted so tightly that they had disappeared between the gaping lips of the wound where Mindy had first slashed her. If she had been alive, she would have been strangled.

Jerry backed away, ushering DI Saunders out of the door. He didn't know if he ought to order Mindy's father and mother to stay where they were, or lie back down on the bed. What do you say to two corpses who have come to life? 'Go back to being dead or you're under arrest?' And in any case, would they be able to hear him?

Mindy's father shuffled closer, half-shackled by his pyjama trousers, and reached out towards Jerry with both hands, like a parody of a zombie. That made Jerry's mind up for him. He slammed the bedroom door shut, keeping a firm grip on the handle, and turned to DI Saunders.

'What the hell do we do now?' he asked. As he did so, two burly officers reached the top of the stairs and came jostling along the corridor in body armour. One of them had a Taser pistol attached to his belt and the other was carrying a Heckler & Koch submachine gun.

DI Saunders had taken out his folded handkerchief and was holding it against his ear. 'I have no idea. They're dead already, although they bloody well didn't feel like it. Any suggestions?'

Jerry said, 'Well – the man has a sweater wrapped around his neck, and the woman has a dress wrapped around hers. Neither the sweater nor the dress were present when we first came up and took a look at their bodies. I reckon that's what brought them back to life.'

He paused, and repeated, 'The sweater, and the dress,' just in case DI Saunders hadn't understood what he meant.

He might as well have been talking gibberish, because DI Saunders could only stare back at him, and the two armed officers turned to each other and both of them looked totally baffled.

'I agree with DC Pardoe, sir,' said Jamila. 'It seems like all of the clothing in this house could have been infected with something similar to Samira Wazir's coat and David Nelson's sweater and Sophie Marshall's jacket. We've already seen how it can take over living people. Perhaps it can take over dead people, too. Sophie Marshall bit my hand and this woman has just bitten your ear. You can't say that there isn't a parallel.'

Jerry said, 'What I'm suggesting is, we Taser them, and take that sweater and that dress off of them while they're still stunned.'

'They're dead,' said DI Saunders.

'I know, guv. But if we take the sweater and the dress off of them, maybe they'll go back to being dead.'

'Well, that would suit me,' said DI Saunders. 'I'll have to go for a tetanus jab after this. Not to mention a bloody HIV test. I might even get sepsis, and lose my whole bloody ear.'

At that moment, there was a loud hammering on the other side of the bedroom door.

'I think they want out,' said Jerry.

'All right,' said DI Saunders. 'Open up and shock them.'

The officer with the Taser stepped forward and stood next to Jerry, while the officer with the submachine gun stayed close behind him. DI Saunders and Jamila retreated a little way back down the corridor.

'OK – ready?' asked Jerry. 'Three – two – one – and go!'

He pushed open the bedroom door. It collided with Mindy's father, who must have been standing right behind it, and so he took a step back and then slammed his whole weight against it. Mindy's father was sent tottering backwards so that he sat down promptly on the end of the bed, but almost at once he stood up again. Mindy's mother had been staring at her reflection in the mirrored door of the wardrobe, but now she turned around.

'God almighty – what the hell's happened to them?' said the officer with the Taser. 'They look like they need a bus, not a Taser.'

'Just shock them, all right?' called out DI Saunders. 'Take the man out first.'

'What, no warning?'

'Do it, for Christ's sake!'

The officer pointed his Taser at Mindy's father, and fired. With a sharp snap, the two barbed electrodes flew out and hit him in the cross-hatched scabs on his chest, trailing their conductive wires behind them. He was shocked by fifty thousand volts, more than enough to give him unbearable pain and violent muscular contractions, and knock him to the floor.

Instead, he gave nothing more than a complicated shudder, his arms flapping up and down dismissively, like a chicken's wings. Then he continued walking forward, with the wires still dangling from his chest.

'What the hell's wrong?' demanded DI Saunders. 'Isn't that bloody thing charged up enough?'

'I gave him maximum voltage, sir!' said the Taser officer.

'It must be because he's dead,' said Jerry. 'The both of them are. You can't shock them because there's nothing to shock. No nervous system. No heartbeat. Nothing.'

'You mean they're really dead?' the Taser officer asked him. 'I thought you meant that they'd been playing dead. How can they be dead?'

'Don't ask me, but look at the state of them. The woman's had her throat cut so deep her head's just about to fall off. And all that blobby grey stuff behind the bloke's right ear, that's his brains.'

'Tell the both of them to lie on the floor,' said DI Saunders. He sounded angry now. 'Tell them if they don't, we'll have to shoot them.'

Mindy's father had nearly reached the doorway now, with

her mother close behind him. If Jerry had taken two steps forward he could have laid his hand on his shoulder and told him that he was arresting him. Mindy's father was chattering his shattered teeth together as if he couldn't wait to take a bite out of Jerry's face, and then he belched. He wasn't trying to speak. He couldn't, because his lungs had no air in them. It was only foul-smelling gas.

'OK – stop!' Jerry told him, although he felt absurd saying it. 'Stop right where you are and lie face-down on the floor, otherwise we may have to shoot you.'

'That'll do,' said DI Saunders. 'I didn't want to open fire without a formal caution.'

He stepped back and said to the officer with the submachine gun, 'Take them down. Go for the legs. That should do it.'

'They're not armed, sir,' the officer protested. 'They're not actually presenting any kind of imminent threat. If I shoot them, that'll be murder.'

'You can't murder them, son, because they're already dead. Haven't you been listening? Can't you see that for yourself?'

'Yes, but—'

'They're dead,' DI Saunders repeated. 'They may be walking and I have no idea how or why but let's just put them out of their misery, shall we? And that's an order.'

'Yes, sir,' said the firearms officer. 'You'd best get back a bit, in case of ricochets.'

Jerry and Jamila and DI Saunders retreated along the landing while the firearms officer cocked his submachine gun. As they reached the top of the staircase, the crime scene manager was coming up, in his white Tyvek suit, carrying a camera.

'OK to process the crime scene now, sir?' he asked.

DI Saunders didn't even look at him. 'Not yet. And if you could clear your people out of the house for a while, I'd appreciate it. We'll call you back in when we're ready.'

'Oh, really? All right, sir – but I have to say that we're a little pushed for time. Three of my team are pretty close to the end of their shift.'

'I said – we'll call you back in when we're ready.'

The CSE started to go back downstairs. As he did so, the firearms officer came backing out of the bedroom doorway, followed by Mindy's father and mother.

Jamila leaned close to Jerry and said, 'This is so wrong. This is going to give me sleepless nights for the rest of my life.'

The firearms officer slowly retreated down the corridor, which allowed Mindy's father and mother to come out of the bedroom and stand facing him, side by side. He was obviously reluctant to open fire. The two of them may have looked bloodied and grotesque, sticking out their blackened tongues and snapping their teeth, but they looked pathetic, too, like two circus clowns who had wandered into the lion's cage by mistake, and been savagely mauled.

'Do we have to do this, sir?' Jamila asked DI Saunders.

'What? Have you got any other suggestions?' said DI Saunders. 'They can't be Tasered, so what else are we going to do with them? Lock them up? They haven't committed any serious crime – not yet, anyway, apart from biting half my bloody ear off. Send them to hospital? They're dead, so what would be the point of that? Besides, they attacked me like a couple of mad dogs, and what do you do with mad dogs?'

Mindy's father suddenly let out a cackling sound, like somebody being violently sick, and stalked towards the firearms officer, flailing his arms. With a deafening bang, the officer opened fire, hitting him in the chest.

Mindy's father was thrown backwards against the wall, but after only a moment's hesitation he launched himself at the firearms officer a second time. The officer shot him again, twice in the chest and once in the stomach, and again he staggered backwards, but yet again he came teetering forward, his fists windmilling like a boxer.

'The legs!' shouted DI Saunders. 'I told you to go for the legs!'

The firearms officer took another step back and then shot Mindy's father in both kneecaps. Mindy's father lurched forward, still trying to walk, but then his splintered shinbones pierced through the skin and he collapsed. He lay on the floor twitching and beating his fist against the skirting-board in frustration.

Now Mindy's mother rushed at the firearms officer, silently, but with a grim expression on her face. The officer shot her in the right thigh, and then the left, and then he pointed his submachine gun downwards and shot her in the right ankle, which almost blasted her foot off. She limped towards him, with her foot bent to one side, but then she too tumbled to the floor and lay beside her husband, face-down, slapping the carpet in the same futile way that he was beating his fist.

The corridor was filled with acrid smoke, and Jerry had to wiggle his fingertips in his ears to clear his hearing. The firearms officer was reloading with another clip.

DI Saunders said, 'OK. If you're right about that sweater and that dress, let's have them off them, shall we?'

'I'll do it,' said Jerry, taking his clasp knife out of his windcheater pocket and clicking it open. He walked back along the corridor and knelt down beside Mindy's father. Her mother twisted her head around to stare at him with those eerie dark grey eyes, and she peeled her lips back in a hostile snarl, but she was too damaged to get up and attack him.

'Sorry about this, mate,' Jerry told Mindy's father, although he had no idea if he could hear him, or even if it was Mindy's father that he was talking to.

He took hold of the sleeves of the dark brown sweater that were wrapped around Mindy's father's neck, and quickly cut into them. They felt soft and crunchy, like wool, but at the same time he was sure he detected a muscular reflex, as if he were cutting into somebody's wrists. Mindy's father kept jolting his head from side to side, but the only sound that came out of his mouth was the faint whistling of gas from his putrefying stomach.

Jerry sliced right through the sleeves, but when he tried to pull them away from Mindy's father's neck, they clung on tight. He took hold of the back of the sweater and yanked it hard, again and again, but it was like trying to pull an octopus away from the piling of a pier.

'Having trouble there, Jerry?' called out DI Saunders.

'Just a bit,' Jerry grunted. He pulled at the sweater again, even harder. There was a tearing sound, and he managed to lift seven or eight centimetres away from Mindy's father's right shoulder, but the rest of the sweater still refused to come free. It was stuck to his skin just like Mindy's jacket and all of the other clothes had been stuck, its dark brown fibres penetrating his pores.

Jamila came up behind Jerry and laid her hand on his shoulder. 'Why not cut it up into little bits?' she suggested.

'What?'

'Perhaps it was only another of her stories, but my grandmother said that when a jinn tried to get into their house one night, my grandfather slammed the door on it, so that it was caught halfway in and halfway out. The half of the jinn that was inside his house, he chopped up with shears and threw them on the fire.'

'Your granny should have been locked up for telling you stuff like that,' said Jerry. All the same, he grasped the sweater in his left fist and started to rip it apart with his clasp knife.

Gradually, as he shredded it up into rags, he could feel its grip on Mindy's father began to weaken. Its sleeves fell away from his neck, and then the rest of it dropped off his shoulders. His dark grey eyes remained open, but now he lay motionless.

'How about that, it worked,' said Jerry. Just to make sure, he pushed Mindy's father with the heel of his hand, so that his body joggled lifelessly against the skirting-board. 'No, he's proper dead now. Like, dead dead.'

Mindy's mother was still feebly slapping her hand on the carpet, so Jerry turned his attention to her, and the long black dress that looked as if it were choking her. Instead of trying to cut through the sleeves that were wound so tightly around her throat, he started to slash at the bodice and the skirts. He felt the dress ripple, like a wave coming in, but he carried on slashing at it until he had reduced it to ribbons, which he then he tore apart with his hands. For almost half a minute, there was no sound in the corridor but the tearing of cotton, while Jamila and DI Saunders and the two armed officers watched Jerry as if they were mesmerised.

He could see it on their faces: *This can't be happening. This can't be real. But I'm here and I'm a witness and it is.*

When the dress was ripped to shreds, the black sleeves slithered away from Mindy's mother's neck as if they were two cowardly snakes. Her hand now lay flat against the carpet, and her dark grey eyes stared at nothing but her dead husband's shoulder.

Jerry stood up and folded away his clasp knife. He felt numb – not just because the whole scenario had been so surreal, but because he felt as if he had taken two lives.

DI Saunders came along the corridor now and looked down at the bodies.

'They're completely dead now?' he said. 'One hundred per cent? I don't want them jumping up and trying to take another bite out of me.'

'Both of them were completely dead before,' said Jamila. 'It was their clothes that brought them back to life. What we have to ask ourselves is who were their clothes possessed by? They could have been second-hand, or from charity shops, like the others, or else—'

'Or else what?'

'I don't know. We have no way of telling for sure, do we, until Dr Fuller has the chance to test them for DNA? But supposing these clothes weren't second-hand? Supposing this sweater and this dress were possessed by Mindy's parents themselves? What if they were trying to reanimate their own dead bodies?'

'You really think it was them?' said DI Saunders. He was still dabbing his blood-soaked handkerchief against the side of his head. 'I wouldn't have thought they were that type of people. You know – the type to bite half your bloody ear off. Too middle-class, if you ask me, and they would have been known to the Tooting nick if they'd ever done anything like that, surely.'

'How about it, guv?' asked Jerry. 'Do you want me to call the CSEs back in?'

'No, not yet. Listen. This is serious. I want this suppressed. This whole clothing thing. We need to sort it out ourselves, root and branch. Like I said before, it's either going to cause widespread panic, or else we're going to end up looking like total arseholes. Or both.'

'But the way it seems to be spreading,' said Jamila. 'Surely the public need to be warned about it.'

'That would cause far more trouble than it's worth, DS Patel. We'll just have to make sure that we've got it under control before it spreads any further. As soon as we've finished here I'm going to contact Dr Fuller again and tell him to pull his finger out. We need to know what it really is that we're up against, and we need to know now. We've agreed it's some kind of infection, so there must be a cure. Look at AIDS.'

'AIDS made live people die, sir,' said Jamila. 'It didn't make dead people come to life.'

DI Saunders ignored her. Instead, he said, 'There's another crucial thing we have to think about these days. If it's splashed all over the media, it's going to be politicised. The bloody liberal left are going to make a meal of it, the same way they do every time some scumbag dies in custody, or some tower block full of illegal immigrants burns down. You know what they're going to be tweeting – "poor people who can only afford clothes from charity shops are being deliberately infected by the Tories, and the pigs are turning a blind eye to it".'

'With all respect, sir—' said Jamila, but DI Saunders interrupted her.

'I know what you're going to say, DS Patel, but if we can't get our heads round this, as professionals, how do you think Joe Public is going to be able to cope with it? It's going to be pan-de-bloody-monium.'

He stepped over Mindy's father's body and into the bedroom. Jerry and Jamila hesitated for a moment and then followed him. One of the sliding wardrobe doors was wide open, and Jerry could see that most of the plastic coat-hangers were empty, and a score of them had dropped in a tangle down to the floor. The whole room was heaped with crumpled clothes: shirts, jumpers, jackets and dresses, as if somebody had gone into the wardrobe and flung everything out of it in a temper.

'So the room wasn't like this when you first came here?' asked DI Saunders. 'Not with these clothes all over the shop?'

'No,' said Jamila. 'The wardrobe door was closed and the rest of the room was tidy.'

'So, unless some third party was on the premises, unbeknownst to you, and that third party came in here and chucked all these clothes around, we have to conclude that the clothes escaped from the wardrobe by themselves.'

'Like Sherlock Holmes said—' Jerry began, but DI Saunders said, 'I know what fucking Sherlock Holmes said, Jerry, but Sherlock Holmes was a story and this is real. We've got clothes that are turning perfectly normal people into murderers and even cannibals. Clothes, for fuck's sake!'

He stood in the middle of the bedroom, surveying all the dresses and jackets and sweaters around him. He was breathing so hard that Jerry wondered if he were going to go into cardiac arrest. Then he said, 'I want all these clothes bagged up, taken down to the Smugglers Way tip and got rid of.'

'What if some of them manage to get away?' asked Jamila. 'What if they manage to cling onto somebody else? What if one of the workers at the tip takes a fancy to one of these jackets and tries it on?'

'I'm not even going to think about that,' said DI Saunders. 'That is beyond sanity. And besides, once they've been disposed of, they won't be our responsibility any longer. If any of them escape, it'll be down to Wandsworth Council, not us.'

'Sir—' Jamila began, but DI Saunders left the bedroom, stepping over the body of Mindy's father again, and went to talk to the two armed officers who were still waiting on the landing.

'I want to make myself perfectly clear about this,' he told them. 'What we have here is a totally unprecedented situation that we haven't even begun to get a handle on. If any word of this incident gets out, especially to the media, it could seriously jeopardise our ongoing investigation, and if that happens we may well expect many more fatalities. So what I'm asking you to do is to keep your lips buttoned. In fact, that's an order.'

'What about the nine spent rounds, sir?' asked the firearms officer. 'I'll have to account for those.'

'You can say that you had to fire warning shots, and I'll back you up on that. You haven't killed or injured anybody, constable, so don't worry about it.'

The firearms officer looked at the bodies of Mindy's father and mother lying in the corridor and shook his head.

'This is the first time I've ever had to shoot an actual live person, and now it turns out they were brown bread already. Believe me, sir, you won't catch me telling a soul. They'll think I'm three stops down from Plaistow.'

32

When they met Dr Fuller at St George's the following morning, all three of them were in a ragged mood.

A thick white dressing was stuck to DI Saunders' left ear with Elastoplast, and he had also cut his upper lip shaving. Jamila's eyes were swollen as if she had been tossing and turning all night, while Jerry had a dull thumping headache because he had drunk three bottles of Stella before he had gone to bed. At least he hadn't had any nightmares about the walking dead – none that he could remember, anyway – and he hadn't woken up until his alarm went off at 7:00.

Dr Fuller was irritable, too. The bodies of Mindy's father and mother hadn't been brought into the mortuary until just before midnight last night, so that he had only been able to give them a cursory once-over. He was still waiting for the latest radiographic results from Block B at Lambeth Road and although he had seen Mindy he hadn't yet attempted to remove her jacket. She was still under heavy sedation in a private room, with an officer posted outside.

'We're a long, long way from finishing all of our tests, detective inspector,' he said, picking up reports from his desk, frowning at them, and then putting them down again. 'Days, if not weeks. And of course I'll have to initiate some new tests once I've managed to take off this young girl's jacket.'

'I just need to know if you've come up with any feasible theories,' said DI Saunders. 'I've got the whole bloody world on my back expecting some realistic progress with this case but there's bugger all I can do until I have at least some idea of what we're dealing with.'

Dr Fuller looked at him over his half-glasses. 'I'm afraid that I'm still as much in the dark as you are, detective inspector. However, I can give you one item of positive news. Lambeth Road got in touch with me late yesterday afternoon and confirmed that the fibre samples that I extracted from Sophie Marshall are an exact match for the fibre samples that I extracted from our nameless drug-addict. Because of that, I can confirm that when they committed their offences they were both wearing the same coat.'

'What about the DNA?' asked DI Saunders. 'Does that match, too?'

'Yes, although it didn't belong to either of them. So far they haven't been able to trace who it did belong to.'

'And what about that headmistress who threw those kids out of the window – what was her name?'

'Laura Miller. Again, we found DNA on the fibres from her coat. It wasn't her DNA, but again we've had no luck in tracing whose it was.'

'And the sweater?'

'Aha, yes. The sweater. It was hand-knitted, and we found traces of DNA on that, too, but they may belong to whoever made it, and not a previous wearer. His wife didn't knit it for him, that's all we know so far.'

DI Saunders was silent for a moment or two, his arms folded, staring at Dr Fuller as if he expected him to know by telepathy what his next question was going to be. Sensing the tension, Dr Fuller looked up from his paperwork and poked his half-glasses back onto his nose.

'Did you find anything in David Nelson's fibres that could have enabled his sweater to move?'

'I'm not sure I understand the question,' said Dr Fuller.

'Well, let me put it this way. There are some drugs, aren't there, which can give you involuntary spasms?'

'Some strong diuretics like furosemide can give you severe muscle cramps, and that could induce spasms. Or donepezil, which is used to treat Alzheimer's. But there was no indication that David Nelson was taking either of those – or any other medication, for that matter.'

'So there was nothing in those fibres that could have caused them to move independently of David Nelson himself?'

'Static electricity, perhaps, but I'm still really not sure what you're asking me.'

Jerry tried to change the subject. 'All these different fibres that you took samples of – do they have anything in common? You know, like a virus? We all seem to be coming around to the conclusion that this is some sort of minor epidemic, don't we, so there must be something that's spreading it.'

'Well, as I've told you, we're far from completing all of our tests,' said Dr Fuller. 'Up until now, however, there's no indication of any viral or bacterial infection, or the presence of any mind-altering substances. That was one of my earliest and strongest suspicions – that the fibres might have been somehow impregnated with LSD or ayahuasca, or in particular with PCP. But no, they're not.'

'Is that it, then?' said DI Saunders, impatiently. 'Apart from telling us that Samira Wazir and that stupid druggie were both wearing the same coat, which we pretty much guessed already, you haven't found out anything? You can't even tell us how Samira Wazir's coat disappeared from her house – or how Sophie Marshall's jacket disappeared, either.'

'No, I can't,' said Dr Fuller. 'I run a pathology laboratory, not a lost property office.'

DI Saunders closed his eyes for a moment and took a deep breath. Then he said, 'Let's suppose for the sake of argument that nobody took them. Let's suppose for the sake of argument that somehow they left the crime scenes under their own steam, as it were.'

'Is that why you were asking me if the fibres were able to move by themselves?'

'Yes,' said DI Saunders. Jerry could tell that he was mortified by having to ask this question, and that he was very close to losing his temper.

'I would have to say undoubtedly not, no, they couldn't have moved of their own volition. It's possible that they could have been highly charged with static, but that would only have had the effect of making the fibres stand on end. You can see the effect yourself if you rub a balloon on your hair. It certainly wouldn't have given a sweater the ability to get up and walk out of the door, if that's what you're suggesting.'

'And you can't work out how those clothes might have affected the mental state of the people who were wearing them?'

'They seem to have induced some kind of schizophrenia, I agree. They may be able to tell you more at Springfield. But from my point of view – so far, no.'

'All right,' said DI Saunders. 'When will you be taking the girl's jacket off?'

'Later this afternoon. I need to take a blood test first.'

DI Saunders stood up, and so did Jerry and Jamila.

'Listen, doctor, I can't tell you how bloody urgent this is,' said DI Saunders. The way he said it made it sound like a threat, as if he would send somebody round to Dr Fuller's house to throw a brick through his window, or worse, if he didn't come up with an answer by the end of the day.

Dr Fuller looked up at him, and although he said nothing, the expression on his face said that he thought that DI Saunders was an irritating ignoramus. Clothes that moved of their own volition? *No, DI Saunders, the clothes goblins carried them off.*

*

As they walked back to the hospital car park, DI Saunders looked at his watch and said, 'You two are going off to the nut house, aren't you, to interview our suspects again?'

'You're not coming with us?' asked Jamila.

'No – I think I'll shoot up to Lambeth Road and have a word with the Borough Forensic Manager. It's not Bob Johnson any more, is it? This investigation needs an urgent kick up the jacksie and we won't get it from Fuller. I know he's supposed to be the great I-Am when it comes to forensic pathology, but he's too bloody hair-splitting for my liking. And too bloody slow. We're going to have to cut some corners if we don't want this clothing fiasco to get totally out of hand.'

'OK, guv,' said Jerry. 'We'll see you when we get back. I can't honestly say that I'm looking forward to this. The last time I interviewed anybody at Springfield it was some basket-case who deliberately shat his pants so that the smell would drive me out of the room.'

'I'll have to remember that next time Callow starts to get sarky with me,' said DI Saunders, although his expression remained totally deadpan.

He climbed into his Insignia and drove off. Jerry looked at Jamila and shrugged and said, 'Right-o, skip, let's do it.'

They crawled through painfully slow traffic to Glenburnie Road, and at last turned into the grounds of Springfield University Hospital. The original building had an impressive red-brick frontage, built in mock-Tudor style in 1840 when it had first opened as a mental asylum, but their suspects were being held in a modern two-storey extension. They parked and went inside, and an orderly pointed them the way to Ward 3.

In the day area they found Dr Dorothy Stewart the consultant, talking to Cherry Mwandi the ward manager. The day area was light and modern, with chunky beige armchairs and a huge flat-screen television. About fifteen patients were sitting watching *Antiques Roadshow*, both men and women. A young woman with wild black hair was humming to herself and repeatedly tapping her fingers against her cheeks as if she were applying moisturiser, and a man with lobster-claw tattoos around his neck kept throwing his head back and staring open-mouthed at the ceiling, but most of the other patients seemed to be lost in a world of their own.

Dr Stewart came forward to greet them. She was a tall, smart woman in her early forties, with a short brunette bob, a grey tweed suit and large Alexander McQueen glasses. Jamila took out her ID, although Dr Stewart recognised Jerry from his previous visits.

'I'm afraid that none of your three are doing at all well,' she said. 'We've carried out some initial examinations, but so far we haven't been able to make a conclusive diagnosis about their mental stability. What's particularly puzzling is that they're all complaining that they feel very ill, even though physically they have absolutely nothing wrong with them.'

'As far as you can tell, do they all share the same mental condition?' asked Jerry.

'Yes, we think so. They're all exhibiting symptoms very much like schizophrenia, but the balance between their dopamines and their serotonin is absolutely normal, which is not what we usually see in schizophrenics. They've also acted aggressively from time to time, especially when they've been questioned by our cognitive behavioural therapist. I know the popular perception of schizophrenics is that they're violent, but in fact most of them are extremely docile and withdrawn.'

'They're conscious, though, and able to speak?' asked Jamila.

'They've been sleeping a great deal, but yes. Cherry will take you to see them now. All I ask is that you don't over-excite them.'

Cherry Mwandi was a chubby but pretty black woman with criss-cross goddess braids. If she hadn't been wearing a pale green nurse's uniform Jerry would have had her down as a singer or a TV chef rather than a mental health ward manager. She led them out of the day area and along a corridor until they came to a locked door with a sign reading SECURITY WING: AUTHORISED PERSONNEL ONLY.

'That Sophie, we've had so much trouble with her,' she said, as she tapped out a four-digit code. 'One minute so sweet and calm, the next minute she's leaping up and trying to take a bite out of my neck.'

Jamila held up her right hand, still covered in a navy-blue cotton glove. 'You don't have to tell me what she's like. She almost chewed off my thumb.'

'Well, you'll be relieved to know that they're all restrained now,' said Cherry Mwandi. 'But like Dr Stewart said, please try not to get them worked up. Until we know for sure what's causing their behaviour, we need to keep them placid. It's possible that if they get too agitated they might suffer a TIA. A mini-stroke,' she added, looking at Jerry, although he already knew what a transient ischemic attack was.

A young police constable was sitting at the end of the corridor, reading a copy of the *Daily Mirror*. He stood up as Jamila and Jerry approached.

'All quiet?' Jamila asked him.

'Bit of shouting and screaming now and again, sarge,' said the PC. 'But nobody's tried to get out – or in, for that matter.'

'Let's see Sophie first,' said Jamila. 'She's the one who interests me the most – well, her and David, but of course David is no longer with us. What she did was so calculated.'

Cherry Mwandi led them to a door further along the corridor. She peered inside through a small window before she unlocked it.

The room was bare except for a bed with two red plastic chairs next to it and a bedside table. There was a single small window, high up out of reach. The only decoration was a reproduction of a David Hockney view of the ocean.

Sophie was lying on the bed facing the wall. She was wearing a plain white nightdress and white bedsocks, and a blue restraint belt around her waist which was fastened to the bed-rail.

'Sophie, love,' said Cherry Mwandi, touching her gently on the shoulder. 'You have visitors.'

'Go away,' said Sophie. Her voice was thin and wheezing, as if she were finding it difficult to breathe. 'Let me die in peace.'

'Sophie, you're not dying. You're perfectly well. Now why don't you say hello to your visitors?'

After a long pause, Sophie turned around. She stared at Jerry and Jamila and it was obvious that she didn't recognise them. Her face was deathly white but her lips were red and swollen and blistered as if she had been chewing them.

Jamila sat down in one of the chairs next to the bed. 'Sophie, don't you remember us? My name's Jamila. My friend here is Jerry. We've come here to try to help you.'

'You can't help me now,' said Sophie. 'Nobody can help me. I'll be dead by morning.'

'What do you think is wrong with you?' Jamila asked her.

'Pneumonia. I caught it here, in the hospital.'

'Sophie, where do you think you are?'

'St George's, of course. But why do you keep calling me Sophie?'

'I'm sorry. What's your real name?'

'Varvara. But most people call me Val.'

'And why were you admitted to hospital?'

''Flu. But it got worse instead of better. You come to hospital to get well but instead they kill you.'

Jamila looked up at Cherry Mwandi, who was standing at the end of the bed. Cherry Mwandi shook her head to indicate that in spite of the hoarse, strained way in which she was talking, Sophie had no symptoms of streptococcal infection in her lungs.

'Val, do you remember what you did to Michael Brent?'

'I did nothing to him. I didn't touch him. It was her.'

'When you say her, who do you mean?'

'It was Sophie, who do you think? Why are you asking me all these questions? I'm dying. Can't you leave me in peace?'

Jerry sat down next to Jamila and said, 'Where's Sophie now, Val?'

'She's gone. Where do you think she is?'

'Gone where?'

'Nowhere. She doesn't exist any more.'

'What do you mean by that? Do you mean she's passed away?'

Sophie frowned at Jerry as if she couldn't make up her mind if he was joking, or stupid, or simply trying to provoke her.

'No – she's gone. There's no room in one body for two people, is there? But now I'm going too and the nurses won't feed me so I'll be dead by morning.'

'The nurses won't feed you? I can't believe that.'

'They won't feed me what I need,' said Sophie, and started to cough. She coughed and coughed until her chest started to heave.

Cherry Mwandi came around and poured her a tumbler of water. She helped her to sit up and held the tumbler to her lips. Sophie took two or three gasping gulps and then spluttered water all over her gown.

'I think that's enough questions for Sophie,' said Cherry Mwandi. 'Perhaps we should go and talk to your other friends now.'

Jerry and Jamila stood up, and Cherry Mwandi ushered them outside. Back in the corridor, Jamila said, 'What did she mean about the nurses not feeding her what she needs?'

'She wanted to eat them – the nurses,' said Cherry Mwandi, as she locked Sophie's door. 'Whenever they came to wash her or to help her to use the bedpan, she kept saying, "Give me a bite of your breast, or your thigh… You won't miss a piece of your thigh, will you?"'

'Blimey,' said Jerry. 'That puts a whole new perspective on hospital food, doesn't it?'

They followed Cherry Mwandi along to the next room. As they walked, Jamila said, 'Calling herself Varvara… I think that's proof enough that she and young Mindy were both wearing the same jacket, don't you? And that's three of them now with an appetite for human flesh. Well, more than appetite – a craving. They seem to believe that if they can't have it, they won't be able to survive.'

33

Laura was wearing a waist restraint, too, but she was sitting up in a high-backed armchair. She appeared to be dozing when Cherry Mwandi let Jerry and Jamila into her room, but when they sat down in front of her, she opened her eyes and stared at them suspiciously.

'Who are you?' she croaked. 'I know you, don't I? What do you want?'

'I'm Detective Sergeant Patel and this is Detective Constable Pardoe. You remember we talked to you before, at the police station? We've come to see how you're feeling, that's all.'

'How do you think I'm feeling, strapped to this chair? I'm feeling ill, and half-starved. I need to go home.'

'Laura, you're in no fit state to go home. Besides which, you're still in police custody. You threw those two poor children out of the window and both of them are dead.'

'Hmph! They deserved it. It's about time children learned to respect their elders and do what they're told.'

'You said before that it wasn't you who killed them. You said your coat did it.'

'You've taken my coat. Did I give you permission to take my coat? You've taken my coat and I've been very sore ever since. My back and my arms – I feel as if they've been sandpapered.'

'Are you still saying your coat was responsible?'

'It's gone now. You've taken it. And she's gone with it. Good riddance, I say. She was always trying to be so reasonable. What a hypocrite. She detested those little brats, just as much as I did. She could never have children of her own and that's why she hated them.'

'Laura – are you admitting now that it was you who killed little Luke and Bishaaro?' asked Jerry. 'You realise you might be given a much lighter sentence if you plead guilty.'

'It was my coat. But the coat was me. It was her, too, the feeble cow.'

'Can I be clear about this? Even though the coat killed them, the coat was you. You were one and the same?'

'And so was she.'

Jerry looked at Jamila. 'I think we've gone about as far as we can go with this, don't you?'

'Yes,' said Jamila, and they both stood up.

Before they left the room, though, Laura said, 'You can rummage through the coat all you like. You won't find her. She'll have gone by now. And I'll be gone, too, before you know it.'

'What do you mean by that, Laura?' asked Jamila.

'What do you think? Souls can't live without bodies. But they won't let me have one.'

'You mean a human body?'

'Of course a human body. What good would a sheep's body do me? Or a dog? That woman who said she was a therapist, I told her I don't need therapy, I need someone to eat. A small child would be enough, even though I can't stand children. An orphan. A stillborn baby. Anything.'

Jerry and Jamila left the room and Cherry Mwandi locked the door.

'Did you know that she had asked for a child to eat?' asked Jamila.

Cherry Mwandi said, 'No. I'm shocked. She's been interviewed by Katharine Worsey, our best cognitive behavioural therapist. But perhaps Ms Worsey thought that she was simply leading her on. Many of our patients do that. They pretend that they've done bizarre and disgusting things, just to shock us. They may be insane, but that doesn't mean they're not clever, or that they don't have a sense of humour. One man told me last week that whenever he feels depressed he cheers himself up by filling a pillowcase with live kittens and jumping on them.'

'I'm glad he found that funny,' said Jamila.

'Sick, I know, but you get used to it in this job,' said Cherry Mwandi. 'Come along, I'll take you to your last suspect.'

When she was out of earshot up ahead of them, Jamila said, 'Honestly, Jerry, I'm about fifty times more confused than I was before.'

'You and me both, skip.'

'Some of the clothes seem to be possessed by their previous owners – well, possessed, or infected, or contaminated or whatever you want to call it. But it seems as if Laura's coat was possessed by her, or another side of her own personality.'

'Like Mindy's dad, with his sweater, and her mum, with her dress?'

'Exactly. Whoever puts these clothes on – whether it's their own clothes or clothes that used to belong to somebody else – they seem to bring out the very worst in them.'

'And the raincoat that ran down the road? What about that?'

'Don't, Jerry. I don't even want to think about it. Like you said, maybe we should put it down to a freak gust of wind, and forget it.'

*

They reached the last door along the corridor, and Cherry Mwandi opened it up. It was dark inside, because the blind was drawn down, so she switched on the overhead light.

Jamie was lying on his back on the bed, dressed like Sophie in a hospital gown, and restrained like her with a blue waist belt. There was an unpleasant smell in the room, like bad breath, and fish.

Jamie looked sicker than either Sophie or Laura. His face was pale and spotty, with two days' growth of gingery stubble. His legs were as thin as two broomsticks although his belly was so swollen that he could have been pregnant.

He was holding up a dog-eared paperback book, although it must have been far too dark for him to read it. As Jerry and Jamila came in, he dropped it onto his chest. Jerry saw that it was *Subud: The Sacred Journey*.

'More doctors?' said Jamie. 'I could really use some white nurse, I'll tell you. That other shit you gave me, that doesn't have any effect at all.'

'Naltrexone,' said Cherry Mwandi. 'But I'm afraid that's all you're getting. It's a very effective opioid antagonist but you have to give it time.'

'I don't have time! Look at me. I'm on the way out. I've got breast cancer but you're not treating me for that, are you? Aren't you going to start me on chemo?'

'You don't have breast cancer because you don't have

breasts,' Cherry Mwandi retorted. 'You were thoroughly examined at St George's and you don't have any kind of cancer. You're addicted to heroin, and malnourished, and of course your back and arms are still abraded from having your coat removed, but otherwise there is absolutely nothing wrong with you.'

'Hey – you're doctors,' said Jamie, turning to Jerry and Jamila. 'You tell her. How can she say I don't have breasts? And please, please, please – just one teentsy shot of white nurse. Don't tell me this hospital doesn't have smack. I feel like I'm on fire, except that I'm freezing, and I can't keep anything down.'

'Unfortunately, mate, we're not doctors,' said Jerry. 'We're police officers and we've come to have a bit of a chat about your shenanigans in the Tooting town centre.'

'You're Old Bill? Shit.'

Jerry and Jamila sat down next to his bed. 'First of all, we need to know your name,' said Jerry.

'I'll tell you if you get me some smack.'

'No, mate, it doesn't work that way. You answer our questions first, and then we'll think about it.'

'I'm really hurting here. I can't tell you how bad. And I've got the runs, too.'

'In that case, the sooner you answer our questions the better,' said Jamila. 'Tell us what your name is and where you live. We've circulated your picture but so far nobody has come forward to tell us who you are, and nobody's reported you missing.'

'I'm—' Jamie began, but then he stopped, and closed his eyes for nearly ten seconds. Jerry and Jamila waited patiently for him to open them again, but when he did, all he said was, 'I'm not sure. I must be her. I am her, aren't I?'

'Who's she?' asked Jamila. 'What's her name?'

'She's me. She must be me, because I've got the tumour, and she's got the tumour.'

'You don't have a tumour, mate,' said Jerry. 'And from where I'm sitting, you don't look like a woman. You look distinctly like a bloke. Feel your chin, if you don't believe me. How many women do you know who've got a beard like Prince Harry?'

Jamie stared back at him in near-panic. 'But I know what my name is. I know where I live. I'm Rachel Beveridge, and I live at forty-three Fontenoy Road. My partner's name is Paul – Paul Johnson.'

He paused, and felt his stubble, and frowned. 'But you're saying I'm not. I can't be, can I? So why do I think I am?'

Next he pressed his hands against his chest. 'I'm not Rachel, am I? And I haven't got breast cancer.'

'No, mate, you're not Rachel,' said Jerry. 'But the question is, who are you?'

'I've – I've forgotten. I'm all full of Rachel. I can even remember where I went to school. Where she went to school. Burntwood.'

'Why don't you relax and see if your real self just floats to the surface?' Jamila told him. 'The more you think about Rachel, the more your real self is going to be suppressed.'

Jamie let his head drop back onto the pillow, and stared up at the ceiling. Although he was supposed to be relaxing, his fists were so tightly clenched that his knuckles were spotted white and Jerry could see that every emaciated muscle in his body was tense. Reaching across the bed, he picked up the paperback that Jamie had been reading, and flicked through it.

'Subud? That's some kind of wacky Oriental cult, isn't it? And look what it says here: "Life is more than a molecular accident." I wouldn't agree with that for a minute. Every single day is a bloody great molecular accident, from the moment you wake up to the moment you go back to bed.'

'James Mullins,' said Jamie, his voice deeper now, but so quiet that Jerry and Jamila could hardly hear him.

'That's your name? James Mullins?'

Jamie nodded. 'Jamie, that's what my friends call me. Used to call me, anyway, when I had some friends.'

'Where do you live, Jamie?'

'No fixed abode, I think you'd describe it.'

'What about relations? Mum and dad? Where do they live?'

'Worthing. Where all the old people live. But they disowned me years ago. They could be dead for all I know.'

'No sisters or brothers?'

'A sister. An older sister, Mary. She lives in Sweden now with some big fat Swede and she never liked me anyway.'

'Where did you get the coat from, Jamie?'

'Found it, lying in the alley next to the library. I was so fucking cold, I thought all my Christmases had come at once.'

Jamila said, 'It's unlikely that we're going to press charges against you, Jamie. You'll have to stay here until you're well enough to be discharged, but in the meantime we'll be arranging for a social worker to come and visit you and see what can be done to find you some employment and somewhere to live. You'll have to get yourself off the drugs, though.'

'It doesn't matter one way or the other,' said Jamie. 'We're dying.'

'Who are you talking about when you say "we"?'

'Me and Rachel. Both of us. I know what she needs but I'm too sick to eat it. I can't even eat a cream cracker without bringing it back up again. Rachel's angry about it but she knows there's nothing she can do.'

'What does she need, Jamie?'

Jamie turned his head away, and when he answered his voice was distinctly higher, like it had been when they first started to question him.

'I'm not going to tell you. You'll only think that I'm some kind of monster. And I'm resigned to it now – dying.'

'Rachel?' said Jamila.

'There's nothing more to say. I died once and that was even worse than you can imagine. You think there's a Hell? You wait until you die. You'll do anything to come back to life again. Anything.'

'Rachel—'

'I'm not talking to you any more. If you can't give him the drugs he needs, then don't come back. You'll be killing me as surely as you're killing him. We'll be gone in a day or two. Don't bother to come to his funeral, either. Our funeral, that is. You won't be welcome.'

With that, Jamie closed his eyes again and lay with his hands crossed over his chest, like the statue of a martyr lying on a tomb.

Jerry and Jamila waited for a minute, but it was clear that Rachel wasn't going to respond to them any further. It was also clear that she was now the dominant personality in Jamie's body, so he wouldn't be responding, either. They got up and left him, and Cherry Mwandi took them back to the day area. Dr Stewart was there, talking to one of the hospital's therapists.

'Well?' she asked them.

'All three of them claim that they only have a short time to live,' said Jamila.

'Yes, they've said that to their therapists, too, several times. It's strange, isn't it? They're obviously not in very good physical shape, but none of them is ill, let alone terminally ill. Apart from that, though, did they give you the information you were looking for?'

'Some of it, yes.'

'And what's your personal opinion of their mental condition? How do you think they compare with other offenders?'

'I can't say at the moment, Dr Stewart,' said Jamila. 'We've recorded everything they said, but we'll need to go through it all again. I'll send you a written report as soon as I can.'

They left the hospital wing and walked back to their car. An airliner was thundering overhead on its way to land at Heathrow.

'That was an expertly non-committal answer,' said Jerry, when the jet had passed over.

'I know. But it wasn't only because we have to keep this under wraps. After talking to those three, my brain is even more muddled up than theirs. I keep thinking, who am I talking about? Sophie or Varvara, Laura or Laura's alter-ego, Jamie or Rachel? And we still have Mindy to interview, when she's up to it, and she says that she's Varvara, too.'

'Life,' said Jerry, as he turned down Glenburnie Road. 'A molecular accident. A spectacular molecular accident.'

34

On their way back to the station, Jamila received a text from Dr Fuller telling her that he had successfully removed Mindy's jacket with far less skin abrasion than he had feared. She would be spending the night in intensive care at St George's and sent over to Springfield in the morning for psychological assessment and further recovery.

'It's my day off tomorrow,' said Jerry. 'If you want me to, though, I'll come over to Springfield when you go to see her. I don't have to pick Alice up until six.'

'Let's see if she's fit to be questioned,' said Jamila. 'Is your Alice staying overnight?'

'Yes, she usually does. We won't be doing anything very exciting – just go to Nando's for a bean burger and then come back to my place and watch *Frozen* for the eleven-thousandth time.'

'How old is she? It must be very hard for you, only seeing her now and again.'

'She was seven in June. And you're right, yes, I've missed out on a lot. She seems to have grown taller every time I see her. But there was no way that her mum and me could have stayed together. Too much alike, that was our trouble. You know what they say about magnets.'

They turned into the police station car park. They didn't get out immediately, but sat together in the car for a while, as if they needed some quiet time to think – not only about their investigation, but about themselves.

'I'd better go and write this up,' said Jamila, at last. 'I don't know how Saunders is going to react, but he needs to know what a confused state our suspects are in. There won't be any future in taking any of them to court, not the way they are now. We'll have to apply to have them sectioned.'

'That's if they live long enough.'

'You don't think they're really going to die, do you? I'm sure that must be a delusion.'

'I don't honestly know any more. The way this case is going, I'm beginning to think that I need to be sectioned myself.'

'I'm going to do some Googling,' said Jamila. 'There could have been similar outbreaks in the past, maybe in other countries.'

'I suppose it's possible, but you'd think we would have heard about them, don't you?'

'I don't know. Perhaps they were so unbelievable that nobody ever took them seriously.'

'So what are you going to Google? "Coats that make you think you're somebody else"? "Jackets that make you want to eat people"? How about "Sweaters that crawl around the house and make a grab for your ankle"?'

'Jerry, we're not going to solve this by making fun of it.'

'Do I look as if I'm laughing? I've never had a case that's given me the willies so much as this one. And the worst part about it is, there's so much evidence, and all our suspects have freely confessed to what they've done, but none of it makes any sense whatsoever.'

Jamila laid her hand on top of his. 'Don't allow yourself to get frustrated. Everything in the world makes sense. It's just that sometimes we can't understand why.'

Jerry looked at her. There was something in her eyes that made him feel both reassured but lonely, as if she had acknowledged that they could never have anything more than a professional relationship. It wasn't only their different ethnicity and their different religions. She would always be DS Patel and he would always be DC Pardoe.

'Come on,' she said, with a smile. 'Let's go and make Smiley as baffled as we are.'

35

Philip had to run across the terminal concourse to catch the
last train from Victoria to Streatham Common, and he was
still trying to get his breath back by the time the train stopped
at Clapham Junction.

Apart from a girl with dreadlocks right behind him who
wouldn't stop talking on her mobile phone, he was the only
passenger in his carriage. He could see his face reflected in
the blackness of the window and he thought that he looked
at least forty years old, even though he was only twenty-
eight. His hair had been thinning lately, but he put that down
to stress.

Streatham Common station was deserted when he arrived,
and so he didn't have to show his ticket. It was nine minutes
past midnight, and a fine rain was falling, so that the
streetlights all shone like dandelion clocks.

He turned up the collar of his jacket and started to walk
down Greyhound Lane. It would take him only five minutes
to get back to his flat, but he was so tired that he felt like lying
down in the nearest front garden and falling asleep, regardless

of the rain. It had been a little over five months now since he had started his first major role as reward manager for Ensurex International, but during that time they had taken over two other insurance companies, which had meant that he was responsible for sorting out hundreds of conflicting demands for bonuses and pensions and other benefits.

He loved figures. He could have happily crunched numbers all day. But it was dealing with foul-tempered managers and whining, discontented staff that he found so exhausting. Ensurex International paid well, but he was beginning to wonder if it was worth all the pressure.

He crossed over to the row of houses which faced the south side of the common. The common itself was dark and empty, with only a sparse line of plane trees separating it from the road. His flat was in a converted Edwardian house on the corner of Braxted Road, with a paved-over garden and a gaggle of green dustbins outside. The couple who lived directly underneath him smoked and argued and played rap music all night and he had wanted to move for months, but he never seemed to have the time or the energy to look for anywhere new.

He was only thirty metres away from his front driveway when he noticed six or seven dark figures standing on the common, roughly in a circle. He stopped and stared at them, shading his eyes from the streetlight with his hand. They were too far away for him to be able to see them clearly, but they all appeared to be hooded, and they were swaying slightly, as if they were performing a ritual dance.

He knew that he should probably mind his own business, but there had been reports in the *Streatham Guardian* recently about a local society of Druids who had been trying to trace the ley lines that ran across this part of South London. Ley lines were supposed to connect one site of supernatural significance to another – such as a Neolithic hill fort at Crystal Palace to a sacred well in Waddon. They interested Philip because he had worked out a way of mapping them mathematically with shape analysis, which archaeologists often used to locate buried ruins.

He admitted to himself that it was nerdish, but he had always loved solving problems with numbers, ever since he was a schoolboy.

The dark hooded figures certainly looked like Druids, and perhaps they had found a ley line crossing the common. After all, Streatham had been named 'street-ham' after the Roman road that had been built through it, and it was conceivable that the Romans had followed the mystical track used by the ancient Britons.

Philip crossed over the road and walked over the wet grass towards the figures. They continued to sway, but they were silent, neither talking nor singing, and under their hoods their faces were in total darkness, so it was impossible to make out what they looked like.

As he came nearer, the three nearest figures turned their heads towards him, but he still couldn't see their faces. It was almost as if their hoods were empty.

'I – ah – I hope I'm not interrupting anything!' Philip called out. 'I saw you all there and I couldn't help wondering if you were Druids. You know – looking for ley lines. I'm very interested in that myself. Ley lines.'

Now the rest of the figures turned towards him. He stopped where he was, concerned that he might have interrupted a family occasion that was deeply personal, like the commemoration of a dead child, or perhaps some kind of fringe religious ceremony. Still, the figures remained silent, although they continued to sway in a way that was beginning to make Philip feel inexplicably uneasy.

'Listen, I'm sorry,' he said. 'I didn't mean to disturb you. It's just that I was reading about Druids and ley lines in the local rag. Sorry. Sorry. I'll leave you to it.'

He started to walk back towards the road. He had only gone a few metres, though, before he heard a very soft rumbling sound behind him, like somebody shaking out a floormat. He started to turn around to see what it was when one of the figures leapt up onto his shoulders and knocked him face-down onto the grass.

For a few seconds he was too winded to say anything. He started to lift up his head but the figure swung its arm around and hit his left ear so hard that his eardrum burst. He tried to roll over and push the figure off him, but two more dark figures dropped down beside him, one on each side, and somehow they wrapped their sleeves around his arms, binding him so tightly that he was unable to move, while another two bound his legs.

He felt as if he were laced up in a straitjacket. The more violently he struggled, the tighter his bonds became, so tight that they were cutting off his circulation. He was desperate to shout for help, but the figure who had first knocked him down was pressing down on his back and he was unable to draw enough breath into his lungs. The figure was so heavy that he thought his spine was going to crack, and all he could manage was a repetitive 'Ah! – ah! – ah!'

While the figure on his back kept him pinned to the ground, the figure who was holding his right arm started to twist it around in its socket. The pain was so excruciating that it brought tears to Philip's eyes, and with his good right ear he could hear the tendons and muscles crackling apart.

'Stop-stop-stop-stop-God-that-hurts-stop!' he begged, but the figure kept on twisting harder and harder until Philip felt his upper arm-bone wrenched right out of its socket. The figure then screwed his whole arm through three hundred and sixty degrees, so that the sleeves of his raincoat and his jacket and his shirt were all ripped off together. It took one final twist to tear his skin apart, too, and with every heartbeat dark red blood was squirted out onto the grass.

The pain was so overwhelming that it went beyond Philip's capacity to feel it. He saw nothing but bright scarlet and then he saw black and then he passed out.

The figure tugged three times at his arm to pull it away from his shoulder, then slung it off into the rain and the darkness.

It was now that the rest of the dismemberment began. Philip's left arm was rotated twice by the figure that had been gripping it, and then once more, until it was suddenly torn free. At the same time the two figures holding his legs bent them sideways at right angles, again and again. It took over twenty minutes of twisting and pulling, with all seven figures clustered over Philip's mutilated body like a clamour of rooks, except that this clamour was deathly silent. Apart from the constant swishing of late-night traffic along Streatham High Road, the only sounds were the tearing of Philip's trousers, the cracking of his thigh muscles as they were stretched to the limit and beyond, and a soft sucking noise from each of his hips as the joints were dislocated.

While they were wrenching off his legs, Philip suffered a massive cardiac arrest. His chest jolted, but if the figures realised that he had died, it didn't deter them from rolling his bloodied torso over onto his back. Huddled over him, they punctured his stomach with scores of pinholes, perforating it so much that they could rip the skin and muscle apart as if they were tearing open a padded envelope. Once they had opened him up, they scooped out his bowels in armfuls.

The figures weren't repelled by the stench, or the blood, or the faeces. They embraced his intestines like long-lost children, passing them around in slippery loops, one to the other, and wrapping their arms around them. After that, they dragged out his stomach and his liver and his lungs, and held them up to their hoods as if they were kissing them.

For nearly an hour they sat in the drizzle with Philip's remains strewn around them, their heads bowed like pilgrims who have at last found the spiritual peace for which they have been searching all their lives. Then, one by one, they rose and silently made their way to the north side of the common, where the trees grew more densely, and disappeared into the darkness.

36

Jamila was walking along the corridor towards the CID room with a cup of latte in one hand and her wet raincoat over her arm when DI Saunders called out to her from his open door.

'Didn't you get my text?' he asked her.

'I'm sorry, no. I forgot to charge up my phone last night.'

'I tried to call your landline too, but your friend told me you'd already left.'

'Yes. I needed to do some shopping before I came into work. Otherwise I never seem to get the time.'

'You've heard this morning's news, though?' asked DI Saunders.

'What? No. What's happened?'

'A young man was found on Streatham Common early this morning. What was left of him, anyhow. He was literally torn to pieces. Both of his arms and both of his legs were ripped off – and I mean ripped off, not cut off. God alone knows how that was done. Not only that, he was gutted, with his internal organs all over the place. Liver, lungs, heart. A dog-walker reported it. He said it was all he could do to stop his boxer snaffling bits of the victim for breakfast.'

'That's awful. Do we know who he is, this young man?'

DI Saunders went back to his desk and picked up his notebook. 'Philip Wakefield, aged twenty-eight. Single, not involved in any current relationship. He was a rewards and compensation manager at Ensurex International. That's a big insurance company based in the Walkie Talkie building. City of London police have arranged to meet his managers this morning to find out if he had any problems at work. Any business enemies, that kind of thing.'

'Who's handling it from here?'

'DI French is taking overall control, with DS Willoughby and DC Bright. But it's possible that you and DC Pardoe might have to be involved, too.'

'Quite honestly, sir, I think we've got enough on our plates. Have you read my report from Springfield yet?'

'Yes, I have. Well – skimmed through it, to be fair. I'll be going over it more thoroughly this morning. But there's a reason why you and Pardoe need to take a look at this case, although I've got my fingers crossed that it's just a freaky coincidence. DI French informed me that when we undertook our preliminary search of the common and the surrounding area, they found a coat.'

DI Saunders hesitated, almost as if he was reluctant to tell her any more. Jamila could tell by his expression that this investigation was vexing him much more than he was prepared to admit.

'A coat?' she coaxed him.

'A black duffle coat. Apparently it was snagged in the thorn bushes on the north side of the common, among the trees. The cuffs and sleeves are soaked in what is almost certainly blood, which was still damp when the coat was discovered. The lining also has bloodstains, as well as faecal matter and shreds of what appear to be human skin and strings of connective tissue. There's bloody tissue and blood clots inside the back of the hood, too.'

'So the coat probably came into close contact with the victim's remains after he was killed?' said Jamila. 'It could have been a futile attempt to cover him up.'

'Maybe. Let's hope so. I think you know what I'm thinking, Jamila, and I think you're thinking the same as me. The ground was saturated because of the rain, and although it's mostly grass it's muddy in places. By rights there should have been dozens of recent footprints around the victim's remains. You can't tear a man to pieces without leaving some trace that you were there. So far, though, the CSEs have found only his footprints – the victim's – and the dog-walker's.'

Jamila said nothing, but her mind was spinning over like a kaleidoscope. It almost sounded as if Philip Wakefield had been attacked by a giant eagle, or a dragon – some creature that had soared down from the clouds and torn him apart without landing on the grass. What else would have been strong enough to pull off his arms and legs? What else could have done it without leaving any tell-tale impressions on the ground?

Of course this was real life, and not *Game of Thrones*, and giant eagles and dragons didn't exist. But who could the coat have belonged to, and why had they left it behind when it was caught in the bushes, when they must have known that it was soiled with incriminating evidence?

Unless, of course, there wasn't a perpetrator – not a human perpetrator, anyway. In her mind's eye she kept seeing flashes of the black raincoat that had run away down the road from

Mindy's house. A coat, running, with nobody in it. Or maybe there had been somebody in it – somebody invisible, or a ghost, or a spirit – but somebody who left no footprints.

DI Saunders was right. Jamila was thinking what he was thinking. There was no question that Philip Wakefield's killing had been far more gruesome than the murders committed by Sophie Marshall and David Nelson and Laura Miller and Mindy. But so far the only circumstantial evidence in every case was the same. An item of clothing – in this case another coat.

'I assume there were no eye-witnesses,' she said.

'Not to the actual killing, no,' DI Saunders told her. 'It must have taken place sometime shortly after midnight because Philip Wakefield had just come off the last train from London Victoria. It was pitch black and it was raining. Of course DI French has got his team knocking on every door along both sides of the common, and he'll be putting out the usual appeal on social media. Meanwhile the victim's remains have gone to the mortuary and the coat was bagged up and sent off to Lambeth Road.'

'I'll call DC Pardoe and get him up to speed,' said Jamila. 'After that – well, I'll just wait for DI French to call us, if he needs us. I was hoping to question that Mindy girl this afternoon. With any luck she might be able to throw some more light on how these clothes make people so psychotic.'

DI Saunders said, 'I don't have to remind you not to mention this coat to a soul, DS Patel. And by that I mean nobody, apart from Pardoe.'

'To be honest with you, sir, I wouldn't know what to say about it,' said DS Patel. 'If the killer left it behind, then we're still looking for him. But if the coat did it? Then we already have it in custody.'

DI Saunders didn't answer that, but closed his office door like a man who needs to be left alone for a while.

*

Jerry had heard the news about Philip Wakefield's murder on LBC News while he was eating a honey-and-oats breakfast bar in the bath. The only information that had been given out on the radio was that a man's body had been found on Streatham Common and that his name would be released when his next-of-kin had been informed. Police were appealing for witnesses but although foul play was suspected, no suspects had yet been identified, and the motive for the man's killing was unclear. It didn't appear to be robbery, since his wallet and his iPhone and his thousand-pound Raymond Weil watch were found on his body, untouched.

'They should have said around his body,' said Jamila. 'There were bits and pieces of him scattered over twenty square metres.'

'Bloody hell. Do you want me to come in?'

'Not just yet, Jerry. There's nothing that you or I can do until DI French has completed his house-to-house and we've had Dr Fuller's autopsy and a full forensic report on the coat from Lambeth Road.'

'All right. But let me know if you need me. The only thing I really must do today is go to the launderette. Have you heard any more about Mindy?'

'No, not yet. Personally I'd be surprised if she's well enough to be questioned today.'

'I'll tell you something, skip, this coat thing's gone way beyond spooky now. I mean, it was weird enough them turning ordinary law-abiding people into homicidal maniacs, but now that they've started running around on their own—'

'Jerry, we have no way of knowing if this duffle coat was running around on its own.'

'But you said it had human tissue and blood clots inside its hood. I mean, think about it – inside its hood? How did those get there? If somebody was wearing it, all that gunk would have splashed onto their face, surely?'

'It's far too early to say, Jerry. We'll just have to wait and see what Block B come up with. Listen, I'll call you later if I need you. Don't worry too much, I can handle things at this end. Enjoy yourself with Alice.'

Jamila put down her phone. This investigation was all becoming so surreal. She was beginning to feel as if she had fallen asleep while her grandmother was telling her one of her stories about jinns and bhoot, the Pakistani house-ghosts, and had never woken up.

She knew that very few people in Britain took the supernatural as seriously as they did in Pakistan, but she had been brought up to believe in the reality of evil spirits, and it was a belief that was hard to shake off. Even now, she still recited the Ayat-ul-Kursi from the Qur'an before she went to sleep and slept on her right side, specifically to ward off any demons that might come sniffing her out in the dark.

Still – when she and Jerry had been eating together, she had noticed that if he spilled any salt on the table he would always flick two pinches of it over his left shoulder, so she supposed that everybody was prone to some degree of superstition. But what was happening with these clothes was so much more than superstition. Ever since she had seen David Nelson's sweater crawling along the floor like a spider she had been completely convinced that they were possessed in some way, and that was why she hadn't hesitated to run after the raincoat and beat it with the garden gate. And what about all the clothes that had come crawling out of Mindy's parents' wardrobe and down the stairs?

She switched on her desktop computer and searched for any references to clothes coming to life. She found several examples of people being frightened to wear clothing that had belonged to the dead, especially in China and Indonesia. In contrast, she also found examples of cultural groups who were happy to wear inherited clothes. They believed that it kept them close to the relatives who had passed away.

Jesus was said to have cursed any clothes that were laundered on Good Friday, because he had been slapped in the face with a wet smock as he carried the cross to Calvary. It was said that if you washed your clothes on that day, they would come to life and strangle a member of your family with their sleeves, or at the very least they would come out of the wash spotted with blood.

Jamila spent over half an hour searching for more background information online. She came across dozens of fairy tales about dresses that danced when their ballerinas were asleep, and ghost stories about vengeful overcoats that roamed through the city streets at night. However she could find no credible accounts of clothes that had appeared to possess whoever was wearing them, or clothes that had appeared to move on their own. Not even in Pakistan.

She was still scrolling through 'Chinese funeral rites' when her phone warbled. It was DI Saunders.

'Jamila? DI French has just received a preliminary autopsy report from Dr Fuller. I'll send you the PDF.'

'That was quick.'

'He didn't have to do his usual dissection, I think that's why. The perpetrator had pretty much done it for him.'

'Has he worked out how the victim's arms and legs were taken off?'

'Twisted off, he says – both clockwise and anti-clockwise.'

'Twisted off? How much force would you need to do that?'

'Well, let me read you what he's written here. *It would have taken between thirty and a hundred kilonewtons to twist off an arm, and possibly up to two hundred to twist off a leg. That's between one to four megapascals if that means anything to you. In English, about fifteen horsepower.*'

'Fifteen horsepower? I'm not a physicist, sir, but surely that's far more than most people are capable of.'

'You're absolutely right,' said DI Saunders. 'According to Dr Fuller, the average healthy human being can produce only one-point-five horsepower, and that's a maximum, and not for any length of time, either.'

'So – if his legs and arms weren't twisted off manually, is there any indication as to how it was done?'

'Dr Fuller says, *the victim's arms and legs all exhibit bruises which indicate that he was forcibly restrained with straps or belts about nineteen centimetres across. This would have kept him pinioned. However to generate sufficient torque to twist off his limbs the perpetrator would have required a mechanical device of some sort, such as a lathe. Or an elephant.*'

'A lathe?' said Jamila. 'But that would have been incredibly heavy, wouldn't it, and I thought there were no impressions on the ground.'

'There weren't,' said DI Saunders. 'And no elephant footprints, either, although I'm not sure if Fuller was trying to be funny.'

'Perhaps not entirely, sir. I've read about several recent cases in Pakistan of wild elephants killing people because we're starting to encroach on their natural habitat. And right up until the end of the nineteenth century, it was quite common in many Asian countries for criminals to be executed by being cut apart by elephants with knives attached to their feet, and then having their heads stepped on.'

'That's very interesting, Jamila – but I'll bet you a tenner that there were no bloody elephants on Streatham Common last night.'

'No, sir. Probably not. But no lathes, either.'

DI Saunders was silent for a moment. Then he said, 'I don't know. I suppose it's remotely possible that the victim could have been dismembered with machinery at another location and his body parts simply dumped on the common. But the grass was soaked with blood, totally soaked, and the way his insides were all scattered about, that doesn't seem likely, does it? I mean, how would they have carried him there? In a bathtub? It's mad. It's totally bloody bonkers. And then there's the coat.'

'Yes,' said Jamila. 'Then there's the coat.'

37

Alice was skinny and pretty and fair and looked just like her mother. Blue eyes, upturned nose.

Jerry drove his six-year-old Ford Focus to collect her from the small terraced house that used to be his, halfway down Lugard Road, in Peckham. Nancy stood in the doorway with her arms folded and her usual sour expression. Jerry always smiled and said, 'Hi, how's it going?' but Nancy rarely spoke to him. If there were any special instructions for Alice – such as her needing to take any cough mixture, or to bring her back early to go to a friend's birthday party – he would find usually them in a computer-printed note inside one of her Wellington boots.

'How's school?' asked Jerry, as they drove back towards Tooting through Peckham Rye.

'It's really good. I got a gold star for my drawing.'

'That's brilliant. Well done. What did you do a drawing of?'

'I drew a dressing-up doll. You know, with lots of different clothes that you could cut out and dress her up in.'

'That sounds like a good idea.'

'Well, I made up a different story for each of her dresses. I drew her a wedding dress for getting married and I drew her a ballgown for going dancing. That was when she was happy. Then I drew her a black dress because her husband had died in a car crash and a ragged dress because she went mad.'

'She went mad? Poor woman. That's not very nice.'

'I know but I wanted to show that you can tell what somebody's like by the clothes they're wearing. I bet you can tell who's a nasty person and who isn't, just by their clothes.'

Jerry didn't answer that. He didn't want to think about the connection between clothes and psychotic behaviour, not on his day off. He had been relieved to have received no more calls from Jamila, either about the man who had been dismembered on Streatham Common, or about Mindy. All he wanted to do was have a good time with Alice. She seemed to have grown another inch since he had last seen her, only two weeks before. Her Little Red Riding Hood coat looked too short for her now, and her sleeves no longer covered her skinny wrists and all her friendship bangles.

It was 6:30 p.m. and dark by the time they reached Tooting. Jerry stopped at his flat to switch on the lights and draw the curtains and drop off Alice's overnight bag, and then they got back in the car and headed to Nando's for supper.

'How hungry are you?' asked Jerry.

'Starving,' said Alice. 'I could eat a baby.'

'Nando's don't serve babies,' said Jerry. He realised that what she had said was only a coincidence, but she was beginning to give him a disturbing feeling that there was an imp inside her that knew what he was investigating, and was provoking him about it.

What had Laura Miller said? *I could eat an orphan. A stillborn baby. Anything.*

'Oh, they don't serve babies?' said Alice. 'I'll have the bean burger then.'

They were driving past Tooting Bec Common when a group of four or five dark figures came running off the common about a hundred metres up ahead of them. Without stopping to see if any cars were coming, the figures ran right to left across the road, and turned down Franciscan Road opposite.

'Did you see those twats?' said Jerry, wishing immediately that he hadn't used the word 'twats'.

'No,' said Alice, without looking up. She was too involved with playing Star Stable on her iPhone. 'What twats?'

On impulse, Jerry turned down Franciscan Road after them, and saw them running close together along the pavement. What had caught his attention was that none of them was wearing running-gear, or a high-viz tabard. Although it was difficult for him to see them clearly because of all the parked cars lined along the road, they all looked as if they were wearing black duffle coats, with their hoods turned up.

Jerry overtook them, and then slowed down and adjusted his rear-view mirror so that he could look back at them. Not only were they hooded, they all appeared to be black, or else they were wearing balaclavas, because their faces were so dark. Strangely, though, he couldn't even see the whites of their eyes. Surely they couldn't be running with their eyes closed.

He continued to drive slowly so that they could catch up with him. Once they had, he crept along beside them for thirty or forty metres, but they didn't appear to be aware that he was there and none of them turned to look at him.

Alice looked up from her game and said, 'Why are we going so slowly? We're not there yet, are we?'

'No, sweetheart. I've just noticed something peculiar and I want to take a butcher's at it, that's all.'

Alice turned around in her seat. 'What? Do you mean those men?'

'Yes, but don't look at them.'

The figures had nearly reached the junction of Franciscan Road and Mantilla Road. They would have to cross over and so Jerry would be able to see them better. As they reached the corner, though, a car was coming up Franciscan Road in the opposite direction, and its driver was indicating that he intended to turn right into Mantilla Road.

The figures didn't hesitate. They ran across the road right in front of the turning car, so that its driver had to step on his brakes. He blew his horn and put down his window, obviously ready to shout something blasphemous at them, but by then they had carried on running and already they were halfway along the next block, a parade of local shops.

Jerry had come to a sudden stop too, because he felt as if he had been hit in the pit of the stomach. When the figures had crossed the road in front of the car's headlights, he had seen that they weren't running at all. They had no legs. They looked as if they were nothing but coats, tumbling along the pavement together as if they were being blown by the wind.

He pulled in by the side of the road and phoned Jamila.

'Jerry? I'm just about to leave for the day. What's up?'

He climbed out of the car and closed the door so that Alice couldn't hear what he was saying.

'I'm halfway down Franciscan Road. I've just seen four, maybe five black duffle coats running on their own.'

'You've seen what? I'm sorry, I can't hear you very well.'

'Five duffle coats, running on their own. Well, not running. They don't have any legs. They look just like that bloody raincoat, skip, although they might have heads. I couldn't be sure because they all have their hoods turned up.'

'Can you keep track of them? I'll ask Sergeant Bristow to send a couple of cars out.'

'I've just lost sight of them, but they can't have got far. I've got Alice with me, but I'll keep in touch.'

He climbed back behind the wheel, started the engine, and sped off down Franciscan Road. The figures had nearly reached the next corner, Brudenell Road. On the opposite side of the road stood a tall tawny-brick church, All Saints. Without any hesitation, the figures ran diagonally across the junction towards it – ran, or flew, or were blown by some capricious wind that Jerry couldn't feel.

Jerry swerved after them, but they didn't continue to run straight down Brudenell Road. There was a low fence surrounding the lawn in front of the church, with a gate in it. They ran through the gate, crossed the lawn, and disappeared into the darkness around the side of the building. They looked like huge black bats flocking back to their cave.

'What's happening?' asked Alice, impatiently. 'What are you doing? I thought we were going to Nando's.'

'We are, sweetheart, but I've seen some suspicious-looking people and I don't want them to get away. If you can wait here for just a moment, I'm going to lock the car doors so that nobody can get in.'

'You mean those men?'

'Alice, I promise you, there's nothing to be frightened about. I've called the station for back-up and there's more officers on the way.'

Jerry took his flashlight out of the glovebox and then he climbed out of the car and walked up to the church. He turned around to Alice as she sat in the car, shining his flashlight up into his face and sticking out his tongue, but he could see that she wasn't amused. He called Jamila again.

'Jamila? I'm at All Saints Church on the corner of Brudenell Road. The suspects went around the back of the church and I haven't seen them come out yet, so I'm guessing that they might have sussed that I'm following them, and they're hiding.'

'There's a car on its way to you now. It was already at Tooting Bec station so it should be with you in only a couple of minutes. But Jerry, be careful. If these coats are anything like the coat that was found on Streatham Common – who knows what they can do. Maybe nothing at all. Maybe they're just ordinary coats. But then maybe they're not.'

'They were running along the road, skip. Ordinary coats don't run along the road. We both know that. There's at least five of them, but don't worry, I'm not going to try to confront them. This time I haven't got an onion with a wrought-iron gate to come to my rescue.'

Almost as soon as he had said 'onion' he wished he hadn't, especially to Jamila. 'Onion' was station slang for 'sergeant' – 'onion bhaji' rhymed with 'sargie'. But she made no comment except, 'Keep this line open, Jerry, and don't try to do anything heroic. What about Alice?'

'She's locked in the car. She'll be safe enough.'

Jerry switched on his flashlight and walked up to the church's main door. He rattled the handles but the doors were locked, so the coats couldn't have gone inside. He made his way around the back of the building. The car park was deserted, so he had to assume that the coats were still hiding themselves somewhere in the shadows behind the buttresses. Very cautiously, shining his flashlight ahead of him, he made his way along the side of the building. His heart was beating so hard that he could hear it, and he was tensed up ready to run if any of the coats came leaping out at him.

After his experience with the raincoat outside Mindy's parents' house, he was no longer sceptical about the possibility of these coats being alive – and not only alive, but highly dangerous. Whatever had possessed that raincoat, he had felt its strength as if a real man had been wearing it. If not a man, then some kind of powerful and aggressive spirit.

He saw two yellow eyes reflected in the beam of his flashlight, and he froze. Only seconds later, though, a grey tortoiseshell cat stalked warily out of the darkness and jumped up onto the fence of the house next door. Jerry thought that the cat was lucky that he wasn't armed, because he probably would have shot it or Tasered it before he realised what it was.

He had almost finished circling the church without seeing any sign of the coats when he heard a loud banging coming from the direction of the road. It went on and on, *bang! bang! bang!* and then he heard a crunch like a window breaking, followed by a high, penetrating scream.

Oh, Christ, that's Alice!

He ran around to the front of the church. The five hooded coats were surrounding his car, and they were beating at the roof and the bonnet and the doors with their sleeves. These sleeves didn't flap, though. They struck the sides of the car as if they were heavy wooden flails, and they had already smashed the rear window and one of the rear side windows.

Alice was cowering inside the car, her hands covering her head, and she was screaming and screaming in absolute terror.

Jerry pelted across the grass and yanked open the gate. He crossed the pavement and seized the shoulders of the coat that was trying to beat open the front passenger door. The coat was coarse and dry, just like an ordinary duffle coat, but he could actually feel that there was somebody or something inside it – something muscular, but muscular like a squid's tentacle rather than a human arm. He tried to drag the coat away from the side of the car, but it swung itself around and one of its sleeves smacked him hard against his cheekbone and sent him flying backwards. He landed on his left hip and knocked his head against the railings.

He felt as if his head had split open and his hair was wet with blood, but he pulled himself back up onto his feet and seized the coat a second time. He managed to grab the back of its hood, but as he tried to pull the hood down, another coat came round from the back of the car and wrapped one of its sleeves around his upper arm, twice, as quickly as cracking a whip. It was like having his blood pressure taken, only ten times tighter.

'Get the fuck – off me,' Jerry panted, but the coat pulled him away from the car and dragged him, stumbling, backwards. The other four coats were still beating at the roof and the bonnet, and Jerry heard another window break. On the opposite side of the street he could see doors opening and curtains being pulled back as people peered out to see what all the noise was about.

The coat dragged him even further back, and as it did so the streetlight shone into its hood, but there was nobody inside it. It was empty, or appeared to be empty, just as it had no visible hands or feet, and all he could see was its tartan lining. Even so, it possessed an extraordinary strength – stronger than any man that he had ever encountered, either in a street scuffle or in the gym when he was kick-boxing. Alice was shrieking in panic, and he felt so angry and helpless that he could have burst into tears.

The coat's right sleeve wrestled towards his neck. He tried to bat it away, but it was relentless. It forced its way underneath his arm and snaked itself around his wet collar, and then it tightened, hard.

Jesus – it's going to strangle me.

He punched the coat as hard as he could, but although it was so strong his fists connected with nothing except thick billowing fabric. He tried to kick it, in the same way that he would have kicked a man in the crotch, but his foot thumped into nothing but coat-tails.

Now the sleeve that was wound around his neck was gripping him tighter and tighter – so tight that he had to tilt up his chin, and he felt that it was going to wrench his head clean off his shoulders. He could hardly breathe, and tiny points of light were swimming in front of his eyes.

His vision began to grow dark, and he was on the point of passing out when he heard a loud metallic screeching sound, followed by a loud clatter. The coat's right sleeve suddenly unwound itself from his neck, and its left sleeve released its hold on his arm. He staggered back, almost losing his balance and falling over again, but he could see why the coat had let him go. Two other coats had torn the passenger door off his car and thrown it across the pavement, and one of them was trying to reach over the top of the front seats. Alice had climbed into the back, and she was pressing herself against the opposite door, so that the coat wouldn't be able to seize her and pull her out. The other coats were clustering around it, as if they were hungry for their share.

Alice wasn't screaming now. Her face was deathly white and her mouth was turned down with absolute dread.

Jerry didn't hesitate. He limped and hopped around the back of the car like Long John Silver, pulling his keys out of his trouser pocket and opening up the driver's door. He dropped down behind the wheel, jabbed the key into the ignition and started the engine. The coat that was leaning into the car hit him hard on the shoulder and then on the side of the head, and then tried to wrap one of its sleeves around his elbow. He forced the gearstick into first and jammed his foot down on the accelerator pedal, and the car shot forward, its tyres screeching in chorus.

The coat tried to clamber right inside, holding onto the handbrake with one sleeve and the back of the passenger seat with the other. Jerry swerved right and left, trying to make it lose its grip, but it kept clinging on. In the back seat, Alice was sobbing with fear, although Jerry couldn't see her in his rear-view mirror because she had dropped down onto the floor.

He tried to change gear because the engine was screaming in protest, but the sleeve was now tangled around the gearstick as well as the handbrake, and preventing him from shifting into third. He tugged at the gearstick again and again, without being able to engage it, but then he saw a lamp-post up ahead, on the corner of the next street. He twisted the steering-wheel sharply to the left and drove up onto the pavement, hitting the kerb with a spine-jarring jolt. With a dull thump that sounded just like a human body, the coat collided with the lamp-post and was knocked out of the car, rolling over and over on the pavement and into the road.

Jerry could see it in his mirror, but he didn't slow down. Instead, he drove at nearly fifty miles an hour until he reached the main Upper Tooting Road, with all its lights and restaurants and shops. It was only then that he pulled into the side of the road and climbed out, although he shaded his eyes and looked back along Brudenell Road to make sure that the coats hadn't come after them. If they were strong enough to tear a car door off its hinges, God alone knew how fast they could run.

He opened the rear passenger door and lifted Alice out. She clung to him, quaking and crying.

'You're not hurt, are you, sweetheart?' Jerry asked her.

'I want Mummy! I want to go home!' Alice wept.

'That's all right, I'll take you back to Mummy. But I can't take you in this car. I'll call DS Patel and she'll send someone to pick us up.'

'Those weren't men!' said Alice. 'They were only coats! How could coats do that? How could coats smash up your car?'

'I'm sorry, sweetheart, I don't know the answer to that any more than you do. But you're right, yes, they were only coats. I just hope you don't have any bad dreams about them. Me and DS Patel, we're going to find out how they can run around like that, scaring people, and we're going to stop them. So you don't need to worry about them any more, I promise you.'

Jerry sat her gently down on the back seat of the car and called Jamila, all the while keeping an eye on the far end of Brudenell Road.

'Skip?'

'Yes, Jerry, where are you? PC Rollins has just called in from All Saints Church and says there's nothing there to see except a ripped-off car door. The local residents have told him that your car was attacked by five black men, and then you shot off.'

'Not black men, skip. Coats. And if you ask me, Alice and me were lucky to get away from there without being killed.'

As succinctly as he could, Jerry told her how the coats had tried to break into his car to get to Alice, and how one of them had nearly choked him.

'Well, there's no sign of them now,' said Jamila. 'Sergeant Bristow sent out another three cars to box off the area but so far there isn't any sign of them.'

'They do know they're looking for coats, and not for black men?'

'Not exactly.'

'"Not exactly"? Either they do or they don't.'

'They don't. But I'm going to have a word with DI Saunders. There's no way that we can keep this a secret any longer.'

Jerry said, 'OK.' He had been about to say something stinging, but he had seen that Alice had found her iPhone on the floor of the car and was calling Nancy.

'Listen,' he said. 'I'm on the corner of Upper Tooting Road and Brudenell Road, and my car's a write-off. Alice is very upset, as you can imagine, and I need to take her back home to her mother. So if you could send a car for us.'

'Is she all right? Those coats must have scared her half to death.'

'She wasn't hurt, thank God. But, yes, she was crapping herself, not to put too fine a point on it. And I can tell you something for nothing – she wasn't the only one.'

38

Jerry didn't get back to Tooting until a quarter to nine, by which time he was feeling bruised and exhausted.

He felt more bruised by Nancy than the knock that he had received on the back of his head, even though Nancy had cleaned it for him. He had sat at what had once been his own kitchen table, and while she had applied Savlon antiseptic cream with her fingertip, he could have believed that the past two years had never happened, and that they had never had to face up to the fact that they were never going to like each other, or even understand each other.

Their attraction had been physical, and that was all. She had always read *The Guardian* while he read *The Sun*. She adored her pet Staffie while he thought it was an ugly, slobbery, expensive waste of space. She was a churchgoing Christian and wanted Alice to be confirmed. He had seen enough killing and villainy and paedophilia to know for an absolute fact that there wasn't a God.

'Alice said you were attacked by coats,' Nancy had said,

almost off-handedly, when she had finished dabbing his wound. 'Why would she say a thing like that?'

'The assailants were all wearing duffle coats, that's correct.'

'Jerry – you're not reporting to your DI now. She said that they were coats – just coats – with nobody in them. I'm asking you why she should say that.'

'I'm not at liberty to discuss it, Nancy. That's all I can say.'

Nancy had dragged out a kitchen chair and sat down next to him. Her expression had been ferocious and he had thought what a great interrogator she would make. Not even the hardest criminal would dare to lie to her.

'Your own daughter has been so traumatised by what happened to her this evening that I doubt if she'll be able to sleep for a month, and I'll probably have to take her for counselling. I'm asking you one more time, Jerry. Why would she say that you were attacked by coats?'

'It was dark and she was very frightened. She could have imagined it, or it could have been an optical illusion.'

'*Was* it an optical illusion?'

'I'm not at liberty to discuss it. That's all I can say. And I've asked Alice not to discuss it with anyone – except for you, of course. But please don't you mention it to anyone, either. It's a question of security.'

'What's going on, Jerry? Are you trying to suggest that Alice is lying, or that she's gone mad?'

'Of course not.'

'Then are you going to tell me who really attacked you this evening?'

'No.'

Nancy stood up. 'In that case, Jerry, get out. I mean, get out now. And I'll be making an application to stop you from seeing Alice ever again. Whatever happened, you had no business dragging her into your police investigation. It was reckless and stupid beyond words and she could have been seriously hurt or even lost her life. As it is she may never get over it.'

Jerry said, 'It's her birthday next week.'

'Don't even think about seeing her. Don't even think about buying her a present or sending her a card. This evening you forgot what it is to look after a daughter. From now on, you can forget what it is to be a father.'

*

Jamila was still at the station when he got back. She was sitting at her desk with a cup of latte and a half-finished plate of samosas. Jerry plonked himself down opposite her and they looked at each other for a long time before either of them said anything.

'We've been sent a preliminary report from Lambeth Road about the duffle coat that was found on Streatham Common,' said Jamila at last, wiping her mouth with a tissue.

'Don't tell me,' said Jerry. 'It sat up and gave a Nazi salute.'

Jamila shook her head. 'No... it's more disturbing than that. It's new.'

'How did they work that out?'

'The only traces of DNA they found on it belonged to the victim, Philip Wakefield. Apart from that, it still has the original maker's label on it. It's a Navy Commander, tall men's size. They cost nearly four hundred pounds new.'

'Is there any clue where it came from?'

'Not so far. But if it originally belonged to that same gang of coats that attacked you and Alice, that means that some shop or warehouse is missing nearly two-and-a-half thousand pounds' worth of merchandise. Don't tell me they're not going to report them stolen.'

'Stolen, or walked out on their own,' Jerry added.

'Whatever. But it was the same type of coat, same colour, same size, and Tooting Bec Common is only just over a mile away from Streatham Common.'

'It's interesting that it got itself all caught up in the bushes, though,' said Jerry.

'What do you mean?'

'Well, when I was trying to pull one of those coats away from my car, you've no idea how bloody strong it was. Like, eat your heart out, Hulk Hogan. If the coat that was caught in the bushes was one of them, it should have been able to tear itself free. And if the other coats were there, too, why didn't they help it to get itself free? Between them, I reckon they could have uprooted the whole bloody bush.'

Jamila sat back, picked up one of the samosas, and then put it down again. 'Do you realise what we sound like? I'm still trying to work out how we're going to put this to DI Saunders, let alone the media. And this latest report from Lambeth Road... this takes all of these cases to a whole new level.'

'You mean the coat being new, instead of second-hand?'

'Of course. The clothes that all of our suspects have blamed for committing their murders might have been possessed or infected by their previous owners. I mean, we've discussed that possibility, haven't we? But this duffle coat didn't have any previous owners. And the coats that attacked you, nobody was wearing them, either.'

'Nobody that I could see, let's put it that way,' said Jerry. 'But I could feel them all right. When that one tried to strangle me – Jesus, it was like being throttled by a bloody great boa constrictor. And my motor's a total write-off. I don't know how the hell I'm going to explain that to my insurance company. I've only got third party, fire and theft. Nothing in the policy about duffle coats.'

Jamila stood up and went to the window. 'I thought we might be able to sort this out without having to warn the public at large. If it was nothing more than a handful of people suffering psychotic episodes because of the second-hand coats and sweaters they were wearing... well, that's bizarre enough, wouldn't you say? But at least we could have explained it, even if we had to bend the truth a little.'

'You're beginning to sound like Smiley.'

'No, Jerry. As I told you on the phone, we can't possibly keep the lid on this any longer. That raincoat that ran down the road and all those other clothes that came down the stairs – that's clear evidence that these incidents are all connected. That sweater and that dress that brought Mindy's parents back to life, they hadn't been worn by anybody except them, had they, as far as we know? And now it looks like we've got brand-new clothes murdering people.'

'So what's the plan?'

'We'll have to discuss this with DI Saunders first. But I'm sure he'll have to take it higher. You and Alice were lucky that you weren't both killed this evening. We can't let that happen to anybody else.'

'I can see the headline in the *Evening Standard* even now. TOOTING COPS LOSE THEIR MARBLES.'

'They won't be saying that if somebody else gets ripped apart.'

*

Sergeant Bristow came up to tell them that a street-by-street search for five suspects wearing black duffle coats had proved fruitless, even though it had covered a three-mile radius from Balham in the north to Collier's Wood in the south. Numerous black men had been stopped in the street and some of them searched, but all of them had been able to give the officers a convincing alibi, although one of them had been arrested for possession of skunk.

Both Jerry and Jamila were aware how racist it was to have falsely put out a shout for five black men, but they knew that if they had done the same for black duffle coats with nobody in them, none of the patrolling officers would have taken them seriously.

Jerry's car had been transported to the garage at Lambeth Road, along with its detached passenger door, and it would be examined by forensic specialists in the morning.

Jamila had sent a text to DI Saunders. Shortly before midnight he came in to the station, wearing a dinner-jacket and a black bow-tie and smelling of cigar smoke. An Elastoplast was still stuck to his left ear.

'You didn't have to come in immediately, sir,' said Jamila. 'We could have discussed this first thing tomorrow morning. DC Pardoe and me – we were both about to call it a night anyway.'

'No – we need to go over this now,' said DI Saunders. 'I've just been to the NUJ Extra charity dinner, and that bloody obnoxious crime reporter from the *Mail* got me in a corner. He said he'd heard rumours that we were deliberately suppressing the connection between several recent homicides. He asked me if the suspects had all been taking some new hallucinatory drug that we didn't want publicised.'

'Did he tell you where he'd got his tip-off from?' asked Jerry.

DI Saunders shook his head. 'No, he didn't. But I reckon it was someone at Springfield. Some nurse or some porter must have heard our suspects babbling all that bollocks about being more than one person at once, and thought they were high on some kind of acid. But these bloody coats – they change everything.'

Jerry and Jamila followed DI Saunders into his office and he switched on all the lights. He hung his dinner-jacket over the back of his chair and unclipped his bow-tie and then he said, 'All right, Jerry. Fill me in. And don't leave anything out. This could make or break my career. And yours. And yours, DS Patel. We all want to get ourselves out of Much-Tooting-on-the-Marsh and back to the Yard, don't we? We certainly don't want to end up in Springfield with the rest of the bloody nutjobs.'

Jerry sat down and described everything that had happened from the moment he had first seen the duffle coats flying across the road from Tooting Bec Common. DI Saunders listened with his head bowed, saying nothing, but Jerry could tell by his expression that he was growing increasingly unhappy with every word he spoke.

When Jerry had finished, DI Saunders leaned back in his chair, tapping his pen on his desk like a metronome.

'They're not going to believe us,' he said. 'Nobody is going to believe us. They're going to say that charity-shop jackets don't make perfectly respectable young women cut the guts out of their boyfriends, and nine-year-old girls slit their parents' throats. They're going to think we're deluded for saying those same dead parents can be brought back to life by a sweater and a frock. And they're going to recommend that all of us need sacking from the force and locking up for frightening the shit out of the public with stories about duffle coats that can run around with nobody in them, pulling accountants to pieces, limb from limb.'

'I know,' said Jamila. 'But the worst part about it is that it's all true.'

Jerry thought for a while, and then said, 'What that *Daily Mail* reporter said to you about a new mind-bending drug... maybe we should drop him a hint that he might be right. I mean, even we don't know for sure, do we? Our suspects could have been affected by some substance that turns them into homicidal maniacs. I don't know... maybe we could call it Scary Spice.'

'Ha ha,' said DI Saunders, sardonically. 'And what about the duffle coats? They're the greatest danger to the public, as far as I can see. How do we explain them?'

'I don't think we need to explain that they don't have anybody in them,' said Jerry. 'And again, I don't think we'd be lying, exactly. They bloody well feel as if they've got somebody in them, so what's the difference? All we have to do is warn the public to look out for a gang wearing black duffle coats, and to stay well clear of them if they see them, because they're dangerous, and call 999.'

Jamila said, 'I think that makes sense, sir. We do need to put out a warning, urgently, but if we tell the public that they need to watch out for coats running around on their own, most of them are going to think it's a practical joke. I know I would. You've seen all the spoof stories that pop up on Twitter and Facebook. There's a serious risk that if a sceptical member of the public sees those coats, they'll approach them and try to show them up for being a prank, and get themselves killed.'

'I have a very bad feeling about this, no matter what we do,' said DI Saunders. 'But, yes, Jerry, I think that we'll tell the media that we suspect some powerful new drug may be responsible, at least for now. What worries me is that somebody might see these duffle coats and take a video of them, and show that they're flying rather than walking, and that their hoods are empty.'

'Even if they do, many people will believe that it is just a spoof,' said Jamila. 'You can Photoshop your videos in almost any way you like these days.'

'All right,' said DI Saunders, looking at his watch. 'Let's meet up again in the morning with the borough press officer, and we can formulate the best way of presenting this to the media. He may even want to involve the director of public affairs. How's progress otherwise?'

'Very slow, I have to admit,' said Jamila. 'In fact almost none at all. We've put out an appeal for any retailers or wholesalers who might have found that their duffle coats are missing, but it's far too early to expect a response yet. I may be able to question Mindy tomorrow, and it's possible that she can give me some clues. If only I could find some key to what is causing these clothes to behave so aggressively – whether it's spiritual or whether it's scientific.'

DI Saunders said, 'Maybe you're right, Jamila, and it is a prank. Maybe it's God, taking the piss out of us poor mortals, and laughing His celestial arse off.'

39

It had stopped raining, so when they left Bill and Sarah's house, Ron and Nuying decided to walk back to their flat on Bickley Street.

'Urrgh, I didn't like that spaghetti Bolognese, did you?' said Nuying, as they walked hand-in-hand down Church Lane. 'It tasted of nothing but tomato paste.'

'Oh, come on,' said Ron. 'Sarah's never pretended that she's Nigella. She served up a roast chicken once but she'd forgotten to take out the plastic bag with the giblets inside it.'

'Tomorrow I will make you Szechuan chicken to make up for it,' said Nuying.

They reached Amen Corner and started to walk along the main Mitcham Road. It was nearly two in the morning now, and the road was deserted, although most of the shop fronts were still lit up, and their lights were reflected in the shiny wet pavements. Somewhere they could hear a dog plaintively barking.

Ron and Nuying had been together for a year as of the previous Saturday, which was why Bill and Sarah had invited them around for an anniversary celebration. Ron was a manager for Budget Car Hire in Battersea – twenty-nine years old, tall and lanky with large ears and a cow's-lick of mousy hair. His three-year marriage to his first girlfriend Kayley had ended in divorce when she had slept with his best friend Pete, and so he had looked for a new partner online, and found Nuying. She was twenty-five, petite but plump, the daughter of a Chinese restaurant owner in Croydon. Both she and Ron were awkward and shy, but they both enjoyed cycling, and Ed Sheeran songs, and watching TV, and in the evening they would sit for hours together – not talking but just pleased that they had somebody to sit with.

'It was nice of them to give us those table-mats, though,' said Ron.

'Yes,' said Nuying. 'All we need now is a table.'

'Don't you worry. I've beaten all my repair targets this year and I'll get a good bonus at Christmas.'

They had nearly reached Bickley Street when they heard a loud crack, and then another, and then the explosive sound of a shop window being shattered. Only twenty metres in front of them, like a furious ice-storm, thousands of fragments of glass burst out across the pavement. At the same time, the shop's burglar alarm began to ring.

'Bloody hell!' said Ron. 'What the hell was that?'

Nuying tugged at his hand and said, 'We should run! We should run! Maybe it's a gas main!'

'That wasn't a gas main,' Ron told her. 'That was more like somebody smashing out the window with a hammer.'

Nuying tugged at his hand again, harder. 'We should still run!'

Ron took a few steps back, but then stopped and took out

his iPhone. He tapped out 999, and he was answered almost instantly.

'Emergency, which service?'

'Police, I think. Maybe the fire brigade too. There's a shop window on Mitcham Road that's blown right out all over the pavement. It could be a gas explosion, something like that. Or maybe somebody's broken it out on purpose. I'm not sure which.'

Before the operator could ask him any more questions, a dark figure clambered out of the front of the shop. It was strangely fluid, more like a large black animal than a man. It was followed by another, and another, all of different colours, and then so many more that Ron couldn't count them. A whole crowd of them were standing outside the shop now, on top of all the thousands of sparkling fragments of glass, except that they didn't seem to be treading on them. They seemed instead to be hovering above them, and jostling silently against each other.

Ron took another step back. Nuying whimpered and held onto his arm. She thought that the figures looked like all the washing that her grandmother used to hang out in her back yard, when she was a little girl in Hong Kong. When the wind had blown and the black and white mandarin shirts had all flapped their arms they had terrified her, and these figures terrified her now. She pulled at Ron's arm so hard that dropped his iPhone onto the pavement.

'Sir? Can you hear me?' said the emergency operator.

Ron bent down and scrabbled to pick up his phone. 'Yes – sorry,' he said. 'I was just—' but before he could say any more, the figures started to rush towards them, making almost the same sharp flapping sound that had terrified Nuying so much when she was small.

As they came nearer, Ron could see that the figures weren't people at all. They were shirts and jackets and coats and dresses. They had nobody in them, no heads and no arms and no legs, but they still came flooding forward with their empty sleeves flailing in the air, and they showed no sign that they were going to slow down or stop.

Ron grabbed Nuying's hand and together they started to run back the way they had come. Neither of them spoke: they were both panicking and they both knew that they would need every last gasp of breath to get away. They could hear the flapping coming closer and closer up behind them, but they didn't dare to turn around.

They reached the corner of the next street, Rookstone Road, and Ron pulled Nuying sharply to the right. The pavement here was much narrower, with parked cars all the way along it, so that the clothes wouldn't be able to chase after them in such a wide-spread pack. Then – if they could make it to the end of the road and take another right, and then a left, and then another right, they would find themselves in Bickley Street, and have a chance of reaching their own front door.

As she ran, Nuying hit the wing-mirror of a parked Toyota, and tripped, and staggered, and nearly fell forward. Ron pulled her upright and they kept on running, but they had lost precious seconds. They were less than a third of the way down the road when a long khaki trench-coat billowed up behind Ron with a soft thunderous sound and dropped onto his shoulders. It was only a coat, but it felt as heavy as if a man were wearing it, and Ron was slammed face-first onto the concrete.

Nuying screamed, 'Ron! Ron! Get up!' and she snatched at one of the trench-coat's epaulettes and tried to wrench it off him, but as she did so a writhing bottle-green dress wound its sleeves around and around her head, so that she could neither see nor breathe. The sleeves of a dark grey sweater tugged at her ankles, and she fell sideways, cracking her skull against the kerb.

Now the pack of clothes began to attack the two of them with blind ferocity. The trench-coat struck Ron's face against the pavement again and again, until his nose was smashed flat and his forehead was split apart and both of his eyeballs were knocked out onto his cheeks. At the same time, three jackets levered off his shoes and dragged down his trousers, and then entwined their sleeves around his legs and started to twist them around in the same way that Philip Wakefield's legs had been twisted. As his femurs were rotated, his hip-joints crackled like a freshly lit fire.

A hunchbacked grey anorak and three thick sweaters crawled crabwise over to Nuying. They rolled her over so that they could drag off her overcoat and then rip the buttons off her dress. Then they wrenched off her bra and dragged down her Spanx. Two of the sweaters wound their sleeves around her thighs and opened up her legs until she was almost doing the splits, and then the anorak forced its sleeve up inside her, right up to its elbow. It pulled and pulled at her womb, its back humping up and down with effort, and at last, in a welter of blood, it tore it right out of her. It waved it around as if it were a scalp that it had taken as a trophy, and then dropped it into the gutter.

It took nearly an hour for the clothes to finish dismembering Ron and Nuying. They clustered over their bodies and ripped them apart layer by layer – skin, fat, muscle, tendons and connective tissue. They heaved out their intestines and unravelled them all the way along the pavement like long slippery hosepipes. Finally they broke open their ribcages and pulled out their lungs and their hearts.

There was no sound except for the squelching of flesh and the snapping of bones.

Eventually, the clothes gathered close together, almost all of them heavily bloodstained, and sat amongst the human devastation that they had created. Anybody who had seen them from a distance and who didn't realise that they were nothing but empty clothes would have thought that they were religious penitents, meditating perhaps, or praying for forgiveness.

After a while lightning flickered in the distance and thunder began to rumble. As the wind grew stronger, the clothes rose from the pavement in twos and threes and started to blow away. They rounded the corner at the end of Rookstone Road like a flock of migrating birds, and then they were gone.

40

Jerry was woken by his bedside phone ringing. He was on early worm today and for a moment he thought it was his alarm going off, because he invariably overslept if he didn't set it.

'Yes, what is it?' he grunted. He squinted at his digital clock and couldn't believe that it was only 4:09.

It was Jamila. She didn't have to ask if she had woken him up. She sounded very calm, and Jerry had already learned to take this as an indication that something was badly wrong.

'Two more people have been torn to pieces, Jerry. From what I can gather they were killed like that Streatham Common murder, only much worse.'

'Oh, shit,' said Jerry, sitting up. 'Where?'

'We found them in one of the side-streets off the main Mitcham Road, Rookstone Road.'

'I know it, yes. Rookstone Road. There's a really good curry-house on the corner, the Krishna something.'

'One of the victims called 999. We couldn't send a car in time to save them, but hopefully we got there before any members of the public could see them, so I suppose we can be thankful for that.'

'Who are the victims? Do we know?'

'DC Malik is in attendance, along with DC Young. He sent me a video from his phone. If you want I'll forward it to you. But I promise you that you'll only want dry toast for breakfast, if that.'

'That bad, is it?'

'Let me put it this way – if the victims' wallet and purse hadn't been left behind, you wouldn't have been able to tell if they were human beings, let alone male or female, or who they are. But – hold on, Malik gave me their names if I can read my own writing. They're a white male Ronald Firbank and a Chinese female Liu Nuying. Ronald Firbank is a deputy manager at Budget Car Rentals in Battersea and Ms Liu is a manicurist at Body Beautiful in the High Street.'

'So, no witnesses yet?'

'No, and no obvious footprints, either, according to Malik, although the CSEs may be able to find some. Ronald Firbank called 999 at 2:33 a.m. to report that a shop window along the Mitcham Road had been broken. He thought that it might have been caused by a gas explosion, or else somebody had smashed it deliberately. Unfortunately that was all he said. The emergency operator said that immediately afterwards it sounded like he had dropped his phone, and then he was cut off.'

'OK,' said Jerry. He had climbed out of bed now and he was opening up his chest of drawers. He picked out a pair of jockey shorts with horseshoes on them. Ever since he had won £200 on the Oaks while he was wearing them, he had always believed they were lucky. He thought he might need them today, more than ever.

'Malik said that there's minimal damage inside the shop, except for some coat-rails knocked over,' Jamila went on. 'There's no evidence of a gas explosion, or any other kind of explosion. The whole front display window has been knocked out, but it's fallen outwards across the pavement, so the obvious conclusion is that it was smashed by somebody inside the shop. But listen to this. It's a charity shop, mainly selling second-hand clothing.'

'Oh, don't tell me.'

'WellBrain it's called, supporting research into brain injuries. It's almost opposite Little Helpers, where Sophie Marshall worked.'

'This just gets worse, doesn't it? Is any of the clothing missing?'

'Malik hasn't been able to contact the shop manager yet, but almost all of the coat-rails are empty and there are dozens of hangers scattered around on the floor, so he reckons that quite a lot of clothes have been lifted.'

Jerry was sitting on the side of the bed, pulling up one trouser-leg. 'Lifted?' he said. 'Or done a runner?'

'We can't know for sure, Jerry, not yet. There's no sign of any abandoned clothing anywhere in the immediate vicinity – not so far, anyway. It's possible that the shop didn't have very much stock to start with, or maybe it was all lifted.'

'Or maybe the clothes managed to break out of the shop on their own and kill two innocent passers-by who just happened to get in their way.'

'Yes,' said Jamila.

'What's your opinion, skip? I mean, serious?'

Jamila still sounded utterly calm. 'I wouldn't have woken you up if I didn't think this was relevant to our investigation, would I? I'll meet you down at Rookstone Road in half an hour.'

The thunderstorm had passed over by the time Jerry reached Mitcham Road and parked, and it was beginning to grow light. The police had cordoned off the entire westbound lane, and a queue of early rush-hour traffic stretched back for over a mile.

Seven patrol cars were lined up behind the police tapes, as well as two CSE vans and three unmarked cars. Three TV vans from the BBC, ITV and Sky News were parked in the next street, and a huddle of reporters and cameramen and sound technicians were standing on the corner smoking and stamping their feet.

Jamila was waiting for Jerry outside the empty window of the WellBrain shop, talking to DC Malik. Two crime scene technicians were walking around inside the shop in their Tyvek suits, taking flash photographs.

'Hi, Jerry,' said DC Malik. He was a serious young Bangladeshi with a neat black moustache and fashionably brushed-up black hair. 'I know I haven't been on the job for as long as you have, mate, but I've never seen nothing as gross as this.'

'I thought you were looking a bit pale,' said Jerry. 'Where are they? Round the corner?'

'What's left of them. And the trouble is, it rained like fuck just after they must have been killed, so a lot of blood and other evidence got washed away.'

'Any witnesses yet?'

'No. We've knocked on almost every door down Rookstone Road, but so far nobody saw nothing and nobody heard nothing. I don't know how you can rip two people to bits without making enough noise to wake people up, but whoever did it did.'

'Do we know why the victims were out on the street at half past two in the morning?'

'We do, as it happens. We had a call from a friend of theirs in Church Lane. The two of them had been to dinner there to celebrate their first anniversary together. Ms Liu had left her umbrella behind and her friend had called her to tell her. She tried three or four times and when she couldn't get an answer she started to get worried.'

'Shit way to end their first year together.'

DC Malik shook his head. 'You think to yourself – why? I mean, what was the fucking point? Whoever it was who killed them, they didn't even steal nothing. So, why?'

Neither Jerry nor Jamila attempted to answer him, but Jerry guessed that they were both thinking alike. Who could possibly understand why clothes would want to dismember human beings? Or more to the point, how? And there was also the worrying question: where were they now, these murderous clothes? Had they simply become lifeless again, like the clothes at Mindy's parents' house, or were they hiding somewhere, waiting for their chance to come out and tear even more innocent people to shreds?

Jamila said, 'Let's have a look at the victims, then, before they're taken away.'

'You're not going to enjoy this, I promise you,' said DC Malik. 'In fact, I guarantee you're going to have nightmares. Or even daymares.'

They walked along to the Jijaya Krishna restaurant and turned down Rookstone Road. For over fifty metres, the pavement on the right-hand side of the road had been completely covered with blue PVC tenting. Forensic experts were coming in and out of the tent flaps like wasps coming in and out of a nest. Behind the blue PVC, flashlights flickered, and every now and then it bulged up as a CSE stood up and moved around inside it.

Jerry looked across the street. The two victims had been killed directly opposite the entrance to the United Reformed Church. A placard on the brown-brick church façade announced I WILL POUR OUT MY SPIRIT ON ALL FLESH.

He nudged Jamila and nodded towards the placard. 'That's a bit too bloody appropriate for words, wouldn't you say?'

'You mustn't start thinking like that,' said Jamila. 'Before you know it, you'll start suspecting that it might have been the church minister who killed them, just to prove his point. As my grandmother used to say, living people are always looking for logical explanations, but ghosts and demons never feel the need for anything to make sense.'

'Pity we haven't got your granny here today, and I mean that. We could do with a bit of the old supernatural guidance.'

A freckly young female CSE was standing beside the tent, and she handed them face-masks and elasticated booties to cover their shoes. Jerry held up the flap so that Jamila could go in first and then he followed her.

Once inside, they stood next to each other, saying nothing. DC Malik had said that he had never seen bodies torn apart like this, but neither had Jerry or Jamila. About ten metres away, Ron and Nuying's heads were lying on the pavement close to each other, face to face, with their eyes bulging out of their sockets like cartoon characters. They were so bloody and raw and so knocked out of shape that it was only Nuying's long black hair that made it possible to tell them apart, and half of that had been torn off the side of her skull.

The remaining parts of their bodies were littered all the way along to the end of the tent. Their two spinal columns, their four deflated lungs, their stomachs, their dark brown kidneys – all with their glistening intestines winding in and out between them. The rain had washed away much of the blood, but dark red runnels were still soaking across the concrete and into the gutter.

Beside a pale severed arm lay a plastic carrier-bag. It had split open and six table-mats with Van Gogh sunflowers on them had spilled out.

Jerry and Jamila stayed for two or three minutes and then pushed their way back outside.

'It's incredible, isn't it?' said Jerry, pulling off his face-mask.

'What's incredible? I think I'm going to throw up.'

'No, but you look at all of that bloody mess – all of those bones and organs and guts and stuff – and you think to yourself – how did all those bits and pieces ever add up to a person – somebody who could talk and think and laugh and have sex and everything? Seeing that lot, that almost makes me believe in God. Or somebody bloody clever, anyway.'

Jamila didn't answer but took out her phone. After it had rung seven or eight times, she said, 'Yes, sir, it's me, sir. Yes, I'm at the scene now and DC Pardoe's with me. We're still scheduled to meet you at the station at eleven, but I believe that you should come and see the victims for yourself. No. I realise that, sir. I do understand. But no photographs or videos can adequately show you what has happened here.'

She listened, nodding, and then she said, 'We'll wait for you, of course. The media are here in force, TV and everything. I don't know if somebody has tipped them off that these murders are somehow out of the ordinary, but it wouldn't surprise me. No, I won't tell them anything until you get here. Yes, sir. No.'

When she had put her phone away, Jerry said, 'How did he react?'

'Well, he's not a happy bunny, naturally. But I get the feeling that he's going to act quickly and decisively, if only to protect his own reputation. He said he'll be here in half an hour, tops, so make sure that the bodies don't get moved until he arrives.'

'Scraped up, you mean,' said Jerry. He looked at his watch and said, 'Look – if he's going to take half an hour, let's go over to Mud and treat ourselves to a treble espresso. I think we deserve it.'

*

DI Saunders pushed aside the blue PVC tent flap and came out looking both shocked and sobered.

'Let me just have a word with the press,' he said, and walked over to the corner where the reporters were gathered. When he spoke, it was very slowly and deliberately, with long pauses in between his sentences: 'All I can tell you at the present time is that a man and a woman had been found dead, presumably murdered. I can't give you any further details until the two of them have been formally identified and their next-of-kin informed.'

'Can you tell us how they were killed?' asked the Sky News reporter.

'We'll have to wait for the post-mortems before I can definitively tell you that.'

'Does that mean it's not obvious how they died?'

'As I say, we'll have to wait for the post-mortems.'

'Do you have any suspects?' asked the BBC reporter.

'Not so far,' said DI Saunders, impatiently. 'But obviously our inquiries are ongoing.'

'There's a suggestion that they were very severely injured,' the BBC reporter persisted. 'In fact, catastrophically.'

'Who suggested that?' snapped DI Saunders.

'Well, I can't reveal my source, I'm afraid,' said the BBC reporter. 'But can you describe the nature of the injuries they suffered? Are we talking about head wounds? Gunshot wounds? Stab wounds? Crush injuries from being run over? That seems to be the favourite M.O. these days, running people over.'

'Their injuries were fatal,' said DI Saunders. 'That's all I can tell you for the time being. If you come to the station at twelve I'll be issuing a more comprehensive statement then, in conjunction with the borough press officer.'

'What about the damage to the WellBrain shop, sir?' asked a woman reporter from the *Wandsworth Guardian*. 'Does that have any connection to these two fatalities?'

'No further comment for the time being,' said DI Saunders. 'I do have to say one thing, though. We would caution everybody in the Tooting locality to be extremely vigilant until further notice, and I mean everybody. We would recommend that you avoid isolated locations – especially at night, and especially if you happen to be on your own or if there's only a small number of you.'

'So what exactly are you warning people to look out for?' asked the BBC reporter.

'Anybody unusual,' said DI Saunders. 'Anybody who doesn't look quite right.'

'That doesn't tell us much.'

'No, and the reason for that is we don't know much ourselves. Not yet. But we're simply making sure that the public at large is aware of the remote but real possibility of random attacks.'

'What are we talking about? Terrorists?'

'Anybody unusual. Anybody who doesn't look quite right. That's all I can tell you for now.'

'Detective Inspector Saunders!' called out the Sky reporter. 'Do you mean ISIS?'

DI Saunders ignored him. He turned his back on the cameras, crossed over to his Vauxhall Insignia and climbed in. The Sky reporter shouted the same question again, but DI Saunders didn't even look at him. He drove away from the kerb, and a PC lifted the tape for him and waved him through, so that he could speed off eastwards along the empty carriageway.

The reporters all turned expectantly towards Jerry and Jamila. The BBC reporter started to approach them, holding up a microphone with a large grey spoffle on it, and closely followed by a cameraman.

Jerry said, 'Come on, skip. Let's hit the bricks. Otherwise they'll have us talking a load of old evasive bollocks, too.'

'I don't think I'd know how to,' said Jamila. 'That was one course at Hendon I must have missed.'

*

At the media conference later that morning, DI Saunders gave out the names of Ronald Firbank and Liu Nuying but little else.

He admitted that their injuries had been 'severe' but went into no more detail than that. He was still holding back the information that Philip Wakefield had been dismembered – saying only that he had been the victim of 'aggravated assault'.

He repeated his warning that the public should keep their eyes open, because 'several highly dangerous individuals are thought to be at large around the area'. The borough press officer sat beside him in her purple tweed suit looking distinctly unhappy about this. DI Saunders had briefed her about the second-hand clothes that seemed to have motivated Samira Wazir to kill herself and their four suspects to commit murder. He had also told her about the duffle coats that had attacked Jerry and Alice. Although he had made it clear that he was deadly serious, she had found it all too far-fetched, and she had said so. 'For goodness' sake, detective inspector, what on earth do you take me for? A simpleton? Coats can't run around on their own!'

Eventually, though, he had managed to persuade her that there was a very real danger to the public, regardless of whether it came from clothes or from humans. Because of that, she had reluctantly agreed to endorse Jerry's line about a new recreational drug that turned its users into schizophrenic killers.

'At least I'll be able to say that I was mistaken, rather than insane,' she had told DI Saunders. 'But – honestly – it sounds to me as if you've all been taking some recreational drug yourselves.'

DI Saunders had pursed his lips but said nothing. On his blotter he had drawn a picture of a cow.

At the media conference, a stringer from *The Sun* raised his hand and called out, 'This drug, detective inspector – does it have a name?'

'Fireball XL5,' said DI Saunders. 'That's all we know. We haven't confiscated any samples of it yet, so we haven't been able to analyse it. But as far as we can tell it makes its users believe that they're another personality altogether, and that other personality can take revenge on anybody who might have upset them. And very violently, too.'

'What about Ronald Firbank and Liu Nuying? Had they upset anybody?'

'Not as far as we know. We've talked to their friends and it seems that they were both very mild-mannered and well-liked. Of course we'll be investigating further but on the surface this appears to have been a totally arbitrary attack, without any discernible motive. That's why we're warning the public to be so careful.'

'Where does this Fireball XL5 come from? Who's selling it? Any ideas?'

'We're still making inquiries.'

The BBC reporter said, 'That protective tenting that was erected at the crime scene – that was over fifty metres long. Can you explain why?'

'That was a matter for the CSEs. I've no comment to make about that.'

'Is it true that the bodies were dismembered?'

'I've no comment to make about that, either. We're still waiting for the post-mortem results, and it could be quite some time before we get those.'

'What about the window that was smashed at the WellBrain shop? I've talked to the manager and he said that almost three-quarters of his clothing stock was stolen. Do you have any suspects, and was that robbery connected in any way to these two murders?'

'We're still looking into that. It's early days yet.'

The media conference broke up with none of the reporters looking at all satisfied. Two of them knew Jerry and they came over to ask him if he could tell them in more detail how Ron and Nuying had been killed. All he could do was shrug and say, 'You'll have to wait and see. Sorry.'

'Oh come on Jerry,' said the reporter from the *Evening Standard*. 'This is worse than trying to get a straight answer out of President Trump. This is me you're talking to, not Up-His-Own-Arse from the Beeb.'

'Listen, you'll know soon enough,' Jerry told him. 'And when you do, you'll wish that you didn't, because you won't be able to find the words to explain it.'

'What the hell does that mean?'

'If I told you, you'd know, but you still wouldn't be able to explain it.'

The two reporters looked at each other in bewilderment. Jerry was about to say more, because he enjoyed teasing them, but then Jamila saw him talking to them and said, 'Jerry,' and beckoned him away. She trusted him, but not them.

41

Jerry couldn't manage anything more than a Ginster's Cornish pasty for lunch and even then he left most of the crust. He had just dropped it into his wastepaper basket when Jamila came in to tell him that she had heard from Dr Stewart at Springfield. Mindy had been taken there about three hours earlier and was now fit to be interviewed.

Jerry put on his raincoat and said, 'What about the others? Any news on them?'

'Not a lot of change, that's what Dr Stewart said, but no improvement. All of them still seem to be convinced that they're going to die, and soon.'

'Well, maybe the spirits possessing them are going to die. They kept saying that they needed to feed on human flesh, didn't they, but there's no way the hospital is going to be serving them fricassee of toddler anytime soon. The question is, will their hosts die, too?'

'I haven't a clue, Jerry. But I don't think we'll have to wait very long to find out.'

As they crossed the car park, Jerry held out the car keys and said, 'Do you want to drive, skip?'

'Do you know something? You are the first man who has ever asked me that. But no thanks. I'm a terrible driver. Not because I'm a woman, but because I'm Pakistani. More than thirty-three thousand people died in road accidents last year in Pakistan.'

'Blimey. That's twice the entire population of Tooting. My offer is withdrawn. If I let you drive, this place would be a graveyard.'

She smiled at him over the roof of the car and again he saw that expression in her eyes: *I like you, and I could have allowed myself to like you even more if only our destiny had been different.* It made him feel pleased and regretful, both at the same time.

*

Cherry Mwandi was waiting for them at Springfield and she led them through to the high-security wing. A young black PC was on duty there, looking infinitely bored. He had a book open on his lap but he was staring at the opposite wall as if he were deep in thought.

'What's that you're reading?' Jerry asked him.

He lifted it up so that Jerry could see the cover. *A Brief History of Time.*

'I'm trying to read it, anyway,' said the PC. 'I thought it would make the time pass quicker, but it seems to make it go twice as slow.'

Cherry Mwandi escorted them along the corridor to the room where Mindy was being treated.

'Has she spoken to you at all?' asked Jamila.

'Not really. When they brought her in she was still very

groggy from the analgesics. She asked where she was, and she asked for a drink of water, and then about half an hour ago she asked for a vodka.'

'Vodka? You didn't give her any?'

Cherry Mwandi shook her head in amusement as she unlocked the door. 'Of course not. And she's still on a saline drip to replace the fluid she lost during her operation.'

Mindy was lying in bed with the sides raised to prevent her from falling out, although Jerry could see that she was wearing a blue restraint belt, too. She was pale, with some red blotches around her mouth, and her eyes were puffy, but her shiny brunette bob had recently been brushed. Jerry found it difficult to believe that this skinny nine-year-old schoolgirl with a turned-up nose had horrifically murdered both of her parents and then cut the penis off a strange man and eaten it.

Jerry and Jamila sat down on opposite sides of the bed. Mindy looked suspiciously from one to the other.

'I know you,' she said, in a husky whisper.

'Yes,' said Jamila. 'We talked to you before, if you remember, outside that house on Pretoria Road. I'm Detective Sergeant Jamila Patel, and this is Detective Constable Jerry Pardoe. We need to ask you a few questions if you feel up to it.'

'What difference will it make?' said Mindy. 'I am dying.'

'No, you're not,' Jamila told her. 'You've had a traumatic experience, and you've had to undergo some quite extensive surgery, but you don't need to worry. Before you know it you'll be feeling much better.'

'You are wrong. I am dying. I know what dying feels like. I have died before.'

'What's your name, sweetheart?' Jerry asked her.

'I told you before. Varvara.'

Jerry looked across the bed at Jamila. 'We were right,' he said. He nodded his head in the direction of Sophie's room and then he mouthed the words 'they're both Varvara'.

'How did you die, Varvara?' asked Jamila, taking hold of Mindy's hand.

'I had the flu. I couldn't breathe. They took me to the hospital but I caught pneumonia. I don't want to die like that again. It was like drowning, except in bed.'

'Varvara, you can't have your time over again,' said Jamila. 'You've taken over this poor young girl's mind and body and you've made her commit the most appalling crimes.'

'What else could I do? I needed to eat,' said Mindy. 'There's only one way that I can come back to life, and that's if I eat. And who cares about this young girl? She's a nobody. My life is the only life that's important.'

'You've had your life, Varvara. Mindy's only nine. She deserves to have hers.'

'Ha! She will now, won't she? If I don't get anything to eat, I'm going to be dead in two days. This time I won't even have a funeral.'

'You have to have human flesh, though, don't you, to stay alive?' Jerry asked her.

'Of course I do, because my body has been cremated. I am nothing but ashes, so I need to rebuild myself. How can I rebuild myself with anything else but human flesh?'

'Is there any way in which I can speak to Mindy?' asked Jamila.

Mindy stared at her for a moment, and then said, 'No. Why would you want to do that?'

'She's still inside you?'

'She's sleeping.'

'But she's still alive, and she's safe?'

'I need to eat. I'm so hungry I could eat my own arms. Can't you please, please find me something to eat? This is a hospital, isn't it? There must be sick or dead people here that nobody wants.'

'Varvara, tell me something about yourself,' said Jamila. 'Where were you born?'

'What do you care? I'm starving.'

'It might help us to understand what's happened to you… How you came to take over Mindy's body. And if we can understand that – I don't know, we may be able to help you in some way.'

'What – you're going to help me die? It was bad enough the first time. This is going to be worse.'

'Please, just tell us where you came from, originally.'

'I was born in Vilnius,' said Mindy. 'October the 12th, 1951.'

'Vilnius? That's the capital of Lithuania, right?' said Jerry.

Mindy looked at him as if he were retarded. 'Of course. Where else?'

'So when did you come to England?'

'In 1991. I met my husband Wiktor when he came to Lithuania to work for Achema the fertiliser company, in Jonava. In 1989 there was a big explosion in the factory and a huge cloud of ammonia gas spread over the countryside. I breathed it in, and after that I always suffered problems with my lungs. Wiktor got a job here, in Merton, and we came here to live, but my chest always hurt and I was always catching cold. That was why I died before my time. Don't you think I deserve a new life?'

'Not at Mindy's expense, love,' said Jerry. 'You've ruined this young girl for ever. She's murdered her own parents and mutilated that bloke who picked her up, even if he was asking for it. When you're dead and she's got her own body back, how do you think she's going to deal with that? I'll be surprised if she doesn't go mental.'

Mindy closed her eyes while Jerry was talking, as if to show him that she wasn't listening. When he had finished, she suddenly opened them again and blinked, and clutched at her sheet. 'What is that light?' she demanded.

'What light?'

'That red light! Why are they shining that red light in my eyes?'

'Nobody's shining any light in your eyes, Varvara. I don't know what you're talking about.'

'It's blinding me!' she said, angrily, covering her eyes with both hands. 'Tell them to stop!'

'I'll fetch the nurse,' said Jamila. She reached over and pressed the button to call for assistance.

'It's blinding me! I can't see!'

A nurse appeared, followed by Cherry Mwandi. Mindy kept her hands pressed over her eyes, but said nothing else, even when the nurse asked her what was wrong.

After two or three minutes, she took her hands away and stared at the ceiling.

'Varvara? Can you answer some more questions?' asked Jamila, but she didn't respond.

'I think it would be better to leave her for now,' said Cherry Mwandi. 'Dr Stewart's anxious that she doesn't get too distraught. We don't yet fully understand her condition, but mentally she seems to be right on the edge, and we don't want her suffering a stroke or any other kind of a seizure.'

'Very well,' said Jamila. 'Perhaps you could call us again when she improves.'

Jerry and Jamila left Springfield hospital and drove through heavy traffic back to the station. On the way, Jamila prodded intently at her iPhone, and didn't look up until they had to stop at the junction with Tooting Broadway.

While they waited for the traffic lights to change to green, Jerry said, 'What do you think that was all about? All that fuss about a red light?'

'I can't even guess,' said Jamila. 'But she's in such a peculiar psychological state, who can tell? What really disturbed me was everything that she was saying about her life in Lithuania. If she isn't possessed by Varvara, how could she possibly know about that explosion at the fertiliser factory? I've just Googled it and it happened in 1989 exactly like she said.'

'Blimey.'

'Yes – it produced a cloud of ammonia gas seven kilometres wide and fifty kilometres long and seven people in the surrounding towns were killed. Hundreds of other people suffered from cardiac arrest and respiratory problems.'

'Well, if it really is her, skip, that sort of fits in with what I was thinking about the red light. It could be that it's infrared.'

'I don't follow you.'

'She's inside Mindy, isn't she, and at the same time she's inside Sophie Marshall, so she can be in two places at once, right? But maybe that means she can be in any number of places at once. Maybe she's still inside her jacket, too. Dr Fuller's sent the jacket to Lambeth Road for forensics, and one of the first things they'll be doing there is putting it under an IR spectroscope.'

'And you think that's what she could see?'

'I'm only guessing, but it could have been. And another thing – if she's still inside that jacket, nobody else had better try it on. They might end up like Sophie and Mindy. The same could apply to that coat that Samira and Jamie were both wearing, and Laura Miller's coat, and David Nelson's sweater.'

'Well, I doubt if anybody will try them on, but I'll warn them all the same. I don't have to explain the reason, do I?'

'No, I suppose not,' said Jerry, as they turned into the station car park. 'But then again, we don't really know the reason ourselves, do we?'

42

Jerry wasn't sure why, but as the afternoon wore on, he began to have a feeling that something bad was about to happen. He hadn't felt like this since he had walked into the Two Chairmen pub in Dartmouth Street near New Scotland Yard and seen two detectives deep in conversation with what they called their CRO friends – meaning convicted criminals whose names were listed in the Criminal Records Office – and then an envelope changing hands.

Although it was only 3:15, the sky had grown almost black, and fat spots of rain started to speckle the windows. At the same time, the station was unnaturally hushed, with nobody shouting or whistling or banging doors. A phone was ringing somewhere along the corridor, and it went on and on ringing as if nobody was ever going to answer it.

He heard squeaking footsteps outside the open door of the CID room, and DI French appeared. He was chafing his hands together and looked extremely pleased with himself.

'Liepa's up in front of the magistrates first thing tomorrow morning, Jerry, so I hope you've got your statement all sorted.'

'Just doing that now, guv,' Jerry told him.

'Shouldn't take long. They'll pass it straight on to the Crown Court. Hope he gets twenty-nine years, the bastard.'

'Do we know a date for Whitey's funeral yet?'

'Oh, yes,' said DI French. 'Next Thursday afternoon, two o'clock, Southwark Cathedral. It's going to be the full ceremonial... Met service colour party, horse-drawn hearse, guard of honour, the lot. Callow's PA can give you all of the details.'

'OK, thanks.'

DI French hesitated in the doorway. 'By the bye... how's it going with those two who got torn to bits on Rookstone Road? I was asking Saunders about it, but he was cagey, to say the least. He told me you suspect that a gang did it, but apart from that he wouldn't elaborate.'

'I don't think he's holding anything back from you, guv. The fact is that we don't have any eye-witnesses and so far the CSEs haven't given us anything to go on.'

'Strange one. Very strange. Reminds me of my very first murder case. A pregnant woman was found floating in the lido with no head and no legs. That was supposed to be gang-related. I always reckoned it was one of the Tooting Trap Stars but we never did find out who did it.'

'Well, maybe this is a little different,' said Jerry.

'Tooting Boys? They're always chopping each other up with axes, aren't they?'

Jerry was tempted to tell him about the empty coats, but all he could do was shrug and go back to his laptop. DI Saunders had insisted that apart from Jerry and Jamila and those officers who had already seen clothes moving on their own, nobody else should be told who their suspects really were – not until it became impossible to keep it under wraps any longer. Even Inspector Callow was still under the impression that they were looking for a marauding gang of young men – maybe Asian or West Indian – and not empty coats.

Jerry continued to prod at his keyboard with two fingers. *The vehicle driven by Herkus Adomaitis with Jokubas Liepa in the front passenger seat was in collision with Police Constable White*

He was still painstakingly typing when he heard a sudden barrage of doors slamming, and shouting, and the sound of running feet. He stood up and went to the door to see what the noise was all about, and as he did so he heard sirens wailing and scribbling outside, and tyres screeching as patrol cars pulled out of the station car park, at least four or five of them, one after the other. Almost immediately, his phone rang.

'Jerry?' It was DI Saunders, and he sounded breathless, as if he had been running. 'I'm in the control room. You need to come down here now.'

'What's up, guv?'

'Come down and see for yourself. About ten minutes ago Sergeant Bristow had a call from the Crime Watch Manager at Wandsworth. Four or five charity shops along the Broadway and Mitcham Road had their front windows smashed, almost simultaneously, as well as Primark and some fashion store called Xclusive. Now there's gangs running through the streets attacking pedestrians, knocking them over and pushing them into traffic.'

'When you say "gangs"—'

'You can't see them too clearly on the monitor. But we're getting dozens of 999 calls, and they're all saying the same thing. They're being attacked by coats and jackets and sweaters with nobody in them. No heads, no legs, but causing multiple serious injuries. It's hard to estimate how many there are, but we've dispatched six units to start with, as well as two ARVs. If this starts to get out of control, though, we may need to call in more.'

'OK, guv. I'll be right down.'

Jerry unhooked his raincoat from the back of the door, slung it over his shoulder and hurried downstairs to the control room. He found DI Saunders and DC Willis and Sergeant Bristow staring at the six CCTV slave monitors that were connected to the main crime watch centre at Wandsworth Town Hall. One of the screens showed the junction of Tooting Broadway and Mitcham Road, where traffic was at a standstill and people were running between the stationary cars in apparent panic.

At first it wasn't easy to see what they were running from, but then twenty or thirty figures appeared around the front of the Tube station, past the statue of Edward VII, and although many of them were hooded, Jerry could see that their hoods were dark and empty, like the coats that had attacked him and Alice. Then he saw headless sweaters, and dresses, too.

When they caught up with any of the fleeing shoppers, they either seized them and started beating them or else they pushed them into the road.

'This is really happening, isn't it?' said DI Saunders, and his voice was flat with dread. 'It's not mass hysteria. It's really bloody happening.'

'Yes, guv.'

'We need to get down there now. Where's DS Patel?'

'She went out about twenty minutes ago to grab a bite to eat at Samrat's,' said Jerry. 'I'll give her a bell.'

'All right. Let me know when she gets back. I'll just go and update Callow and I'll meet you out front.'

Jerry went down to the front desk and picked up a set of car keys. Sergeant Clark was there, grizzled and paunchy and grey-haired. 'Bleeding pandemonium out there,' he said. 'Bleeding World War Three.'

Jerry went out to the car park. He had to jump back when another patrol car came speeding out with its blue lights flashing and its siren blaring. Then he went over and climbed into an unmarked silver Mondeo, driving it out of the station and parking across the road to wait for Jamila. While he waited, he listened to the frantic reports that were coming in over the Airwave radio.

'There's more than a hundred of them gathered outside the Tube station. I don't believe what I'm seeing! They're fucking coats!'

'We've got more of them running south on the Broadway from Garratt Lane. Fifty or sixty at least. Coats and jackets and shirts and Christ knows what.'

'They're all across the road and they're not stopping for nothing – not even for buses.'

Jamila reached the car and opened the passenger door, and Jerry caught a waft of curry. As she climbed in, DI Saunders came hurrying down the steps in front of the station. He crossed the road and sat himself down in the back.

'Right, let's go,' he said. 'I need to see this with my own eyes. Callow's arranging back-up with riot gear from Sutton nick, and the ASU are sending a helicopter over from Lippitt's Hill.'

Jerry pulled out and started to drive towards Amen Corner, but as soon as he reached it he found that the main Mitcham Road was gridlocked with cars and buses. Some drivers had climbed out of their cars to try to see what the hold-up was. He switched on the Mondeo's blue flashing lights and gave occasional whoops on the siren, and when two cars had backed up to let him through, he managed to steer his way slowly down the centre of the road in between the two opposing lines of traffic.

They had only reached the Granada Bingo Hall when they saw the first people running. They looked as if they were trying to get away from a terrorist attack – only a few at first, but then more and more. Jerry saw mothers desperately pushing baby buggies and carrying small children, while some shoppers were throwing aside their carrier-bags so that they could run faster. One Asian man was even carrying an elderly woman in a hijab over his shoulder, with her skinny ankles dangling.

Then, close behind the crowds of running people, the coats and the jackets began to appear. Jerry could see them bobbing up and down – black and khaki and navy-blue coats, as well as brown and chequered jackets and dark grey anoraks. They were headless, but whirling their sleeves, and billowing along the pavement in the same way that the black raincoat had flown down the road when Jerry was chasing it.

Whenever the coats caught up with any of the fleeing shoppers, they snatched at their arms and wound their sleeves around them. Then they swung them violently sideways, so that they were thumped against the nearest shop frontage, or doorway, or lamp-post. If they weren't concussed the first time, the coats swung them again and again until blood was spattered across the pavement and up the shop windows. After the shoppers had dropped to the pavement, the coats rolled them over so that they were lying face down, and then twisted their sleeves around their heads and jerked them back, and it looked as if they were breaking their necks.

There were scores of assorted clothes, and they were tumbling along so fast that they began to overtake the shoppers, only to turn around and snatch at their arms as they desperately tried to dodge their way past. So many beaten and bloody bodies were now heaped on the pavements that the shoppers following them were stumbling over them, and that made them easy pickings for the hordes of coats and jackets coming up behind them.

'Christ, it's a massacre,' said DI Saunders. Even though the car windows were all closed, they could hear the fleeing shoppers screaming in terror, and another sound, too, deep and blustery, like a strong wind blowing.

The police messages on the radio were becoming increasingly panicky.

'—we've got three more men down – we can't—!'

'—there's too many of them – get back!—'

'Oh God, it's pulled his head off! It's only gone and pulled his fucking head off!'

Among the crowds who were rushing along the pavements, they could now see police officers, too. They were beating at the coats and jackets with their batons to keep them away, but it was obvious that they too were running for their lives. Three hooded coats leapt on top of one PC and brought him to the ground, and then more coats piled on top of them until he was almost completely buried.

They heard three shots, and then another two, but they couldn't see any armed police, and none of the coats seemed to have been hit.

Jerry tried to drive forward, but a bus had pulled out halfway across the road, and the gap was too narrow. He thought at first that he might be able to force his way through by ramming aside the cars on the opposite side. With a harsh metallic squeal, he started to scrape his Mondeo along the side of the Jaguar next to them. The driver shook his fist and started shouting, although Jerry couldn't hear him, but the two cars were so tightly jammed together that the driver couldn't open his door.

Jerry revved the Mondeo's engine, but before he could push any further forward, coats and jackets and dresses began to appear between the cars, beating on them with their sleeves. They flooded across the road, hammering at every car they reached, shattering their windows and reaching inside them to drag out their drivers and their passengers.

A trench-coat came running up to the front of their car and beat its sleeves on the bonnet, denting it. Jamila said, 'Jerry – we need to get out of here, and fast!'

Jerry put the Mondeo into reverse so that it slowly screeched free from the Jaguar. Then he turned around in his seat, put his foot down, and drove backwards the way he had come, in the middle of the road between the two lines of traffic. He collided four or five times with other cars, and once with an Ocado van, but at last he reached Amen Corner, and managed to reverse the Mondeo into the police station car park, although he hit the wall as he did so, and then knocked over a police motorcycle.

They all climbed out, shaken. DI Saunders said, 'Let's find Callow, pronto. He's probably watching all this but he needs to know that it's a full-scale Code 13.'

The three of them hurried upstairs. Officers were running up and down the corridors and phones were ringing on every floor. They found Inspector Callow in the control room. He was very tall, with thinning brown hair, glittery little eyes and a long, pointed chin. He was watching the closed-circuit TV screens with his hand pressed over his mouth, as if he couldn't believe what he was seeing. When DI Saunders and Jerry and Jamila came in, he turned to them and shook his head and said, 'They're nothing but clothes. There's nobody in them. I think I must be going mad.'

The shirt-sleeved officer who was operating the camera said, 'They're definitely coming this way, sir. They've just crossed Avarn Road.'

'Right,' said Inspector Callow. 'I want the station locked down, but keep a couple of PCs on the doors in case any of our own people need to get back in.'

'What's the SP?' asked Jerry.

'Absolute chaos at the moment,' said Inspector Callow. 'They sent us twenty-seven men from Sutton, complete with riot gear, and two armed response vehicles. They tried to kettle the rioters outside the Tube station but they were totally routed. They're still running. Look at the monitor. There's one of them. There's another. They've even dropped their shields.'

'"Rioters"?' asked Jamila.

'Well, I don't know what else to call them,' said Inspector Callow. 'It's surreal. But it's also real. Two of the armed response officers fired at them, not just once but three or four times. It had no effect on them at all. Why would it? They're not people – they're clothes.'

He paused, watching the tide of panicking shoppers as they came nearer and nearer along Mitcham Road.

'I contacted Deputy Commander Broadbent as soon as I saw that things were getting out of hand. He didn't believe me at first and I can't say I blame him. He even asked me if I'd been drinking. Then I sent him the CCTV link and he saw what was happening for himself. He's appointed me gold commander and I've already called for urgent reinforcements from all around the borough. He says we may have to bring in the SAS if we can't contain the situation within the next couple of hours. God knows what the final death toll's going to be. How the hell do you stop clothes?'

Jamila said, 'They're possessed, sir. Possessed by spirits of some kind, most likely the ghosts of dead people.'

'Spirits?' said Inspector Callow. 'Ghosts?'

'I know it sounds far-fetched, sir, but look at what we are witnessing here, right in front of our eyes. DC Pardoe and I have interviewed the suspects who claimed that their clothes were responsible for turning them into murderers, and we have both become convinced that possession is the most likely explanation. You can call it "infection" if that sounds more rational. In Pakistan and other Asian countries there are many stories about such possessions. Most of them are simply folk tales, but there are so many and they are so similar – and similar to what is happening here – so I do believe there is a nub of truth in them.'

Inspector Callow turned to DI Saunders. 'Simon? You've been in charge of these investigations. What's your opinion?'

DI Saunders nodded towards the CCTV screens. Each was showing Tooting Broadway and Mitcham Road from a different angle.

'Like DS Patel says, sir, we can't pretend this isn't happening, just because it's so bloody weird. I was the same as you, sir, I didn't want to believe it at first. None of us did.'

'So you think those suspects were actually telling the truth, and it was their clothes that made them do it?'

Jerry and Jamila knew that DI Saunders hadn't told Inspector Callow about the way he had been attacked by Mindy's dead parents – and how they had been stopped by

Jerry cutting off the sweater and the dress that had been clinging around their necks.

'I think there's a strong possibility,' said DI Saunders. 'I mean – up until now I've never had any time for psychics or mediums or people who try to make out that there's life after death. I've always thought that when you die, that's the end of you. Before you were born you were dead for a billion years and it didn't bother you, did it? But I can't think of any other explanation for those clothes running around and killing people.'

On the CCTV screens they could see two hooded coats gripping a young woman's arms and repeatedly hitting her head against the corner of a glass phone box. Blood and brains burst out of her black cornrow hair and splashed across the phone box's door.

'My God,' said Inspector Callow, under his breath. 'How is it possible?'

'I have no idea, sir, but there it is, right in front of our eyes,' said DI Saunders. Jerry had never heard him sound so miserable. 'Unless somebody else can prove her wrong, I'll go along with DS Patel.'

Jerry was relieved to hear him say that, and he could see that Jamila was, too. They knew that he had been suppressing the supernatural aspects of these cases for as long as he could, for fear of being ridiculed, but now there was no denying what was happening.

'Sir – riot squad from Wandsworth nick have just arrived,' said the CCTV operator.

'How do you want to deploy them, sir?' asked DI Saunders.

'We'll line them up outside here first and then see if we can push the clothes back along the Mitcham Road,' said Inspector Callow. 'There's reinforcements coming from

Feltham and Shepherd's Bush and they can bottle them up at the Broadway. A couple of Jankel armoured trucks are being sent down from Heathrow, too, and they should be able to contain them.'

'And once we've contained them?'

Jerry could see by the expression on Inspector Callow's face that he had no idea what they would do, even if they did manage to kettle the clothes between here and Tooting Broadway. They had been beaten and even shot but it hadn't deterred them at all. What else could be done to stop them?

43

Three police Transit vans had arrived from Wandsworth and parked nose-to-tail outside the station. DI Saunders went down to meet them, and Jerry and Jamila went with him.

The noise in the streets was hellish. From the direction of Mitcham Road there was screaming and shouting and police sirens, as well as the intermittent banging of gunshots and the smashing of car and shop windows.

Thirty officers in full black riot gear had jumped out of the vans and were lining up along the pavement. DI Saunders went up to the sergeant in charge and said, 'They're heading this way. We need to stop them before they come any further, and see if we can push them back towards the Broadway.'

'You say "they", sir,' said the sergeant. 'Who exactly are we talking about?'

'They're coats and jackets and other clothes,' said Jamila. 'They've become alive, and they're extremely violent.'

'And they're bloody strong, too,' Jerry put in. 'Don't underestimate them, just because they're clothes.'

The sergeant stared at them. 'Coats and jackets? Are you serious? I was told they were rioters, that's all.'

Jerry was about to say more when the first of the coats appeared around the corner. They were still beating at cars and shattering their windows, but they were advancing more slowly now, fanning themselves out across the road. There was no sign of any more shoppers. The coats must have killed most of them, although Jerry hoped that some of them had managed to escape down one of the side-streets, or hidden in cafés or shops.

'God almighty,' said the sergeant. 'I'm seeing things.'

The coats were joined by jackets and windcheaters and long black dresses. They stopped for a few moments, lined up like warriors in some film about a medieval battle, their sleeves flapping in some unfelt wind. The feeling of war was heightened by the sound of drumming, because the coats that were coming up behind them were beating relentlessly on the bonnets and rooftops of the cars that were jammed along the Mitcham Road. Those drivers who hadn't been dragged out of their vehicles remained trapped, cowering, behind the wheel, although many of them had managed to climb out of their cars and run away down Southcroft Road.

The sergeant shouted to his men, 'Let's have you all spread out across the street! We need to push these buggers back, OK? Move forward slowly, keep your shields together, and don't let any of them get behind you!'

'OK, sarge, but what the fuck are they?' called out one of his PCs.

'That doesn't matter! Just push them back and keep on pushing them back!'

The riot squad lined themselves up to face the coats, drawing their batons and shuffling themselves close together so that their transparent shields overlapped. Almost as if the weather could sense the drama of this confrontation, it began to rain again, suddenly and heavily.

Jamila said, 'I think this is when we pray.'

The first clothes began to float eerily forward, with hundreds more clothes massing behind them. The drumming stopped. There was no sound now except for the pattering of rain on the tarmac, and two distant sirens warbling, and somewhere a woman's voice calling out 'Help me! Help me!' although it was hard to tell where it was coming from.

As the coats approached, the riot police moved to meet them, until they were only ten metres apart, when they both stopped.

Although he couldn't see their faces, Jerry could guess from the way in which the riot police were uncomfortably shifting their boots that they were deeply unnerved. In front of them, in the drifting rain, they were confronted by parkas with empty hoods, as well as dripping sweaters with nobody in them, and long dresses that were twisted like tied-back curtains. All of these clothes were swaying inches above the roadway, and it was impossible to imagine what was keeping them up.

'Come on, advance! Push them back!' the sergeant shouted. He was almost screaming, which showed that he was just as frightened as his men.

The riot police took another few hesitant steps forward, but as soon as they did so the clothes rushed at them with the force of a tidal wave. They collided with the line of riot shields and knocked almost all of the officers off their feet. Some of them fell backwards onto the wet roadway, their shields clattering on top of them. Some of them staggered sideways, but were instantly jumped on by hooded coats and rain-soaked sweaters and dragged down onto the pavement. They started shrieking in fear and agony as the clothes wound their sleeves around their arms and legs and started to wrench them out of their sockets.

DI Saunders hesitated. It was obvious that he didn't want to look like a coward and abandon all of these officers, but now a whole army of clothes was pouring down the road towards the police station and there was no chance that any of them could be saved. Even the riot squad's sergeant turned around and started to run. He was almost halfway back to the police station when a grey raincoat came slithering along the ground and entangled his ankles and then a bronze padded anorak with a thick furry collar leapt onto his shoulders. He fell to the ground face-first, his forehead hitting a kerbstone with a crack.

DI Saunders didn't have to give an order to run. Jerry and Jamila and DI Saunders began to bound up the steps that led to the police station's front doors. A PC was holding the left-hand door open for them, but Jerry had the horrible feeling that if the clothes caught up with them before they could reach it, he would slam it shut in their faces.

They had nearly reached the top of the steps when Jamila let out a piping scream. Jerry turned to see that a long dark brown dress had caught hold of her arm, and was starting to wind one of its sleeves around her upper arm.

He seized the sleeve and prised it off her. It was so wriggly and strong that it nearly twisted itself free, but he clenched his left fist firmly around it and wouldn't let it go. Then he reached over with his right hand and snatched at the other sleeve.

For a few moments the two of them were locked in a struggling dance. The dress tried to pull Jerry back down the steps, and he tripped and almost lost his balance, but he managed to steady himself, lean back, and heave the dress back up again.

'Jerry!' shouted Jamila. 'Let it go!'

Jerry was struggling so hard to keep hold of the two wet woollen sleeves that he could only grunt. But he could guess what would happen if he let it go. It wouldn't try to fly away – it would launch itself at him even more fiercely and wind its sleeves around his neck and try to choke him, just like that duffle coat.

Still gripping the right sleeve, he pushed his fist down between the two white iron handrails that ran up the centre of the steps. Then he forced the left sleeve underneath the nearer handrail, so that he could knot the two together.

The dress struggled against him so fiercely that it took every ounce of strength that he could summon up, but with his teeth gritted he managed to tie one wet sleeve around the other and pull it tight. The dress was now fastened to the handrail, and even though it flapped and curled and lashed against the steps like a landed manta ray, it couldn't get free.

'Jerry!' shouted Jamila, and this time she sounded almost hysterical. He backed away from the furiously struggling dress, catching his heel on the top step behind him so that he sat down, hard, jarring his spine. As he stood up again, he saw that the clothes had reached the bottom step, a sinister crowd of dark hooded coats and jackets, and that they were already floating up towards him.

He turned and with three gazelle-like bounds that would have made him laugh if he hadn't been so terrified, he reached the front doors of the station and staggered inside. The PC who had been holding the door open immediately slammed it shut, and shot the bolts across it, top and bottom. Two seconds later, the doors thundered and shook as the clothes piled into them.

DI Saunders looked grey. 'Thought you were done for there, Jerry, like those other poor bastards.'

Jerry stood there, panting, trying to get his breath back. He was tempted to say, *It takes more than a wet brown dress to get the better of me, Smiley*. Instead, he simply nodded. He felt a sharp pain in his left thumb and guessed that he might have sprained it when he was tying the sleeves together.

Jamila came over and without any hesitation or embarrassment she wrapped her arms around him and hugged him.

'You saved my life, Jerry,' she said, looking up at him, and her dark brown eyes were glistening with tears. 'I would have died if it hadn't been for you.'

The reception area was crowded with sergeants and acting sergeants and PCs and PCSOs and other station staff, and they were all milling around looking frightened and utterly baffled. They were being besieged by clothes? All Jerry could do was pull a self-deprecating face to show them that he wasn't a hero and that he hardly understood what was happening any more than they did. He didn't want them to realise that he was still trembling from fear and physical strain and the sheer unreality of fighting a dress that had been determined to tear him apart.

The lift doors opened and Inspector Callow quickly walked out. Jamila let go of Jerry and stepped away, but she gave his hand a last affectionate squeeze, right on his twisted thumb, so that it was as much as he could do not to yelp out loud.

Holding up his hands for attention, Inspector Callow said, 'It's hard to accept, I know that. It seems like science fiction. But as most of you are now aware, some unknown force has enabled all kinds of clothing to come to life. Coats and shirts and sweaters and dresses: they can walk and run as if they have people wearing them, even though they don't. Even more alarming than that, they seem to be determined to attack and kill every person they come across.'

DI Saunders said, 'From what we've seen first-hand on the streets and from CCTV, they may already have killed and injured as many as two or three hundred – possibly more. Innocent shoppers and cyclists and motorists and bus passengers, not to mention the entire riot squad team that was sent down from Wandsworth to give us back-up.'

'Right now, they've surrounded the station on all sides,' said Inspector Callow. 'They've broken some windows at the rear of the building but of course they're barred and they haven't been able to gain access. I've called for more reinforcements and they should be arriving within twenty to twenty-five minutes, including anti-terrorist teams and a specialist SAS squadron. Meanwhile there's not a lot we can do except sit tight and repel any attempts to break in.'

He hadn't finished speaking before the front doors thundered again. The clothes had collided with them with such force that plaster dust sifted down from the lintel.

'Don't let's lose our nerve,' said Inspector Callow. 'I fully realise that we're up against a threat that's unlike anything we've ever had to face before. Infinitely greater in numbers than any jihadi attack. Infinitely more aggressive. And infinitely more difficult to counter.'

Sergeant Bristow raised his hand and said, 'Do we have any idea why they're attacking us, sir? I mean, why would they want to go for the very people who have the best chance of stopping them?'

'I can't answer that, sergeant,' said Inspector Callow. 'But perhaps that's the reason. They want to neutralise us so that they can be free to cause whatever havoc they have in mind. Although that suggests, doesn't it, that they have minds, and that they can think, and communicate with each other? They're nothing more than fabric. How can cotton and wool and nylon think for themselves? Because that's all they are.' He turned to DI Saunders and Jerry and Jamila. 'Let's go back to the control room. We need to keep a close eye on what they're doing, these – clothes.'

They all went upstairs. On the CCTV screens in the control room they could see that the building was completely surrounded, and that at least a dozen hooded coats were relentlessly beating at all of the outside doors with their sleeves. They could hear the dull thumping sound of it, even up here in this soundproofed room.

DI Saunders stared at the screens for almost a minute before he said, 'What if they can't be stopped? We know they can't be Tasered, and they can't be shot, and they haven't got eyes or lungs so tear-gas isn't going to work, is it? What if they manage to break the doors down and get inside? What the hell are we going to do then?'

'I have been thinking about this, too,' said Jamila. 'In the stories my grandmother used to tell me in Pakistan, evil spirits were usually banished with religious incantations. But we don't know if these spirits have any religion, and if they do, what religion it might be. We can't even be sure that they are spirits, or ghosts, not in the sense that we usually understand them.'

'Well, let's hope we can hold out until the SAS get here,'

said Inspector Callow. 'I'm sure they can work out a way of dealing with them, especially if any of them have experience of fighting ISIS and the Taliban.'

Jerry said, 'Those clothes at Mindy's parents' house... they came to life, didn't they? But they didn't stay alive for long. They just about made it down the stairs and that was as far as they went. And all three of our suspects at Springfield told us that the personalities that have taken them over are dying. Maybe these clothes are going to do the same and simply run out of steam.'

There was renewed thumping on the back door that led out to the car park. Then they heard a grinding crash, too, and when they looked at the CCTV screens they saw that a cluster of clothes had heaved a patrol car onto its side and were smashing the windows and denting the doors.

'Running out of steam?' said DI Saunders. 'Not this lot. Not yet, anyhow.'

'Anti-terrorist unit are just passing Wandsworth Common,' said the radio operator. 'ETA twelve minutes.'

It was then that the CCTV screens died and turned black, and immediately afterwards, all the lights went out.

44

There was a moment of utter silence and darkness before the emergency generator kicked in and all the lights flickered back on.

'This is getting more than serious,' said Inspector Callow. 'Have you had an update from the SAS yet?'

'About thirty-five minutes, they told me,' said the radio operator. 'The traffic's a nightmare.'

There was nothing more they could do but watch as the clothes that were clustered around the police station continued to pound at the door-panels. Jerry said nothing, but he had seen how the duffle coats had torn off the door of his car, and he wasn't at all sure that the police station doors would be strong enough to keep them out for very much longer.

'Anti-terrorist unit's come back,' said the radio operator. 'Garratt Lane's blocked solid and they're trying to find an alternative route. ETA maybe twenty.'

Sergeant Bristow came into the control room. He went straight over to DI Saunders and said, 'Liepa says he needs to talk to us, urgent-like.'

'Liepa? What the bloody hell does he want? Doesn't he realise we've got a crisis on our hands?'

'Well, that's it, sir, he does. We've had to tell him what's going on in case we have to evacuate the cells. He says that he can help.'

'Help? How?'

'He didn't go into any detail, sir, but he said that he knows how these clothes have come to life.'

'He's blagging it,' said DI Saunders. 'Go back and tell him we're not interested.'

'Hold up a minute, guv,' said Jerry. 'Liepa deals with second-hand clothes all the time. That's his racket. Maybe he does know something. It might be worth hearing what he's got to say.'

'He's responsible for killing one of our officers,' DI Saunders retorted. 'Why should he care what happens to the rest of us?'

'He probably doesn't care two hoots,' said Jamila. 'But maybe he cares about his own survival. If the clothes manage to break in, he's going to be in just as much danger as we are.'

'He's locked in a cell.'

'I don't think that's going to save him, guv,' said Jerry. 'I reckon that some of those coats could tear a cell door off, no trouble.'

'I would like to hear what he has to say,' said Jamila, firmly.

Sergeant Bristow looked at DI Saunders, and DI Saunders thought for a moment and then shrugged. 'OK. Bring him up to interview room two. But as soon as we've heard him out, I want him banged up again straight away.'

When Sergeant Bristow had left the control room, Jerry said, 'You're right, guv. Liepa's probably going to come out with a load of old moody, but like I say, he's been handling second-hand clothes for years, and maybe he can give us a hint.'

'I'll believe it when I hear it,' said DI Saunders.

*

Jokubas Liepa was already sitting at the table in interview room two when DI Saunders came in with Jerry and Jamila. Two PCs were sitting at the back of the room with their arms folded. On normal days, they would have been looking bored, but with the persistent sound of thumping echoing through the station, they both appeared edgy, and one of them kept letting out nervous little coughs and licking his lips.

Liepa was unshaven but still resembled a movie villain, with his long black hair curling back over his shirt collar. When DI Saunders and Jerry and Jamila pulled out their chairs and sat down opposite him, he gave them a humourless smile, as if he regarded them with nothing but contempt.

'We understand you have something to say to us regarding the present situation,' said DI Saunders.

'"The present situation"?' echoed Liepa. 'I think that is what you might call an understatement. Your police station is surrounded by clothing which has life of its own, and which is determined to kill all of you. I think that is more than just a situation.'

'So what do you know about this, Mr Liepa?' asked Jamila.

'I know everything about this. I know why and how this clothing has come to life, and I also know why it is hammering at your doors.'

'All right, then,' said Jerry. 'Why don't you tell us?'

'You can never have something for nothing, you should know that,' said Liepa.

'So if you deign to enlighten us, what do you want in return?' asked DI Saunders.

'What do you think? I want a guarantee here and now that you will release me without charge for manslaughter. Cast-iron guarantee.'

'Forget it,' said DI Saunders. 'You were party to killing one of our officers while involved in organised robbery. I can't let you get away with that.'

'Do I have to remind you that it wasn't me who was driving?' said Liepa. 'And now you have a choice. Either you decide to drop the charges against me for killing one policeman, or else all the officers in this station could die.'

'You're just as much at risk as the rest of us,' said DI Saunders.

'No, that's where you're wrong. And that's what I can tell you, if you give me that guarantee. Otherwise – well, I have to leave you to your fate, which will not be pleasant, I can assure you. Have you ever wondered what it feels like, to have yourself torn to pieces, limb from limb? To have your guts dragged out of your stomach?'

Jamila looked at DI Saunders and gave him an almost imperceptible nod. From downstairs, there came a loud splintering noise, and the sound of officers shouting.

DI Saunders thought for a few moments and then he said, 'Very well. It doesn't seem like I have much of an alternative, does it?'

'These detectives are my witnesses to your promise,' said Liepa. He turned around in his chair and added, 'These two constables, too.'

'Go on, then,' DI Saunders told him. 'What do you have to tell us?'

'As you know, I collect second-hand clothing and send it to Lithuania to be processed,' said Liepa.

'You steal second-hand clothing and send it to Lithuania,' DI Saunders put in.

'That is a matter of opinion. Once somebody has decided that they no longer want an item of clothing, who does it belong to? Nobody. If they throw it in the dustbin or leave it out for charity, what's the difference? Stealing means taking something from somebody who still wants it.'

'Don't let's argue about that,' said Jamila. 'Tell us more about this second-hand clothing that you send to Lithuania.'

'All of it goes to our textile mill in Šiauliai, that is run by my uncle Dovydas. If the clothes are nearly new and in good shape, our girls will repair them and alter them so that they look more modern, and then we resell them. If they are not so good, the fabric is sorted and recycled and carded into new yarn, which will be used to make new clothes.'

'I think we already knew that,' said DI Saunders, impatiently. 'What does that have to do with these clothes that are trying to break our doors down?'

'What you don't know is that many of the clothes we recycle are infected, because the people who used to wear them were sick. They may carry some fungus or some disease like ringworm or bronchitis or HIV. But sometimes they're infected with what we call *vaiduoklis virusas*. I suppose in English you would call that "ghost virus".'

'And what exactly is a "ghost virus" when it's at home?' asked DI Saunders.

'When a person wears a coat, say, sometimes they leave not only their sweat and their perfume and their tiny flakes of skin in it, too small to see. If they are highly stressed, or unhappy with their life, or frightened to die, they infect it with themselves. How would you describe that?'

'You mean their personality,' said Jamila.

'That's right,' said Liepa. 'Their body is buried, or cremated, but in their clothes they have left behind their personality. You must know this for yourselves. How many times have you tried on a coat that belongs to somebody else and felt like them?'

'So this "ghost virus" can infect people who wear a dead person's clothes?' asked Jerry.

'Exactly – if the dead person was angry enough at dying. At least that's what my uncle and I believe. People who die happy, I don't think they infect their clothes in so much the same way. Maybe they make the people who wear their clothes happy, too, but I have never come across that. Only anger at being dead. Only desperate to come alive again.'

'Once a dead person has infected a living person, what then?' Jerry asked him, being careful not to mention the word 'cannibalism'.

But Liepa didn't hesitate. 'They want a new body of their own. They need a new body of their own, otherwise they cannot survive for very long. That's our experience. And to get that body, they need to kill other people and eat them. As far as we know, that is the only way they can come fully back to life. Otherwise, if they can't have human flesh to eat, they starve, and they die a second time.'

Jerry and Jamila looked at each other. Liepa had to be telling the truth. This was exactly what Sophie Marshall and Laura Miller and Jamie Mullins had told them – or, rather, what they had been told by the personalities who were hiding, cuckoo-like, inside them.

Liepa said, 'This *vaiduoklis virusas* – this ghost virus – it's very catching. What do you call it? Contagious. Sometimes at our factory we have stored clothes together and later we have found out that all of them have been infected by the same dead personality. A strong and revengeful personality can go through somebody's wardrobe like the wildfire, until every item of clothing that you own is infected. Not only a wardrobe, but a shop, especially a shop that sells second-hand clothes. Those charity shops – they are like crowds of dead people, hanging there, waiting to come back to life.'

'What about new clothes?' asked Jerry. 'Like, clothes that have never been worn by anybody, or hung up anywhere near second-hand clothes? Those clothes outside, there's nobody in them. They're empty. And I've seen some coats for myself that were absolutely brand new, as far as I could find out.'

'It is the same with new clothes but different.'

'Different how?'

'Almost all of the new clothes that you can buy have fibres in them that are recycled from old clothes – even from the best shops. If the fibres are infected with the *vaiduoklis virusas* then the new clothes will be just as desperate to come back to life as clothes that have only been restyled.'

'But they don't need anybody to be wearing them, do they, before they come to life? And when they do, they don't eat people, they rip them to pieces.'

Liepa nodded. 'You're right, of course, they don't eat people. They would, if anybody was to buy them and put them on. But until that happens they can't eat people because they don't have mouths to eat with or hands to cook. So, yes, they tear them apart, so that they can take out of them the most important thing that they lost when they died.'

'You're talking about their soul,' said Jamila. 'That's what they're after when they rip people to pieces, isn't it? They still have their personality. They still have their anger. But when they died they lost the one thing that makes us human.'

'You are a very clever lady,' said Liepa. 'Yes, these new clothes are searching for souls, or whatever you want to call the human essence. For the second-hand clothes, it's easier, because they can feed from the souls of whoever puts them on. But the new clothes have to go hunting for them, and as far as they are concerned, nobody else's life is as important as their own.'

DI Saunders was clearly growing impatient. 'This is all very well, all this mumbo-jumbo about souls, but I thought you said that you could help us. That was the deal, wasn't it? If you can't help us, there's no way that I can consider dropping the charges against you.'

Liepa closed his eyes, and for a moment Jerry could have believed that he had fallen asleep. What he was doing, though, was showing DI Saunders that he needed to be patient, and that all would be explained in due course.

When he opened his eyes again, he said, 'In our factory, in Šiauliai, we began to see signs of the ghost virus only late last year. Maybe just one article of clothing that came in for recycling was infected with it, but before we knew it the whole factory was infected. Some of our seamstresses were trying on clothes while they were restyling them, and they couldn't get them off. Dresses, skirts and suits. And then one of our girls went home and murdered her husband and her baby daughter, and we found out later that she had cut them up and cooked them in a *čenakai*, which is a stew.

'After that, some coats began to move around the factory by themselves – only at night, at first. But one morning my uncle came to the factory and found our night-watchman had been torn wide open. His feet were fifty metres away from his head and his *žarnos* were hanging from the ceiling. His intestines.'

'I presume you called the police,' said DI Saunders. 'What did they say?'

'*Policija*? No – why would I do that? It would only get us into trouble, and what could they do against a virus? Also, I knew already what the *vaiduoklis virusas* was. There was an outbreak in another textile mill in Kaunas about six or seven years ago, and my friend who ran the mill told me all about it. Not only that, there are many stories about it in Lithuania. The virus was supposed to have come from Russia. It was one of the ways in which they tried to take over our country.'

The thumping downstairs was growing increasingly frantic, like very fast drumming. The shouting was becoming more panicky, too.

DI Saunders said, 'Come on, Liepa, get to the point. We haven't got all bloody night.'

'All right, all right, I will tell you how I can help,' said Liepa. 'The way my uncle and I learned how to control the clothes was to shut down the factory, switch off all the carding machinery, all the lights, everything. At first we did it because we didn't know what else to do, even though every day it was costing us so much money. But when we went back after three days to see what would happen if we started up again, we had no more trouble. The new clothes stayed where we had hung them up, ready for packing. My uncle took a risk and tried on a second-hand jacket. It made him feel strange, he said, like there was somebody whispering to him, in his ear, but he was able to take it off again easy, and it did him no harm.

'That was when we understood that the ghosts in those clothes thought of my uncle and me like gods. They depended on us to come back from the dead. If we didn't restyle the second-hand clothes, they would never go back on the market to be sold and find new owners. If we didn't card all of that fabric, the fibres from recycled clothes would never be woven into yarns and become new clothes.

'For all of those clothes, new and second-hand, we are the difference between death and life after death. We are their only hope of resurrection.'

'But at what price?' said DI Saunders. 'Your clothes have killed hundreds of living people – people who never had the chance to live their lives to the full, like they have! Do you know what you're talking about here? Mass murder. Deliberate, pre-meditated mass murder, and you're responsible for it. And you seriously expect me to drop all the charges against you?'

Liepa pointed a finger at him. 'Do you know why those clothes are trying to get in here? Do you know what they want? Why have they come to this police station rather than anywhere else? Like I told you, I am one of their gods. I gave them life. They have come here to rescue me. Think about it. If Jesus had been born again, and unjustly held prisoner, don't you think that crowds of Christians would come flocking to set him free?'

'All right,' said Jerry. 'How did they know you were here? They haven't got eyes so they couldn't have seen it on telly, and they haven't got ears so they couldn't have heard it on LBC.'

Liepa pressed the fingertips of both hands to his temples. 'I called them, detective. Don't forget that they are ghosts – whatever it means to be a ghost. They can pick up a thought from thin air as easily as we can receive a text, especially when somebody is concentrating on sending them a message.'

'So what are you trying to tell us?' said DI Saunders. 'If we let you out of here, they'll all go away?'

'Of course. They have no interest in harming any of you. They only want to see me released, so that I can carry on bringing more and more of them back to life.'

'And what will they do, after we've let you out? That's always assuming that we do let you out?'

'They'll go back to wherever they came from... back to their shops. They'll lie down again, like the clothes that they are, and it will be hard for you to believe that they ever came to life. They won't attack anybody else, once they know that you've let me out.'

DI Saunders stared at him, and it was obvious that he was wracked with indecision. Liepa was calmly admitting that by continuing to sell clothes infected with the ghost virus, he was making a profit out of mass murder and cannibalism, and that if he were released he would continue to do so. It was plain that he had no qualms about making that admission, because it would be impossible to prove in court. Even with all the forensic evidence that Dr Fuller and the laboratory technicians at Lambeth Road had amassed, there was no way in which Liepa could be indisputably connected with any of the killings that had taken place over the past few days.

Jerry doubted that they would even be able to trace Liepa's company back from the second-hand clothes that had been sold in Tooting's charity shops, or the yarns that had been used to make all the duffle coats and other clothes. And if he were questioned by the prosecution about the ghost virus, he could always say that he had made it all up, as a joke. How could anybody scientifically prove the existence of *vaiduoklis virusas*?

DI Saunders was faced with the starkest of choices. Should he let Liepa go, or should he risk the lives of all the officers and staff who were trapped inside the station, including his own?

His mind was made up by a thunderous crash from downstairs, and an officer shouting, 'They're in! They're in! They've broken the fucking door down!'

DI Saunders stood up, and so did Jerry and Jamila and the two PCs. Jamila looked at Jerry as if she wanted to tell him something important, but DI Saunders said to Liepa, 'Come on, then. Let's go. Now you can show us just what a god you are.'

Liepa stood up, and gave another one of his humourless smiles. 'In another life, you know, detective inspector, you and I could have been very good friends.'

'Don't you worry,' said DI Saunders. 'If there is another life, I'll come back and haunt you.'

45

They clattered down the staircase, not using the lift in case the power cut out. Halfway down, they heard more shouting and a crackling volley of shots from an automatic rifle.

As they reached the first-floor landing, they saw below them a battleground. The double front doors of the police station had been smashed down flat, and a host of living clothes was swarming over them and into the reception area. A variety of coats was leading the assault, but they were followed by scores of jackets and anoraks and dresses and sweaters.

About twenty police officers were lined up beside the front desk. Five or six of them were kneeling, and pointing their Heckler & Koch machine guns. The rest were wielding batons and holding Tasers and pepper sprays. Most of the volunteer officers and clerical staff had fled upstairs.

Apart from the banging of sporadic shots, the whole station was eerily quiet. The police officers were no longer shouting, and the clothes had stopped drumming at the back doors. All that Jerry could hear was the breath-like sound of clothing as the coats and jackets came swaying across the reception area.

DI Saunders turned to Jokubas Liepa and said, tersely, 'Go on, then. Do your god thing.'

Liepa didn't answer him, but walked down to the bottom of the staircase and held up both of his hands.

'I can't see this working,' said Jerry.

'Me neither,' said Jamila. 'He was lying about something. I'm not sure what. Towards the end, his eyes went black.'

'What? You're kidding. Tell Smiley.'

'What's the point? He won't believe me, and anyway we've run out of time.'

Liepa walked right out in front of the oncoming coats, still with both hands raised. For a moment, Jerry thought that they were going to keep on floating forward and beat him down with their windmilling sleeves. But then he cried out, 'Stop! *Tu mane pripažjsi, ar ne?* You recognise me, don't you?'

Although they were still swaying, the coats stopped, and hovered, and one after another they dropped their sleeves slackly by their sides. Liepa lowered his hands and walked towards them, and when he reached them, they parted to let him through. They allowed him to walk all the way to the fallen front doors, and when he was standing on one of the doors he turned around and lifted his hands again.

'You see?' he called out. 'I am a god!'

With that, he walked out and disappeared into the rain.

'Liepa!' screamed DI Saunders. 'Liepa! What about all these bloody clothes?'

But as soon as Liepa had gone, the clothes began to surge forward again, and three or four black duffle coats rushed up to the line of police officers together and started to beat at them with their sleeves. The police fired at them again and again, and dozens of fragments of dark cloth were blown up into the air, but the coats kept on coming, even when their hoods had been shot into tatters. They were followed by a tumultuous horde of jackets and dresses, overwhelming the officers and piling themselves on top of them, until they were lost from sight. Jerry could hear muffled screaming, and one or two gunshots, but then nothing except that strange deep breathing sound that accompanied the clothes, as if they had lungs.

DI Saunders said, 'Back upstairs! Back upstairs! We can lock ourselves in! The SAS will be turning up in a minute!'

As she turned around to follow DI Saunders back upstairs, Jerry caught hold of Jamila's hand.

'No,' he said. 'If we go back upstairs, we'll be trapped.'

Jamila looked down at the mass of clothing writhing on top of the officers. Some of the shirts were already stained with blood.

'Where else can we go?' she asked him. Her eyes were wide with fear, and she was tugging at his hand, trying to get free.

'There – out through the door. Look at them, they're all too busy trying to get a share of those poor bastards' souls.'

'Come on!' shouted DI Saunders. 'You don't want to get locked out!'

Jerry held Jamila's hand firmly. 'We need to go now, Jamila! It's the only chance we're going to get!'

Jamila could see that there was a clear space between the bottom of the staircase and the front door, and if they went now, and ran fast enough, they might just be able to make it outside. But if the clothes realised that they were trying to escape, would they leave the squirming bloodstained heap and come after them? And if they did, how fast could they fly?

Without saying anything, she launched herself downstairs, pulling Jerry after her. When they reached the bottom stair, she tripped and almost fell, but Jerry yanked her upright, and together they ran for the space where the front doors had been.

Jerry didn't turn his head to see if any of the clothes were chasing after them. Still holding Jamila's hand, he sprinted through the doors and into the rain, and together they leapt down the police station's front steps as if they were dancers in a stage musical.

They both stopped when they reached the pavement, and looked around. None of the streetlamps were lit and there were no lights shining in any of the shop fronts or upstairs windows. Even though it was raining so heavily, and it was so gloomy, they could see that at least a score of coats and jackets were hunched over the bodies of the riot officers, and that they looked as if they were tearing them apart. They could also see Jokubas Liepa, standing in the road at Amen Corner, watching this grisly dismemberment with his hands in his pockets. He was too far away from them to be able to see the expression on his face, but Jerry imagined that it was grim satisfaction.

You see? I am a god!

'I don't think he's seen us,' said Jerry. 'Let's head this way, but we should nip down a few side-streets in case he sends any of those clothes after us.'

They started jogging south towards Tooting railway station. There were only twenty or thirty cars along this stretch of Mitcham Road, and all of them were abandoned. Most of them had dented bonnets and broken windows, and one or two of them had runnels of blood down the sides of their doors. There were no pedestrians around, either, and every shop and restaurant and pub was in darkness, although some of their doors were open.

Outside the railway station entrance, they saw bodies lying on the pavement in the rain – men, women and several small children. Some of them were severely mutilated, with their heads so badly crushed that their faces were unrecognisable, and their arms and legs twisted off. One small boy had been torn in half, with his upper body only connected to his hips and his legs by yards of intestines. His eyes were open and he was staring at the pavement through spectacles with cracked lenses.

'God almighty,' Jerry panted. 'Hundreds of clothes must have come charging through here. Thousands. This is like a bleeding ghost town.'

He took out his phone to see if he could make contact with the CCC – the Met's central communication command at Lambeth Road. He knew that his battery was charged but the screen remained black. Jamila tried her phone, but hers was dead, too.

'The landlines should still be working,' said Jerry. 'Let's knock on somebody's door and ask to use their phone.'

They looked around to make sure that they weren't being followed, and then they crossed over to Finborough Road. As they did so, a police helicopter roared overhead, very low, with a spotlight shining along the road.

Finborough Road was narrow, with terraced Victorian houses on both sides. Jerry went to the front door of the first house and rang the doorbell. There was no response at first so he rang it again. The curtain was drawn aside from the living-room window and a pale bald man in glasses appeared.

'Who are you?' the man shouted, barely audible through the glass. 'What do you want?'

Jerry took out his warrant card and pressed it against the window. 'Police. We need to use your phone.'

'It's not working. Nothing's working.'

'I'm not talking about your mobile. I mean your landline.'

'It's not working. Ever since those coats came past and knocked at the door and tried to get in. Nothing's working.'

They tried another house, further down the road. A very polite Indian woman refused to open the door but spoke to them through the letterbox. She had no electricity, either, and her landline was dead. 'I am sorry. I would like to help. But I am too frightened. Ghosts came down this street, knocking at all of the doors, and I heard screaming.'

'What did they look like, these ghosts?'

'Invisible people. But wearing clothes. I don't care if you don't believe me. That is what they looked like.'

They tried one last house, but this time nobody answered, although Jerry was sure that he saw a woman's face at an upstairs window.

'Well, sarge, it looks like we're on our tod,' said Jerry.

'The SAS squadron must be very close now,' said Jamila. 'Since we can't make contact with anybody, let's head in that direction and see if we can meet up with them.'

'That sounds like a plan. The last time they got in touch they said it was going to take them about thirty-five minutes to get here. They must have reached the Broadway by now.'

'We won't have to go back the way we came?'

'No… there's a pedestrian cut-through between the end of this road and Robinson Road, and that'll take us straight to the High Street. It's only about half a mile to the Broadway from there.'

They jogged along the dark wet suburban streets, not talking. Every now and then Jerry took out his phone to see if he could get a signal, but the screen stayed blank. The police helicopter roared over them again, and for a split-second they were lit up by its spotlight, but it carried on flying north-eastwards, towards Streatham. Either its crew hadn't seen them, or else they had more urgent business to attend to.

They had almost reached the High Street when Jamila said, 'Look – on the corner – are those—'

Jerry strained his eyes to look up ahead. His optician had told him several times that he needed to think about wearing glasses, but he had kept putting it off. Although they were blurry, he could just make out four or five dark figures gathered beside a motoring shop on the corner, and from the way they appeared to be bobbing and floating he guessed they were coats.

'Damn,' he said. 'We'll have to make a detour.'

'What about that street we just passed? Can't we go up there?'

'It's a dead end. They all are, along here. The bleeding River Graveney's in the way.'

Jerry was still trying to think of the best route to reach the Broadway without having to walk miles out of their way when he noticed that the dark figures on the corner were moving. Not just moving, but crossing the High Street and coming towards them, and quickly.

He touched Jamila's shoulder and said, 'I think they've spotted us.'

'I think you're right,' said Jamila. 'Quick – which way shall we go?'

'Down here,' Jerry told her, pointing to the next street on the left, Park Road.

They started running, but as they reached the corner of Park Road they could see that the coats were clearly coming after them, and very fast – flapping along the pavement as if they were being blown by a hurricane.

'Allah, give me wings!' gasped Jamila. But as they sprinted down the middle of the road, Jerry quickly looked behind him and he could see that the five dark figures were less than a hundred metres behind them.

On either side of the road there were nothing but two-storey terraced houses, and every window was dark. Even if they knocked and someone came to the door and was prepared to let them in, the figures would have caught up with them by then, and the house-owner would probably be killed, too, along with anybody else in the house.

About sixty metres up ahead of him, though, he saw a gap between the houses. It was fenced off from the street, and behind the fence he saw a half-demolished brick warehouse, and three parked vans, and a builders' hut, and two workmen's chemical toilets.

'In there!' he panted. 'Maybe they won't be able to follow us – over the fence!'

There were double swing gates in the centre of the fencing. He ran straight towards the gates and jumped at them, grabbing the topmost rail with both hands and sticking one foot into the gap beside the catch. He managed to swing his leg over the top of the gate and once he was sitting astride it, he twisted around and leaned down so that he could grasp Jamila's hand and help her to climb up.

'I can't do it!' she shrieked, but Jerry leaned over even further and grabbed her left sleeve as well as her hand, and once he had a firm grip on her he threw himself sideways. Jamila scrambled up the gate as he fell, and when he landed on his left shoulder on the ground, she came tumbling down on top of him.

Only a few seconds after they had fallen, the dark figures collided with the gate, so that it rang like bells. Jerry struggled back onto his feet, and it was then that he could see them for what they were: five black and navy-blue coats, with hoods, and flailing sleeves. The gate shook as they threw themselves against it again and again. Inside their hoods, there was nothing, only darkness.

His shoulder was bruised and he was winded, but he helped Jamila to stand up, and together they hobbled around the last remaining wall of the warehouse, so that the coats could no longer see them.

'Do you think they can climb over?' asked Jamila.

'I have no idea,' said Jerry. He was looking around for a gate or an alleyway at the back of the warehouse yard, but it was surrounded on all three sides by high brick walls, dividing it from the next-door gardens, and he could see neither. 'I thought there might be a way out of here, but it doesn't look like there is.'

Although they could no longer see the coats, they could hear that they were shaking the gate so violently that it couldn't keep them out for very much longer.

Jamila took hold of Jerry's lapels. The whites of her eyes were shining in the gloom, and the rain was sparkling on her headscarf.

'Will they tear us into pieces, like those other people?' she asked.

Jerry looked over at the builders' shed. 'Not if I can help it,' he said. 'Maybe there's something in there we can beat them off with.'

'Jerry – even if you shoot them they don't die – and you haven't got a gun.'

Jerry crossed over to the shed. He peered through the window but the glass was too grimy and it was too dark to see anything inside. There was a heavy padlock on the door, so he went over to the warehouse wall and picked up a broken brick. He smashed it against the padlock as hard as he could, and after the third smash both hasp and padlock dropped off onto the ground. Jerry opened the door and stepped in.

Inside, the hut smelled strongly of stale cigarettes and sweat and oil. A collection of picks was stacked up against the wall on the left-hand side, and piled on a shelf above them was a cluster of yellow and white hard hats. On the right-hand side, at least seven donkey-jackets stained with mud and brick dust were hanging from a row of pegs, and at the back of the shed there were more shelves, with long-handled mallets and crowbars and two chainsaws, one with no chain. A picture of this year's Miss BumBum had been cut from the *Daily Star* and nailed to the front of the middle shelf.

Jamila looked anxiously back in the direction of the fence. The shaking sound was growing more and more furious, and she was sure that she heard a metallic creak as if one of the gateposts were giving way.

'Jerry! What are we going to do? Maybe you could hit them with one of those picks.'

Jerry said, 'Wait – the way we cut up that sweater and that dress, when Mindy's parents came back to life. That worked, didn't it? Just like your grandfather cut up that what's-it's-name.'

'That jinn, yes. But maybe these are different. The sweater and the dress, they were attached to people. They were parasites. These coats, they have a life of their own.'

'Didn't the jinn have a life of its own?'

'Jerry, I know that worked with Mindy's parents, but that was a story! And listen – did you hear that? It sounds like they've knocked the gate down! They must be coming!'

Jerry pushed his way past the donkey-jackets to the back of the hut. He lifted up the chainsaw and carried it outside. Jamila watched him as he set it down on the ground and put his foot on it to hold it steady, although she kept glancing nervously back towards the corner of the warehouse wall for any sign of the coats appearing.

Jerry pulled out the choke lever, pressed the decompression button and then started to yank at the pull cord. He yanked it five or six times but the chainsaw still wouldn't start, and he had the chilling feeling that it might be out of petrol.

He was still tugging at it when the five coats appeared around the side of the last warehouse wall. They were floating towards them more slowly now, all spread out, like a gang of gunfighters in a Western. They obviously realised that the warehouse yard was totally enclosed and that Jerry and Jamila had nowhere to run.

'Please, Allah, protect us,' prayed Jamila, laying her hand on Jerry's shoulder.

Jerry tried pushing the choke lever back in a little, and yanked at the pull cord again. Immediately, the chainsaw roared into life.

He picked it up and stood his ground, with his feet planted firmly apart. 'Come on, then!' he shouted, over the buzzing of the chainsaw. 'If you want us, come and fucking get us!'

The coats didn't hesitate, and kept on coming. It occurred to Jerry that although they could probably sense him and Jamila, they could neither see them nor hear them. They had no eyes or ears, after all. But they were spirits. They were ghosts. They were desperate to come alive again, and that desperation must alert them to the presence of any living soul.

Two of the coats suddenly came rushing towards him, their

sleeves whirling. Jerry lifted the chainsaw and one of them flew right into it. One of its sleeves was instantly ripped into shreds, and then Jerry swung the chainsaw from side to side and the coat was torn apart so violently that it looked as if it had exploded.

Jerry advanced on the second coat while fragments of the first were still fluttering all around him like a swarm of black moths. Now it was plain that the coats were either blind or suicidal, because this coat flung itself at him without any hesitation. He lopped off its hood before he zig-zagged the chainsaw all the way down it, reducing it to tattered grey ribbons.

Now I've got the better of you, you bastards, thought Jerry, and his whole body surged with adrenaline. He stalked towards the remaining three coats and when they came flying towards him he swung the chainsaw in a criss-cross pattern so that he could chop up all three of them at once. For almost a minute the chainsaw screamed and gnashed and growled and Jerry almost disappeared from Jamila's sight behind a blizzard of dark wool.

At last Jerry switched the chainsaw off, and the warehouse yard fell silent, while the remains of the coats drifted slowly to the ground all around him.

He walked back to Jamila and put down the chainsaw. They held each other tightly, so tightly that they could almost feel each other's hearts beating.

After a while, Jerry said, 'There. It worked on jinns, and it worked on Mindy's mum and dad, and it works on these buggers too. We need to find that SAS squadron and that anti-terrorist squad, and tell them.'

'There is one more thing I think we should do,' said Jamila. 'My grandfather not only cut up the jinn into pieces, he burned the pieces, too. I believe we should do the same. Liepa said that the virus kept people's spirits alive in the fibres of the clothes they once wore. If their spirits could survive their clothes being torn apart and spun into yarn and remade into other clothes, maybe they can also survive you cutting them up.'

'Well, you could be right,' said Jerry. 'And who am I to argue with an onion?'

He went back into the shed and found a rake and a plastic container full of petrol. It took him only a few minutes to scrape up most of the woollen fragments and heap them in a metre-high pile on the warehouse's concrete floor. Then he poured petrol all over them.

'Don't happen to have a light on you?' he asked Jamila.

She stepped forward and handed him a book of matches from Samrat's. 'You're lucky. I only took these today so that I could make a note of their number.'

Jerry tossed a lighted match onto the heap of rags and with a soft *whoomph* it burst into flame. They stood and watched it, with Jerry's arm around Jamila's waist, holding her close. Raindrops spat and sizzled as they fell on the fire, and the flames threw shadows on the white-painted interior wall of the warehouse.

Jerry looked up at the shadows and he was sure that he could see ghosts dancing and waving their arms, but in the state of mind he was in at the moment, he knew that he was prepared to believe almost anything.

Jamila looked at her watch. 'Now we need to go and find the SAS and tell them to equip themselves with chainsaws,' she said.

Jerry hefted up the chainsaw that he had left on the ground. 'That shouldn't be difficult. There's a Screwfix shop on the

High Street, only just up the road from here. They should have enough chainsaws in stock.'

They left the fire burning and went out through the broken-open gates. They were both shocked by their experience, and feeling detached from reality, but they walked as quickly as they could, with Jerry lugging the chainsaw. They knew that every minute could mean the difference between innocent people being spared or being savagely dismembered.

What they didn't see as they made their way up Park Road was a fiery figure floating out of the gates and starting to follow them. It was made entirely out of flames, but it had the vague appearance of a person walking. The figure hadn't gone more than fifty metres, though, before the flames started to subside, and the last few flickers were quickly extinguished by the rain. Then there was nothing left except a wisp of grey smoke, and that soon drifted away.

46

It took them less time to find the SAS squadron than they could have hoped. As they walked up the High Street towards Tooting Broadway station, they saw at least eight khaki Land Rovers parked in a line, as well as three camouflaged personnel carriers. About forty blades were gathered around the station entrance, all wearing black helmets and black combat uniforms and body armour.

Jamila took out her warrant card as they approached, and held it up so that the blades could see it.

'Police,' she said. 'Can you tell me who's in charge here, please?'

A sergeant took her card and examined it carefully. Then he said to Jerry, 'What are you carrying that for? That chainsaw?'

'We can explain that,' said Jamila. 'Please just let us speak to whoever's in charge.'

An officer in a black beret came forward. Jerry thought he was far too young to be an SAS officer. He had blue eyes and a fresh face and he looked more like the captain of a public school rugby team.

'What's going on?' he demanded. 'Who are you?'

'Detective Sergeant Patel and Detective Constable Pardoe, both attached to Tooting CID. We only just managed to escape from the police station after the clothes broke in. You've seen the clothes? The coats and the jackets and the sweaters?'

The officer nodded. 'We've lost three men already. That's why we're here, to regroup. We're all pretty stunned, to tell you the truth. We were told we were going to have to deal with rioters. We had no idea they were going to be – well, whatever the hell they are.' He held out his hand and said, 'Major John Wallace, by the way. SAS CRW.'

'What happened?' asked Jerry.

Major Wallace turned around and looked back along Mitcham Road. It was still jammed solid with abandoned cars and buses, and the pavements were still strewn with bodies, and it was still raining, hard.

'We tried to call your control room to let them know that we'd arrived,' he said. 'There was no response. And then our own radios cut out. We haven't been able to get into contact with anybody, not even with mobile phones.'

'Same problem,' said Jerry, lifting up his iPhone. 'Dead as a dodo. No landlines working, either.'

'I'm guessing that our rioters have set off some kind of electromagnetic pulse device,' said Major Wallace. 'They're designed to knock out anything electric – phones, radios, as well as computers. We know that the Russians and the North Koreans have got them, but these aren't Russians or North Koreans. For God's sake, they're not even people.'

'How did you lose your men?' asked Jamila. She spoke so sympathetically that Jerry thought Major Wallace was going to start crying.

'We couldn't get the Jackals anywhere near the police station because of all these abandoned vehicles, so we went on foot. We came across the – rioters, whatever they are. They were swarming in front of the police station and it looked like they were mutilating a number of dead police officers. We fired some warning shots but they came straight for us.'

Major Wallace paused to take a deep breath. Then he said, 'We shouted another warning and then we opened fire. There must have been about two dozen rioters, and it was only when they came closer that we realised what they actually were. I couldn't tell you how many rounds we pumped into them but it didn't make any impression on them at all. They kept on coming and they brought down three of my best men while they were still firing. Literally buried them. That's when I called for an immediate retreat.'

He paused again. 'What we're going to do now, I have no idea.'

'Well, let me tell you this,' said Jerry. 'Because they're just clothes, they can't be stopped by shooting at them. They can't be Tasered, either, and I don't think that tear-gas would have any effect, either. They haven't got eyes and they haven't got lungs.'

'So how in the name of God can they be walking around, attacking people?'

'It has been explained to us,' said Jamila. 'But it is a long and complicated story, and even then what we were told may not be true, or not completely true, anyway. It is some kind of virus which infects clothes and gives them the personality of people who used to own them, but are now dead.'

Major Wallace frowned at her. Jerry could tell that if he hadn't seen the clothes for himself, he would have thought that she was raving.

'DS Patel and me, we managed to escape from the nick,' he said. 'We were trying to get here to meet you when we got spotted by five coats. They chased us into a building site and that was where I found this chainsaw. When they came for us, I cut them up into literally hundreds of pieces. DS Patel told me her grandfather used to do that to jinns when they tried to get into his house. A jinn – that's a ghost, or a demon thingy.'

'That was only a story,' Jamila insisted.

'Yes, but it killed them, didn't it, cutting them up?' said Jerry. 'And just to make sure, we made a bonfire out of them afterwards.'

Major Wallace said, 'All right. And you think that we'll be able to deal with the rest of them the same way? We've a chainsaw aboard one of the Jackals, but we're going to need a lot more, aren't we? These clothes – there must be hundreds of them.'

'There's a Screwfix shop just down the road there, and there's a Wickes hardware store in Plough Lane, just the other side of St George's Hospital,' Jerry told him. 'Between the two of them they should have enough chainsaws in stock, and if not there's a Toolstation in Wimbledon.'

Major Wallace said, 'Did you catch that, sergeant?'

The sergeant had been standing close behind his right shoulder, so Jerry thought that it would have been amazing if he hadn't. 'Yes, sir,' he snapped. 'Chainsaws, sir.'

'That's right, sergeant. As many as possible and as quickly as possible. You'll probably have to ram your way into the shops but we'll worry about that later.'

'Yes, sir.'

The sergeant picked out half a dozen men. They all climbed into one of the Jackal armoured vehicles, started up the engine with a loud bellow, and U-turned across the road, colliding with three abandoned cars and forcing them, deeply dented, out of their way.

Major Wallace said, 'All we can do now is wait for them to come back. Let's go and sit down and you can brief me some more about this virus.'

Next to the station there was a Starbucks coffee shop. Its front window was smashed and its front door was hanging by its hinges. They went inside, their feet crunching on broken glass, and sat down at one of the tables.

'Shame there's no power,' said Jerry. 'We could have made ourselves a double espresso.'

Another helicopter passed overhead, so low that that the whole coffee shop shook.

'That sounded like one of ours,' said Major Wallace. 'Central command will have seen what's going on so we're sure to have reinforcements pretty soon. It's so damned frustrating having no way of getting in touch with them. As I said, I can only guess that these clothes have an EMP device, although I always thought you needed a high-altitude nuclear explosion to fry a country's electronics.'

'Yes,' said Jamila. 'But instead there is some extraordinary psychic power at work here. If the virus is able to give clothes the power to come alive, who knows what else it can do? My grandmother told me about a bhoot which could set fire to somebody's house even if it was miles away. It could also kill people who had antagonised it during its lifetime just by dreaming about them.'

'Don't tell me any more,' said Jerry. 'Too much of what your grandmother told you is coming true.'

*

More than an hour and a half passed before they heard the bellowing engine of the Jackal coming back, and a loud crunch as it drove over an abandoned motorcycle.

Jerry and Jamila followed Major Wallace out of the coffee shop. The sergeant climbed down from the Jackal brandishing an orange Husqvarna chainsaw, and his blades came out carrying two chainsaws each. Three of them went back to the Jackal and brought out more.

'Well done, sergeant,' said Major Wallace, inspecting the chainsaws all laid down in a row on the pavement. 'How many altogether?'

'Twenty-three, sir. I reckoned that would be enough. They're all petrol, and we've topped them all up. They had your cordless electric chainsaws, too, but none of them were charged and of course there's no power to charge them up with.'

'Right – plan of action,' said Major Wallace. 'We divide into three squads of chainsaw operators and we attack the police station simultaneously from the north, the centre and the south. The main doors in the centre have already been breached, so we won't have any trouble gaining access there. The doors on the north and south sides you'll almost certainly have to blow.

'Any clothes we encounter on the way there we rip to bits, and when we attack there can't be any hesitation, and I mean none. I want you going after those coats and jackets as if you're berserk. The Tooting Chainsaw Massacre. Do you understand me?'

'Yes, sir,' said the blades, in unison.

'Once we've chopped up these clothes, I've been discussing with Detective Sergeant Patel here what we should do next, because she's something of an expert on bizarre happenings like this – well, more of an expert than any of us. She says we need to burn them, so that we make absolutely sure that the fibres they're made of can't come back to life. Yes, I know. None of it makes any sense. But they've already accounted for three of us, and if that's what it takes to kill them off for good and all, that's what we'll do.

'So – while the chainsaw squads are doing their worst, another squad will be scouting around the area to requisition any trucks that aren't stuck in a traffic jam. They'll bring those trucks to the police station and load them with the chopped-up clothes, so that we can take them away to build a bonfire out of them. DC Pardoe has suggested that a place called Figges Marsh is the best place to burn them… he says it's a recreation ground just south of the police station. Apparently it's not too far away and we should be able to get there easily by the back streets even if the main road's blocked.'

Major Wallace looked around at his squadron in their black kit and goggles, and said, 'Any questions? No? Right then, chainsaw squad, fire up your chainsaws!'

Jamila came up to Jerry and said, 'What are you going to do?'

Jerry already had his foot on his chainsaw, ready to start it. 'What do you think I'm going to do? I'm going to go with them. I'll be making up the numbers, and besides that I know that nick like the back of my hand and these geezers don't, do they? There's loads of places where those coats could hide. They could hang themselves up from the back of a door and pretend they were ordinary coats and who would know?'

'If you're going, then I'm going with you.'

'Sarge – you haven't got a chainsaw.'

'I don't care. I wouldn't know how to use it, even if I did. But I've been involved in this investigation right from the beginning, and I want to see it through to the end.'

'Jamila – no.'

'Jerry – yes. And that's an order. I'll stay close behind you.'

'If you get yourself killed, I'll never speak to you again.'

'If I get myself killed, I won't be able to hear you, anyway.'

Jerry said something else, but all around them twenty-three chainsaws were starting up in chorus, so that she couldn't hear him. He bent down and tugged at the pull cord of his own chainsaw, and that stuttered into life, too.

The twenty-three SAS blades of the chainsaw squad divided themselves into three columns – two of them walking along the pavements and the third down the middle of the road, in between the lines of damaged cars, their chainsaws idling like twenty-three softly growling pit bull terriers. Jerry and Jamila walked down the middle of the road, too, at the rear of the column. Jamila hadn't wanted to walk along the pavements because there were too many bodies to step over, and some of them were grotesquely mutilated. In spite of the rain, there were still deltas of blood running into the gutters.

When they reached Byton Road, the eight blades who were going to attack the police station from the south turned right. They would go down the side-streets and then double back. The other fifteen kept on going. As they came around Amen Corner they could see that a few dark coats and jackets were still crouched like hunchbacks over the bodies of the Wandsworth anti-terrorist team, tearing them open and dragging their glistening insides all across the road. The three SAS men who had been overwhelmed by the clothes were lying there too, somewhere, and one of the blades in front of Jerry revved his chainsaw as if he couldn't wait to get his revenge.

'Hold your horses, Branning,' said the sergeant, without even turning round to see who it was. None of the squad wore name-tags on their uniforms, so Jerry was doubly impressed.

They held back, waiting for a signal from the squad who were coming from the south. Jamila, close behind Jerry, tapped him on the shoulder and said, 'If this goes wrong...'

'What?' said Jerry. 'I can't hear you!'

She held onto his shoulder and said loudly in his ear, 'If this goes wrong, I want you to know how I feel about you!'

He turned and looked at her. She didn't say anything else. She didn't have to.

Jerry smiled and said, just as loudly, 'Me too!'

At that moment they saw a flashlight further down the road. The south squad were in position and ready to advance.

'Right!' screamed the sergeant. 'Let's get in there and chop the bastards to bits!'

The SAS blades all started to run towards the police station with their boots pattering on the tarmac and their chainsaws roaring. The coats and jackets that had been dismembering the anti-terrorist squad stood up straight, but they made no attempt to flee. If they were capable of thought, they obviously believed that nobody could hurt them. The blades tore into them, swinging their chainsaws up and down and side to side, and sleeves and collars and lapels and long strips of lining flew all around them.

Eight of them ran through the car park gate at the side of the station, while the other eight bounded up the steps towards the front entrance. Jerry and Jamila followed them. The long brown dress that Jerry had tied by its sleeves to the railings was still lying there, flapping, and he saw one of the

SAS blades ripping it in a few roaring seconds into chaotic shreds of wool.

It was pitch dark inside the station, but one of the blades tossed two white chem lights across the reception area and abruptly the whole grisly scenario was brightly lit up. On the far side of the reception area there was a struggling mass of clothes, like a heap of giant maggots. They were heavily bloodstained and some of them were draped in long strings of membrane and intestines. There was hardly anything recognisable left of the police officers who had tried to fight them off, only the tatters of uniforms and boots with torn-off ankle-bones sticking out of them.

Now that they had almost finished dismembering the officers in the reception area, more clothes were ascending the stairs, and over the roaring of chainsaws and the shouting of the SAS blades, Jerry could hear screaming from the upper floors.

With no hesitation the SAS squad ran across the blood-streaked floor and started to tear the clothes to bits. The clothes struggled and flailed, but there was nothing they could do to save themselves from the jagged teeth of eight chainsaws.

Jerry heard a loud bang from the back of the station and a few seconds later the north squad came running in.

'Get upstairs after that lot!' bellowed the sergeant, and they crossed the reception area and started to attack the heaving crowd of shirts and jackets that were mounting the staircase.

The air was thick with a storm of ripped-up fabric – wool and nylon and cotton and silk – as well as zips and buttons that were scattered across the floor. Jerry could hear that the south squad had broken into the cells, and from the screeching sound of chainsaws against metal bars, he could only imagine that there must have been be coats in there, too, probably trying to get at their prisoners.

He saw a trench-coat flying towards the back of an SAS blade, clearly intending to jump on him. He ran over, snagged its belt in the teeth of his chainsaw, and then sawed it upward in a tangle of khaki gabardine and black wool lining.

As the south squad climbed up the stairs, strewing them with fabric, Jerry and Jamila climbed up behind them. Only three or four chainsaws were still roaring at full throttle now, although the rest of them were keeping up a menacing burble as the SAS blades scoured the station for any clothes they might have missed, or which were hiding.

Jerry and Jamila followed the south squad along the corridor to the control room. The door had been broken off its hinges and was lying flat on the floor. By the light of the soldiers' torches, they could see Inspector Callow and DI Saunders and Sergeant Bristow and three other officers, or what was left of them. One was still sitting in front of the dead CCTV screens, his white shirt soaked with blood, headless. His head was lying on the floor, his eyes wide open, staring at his shoes as if he were wondering how he had managed to get down there.

'Bloody hell,' said Jerry. 'Smiley. What a bloody awful way to go.'

At last, one after another, the chainsaws fell silent. Along with the sergeant and four of his blades, Jerry and Jamila searched the station from the top floor back down to the reception area, but they found no more living clothes.

Major Wallace was waiting for them outside, by the front steps.

'This is a great start, DS Patel,' he said to Jamila. 'I'm receiving reports that there are still random groups of clothes roaming around the neighbourhood, attacking anybody who's out on the streets. Now that we've dealt with this lot I'm going to send out five patrols armed with chainsaws to hunt them down.'

He looked back inside the police station. 'I hope we've done for most of them. But we'll get any strays and chop them up, too, don't worry. I can't thank you enough for the help you've given us. And you, DC Pardoe. Bloody good show, the both of you.'

He had hardly finished speaking when the streetlights started to flicker on, and lights in the police station came on again, too. Shop fronts all the way along Mitcham Road were suddenly illuminated again. It was only then that they could see the full horror of the bloody carnage on the pavements, and the dismembered bodies lying across the road.

In his pocket, Jerry's iPhone began to ping with messages and texts, but he felt too numb to take it out and answer them. He set his chainsaw down on the steps.

Jamila linked her arm through his. 'What next?' she asked.

'It's time for the big clear-up,' said Major Wallace. 'Then we'll be lighting our bonfire. I very much hope that you two can join us.'

414

47

Jerry found a patrol car at the rear of the station, undamaged except for a broken blue light and a dented bonnet. While Jamila waited for him in the car park he took the keys from the reception desk, trying to keep his eyes averted from the mess of mutilated bodies. At least ten SAS blades were clearing up heaps of bloodstained fabric, using the station's snow-shovels. Three trucks were lined up outside, waiting to be filled with all the hundreds of items of clothing that they had sawn to pieces.

Jerry drove them back to his flat. They hardly spoke, but after what they had been through and what they had witnessed, neither of them had very much to say. Jerry was glad in a way that Jamila had stuck with them until the very end, because he didn't have to describe how gruesome it had been.

He made coffee for them both while she took a shower. When he came out of the shower himself he found her sitting wrapped in a towel in the living-room watching the television news. The newscaster was saying that there had been rioting in some areas of South London, causing multiple casualties and a temporary blackout, but he said nothing about clothes that had come to life or dismembered shoppers, and neither did he mention the SAS assault on Tooting police station.

'Heavy, heavy censorship,' said Jamila.

Jerry sat down on the couch beside her. 'It'll have to come out sooner or later. Too many people saw those clothes running around to keep it under wraps for very long.'

'Has anybody from the Yard been in touch?' Jamila asked him.

'Not yet. I doubt if they know yet who's still alive and who's snuffed it. They're probably more worried about poor old Callow than anybody else. It's all total chaos at the moment.'

They finished their coffee and dressed. They hadn't eaten all day but neither of them could face the idea of food. Jamila closed her eyes and fell asleep on the couch for nearly an hour while Jerry continued to watch television. There were constant reports about the 'rioting' and a phone number was posted on the screen for anybody concerned about missing friends or relatives, but there was still no word about how many people had been killed or injured, or how.

Jerry was just coming out of the toilet when his iPhone pinged. It was Major Wallace, telling him that almost all the clothing had been gathered up and tipped into the middle of the Figges Marsh recreation ground.

'We'd really appreciate it if DS Patel could come along and see it. She seems to know all about this kind of ghost malarkey.'

'Sure. We'll be there in ten.'

He woke Jamila. She blinked at him and said, 'Where am I?'

'Chez Pardoe. Sorry to disturb you but the major's ready to light the bonfire. He says he'd like you to be a witness.'

'Don't worry about waking me. I was having a horrible dream about black hairy caterpillars crawling around inside my clothes. Do you have any Listerine? The inside of my mouth tastes as if I've been licking scaffolding poles.'

They drove down to Figges Marsh, a flat grassy triangle opposite the London Road Cemetery, bordered by oak trees. They parked in front of the houses in Manship Road and walked across the grass to the huge pile of torn clothing that the SAS had cleared out of the police station. Major Wallace was there, as well as twenty of his squadron. Some of them had taken off their black Kevlar helmets, and were bareheaded, or wearing berets.

As they came nearer, Jerry could smell petrol. Two SAS blades were walking around the pile of clothing, sloshing out the last of two twenty-litre jerry cans. The pile was at least a metre taller than they were.

'Lighting-up time,' said Major Wallace. 'I've heard from two of our chainsaw squads. They've already located and ripped up five gangs of coats and jackets between them, so there'll be much more to burn later. I just thought it would be a good idea to get this lot cremated first.'

He turned to one of the soldiers beside the pile of clothes and said, 'That's it, corporal! You can get it going now!'

The corporal struck a match and dropped it onto the clothes. With a soft rumble, the whole petrol-soaked pile went up in flames, and it gave out such a blast of heat that Jerry and Jamila had to take a few paces back. They stood in silence as the flames leapt and curled and seemed to form patterns in the air.

The fire was still blazing furiously when Jerry heard somebody shouting. He looked around the recreation ground but at first he could see only trees. Then he heard the shouting again, closer, and saw a man running towards them across the grass.

'Bloody hell,' he said. 'It's Liepa!'

Jokubas Liepa came up to them, gasping for breath. His long black hair was wild and his eyes were staring like a man gone mad.

'What are you doing?' he shouted at them. 'What are you doing? These are souls! These are people! You are burning them alive!'

Jerry circled around behind Jamila and caught hold of Liepa's left arm. 'These may be souls, mate, but they're mass-murderers, and they're getting their come-uppance. And you – you're getting your come-uppance, too. You're under arrest for just about everything you can think of.'

'You can't do this!' Liepa protested. 'These are human souls! These are my followers! Don't you understand what pain they must be suffering? Put out the fire! Put it out, before all of those poor souls perish!'

'Not a chance, tosh,' said Jerry. 'And how are we going to put it out? Piss on it?'

'You can't do this!' Liepa raved at him. 'You – you are the killers! You can't do this!'

He was still shouting when a pattern of flames leapt out of the fire and came dancing towards him. It kept changing shape, so that it was difficult to see exactly what it was, but more than anything it resembled a burning man. It rushed up to Liepa and threw its fiery arms around him.

Jamila screamed, 'Jerry!' and seized his coat collar and pulled him away. The burning man embraced Liepa with flames and

Liepa threw back his head and let out an extraordinary dog-like howl. As Jerry staggered back, he could see that Liepa's face was already seared scarlet and that his long black hair was alight.

One of the SAS blades whipped off his jacket and approached Liepa, holding his jacket up ready to wrap it around him, and stifle the flames. But the heat was far too intense for him to be able to get close enough.

Liepa stumbled around and around, blazing from head to foot, and there was nothing that Jerry or Jamila or the SAS men could do to save him. As he stumbled around another fiery figure came leaping out of the pile of burning clothes, and then another, and another, and they all went rushing towards Liepa and clung to him like napalm.

For a few seconds Liepa looked like nothing except a rippling pillar of flames. Watching him, one of the SAS blades crossed himself. Jerry knew that by now all Liepa's nerve-endings would have been burned away, so that he would no longer be capable of feeling any pain, but when he thought of all the people he had caused to suffer, he almost wished that he was in agony, right until the very end.

At last Liepa collapsed and fell to the grass. The flames dwindled and died out, and soon there was nothing but smoke drifting across the recreation ground. Liepa's body was totally black and crusted, like a man made out of charcoal.

The bonfire, too, began to subside. It had stopped raining now and a faint night breeze was blowing, so ashes tumbled away towards the trees.

'What the hell was that all about?' said Major Wallace. 'Who was that man? And how the hell did that happen?'

'That man was Jokubas Liepa,' said Jamila. 'It was him who claimed to be responsible for bringing all these clothes to life. Because of that, he said that they regarded him as their god.'

'My head's spinning,' said Major Wallace. 'This gets harder to understand by the minute.'

'Don't you see?' Jamila told him. 'When we cut these clothes up and set fire to them, the spirits inside them were faced with dying a second time. So when they felt Liepa's presence close by, they believed that he could rescue them. They weren't trying to kill him. They were begging him for salvation. That's what I believe, anyway.'

'I suppose that's as good an explanation as any,' said Major Wallace. 'What's your opinion, DC Pardoe?'

'Don't ask me,' said Jerry. 'The only spirit I know anything about is Jack Daniel's.'

Major Wallace thought for a moment. He looked down at Liepa's charred body, and then he said, 'This didn't happen, OK? I think it's going to be far better for all of us if we keep our lips zipped. All right, corporal. Carry on.'

*

Jamila spent the rest of the night at Jerry's flat, sleeping on the couch. By the time Jerry was making toast and coffee for them in the morning, they had still received no contact from the Yard or the Lambeth borough commander, but both of them were reluctant to try to get in touch and report that they had survived.

Although neither of them said anything, they both felt that they needed at least a day to recover from what they had been through. Not only that, the television news programmes were still describing the mayhem that had killed so many innocent people in Tooting as a riot. If Jerry and Jamila checked in and described what had actually happened, they were sure that they would be told to forget it, and that they must have been suffering from overwork. Either that, or they would be accused of trying to cover up the murderous behaviour of some black or Asian gangs in order to be politically correct.

As she spread butter on her toast, Jamila summed up both of their feelings. 'You know what will happen if we tell the powers that be all about it? They'll sack us. And if we tell the media, the Met will ruin us, believe me. They'll make out that you're a paedophile and I'm a terrorist. There's no such thing as clothes that come to life and kill people.'

Halfway through the morning, Jamila's phone rang. It was Dr Stewart, from Springfield hospital.

'Detective sergeant Patel? Oh, good. I tried to get through to the police station but I got no answer. I gather from the news that there's been some trouble.'

'How can I help you, doctor?' asked Jamila.

'Well, I'm just calling to tell you that all three of your suspects have made a remarkable overnight recovery. They all seem to be their old selves again. None of them are saying any longer that they have another personality inside them who's going to die if they're not fed with human flesh, which I must say is a great relief to all of us. From a psychological point of view, I would say that all three are ready to be released from our care back into yours.'

'Oh, I'm afraid there might be some problems with that,' said Jamila. 'As you rightly say, there has been some trouble, and we may not have any secure accommodation available for them just at this moment in time.'

'I see,' said Doctor Stewart. 'But you can understand that we're a hospital, not a prison, and if an individual is mentally competent, we cannot be expected to keep them incarcerated.'

'All right,' said Jamila. 'What I'll do is, come to the hospital and interview each of them, if that's all right with you. If they're not trying to pull the wool over your eyes, I'll see what I can do to have them moved.'

'DS Patel,' said Dr Stewart, frostily, 'I have been a psychiatric consultant for twenty-seven years. Patients do not "pull the wool over my eyes", as you put it.'

'I'm sorry,' said Jamila. 'It's just that many offenders have a great talent for deceiving almost everybody, including us.'

'Perhaps you'd like to come this afternoon,' said Dr Stewart. 'The sooner the better.'

Jamila put down her phone and said to Jerry, 'That was Dr Stewart. She says they're better – Sophie and Laura and Jamie and Mindy. They've all made a miraculous overnight recovery.'

'You're kidding. Maybe it was something to do with those clothes. After all, the power came back on after we'd chopped them up, didn't it? Or maybe it was something to do with Liepa snuffing it.'

'I've said that we'll go to Springfield this afternoon and talk to them. I don't want to take them back into police custody until I'm sure that they're not dangerous any more. You know what some of these schizophrenic murderers are like. They can convince you that it wasn't them who strangled their wives, it was the fellow next door but one.'

'All right, sarge, if you say so. Although I must say I've had it up to here with homicidal clothes.'

*

It took them nearly three quarters of an hour to drive to Springfield hospital that afternoon, because the centre of Tooting was still cordoned off, and most of the town-bound traffic had been diverted along Tooting Bec Road and Trinity Road.

Dr Stewart was there to meet them herself.

'We thought you must have had some inkling that they were better,' she said, as she led them along the corridor. 'You didn't send your officer this morning.'

'No, well, there was some trouble at the police station, as you said.'

'A riot, that's what it said on the news. Who was rioting, and what were they rioting about? They didn't say.'

'I'm not sure,' said Jamila. 'Some protest about somebody who'd been arrested, I think.'

'I blame social media, myself,' said Dr Stewart. 'It's the way that people work themselves up into such a frenzy on Twitter, or Facebook, or whatever. They get quite hysterical about things that are none of their business, and personally don't affect them in the slightest.'

'This isn't the way to your security wing,' Jerry put in.

'Oh, no. Their recovery is so complete that we've let them out of there. They're in the quiet room now with Cherry Mwandi. She's encouraging them to share their experiences. We're hoping that it will help each of them to understand how they came to be in such an unusual state of mind.'

Jamila glanced at Jerry as if to say, *We already know how they came to be in such an unusual state of mind, don't we? It was the clothes they wore, and the ghost virus that was infecting them.*

Dr Stewart led them to the door marked QUIET ROOM. She knocked, and then she entered. 'Come along in,' she said.

But then she stopped dead. All of the chairs in the room had been pushed back to the walls so that there was a wide clear space in the centre. Sitting cross-legged around this centre space were Sophie and Laura and Jamie and Mindy. They had looked up as Dr Stewart came in, and their chins were all red-bearded with blood. Their hands, too, wore glistening red gloves.

Lying spread-eagled in between them was Cherry Mwandi. She was staring blindly at the ceiling and her mouth was open as if she were finding it difficult to breathe. She was naked, and all of her clothes were lying on the floor under the window. She had been cut open from her breast bone to her curly black pubic hair, and all of her intestines dragged out, as well as her stomach and her womb. The whole room smelled of blood and excrement.

Jerry and Jamila stood in the doorway, so shocked that they didn't know what to say. Dr Stewart turned around, pushed her way back into the corridor, and vomited on the floor.

It was Mindy who spoke first. 'It's all right now,' she said, quite chirpily, wiping the blood from her chin with the back of her hand. 'We've found something to eat.'

A letter from the publisher

We hope you enjoyed this book. We are an independent publisher dedicated to discovering brilliant books, new authors and great storytelling. If you want to hear more, why not join our community of book-lovers at:

www.headofzeus.com

We'll keep you up-to-date with our latest books, author blogs, tempting offers, chances to win signed editions, events across the UK and much more.

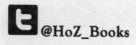 @HoZ_Books

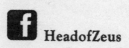 HeadofZeus

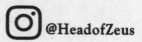 @HeadofZeus

HEAD *of* ZEUS